Praise for *Going to the Sun* by James McManus

"An extraordinary work. McManus's pre⸺
love and chronic illness are simple and po⸺

"As Penny pedals along with Beckett, her beloved invisible companion, her joy in shaping her mission is palpable (McManus gets the voice just right). He manages a delicate balance between Penny's meditations and episodes on the road. . . . McManus takes big risks here. He sets off his fireworks at the start; furthermore, the problems of a blocked Ph.D. candidate are not guaranteed to get the heart racing. Yet, against the odds, he succeeds; his portrait of a gutsy lady dueling with death is both exhilarating and moving."

—*The Washington Post Book World*

"Absolutely spellbinding . . . seldom have I read a novel that succeeds on so many levels as this one does."

—*Chicago Sun-Times*

"A road novel with a difference . . . An absorbing, heart-tugging story."

—*Newsday* (New York)

"Exquisitely crafted, heart-wrenching."

—*Chicago Tribune*

"Fluid and captivating, filled with disturbing insight . . . grotesque and powerful. Penny is an extremely captivating character . . . Scenes of love and desire, life and death, identity and disguise constantly unfold . . . McManus has created one of the most engaging heroines of the year out of a multitude of everyday details and his sharp insight into the soul of a brilliant and deeply disturbed young woman."

—Alan Cheuse, *All Things Considered*, National Public Radio

"McManus has crafted a story that's both a rugged adventure and a mesmerizing inner monologue, a tale that finally becomes a love story, minus the mush."

—*Entertainment Weekly*

"One woman's amazing journey, a novel of search and discovery. . . with nuance, detail, and wonderful dialogue . . . full of sensuality, humor, and vibrant life."

—*Atlanta Journal-Constitution*

"Poet and novelist McManus makes interesting use of Beckett, relating his obsession with physical decay to Penny's diabetes, but ultimately this novel could not be more American. . . . Penny's narrative—by turns lyrical, pissed off, and longing—is a triumph."

—*Publishers Weekly*

"A well-crafted tale of grief, introspection, and courage."

—*Booklist*

"The admirably edgy energy that runs through James McManus's five previous books is a kind of signature. But in *Going to the Sun* there seems to be a special urgency about his writing that powerfully portrays the consciousness of his diabetic central character, Penny Culligan; it's an urgency capable of conveying not only her cross-country flight but the very spikes and plunges of sugar in her blood. It's an urgency that is finally a measure of the deep compassion in this intense novel."

—Stuart Dybek

"Engaging and challenging, and has a gripping ending."

—*Library Journal*

"Death hovers over *Going to the Sun* as if it's a guardian angel—a watchful, benign spirit of calm assurance. . . . McManus has rendered the specifics of Penny's story with loving attention, even when the specifics are unlovely in the extreme. . . . *Going to the Sun* shimmers with McManus's storytelling . . . a compelling page-turner that deftly straddles the line between art and titillation."

—*Citypaper* (Baltimore)

"Perhaps the most compelling elements of this beautiful novel are McManus's ability to write in a woman's voice and his descriptions of being diabetic. . . . *Going to the Sun* is a meditative road story, but it is more profound and more intimate. . . . McManus proves that he is both a gifted wordsmith and a great storyteller. *Going to the Sun* is chilling and riveting; this story will haunt you long after you have put it down."

—*Chicago Books in Review*

"Reversing the role of her Homeric namesake, Penelope sets off on a 3000-mile odyssey. . . . An acute observer of the detritus of North American culture . . . A tour de force account of trauma, disability, the triumphs and limits of the human spirit . . . and the bleak metaphysics of a savage and meaningless universe."

—*The Boston Phoenix*

"With lyrical precision and solid, unpredictable storytelling, McManus—a poet and novelist who displays here the skills of both genres—creates a contemporary picaresque. . . . It's a strong storyteller who can bring so elliptically to a close such an emotionally affecting tale—which is exactly what the sensitive and talented McManus manages to do."

—*Kirkus Reviews*

Going to the Sun

A

NOVEL

JAMES McMANUS

PICADOR
FARRAR, STRAUS AND GIROUX
NEW YORK

For Bridget

www.picadorusa.com

Picador® is a U.S. registered trademark and is used by Farrar, Straus and Giroux under license from Pan Books Limited.

For information on Picador Reading Group Guides, as well as ordering, please contact the Trade Marketing department at St. Martin's Press.
Phone: 1-800-221-7945 extension 763
Fax: 212-677-7456
E-mail: trademarketing@stmartins.com

Designed by Nina Gaskin

Library of Congress Cataloging-in-Publication Data

McManus, James.
    Going to the sun : a novel / James McManus.
        p. cm.
    ISBN 0-312-42329-2
    1. Young women—United States—Psychology—Fiction.
    2. Diabetes—Patients—Fiction. 3. Loss (Psychology)—Fiction.
    4. Assisted suicide—Fiction. I. Title.

PS3563.C386G65 1996
813'.54—dc20   96-46707

First published in the United States by HarperCollins*Publishers*

First Picador Edition: March 2004

10 9 8 7 6 5 4 3 2 1

ma già volgeva il mio disio e'l velle
sì come rota ch'igualmente è mossa,
l'amor che move il sole e l'altre stelle.

—Dante, Paradiso, XXXIII, 143–145

all the livelong way this day of sweet
showers
  from Portrane to the seashore
Donabate sad swans of Turvey Swords
pounding along in three ratios like a sonata

—Samuel Beckett, from "Sanies I"

The author is grateful to

Robert Jones
Jennifer Arra
The John Simon Guggenheim Memorial Foundation
Sheila Gillooly
David Breskin
Isabel Thompson
Terry McManus
Mary Ellen McManus
and
Bob Cornfield

PART 1

This isn't really a horror story, but for the last seven years just the thought of what happened to David, of what I did to my Saint, has burned in my blood like cold powdered glass for an hour or two every day, sometimes all day and all night. Sometimes for eight or ten nights in a row, whether or not I'm awake. I can't make myself not remember it.

The day the ferry dropped us off at our campsite, June 28, was clear, crisp, and reasonably warm, about sixty-five degrees, but thirty degrees cooler when the sun sank below the mountains. The top third of the Alseks were covered with snow, and some of the shallower inlets were frozen. Four humpback whales breached and showed us their flukes as we cruised up the bay. Miniature icebergs tilted and spun in our wake.

It was the first time I'd ever seen mountains. Our campsite, on the northeastern shore of Tarr Inlet, was surrounded by them: the Alseks behind us, rising twelve thousand feet from the water, and the Fairweather range to the west—higher, more jagged, cutting the sun off six hours before it actually set in the Pacific.

Between the two ranges were the Margerie and Grand Pacific glaciers, which came together at the northern tip of Tarr Inlet in a four-mile-long wall of ice the color of road salt. Fruzen Velva, Saint called it. When a glacier calved—as one of them did every fifteen or twenty minutes—blue bergs the size of six-flats ripped away from the wall and belly-flopped into the water. It sounded like planes taking off.

Our campsite was almost three miles from the ice, directly across the inlet from Margerie Glacier, but the intensity of the light bouncing back through the crystalline air made it seem like three blocks. Even with sunglasses on, it was painful to do more than glance at it. The way it just *glowed*, the blue ice looked plugged-in or somehow on fire. Our plan was to paddle our kayaks along "her" (Saint's designation) the following morning, drifting up close without getting too reckless.

We pitched our tent on a flat patch of turf twenty yards from the water in a clearing surrounded by alders and birch trees not much taller than me. The closest other campsite was three hundred yards to the south.

David took out his rod and tackle box and caught three gorgeous trout in ten minutes; he was more of a firing squad than a sportsman. I walked down the inlet and took a roll of pictures of eagles and mountains and glaciers. I didn't take any of David that afternoon; I figured it could wait till after dinner—or the morning, when he got in his kayak. I was also planning to use the timer and set up some pictures of both of us.

Sitting on our zipped-together sleeping bags, I loaded a syringe in the light from our reading lamp. (For passionate young lovers communing with unspoiled nature, we'd sure packed a lot of CD's and books and syringes.) I brushed away an especially ferocious mosquito before hitting myself up in my lower-left thigh—my first and last shot in the wilderness— then stowed the syringe in our trash bag. We'd been instructed in no uncertain terms by the rangers to "pack out" all non-biodegradable refuse. I figured this meant used syringes.

I was more concerned with staying warm, brushing my teeth, and coming up with a plan for washing my hair without going hypothermic; the idea of dunking my head into an inlet of Glacier Bay made my molars ring out sostenuto. Once the sun went below the Fairweathers, it was hard to stop shivering, though the sky was still bright overhead. I was wearing a quilted down vest, insulated hiking boots, jeans, a flannel shirt, and long underwear. *Brrr!* It was gorgeous and horrible, camping. I firmly decided never to do it again, changed my mind several times, never achieved any closure. But I loved being out there with Saint.

My image of him in Alaska: sitting cross-legged on top of the boulder in front of our sleek yellow tent, reading the booklet of liner notes to a Mingus CD while swatting bugs from his face. Incipient dark-brown goatee, black plastic sunglasses with green prescription lenses for his weak gray-blue eyes, brown hair swept back behind his ears, pushed down across the top by the headphones. Behind him the Alseks are dull gold and black, backlit with sapphire sky and gray cotton clouds tipped with pink. But above all his face. Just his face.

When I experimented with my kayak, practicing for our trip to the glacier, it wasn't as unwieldy or prone to flip over as I'd thought it would be. It went more or less where I aimed it. I made two wobbly arcs out and away from Saint's boulder, then rested my paddle across the bow and mock-flexed my biceps to show him how pumped I was feeling. I knew he was anxious about whether the pancreatically challenged were up to this level of roughing it. So. I was showing him.

He grinned and flexed back at me. Now that I'd stopped paddling, I could hear "Fables of Faubus" leaking out the sides of his headphones.

"Any no-see-ums out there?" he called, much too loud.

I shook my head no and kept flexing.

Less loudly, he asked, "There are but you just can't see um?"

When I pretended to grab one from out of the air and squish it by clapping my hands, he applauded in time to the music.

We scoured the campsite, then got into the tent a little after eleven. It had already been a long day, and it was two in the morning Chicago (and my body clock's) time. *Ah Um* was playing on the little foam Discman headphones, which were down by the ends of our sleeping bags. Even with the volume on ten, it was distant and comically tinny. Outside the tent the bay rippled gently, incessantly, lapping the pebbles beneath our beached kayaks. I felt horny and cold and sequestered, alone in the wild with my Saint.

He pulled off his sweatshirt, cursing and swatting mosquitos. I leaned back on the egg-crate foam mattress and watched him. He was pretty in daylight with clothes on; he was pretty in moonlight soaking through yellow Gore-Tex. Bugs whined behind and between us as I rolled back and shimmied from my jeans. It felt like I was sitting on soft little mountains—as though my thighs had expanded to vast, continental proportions. Saint stroked the inside of one, then the other, using the back of his hand, one too-brief, unhasty stroke each. I couldn't stop shivering, but I didn't feel cold anymore. From the short streak of gray on his chin, I could tell that he'd just brushed his teeth.

He pulled off his boots and socks. His legs were tanned from the middle of his thighs to his toes except for the lines from the straps of his sandals, which glowed in the dark at the other end of the tent, a million and a half miles away.

"Ghosts," I said, pointing them out.

He squinted. "Iridescent puppies," he said, wiggling his long, bony toes. The white wishbone lines bent and shimmered.

"Like the fruzen velva glaciers," I said.

"Oh, I don't wanna lick them," he sang. "I just wanna be their victim."

"Lick who?"

He kissed me. The cathedral vault of the tent was brushing our hair and the sides of our faces. We knelt there and kissed for a while. It was only our fifth night together, and sometimes I don't even count it.

Eventually David pulled back his knees and slid off his shorts. In the moonlight his olive-drab boxers looked black against his pale skin. I could see his erection slanting up toward the waistband. I was trying to decide whether to make a friendly remark about that when he put his hand on the side of my neck and kissed me again. No tongues in play, just lips lightly brushing. I tasted a soupçon of baking soda as I ran my hand over his chest.

We knelt on the mountainous foam and fondled each other as the mosquitoes and no-see-ums attacked. I ran my nails over his nipples. I knew David liked that; I loved when he did it to me. We nibbled on each other's lips. I hoped that my breath wasn't horrible. Gently, our lips barely touching, then with sudden ferocity, we kissed. We were starting to get pretty good at it.

But the mosquitoes were still a huge nuisance, even inside the zipped tent. We'd been careful all day to keep the mesh doorway zipped, but there were still five or ten of them buzzing us. I'd read in a guidebook that only the females would sting you for blood—but so what did the males do for nourishment? Rely on their wives or their girlfriends? Whatever their gender, the ones in our tent were half an inch long and persistent.

Saint sprayed some Jungle Juice on his fingers and painted my neck, my forehead, my cheeks, the insides of my wrists . . .

"Hold still," he told me.

"It's cold, plus it tickles," I said, holding as still as I could.

He lifted my sweatshirt and rattled the can back and forth. I swallowed. Gingerly, watching me, taking his goddamn sweet time, he fingerpainted each of my nipples. All in good time, I reciprocated, daubing chevrons of invisible war paint onto his nose, cheekbones, forehead. I told him to take off his shirt.

"Yes'm," he said shiveringly, mocking me. "Whatever you s-say. A-a-absolutely."

"Turn around." I squinted, the better to see him obey me. "Yes'm."

Still kneeling, he turned. I sprayed his shoulders and back, then used my hands to smooth it over his back, arms, and legs, memorizing (I thought) every last detail with my too-hungry fingers. I remember his eminent little buttocks when I tugged down his boxers. I smoothed and bit and kissed them, then moved up and licked the downy hairs in the small of his back, tasting the sticky martini of bug spray. It could have been gasoline, transparent blood, or curare. I loved it. I painted and tasted him, watching him shudder and listening to his suggestions, and in roughly this manner the bloodthirsty female mosquitoes became even less of an issue.

That spring we'd been in Christina Zorn's seminar on contemporary Irish poetry. Saint never said much in class, but judging by Zorn's sotto voce comments when she handed back the papers, you could tell that she thought he was brilliant. And funny. I was getting A's and A-minuses on my own papers, but Zorn never muttered "Indeed" or shuddered with mirth when she handed them back or discussed them with me.

She also never invited me to Starbucks after class. That Parnassian compliment was reserved for Mr. David St. Germaine and another guy in the class named Bill Hill. My brain popped and sizzled with the various permutations and combinations of Zorn and either or both of those guys in the sack together, not one of them founded on even the most gossamer filament of evidence. There was also a rumor that Zorn had taken up with Leona Marvin, who in those days was UIC's resident light-heavyweight critic.

As the semester wore on I became almost frantic to get to know David, or at least get my hands on one of those "deftly convincing" papers of his. I was too insecure to simply show up at Starbucks alone, or to straightforwardly introduce myself after class. The day before May Day, a Wednesday, I came up with a fairly convincing faux-impromptu explication of Eavan Boland's "Spring at the Edge of the Sonnet," eliciting at least two nods from David and a low-key *mm-hmm* from Frau Zorn. After class I summarily decided I'd be well within my rights to tag along to get coffee, pretending at the outset to be headed in that direction myself.

As we moved up toward Morgan Street, we configured ourselves mostly as twosomes in a series of raggedy parallelograms: first Zorn and me in front with Bill and David behind us, then me in the back with Bill Hill. I couldn't get paired off with David.

"I mean, who *doesn't* wanna kill Ronald Reagan and fuck Jodie Foster?" Bill Hill asked rhetorically, taking up a thread I hadn't been privy to.

David just shrugged, but Zorn burst out laughing.

"I doesn't," I blurted—to assert myself, I suppose. Own my anger, or something like that. Own Zorn's laughter, perhaps. I said it, in any event. I didn't say it confrontationally; I admitted it as a matter of fact, for the record.

"Sure, right, okay, but—you *don't?*" said Bill Hill, while subtly but witheringly, spiked head thrown sideways and back, Frau Zorn said, "Ah."

David, for his part, said nothing.

"Um, not particularly," I said. I was being a stick in the mud pie they were joyously baking. I don't really know what my point was.

"That's what they all say," David piped in, and not too sarcastically either. Had he come to my rescue? Sort of, I thought. I was hoping. But *they?*

"But that doesn't prove she's insane!" Bill Hill claimed triumphantly.

In response, Christina Zorn made several wet lip farts, which left me too startled to answer Bill Hill. The three of them were already off again on what I gradually understood to be a running debate as to the difference between actors and movie stars. Billie Whitelaw had ceased to be a legitimate actor when she cut short her stint in the London production of *Happy Days* to take the part of Damian's nanny in *The Omen*. Ronald Reagan was an actor as president and he was not an actor as an actor. Roy Scheider was an actor in *Sorcerer*, but in all his other films he was a movie star. Harrison Ford was a squinter, a newt, a torso with limbs, monolithically intense, a wally, and (according to David) a mook. Dustin Hoffman and Anthony Hopkins and Danny Glover were actors who happened to be movie stars. Robert De Niro was becoming a mook if he didn't watch out. Roman Polanski was a century-class director and child molester *as well as* a half-decent actor. Jane Fonda was an aerobics instructor and, worse, a wife. Madonna could act like a mother; no she couldn't; the fuck she couldn't; she could—if you'd seen her on Broadway in *Speed-the-Plow*, bud, you'd know that. When she wasn't being too tomboyishly cutesy or "lizardly," according to Bill Hill, Jodie Foster was a convincing and serious actor. They went on and on in a series of flamboyantly opinionated exchanges that startled me further when it managed a measure of closure: however sane John Hinckley might be, he was not, in Bill Hill's humble opinion, an actor.

Half a block from Starbucks, Zorn and Bill Hill simultaneously discovered that they needed to get home immediately— to their separate apartments, that is. At least that's what I thought was being communicated. They were speaking to one another with cryptic signals and pauses that I couldn't decode. They said they'd catch up with us later.

David shrugged. He was wearing a blue hooded sweatshirt with the sleeves pushed past his elbows and black rugby shorts. His limbs had looked delicious all afternoon, but I would have been willing to bet he was about to make his own excuse, or just make a run for it, using those same sightly limbs.

We stood there, everyone smoking but me. I watched the three of them carefully, trying to read the unfolding, four-part departure. David and Zorn raised their eyebrows a fifth of an inch. Bill Hill's right thumb almost, then *did* touch, Zorn's elbow. Nothing else happened of note. And then Zorn and Bill Hill were gone, headed in separate directions, and David and I were walking up Morgan alone.

We sat on tall stools at a little round table in Starbucks. David had paid for our coffees at the register but allowed me to hand him two dollars. We rotated our cups with our palms as though they were tiny LP's that we wanted to fit on a spindle. David was asking me questions and I was answering them; I cannot remember the subject. I do recall snapping the upper corners of the Equal packet before I tore it open, making sure no granules were stuck in the crevices, then snapping the bottom corners after I'd emptied it into my cup. David continued to talk to me.

I sipped the strong coffee. I swallowed. "So what's so funny about those papers that Zorn's always joshing you?"

"Joshing me?"

Why had I said that? It definitely wasn't a word I would use. No one would use it unless they were deranged with anxiety. "She must think they're terribly witty," I said. I couldn't have felt too much less so, myself.

"What makes you think she thinks they're so funny?"

I haltingly managed to recount my process of deduction.

David shrugged. "She never told *me* they were funny."

"Be that as it may. I'd still like to read one sometime."

He shrugged, said, "Okay." The way his jaw would move under his skin—I adored it; I wanted my own jaw to move that way too. Plus his eyes looked so angry and confident, while his voice was so sad. I suddenly felt very . . . *invaginable*, if that's the right word. I think I'd become slightly delirious. I needed to get some glucose into my system. I therefore couldn't be held accountable for what I was saying, and I knew that I would be.

I imagined him saying, "I orchestrated all this, you know, with Christina and Bill."

"Oh, really," I planned to say coolly. "How candid of you to admit it."

What actually happened was—as I sucked on butterscotch Lifesavers two at a time—David and I discovered we could talk. It was good. I told him about my father getting arrested for shoplifting at Tower Records. About how much I'd hated New Trier. About running over the bright orange cord of our electric lawnmower, having it repaired at the hardware store, shredding it again the next time I mowed the backyard. When I told him I had diabetes, he nodded and asked me since when. He didn't ask me twenty questions, but it also wasn't like it hadn't registered, either. He listened to me without cringing—not that I went into any of the gory details. But he wasn't grossed out. It wasn't the end of the world.

He told me about his father's MS, that he'd died five years earlier; then he changed the subject back to movies. He'd just been accepted into the filmmaking program at NYU; he was going to start in September. As I furiously made plans to move to Manhattan, he asked if I'd seen *Rikki's Number*. I hadn't. We talked about *La Femme Nikita* and *The Plumber* and *Eraserhead* and *The Piano*. He told me he wanted to make a film of *Molloy*.

"You do."

"Yeah, I do."

"I doubt that's a real good idea," I said. Rather bold.

"Why is that?"

I nodded with re-trebled boldness. "It's much, much too inward. All the humor's in the narrator's voice."

"Exactly. In voice-over. Then you braid the two stories together. Molloy on his way to his mother's, Moran and his son tracking him down on their bike . . . "

"Where's this gonna happen? On location in Wicklow?"

"On location in Wicklow and the Vaucluse." He was getting excited. "Though I think a lot of it could be shot in upstate New York. In the Catskills."

I asked him to let me think about that. He said that he would. He did not mention Emma, his previous girlfriend. He did let me buy the last round.

We stood outside Starbucks, surrounded by hookers and students and kids in long shorts and no socks on oversized translucent skateboards.

"I'll talk to you," David said finally.

I nodded.

"So, okay," David said.

"We'll definitely talk then," I said. "I gotta read one of those papers."

He kissed me good-bye on the cheek, three fourths of an inch from my mouth. "Absolutely."

I walked and danced and trotted the six blocks to my apartment and immediately tested my blood. I was low— about twenty, I think.

I was shaky.

I'd known him for less than two months when we went to Alaska. Depending on what things you counted, the trip was either our fifth or sixth date. We had coffee at Starbucks, we saw Ray Charles at Ravinia, he brought about fifty CD's over to my apartment and gave a two-hour disquisition on Coleman Hawkins and Coltrane and Sonny Rollins and Wayne Shorter and Joe Zawinul while we watched a Bulls play-off game; I made broccoli and shells and answered some more of his queries about diabetes. We went out to dinner at Mare. We also stayed home a few nights and read things we liked to each other. He read me the end of *Molloy*.

I didn't want to take things too fast. I was feeling so happy, I was petrified that it would stop. People protect themselves emotionally by keeping their distance from me. They know I'll get sick on them, make them feel guilty, somehow responsible even. They think they'll have to take care of me. They sense that I might die on them.

David wasn't obsessed about sex the way most straight guys were in Chicago, at least the ones I'd met. He did show me the results of the HIV test he'd taken in February: negative. "Just in case you were wondering," he told me. But it wasn't a come-on; he was simply letting me know, for the record. He was blushing, in fact, as he usually did when the subject of sex came up.

"I wasn't," I told him. He wouldn't stop blushing, so I

changed the subject, and he put the xeroxed certificate back in his pocket. Not that I wasn't interested in the results of his test, or that I wasn't interested in having sex with him. I was confident that both of us knew what the other one wanted to happen, though I can't say exactly what this confidence was based on. I'd assumed he was negative, but it wouldn't have been the end of the world if he wasn't.

We made love fourteen times. At least that's the number I've settled on. I've gone over these sessions so manically so many times that a couple of similar ones may have merged, but I know I haven't forgotten any. What kills me is the way crucial details have started to fade. I remember what David looked like and the "plot" of what we did to each other, whereas what his skin on mine actually felt like is no longer available. The only time I can get back those feelings is when I dream about us. But since I can't control the rhythm or intensity, and since by the end of these dreams we're never together, I'd rather not have them at all.

We made love two times in Alaska, the other twelve times in my apartment. The first three or four times were awkward but terribly wonderful. I waited till I got out of bed and into the bathroom to cry. I thought he was beautiful, and I sensed that he loved me.

I knew I loved him.

As far as the mechanics were concerned, we began to get better. First gradually, then rather suddenly. When he asked me to go to Alaska with him, I said yes. I'd never been the outdoorsy type—I was a girl from the suburbs going to college downtown—but the decision was not a close call.

The night and morning before our plane left for Seattle, we made love four times; we couldn't stop tasting each other. We rubbed through our flesh. It was more or less continual, with some dozing and food and syringes spliced in, but four is the number I've assigned to it. We couldn't stop fucking. I cried that time too.

We were something.

*   *   *

David and Emma Pitt had gone camping twice: once in the Ozarks, once on a dory trip down the Colorado River. When he asked me to go to Alaska with him I was thrilled, but I worried that the trip would be an experiment to help him discover whether he was better off—as happy, as horny, as intellectually fulfilled, or whatever—with me than he had been with Emma.

I don't think he ever decided. I do know that he never seemed altogether contented at any point in the month and a half I knew him. I was always afraid he missed Emma. I once heard him refer to her as "the Pits" in a tone that was not unaffectionate while he was talking on the phone with his mother.

And it's not that he was always melancholic; it's more accurate to say he had a nervous, sort of bluesy, reserve. Like me, he was a natural isolate. He often seemed slightly exhausted. He didn't talk much, except for brief, sudden outbursts in which he'd wax elegiac about Beckett, Miles Davis, Coltrane, Mingus, Richard Pryor, Nusrat Fateh Ali Khan, Martin Scorsese, Pernell Whitaker, Julius Erving, Scottie Pippen—I never really noticed his aproportional affinity for the exploits of black guys until after he'd died. I wish we could've talked about that.

Even when he was clearly enjoying himself there was always some blues in the grain of his voice, something I heard as a sadness. Maybe it was simply the way his larynx or vocal cords were constructed. His eyes never looked all that sad.

I don't know. It was one of the things I liked most about him, since happy talk has always been my least favorite mode of expression. How much of his sadness got generated by his separation from Emma I'll never be able to know.

Another key factor: His father had MS for ten years and had died of a heart attack when he was forty-six, when David was seventeen. David inherited a trust fund that kicked in when he turned twenty-one. I never knew how much money was involved, except that it was enough to be able to book trips for two to Alaska without worrying too much or saving up ahead of time. He tapped his foot and played with my hair while reading his credit card number over the phone to the travel agent. He had five or six hundred CD's.

That his father had died of a chronic disease was one of the things that attracted me to David: the fact that he understood illness, or at least had had to deal with it. The only problem was that he might have already been close to the end of his rope as far as sick people were concerned. When the subject of diabetes came up, he didn't exhale and smile and turn away slightly. He did not—like some of my girlfriends in high school—ask to check out my "tracks." He did not change the subject. The questions he asked tended toward the practical: how many shots a day, what would happen if I skipped one, etc. He didn't ask whether it was sexually transmittable, but after we'd exchanged fluids a few times I decided to volunteer that it wasn't, just in case he was wondering. He told me he already knew that.

He also didn't flinch the first time I showed him my works. If anything, he seemed almost too fascinated by the lancets and logs and syringes. One night he pricked his own finger and tested his sugar; he was 117, slightly high. (I think I remember this number because that's how much I weighed at the time.) We'd just spent an afternoon and half of an evening in bed together, and I was starting to feel pretty shaky. It was the first time I'd had an orgasm with anyone other than myself. I'd spent most of the previous decade wondering whether I'd be able to tell the difference between an orgasm caused by a man and the early stages of an insulin reaction, but now I'd experienced both in one evening and I'd definitely been able to distinguish between them. Once I found out the answer to *that* question, I wanted to know whether David was feigning all his unfazedness about diabetes in order to make me feel "comfortable." To make me feel loved? That's probably what I would've done, and I don't think it would've been such a bad thing, but I still wanted to *know* how he felt about my disease. About what were, for me, all the humiliating details. Did he have some sort of kinky fascination with needles and bubbles of blood? If he did, it never had a chance to come out. Maybe he thought my works might come in handy someday. I don't know.

Two nights before we left for Alaska, we went to see Ray Charles at Ravinia. Our seats were way down in row seven. The Raylettes wore stylish but relatively loose-fitting, knee-length red dresses. They looked almost dowdy compared to the versions I'd seen in the Pepsi commercials—those women were models, whereas the five women on the stage singing with Ray and his band were real singers; they played tambourines and did call-and-response stuff, teasing Ray into several huge grins. He played "Hit the Road" and "The Right Time" and "I Want A Little Girl." Before he played "Georgia" he explained that it was a song about a woman he'd loved but also about the last place he saw before he went blind. Then he played it. I was crying and swaying and dancing right there in the seat. I wanted to know what David was thinking, but I didn't think I knew him well enough yet to ask questions like that. He was watching Ray Charles bounce and rock back and forth on his black leather bench, belting the words out and banging away on the keys.

On the flight from Chicago to Seattle we gained two hours, then another hour flying up to Juneau. I followed the "Diabetic Traveler" chart: my usual dosage that morning and evening, plus one third of my morning dosage at 3:00 A.M. Chicago time. In the morning I set my watch to Juneau time and began to give myself the usual breakfast and dinner doses. I'd thought it would be much more complicated.

On the flight up to Juneau the signs in the cabin were printed in English and Yupik. FOR YOUR SAFETY, they said. PIYAQQULUKTAIRRUTIKSRAGNUN.

"You got that?" said David, pointing one out as we both stood in line for the john.

I pronounced it as well as I could.

"Then put out that reefer this instant!"

That got us two or three looks. He ignored them. I stood there and giggled and yawned. I was still kind of nervous around him.

Back in our seats, he grilled me about how to recognize the symptoms of an insulin reaction. If I started slurring my words or became stuporous he should force me to swallow some fruit juice or non-diet soda; if necessary, he should slap me in the face to focus my attention. If I still ended up passing out, he knew how to load the syringe with glucagon and administer the injection, but I emphasized that this was definitely a *last*-last-ditch measure. I also let him know that my tendency to "run high" made it extremely unlikely that I'd have a reaction. I told him not to worry, and he promised me he wouldn't.

"Just do what I'll do if you have an erection," I whispered.

"What's that?" he asked, turning pink.

"Just remain calm and, you know, *tair rutiks ragnun.*"

"Absolutely. Though I don't even think you can get them when you're out in the bush, getting eaten alive by mosquitoes."

Ms. Pitt flashed to mind, slim legs doubled back on the needle-strewn floor of some federally protected virgin timberland, getting zapped by mosquitoes and David in all her cuntorial splendor. I exhaled and steadied myself. "Then you simply unpack some of that high-powered repellent we've got. That stuff you picked up at the REI store."

"Jungle Juice."

"Right. Massage well into all exposed surfaces, avoiding exposure to eyes, mouth—"

"And tongue?"

I patted and rubbed the inside of his thigh, keeping my hand near his knee in case any high-minded Air Alaska flight attendants were in the vicinity, then put my mouth next to his ear. "And keep out of reach of small children."

We spent the first night in Gustavus in the Glacier Bay Lodge. The boat that took us out to our campsite left the next morning at seven. Our plan was to camp alongside the Tarr Inlet for four days, then fly up to Denali. Neither of us had ever paddled a kayak, but we'd rented two anyway. The outfitter's package also included foam mattresses, sleeping bags insulated to zero degrees, a mosquito-proof tent, a flashlight, four days' worth of meals, and a short-wave radio.

A gold-toothed, ponytailed Park Service ranger named George briefed all the campers and backpackers. There were twenty-five or thirty of us, standing around in a semicircle. Except for all the Gore-Tex and capilene, it looked like a sixties convention: long hair and beards on the men, long hair and beatific smiles and no makeup (and only one peach-fuzz mustache) on the women. We were formally handed brochures with camping advice and park regulations: do not feed bears, keep a clean camp, do not camp on bear trails, do carry firearms. No one I saw had a firearm. One entire brochure was devoted to the issue of giardia, but George added a personal note. Animals shat in the water, he informed us. This spawned strains of bacteria that in humans caused "some fairly mind-bending diarrhea. So please be advised." So we were.

After determining what my insulin dosages would be, what I most wanted to know was, what does one do with one's hair when camping outside for four days and nights? If I don't wash my own every day it quickly begins to resemble a Valdez-caliber oil slick with frizz. My provisional plan was to keep it braided, wear my cap, play it by ear. We would, after all, be wearing our stocking caps to bed, would we not? I'd disguise myself as The Edge. We were to brush our teeth and sponge ourselves off in the bay—Glacier Bay—dodging the giardia as well as we could while we gargled, treating the water we drank with iodine tablets. I tried to convince myself that David and I were beyond worrying about mere appearances or the way our breath smelled. We'd known one another for almost six weeks, after all.

Our instructions with respect to wild animals and calving glaciers were detailed and explicit. Stay at least a mile from the Margerie Glacier; a safe distance could be determined by approaching the glacier very slowly from a perpendicular angle and watching it through binoculars; when part of it calved, you checked to see how far the resultant miniature tidal waves extended; if one of these waves rocked your kayak even slightly, back off—the next one might be twelve times as large.

Campers would be deposited within a quarter mile of each other. Our campsites had been selected for their lack of proximity to salmon streams, berry patches, whale carcasses—anything that might attract bears. Some of the brown bears in this part of Alaska stood nine feet tall and weighed twelve hundred pounds. We were repeatedly reminded to keep a clean campsite. We should not get between a sow and her cubs. If confronted by a bear, we should turn sideways and crouch down to make ourselves appear less imposing, then back away slowly while keeping our eyes on the bear. In the unlikely event that one were to charge, we should drop to the ground, cover our crotch and head, and play dead. As the group awaited the ferry, we practiced this maneuver, tripping over backpacks and rocks as we crouched and shuffled unimposingly sideways and covered our crotches, producing much mirth. Two students from Scotland, Barbara and Willie, would be camping about five hundred yards from our site. We played dead with them and made friends.

It now seems stupefyingly irresponsible to me that humans would be permitted to camp anywhere near a grizzly habitat. I've read up on the subject. (Not exhaustively, of course. There are well over five thousand articles and books in print about grizzlies. But still. I know some things now.) The central fact is that wolves and coyotes and moose do not attack humans, but bears attack and kill humans on a regular basis. Since 1975 seven people had been killed by grizzlies within Glacier National Park alone, and thirteen others had been mauled. The moment that ferry off-landed us along the Tarr Inlet we'd reentered the food chain, and not at the top. Rangers had briefed us in detail, we'd been handed brochures, but no one had proposed that we not camp there. There were, granted, signs posted prominently and designed to give pause. ENTERING GRIZZLY COUNTRY, they said in bold black letters beneath a graphic rendering of a rabid-looking grizzly. *You have come here voluntarily to enjoy this natural scene. There is no guarantee of your safety. Bears may attack without warning and for no apparent reason. Respect this wild country and its inhabitants. Follow the rules posted at the trailhead. Visitors have been injured and killed by bears.*

Nothing unambiguous about it. The signs were printed on brittle orange plastic, then slashed diagonally six or eight times before being stapled to trees. It was immediately clear to me why the signs had been slashed: to discourage people like me from trying to remove one intact and taking it home as a souvenir—to hang on the door of my room when I felt especially grouchy, for example. And for people like me who found the prospect of spotting a grizzly invigorating.

I don't think David was apprehensive about grizzly bears either, probably for the same reasons I wasn't. We flew in airplanes and lived in big cities and drove on expressways: it was dangerous, possibly fatal, but the odds were still with us. We were talking about one in a million—in ten million, probably. We were talking statistics. We were talking about some other person.

The fact is that David very much wanted to encounter a grizzly in the wild. He had two books about them in his day pack, and we both expected to see bears when we got to Denali; according to the guidebooks, it was virtually guaranteed that we could watch them up close, from a bus. People in Gustavus made jokes about them, especially when they heard we were from Chicago: da Bears. But Glacier Bay was where you went to see glaciers and seabirds and whales. David was mainly up there for the air and the visuals—and to compare me with Emma as a tentmate and hiking companion. He also probably assumed, as I did, that if rangers with government patches stitched to their hats were permitting us to camp along the Tarr Inlet, it was safe for us to camp there; that the brochures and oral caveats and slashed plastic signs were pro forma.

I woke up that night with my whole body caught in the grip of a nightmare I'd already forgotten. Bewildered and shivering, saliva and bugs on my face. I was still half asleep when I heard someone hollering. Shrieking. I didn't know where it was coming from.

It dawned on me then: David was outside the tent. I noticed that the flap was unzipped when I began to crawl out, then almost sobbed with relief when I bumped my forehead against bony white knees.

They were Willie's. He was squatting in front of our tent and yelling at me. Why had this crazy man unzipped our tent? It took me a moment to connect the Scottish accent with the man we'd been introduced to the previous morning. All I had on was David's NYU sweatshirt and a wad of Kleenex stuck between my legs.

A hundred-pound bear cub bounded through the campsite, skidding to a stop near the kayaks. It grunted and sniffed, looked around. Its fur was ash blond, long and matted everywhere except for its glittering snout. It was easily as large as an adult German shepherd, but thicker and hairier—wilder. And scared. It trembled with fear and confusion. When Willie cursed it and told it to go, it obediently took off down the shore of the inlet—the same direction from which we now heard a blood-freezing roar as well as choked, desperate hollering.

"He's no in there with ye?" said Willie.

I stared at him: No! And yet I was still strangely calm. It hadn't sunk in yet what had happened. The cub hadn't looked like a killer.

"Oh Christ!" Willie said.

Barbara appeared now beside him with a Day-Glo orange blanket wrapped around her shoulders. She was sobbing and shivering. Willie told her to get on the shortwave and call the ranger station. We'd all received detailed instructions on how to transmit a distress call. I didn't remember a word.

More roaring then, and much more loud screaming. I knew. I ran in the direction of the screams and the roaring, but as soon as I began running toward them, they stopped. The order of events isn't clear. I ran toward the places I thought David was. There were trees and small bushes. Willie ran after me, holding my elbow, yelling at me to please stop.

I climbed a small hill and peered down the shore of the bay. It was still too misty and dark to see very far, but the growling was unmistakably closer.

Dimly at first, about forty yards away in faint blue dawn light, I saw it: an enormous blond bear was shaking a naked gray body. I understood that it was David.

I ran in that direction. I fell and got up and kept running. I couldn't catch my breath or stop sobbing. Willie was screaming at me, at the bear. I don't know. I called David's name. His body was running with blood.

It seemed altogether impossible that the bear was that big. Saint's body looked like a rag doll in the mouth of a very large dog. Willie threw baseball-sized rocks, and the third or fourth one hit the bear in the side. It turned and glared at us, still holding Saint by the shoulder. It grunted and shook him. I screamed. Its eyes were small coals.

The cub we'd seen in the campsite appeared by its mother. The sow gave Saint's body another vicious shaking, then turned from the shore and carried the body beyond some large rocks. The cub trotted briskly behind her. They disappeared into the mist and the boulders.

I ran toward the gap in the rocks. Willie caught up with me, grabbed my elbow. "Don't be stupid!" He held my wrist with both of his hands while we screamed at each other.

I broke free and ran. I couldn't hear the bear anymore as I ran through the gap in the rocks. All I could see were some trees. I ran and kept calling for David.

Willie tackled me. He held me against the ground, pressing his weight against the small of my back. His teeth were chattering, and I smelled his rank breath. The wet ground was rocky and cold. Corners of shale stones cut into my belly and legs. Willie Harris from Largs, Scotland, pressed me down with his shivering body. He held me there like that.

Medics arrived by helicopter. Rangers with rifles and special binoculars arrived in a float plane. It was light out. The pilot and one of the rangers were talking to Barbara and three other campers. We all had some clothes on by now.

It was originally determined that the sow was wearing a radio collar, but that turned out not to be true. I was given to understand that David had gotten up to urinate and somehow found himself between the sow and her cub. I nodded. I didn't ask how they could know that.

After a heated discussion between two of the rangers, I was permitted to join the search party. We followed the trail of prints, flattened grass, smears of blood. The rangers were hyper-alert; it was easy to see they were scared. One of the rangers was Tlingit.

After an hour or two—fifteen minutes?—we stopped. Someone had found blood-smeared grass. Two rangers got down on their hands and knees to examine the evidence. One put a hand on my shoulder.

The lead ranger leveled his rifle as he slowly moved forward. He stopped. I was told later on that I tried to rush past him. A second ranger grabbed my arm firmly.

"Please, ma'am. We're going to find him."

"Just found him," the lead ranger whispered.

They moved forward, crouching, covering each other with

oiled steel rifles. The lead ranger held up his hand.

We'd entered a clearing defined on one side by the horizontal trunk of a dead fir tree. Charred bark and sap, white wood exploded by lighting. The long tufts of grass in the clearing were matted and torn. There was blood.

I'd calmed down a little by now; my panic was coming and going in waves. Then I saw it: what was left of David's body wedged between the ground and the trunk, three fourths of it covered with stones, dirt, and brambles. It would have been difficult to recognize because of the mud and dried blood smeared across most of the unburied flesh, but I knew what it was. Everyone knew what it was. It seemed to be missing its head, an arm, at least part of one leg. Other than a line of red ants swarming around a deep gash, and huge horseflies diving and buzzing, there were no signs of life.

"She was coming back later to eat him."

"Finish eating him, it looks like."

I edged a step closer. I could face this grotesque thing stashed away on the ground in front of me only because it so little resembled my Saint.

Somebody whispered, "Oh Jesus." A tall man was crossing himself.

I turned to my left. One of the rangers was standing on a blood-matted patch of brown hair. David's scalp. I looked away, calm, staying calm, fairly calm, then turned to my right. I saw David's hand make a fist.

He was medevaced by the Coast Guard to St. Jude's Hospital in Juneau. Four surgeons worked for eleven hours to keep him alive. What the sow had done to him was enough to kill him eight or ten times. But it hadn't.

Much of this part is a blur. My whole brain felt vacant and sizzling. I don't remember much about my own trip from the campsite to Juneau. It was only sixty miles, but it apparently involved a float plane, a helicopter, and one or two ground vehicles.

I remember strange details. Two black-haired boys with tubes up their noses getting pushed in black wheelchairs by very old nuns. A small, skinny boy on a gurney, white plaster casts on both legs. One of the doctors had on an inside-out argyle sock, which I took as a clear indication of carelessness, of the amateur-hour medical attention David was getting.

I was semi-catatonic but frantic. That I hadn't done my shot or eaten a meal made me feel even more like a zombie. By the time I did my shot two days later, I was probably spilling some serious ketones, about to go into a coma myself.

I'd always hated hospitals. I hated their low, well-spaced, stainless-steel drinking fountains, gleaming tile floors and humming machinery, hoses and latex gloves and catheters in every other drawer. I hated them because I'd spent enough time in them to know what was in store for me. I hated them with a visceral intensity I've always understood I had to get over and now know I won't.

I was introduced to Dr. Florence Koo, a Korean woman in her middle or late forties. It was Dr. Koo's job to prepare me for what I would encounter when they finally let me in to see David. I shook her cool, tiny hand; she held onto mine and looked up at me. She was almost comically short, and she couldn't have weighed eighty pounds. She was searching my eyes, asking innocuous questions, gauging how much I could take at this stage.

"Tell me," I said. "I'm okay."

One of her eyebrows went up half an inch. She asked if I'd like to sit down.

We sat at right angles on mauve plastic chairs. She told me that David had lost both his legs and his eyes. Because of the grizzly's saliva, several of his wounds were infected. In his weakened condition, any of these infections might be life-threatening. His left hand had been amputated. Other things. I may have stopped hearing her after a while; sitting there with my eyes open, facing her, listening, I may have blacked out. I'd already known it was bad—that the grizzly had started to eat him alive, stopped for some reason, then partially buried him—so the kinds of details Dr. Koo was enumerating really didn't matter that much. She told me that the grizzly had ripped off his penis. I nodded. I was desperate to demonstrate my composure, that I could be entrusted with all pertinent information; if I lost my composure, the doctors wouldn't tell me everything, including some detail that could help Saint recover more quickly. This was my logic. Dr. Koo's English wasn't perfect, but I was able to understand what she said. She spoke much too slowly, I thought.

I wanted a cigarette. I was surprised to note how similar the inside of an Alaskan hospital was to the inside of a hospital in Evanston or Chicago. As Dr. Koo continued her summary, I saw David walking toward me down the hallway—his eyes, his goatee, his chest-forward saunter—but it turned out to be one of the maintenance men. I purposefully breathed in and out as Dr. Koo listed more of the measures being taken to keep him alive.

"... although grafts of that type usually don't take, any-way."

I shook my head, nodded. Not that type. Wouldn't take. No, of course not.

I wanted to see him. I did not want to wait anymore. Dr. Koo told me I was going to see him, but that she had one more thing to tell me. I listened.

She told me that David wanted to die. She told me that he'd wanted to die from the minute he'd arrived at their unit. I looked at her plastic ID badge. Her picture. A number. Her signature.

I didn't doubt it. I looked at the legs of a man who was taking a drink at the water fountain. His light-khaki pants were wrinkled and stained near one of the pockets, but they fit him just right. Was it David?

"I thought you should be aware of that," Dr. Koo told me.

I must have agreed.

"David remains adamant. He's been demanding that we disconnect—that we stop feeding him intravenously, though his mother is firmly against that. He's also still in shock."

I inhaled and exhaled. Dr. Koo kept on talking.

I nodded.

Dr. Koo eventually took me in to see him. His mother had already seen him, apparently. She'd flown up the previous day from Chicago. Three days had gone by since we'd found him. It felt like I'd been awake the whole time, but I was told that, at least once, I'd slept for ten hours straight on a couch in the solarium.

As Dr. Koo walked me down to the intensive care unit, I was nauseous and dazed but determined to do right by David, whatever that might turn out to require.

"Just try to stay calm, not react too much," Dr. Koo told me. "He won't be able to see you, but he'll probably sense it if you panic."

"I won't panic."

I didn't. What I saw on the bed when I entered the room was a tape and gauze sculpture connected by cables and tubes to various monitors and stabilizing devices. My Saint.

I stood alongside him. From the contours of the bandages you could tell that the left leg had been amputated above the knee. The right leg had been amputated, or torn off, even higher. A translucent tube ran from the scrotum to a plastic bag half-filled with blood-marbled urine. His left hand was gone, but his right arm and hand were intact. It was being used as the entry point for three catheters.

I took this pale-purple hand into mine.

"David? Sweetheart?"

He seemed not to hear me. His hand was so swollen and hot.

"I'm here," I whispered. "It's me."

No response. His head was entirely bandaged except for the slits where his nose and mouth should have been. There was no noselike rise in the gauze.

I looked at Dr. Koo. She signaled with a nod that I should keep trying.

"Sweetheart, you're going to be okay. The doctors all say . . . Can you hear me?"

As I looked at Dr. Koo again, the hand began squeezing mine—hard. I gasped and jerked sideways. All the strength he had left must have been concentrated in his thick, trembling hand.

I sat on the side of the bed and told him it was going to be all right, that the doctors were doing whatever it took, but I was interrupted by a ferociously sobbing howl the violence of which might have knocked me off the bed if his hand hadn't been gripping mine so tightly. His howl continued, got louder. One of his catheters got ripped out somehow, and the bag of bloody urine hit the floor and splashed open.

As Dr. Koo and one of the nurses tried to disengage our hands, David's fierce howling finally resolved into words: *I CAAAAAAAANNN'T . . . !*

But we held on as well as we could. And I listened.

*   *   *

Dr. Koo outlined David's legal position. He was an adult, but he had not left a living will. He wanted to die. His request had been tape-recorded; he would sign any papers. He did not want to live in the condition he was in. He did not want to be kept alive artificially. He wanted to die right away.

His mother and uncle were insisting he be fed intravenously, that all medical procedures be continued in order to keep him alive. His mother was not his legal guardian, but she was his next of kin. She was his mother. She planned to have David flown back to Chicago as soon as he was capable of surviving the trip.

"Has she seen him?" I asked Dr. Koo.

"She has seen him."

I shook hands with Mrs. St. Germaine and her brother, Paul, in one of the brightly lit waiting rooms. Corduroy couches, miniature evergreens in big ceramic pots, get-well cards and children's drawings taped to one wall. A small plastic ashtray. For a minute or so, I was angry at David for not introducing me to his mother before we left for Alaska; he should have understood that something like this might have happened.

An Inuit woman was sitting with her back to Mrs. St. Germaine and her brother; she was knitting the sleeve of a sweater. Her three-year-old son squirmed on the couch alongside her. He was wearing Chicago Bulls sweatpants.

Mrs. St. Germaine spoke right up. "It seems, although we all don't completely agree, that David's position—that it might be better if we waited for a while, to see . . . He is, after all, still in shock." She wasn't trying to reason with me. She was telling me.

Her brother was in his late forties: gray hair, camel sport coat, distinguished and prosperous-looking. He was there to support his big sister, but he really didn't say very much. I recognized David's high forehead and the shape of his eyes. He'd gotten his cheekbones and slenderness and the glinting cool blue of his eyes from the woman across from me. She was decked out in cashmere and silk, which offended me more than a little. Why get dressed up?

"We're still waiting to see what all these local doctors can do."

I nodded—I'm sure that I nodded—but I also must have exhaled somewhat skeptically. I don't think I laughed. I may have shaken my head.

We stared at each other. The lower-left part of her face was collapsing. She fought it. "Do you think we're just going to allow them to let David die?"

"I don't think that. No. But—"

"We're not!" she said. "At least *I'm* not." She looked at her brother, then glared back at me even harder.

I understand now that I should have expected it, but her ferocity took me aback. It was also apparent that she held me at least partially responsible for what had happened to her son, as well as for what was now being done, or not being done, to help him recover.

"Not 'just' let him die," I began. I had to speak up for David's position, but I couldn't really get very far.

"I'll certainly not let that happen!"

The Inuit woman was eavesdropping; she didn't try hard to conceal it. Her son, fidgeting beside her, had started to peek at me over the back of the couch. I tried to smile back, but I don't think I did a good job. I lit a cigarette.

Red-eyed with anger and grief, Mrs. St. Germaine continued her soliloquy. Her point was that she was in charge. As David's mother, she had legal standing. I didn't know what David had said to her, but I assumed that Dr. Koo had informed her of his position.

I must have eventually tuned her out. I exhaled some smoke, started coughing. The Inuit boy was peeking again.

I put out my cigarette and decided I needed to eat something. A doctor had supplied me with syringes and insulin. I didn't know what to do next.

"And he never said anything to us about suicide," said Mrs. St. Germaine.

"I really don't see how much clearer he could be that he doesn't want to live anymore." For some reason it was easier to say this to her than to convince myself that it was true. "He refuses to lie there like that."

"Not that it's any of your business."

I lit another cigarette. This desperate, angry woman wanted the same thing that I did: for David to be sewn back together, to not have been mauled in the first place. But there it was.

"All I know is what he just told me," I said. "There's nothing unclear about what he's decided."

"We're going to see about that."

The Inuit boy was still playing peekaboo. I finally covered my eyes with my cigarette hand and briefly peeked back. He dove down behind the top of the couch. A few seconds later his hands reappeared, then his shiny black hair in between them.

I did not want to argue with David's mother, but David's case had to get made. He wasn't there to make it himself, and he apparently lacked the legal wherewithal to execute his decision. His mother and her lawyer, who was supposed to arrive the next day, had the ears of the doctors. That was how I saw it.

Somehow I ended up trying to tell Mrs. St. Germaine and her brother how happy David had been on the trip. "I mean, even just doing the dishes, or reading, listening to music, cruising up the bay in his kayak. He was really looking forward to that. And I know that he wanted—"

I was starting to lose it. I put out the cigarette. The Inuit woman was watching me frankly.

"What did he want?" said Paul. "What I mean—*would* he want. Did he say?"

"We've still got to see what the doctors can do for him here," said Mrs. St. Germaine. "If not here, then the ones at Northwestern."

"What do you think he would want?" Paul repeated.

"What he wouldn't want, I don't think, as he's *said*, is to spend the whole rest of his life—"

Mrs. St. Germaine shook her head so violently that I was convinced she was going to launch herself off the couch and claw at my face. She glared back and forth, bug-eyed and flushed, between me and her brother. "He *never* said that! And didn't that doctor just promise us—"

Paul interrupted her. "What?"

The Inuit woman kept knitting, all ears. Her son stared at Paul, then at me.

Mrs. St. Germaine huffed and grunted. "Doing the *dishes!?*"

"Doing the dishes," I told her.

Paul asked me, "What else do you think he would've wanted?"

"What he wants to do is get better, of course," said Mrs. St. Germaine. "To see what the doctors can do for him here. After that, we'll be flying him back to Chicago."

Her brother now looked at me oddly—a smile?—then opened one palm. His wedding band shone in the too-bright fluorescence. "What would he want us to do?"

"Didn't you see him in there?" I said. I'd intended to sound more conciliatory, since he seemed to be taking my side. David's side. "We've all of us heard what he wants."

"Did I see him?" said Mrs. St. Germaine. "You can ask me that question? He's my son, and I certainly have seen him in there." She was sobbing, but violence still didn't seem out of the question. Just the opposite: she seemed to be getting more desperate. "Were *you* there to see him, out there, where he never should've gone in the first place?! Where were *you?!*" Trembling, she turned to her brother. "Don't you know what these doctors can *do?*"

Paul hugged her hard, patting her head and her back, but she couldn't calm down.

"But what are we talking about?" said Paul. "Plastic surgery? Glass eyes? Prosthetic—"

From somewhere not far down the hall came a thunderous crash of metal trays and cutlery. We were all rattled speechless for several long seconds. The Inuit boy started laughing.

"What did he tell you, Penny?" Paul asked me finally. He'd let go of his sister with one of his hands. He scratched his tanned cheek and leaned forward. "Did you two ever discuss—what he wanted?"

Was he asking me whether David and I had discussed heroic measures and life-support systems before we'd gone camping? Or did he simply want to know what David had told me since he'd been in the intensive care unit? Either way, it sounded as though he was asking me to decide what to do.

I gathered my thoughts and resisted lighting a cigarette. "I've really only known him since May, although—" I wanted to add that we hadn't even got around yet to discussing whether I'd move to New York in September.

"You see?" said Mrs. St. Germaine.

"What?" said Paul. "Let's please let her answer. Okay?"

She was muttering now. Her eyes were bulging and bloodshot behind her swank metal glasses. "Going off with strange little girls on these dangerous trips to begin with . . . "

I got up from the couch and walked out.

I sat on the bed beside Saint. We held hands. I caressed his right shoulder, kissed his forehead through the gauze. Blood and clear pus seeped through the gauze near the end of one leg. He smelled like stale milk and ammonia.

When he finally spoke, his ability to enunciate was impeded by the tube down his throat, but in timbre and grain it was still very much his old voice. I pieced together what he was saying as well as I could from various syllables and the gist of his syntax. The tube down his throat seemed thinner, slightly less uncomfortable for him, than the one he'd had earlier. The gauze on his face barely moved when he talked.

"I'm sorry about before."

"That's okay, sweetheart. Are you kidding? All I want is for you—" I kissed his hand. It seemed like the best thing to focus on: the strongest, most intact part of him. That and his forehead. The skin on the back of his hand was pale green and purple; the inside was clammy and hot. I felt his weak pulse tapping crazily.

"You thought about, shit, what I asked you?"

"What you asked me?" He hadn't yet asked me directly—that was the thing. I only knew what Dr. Koo had told me, and some things I'd inferred from his mother.

He began to curse violently while his sightless head jerked back and forth. I held him, whispering for him to just shush. He finally calmed down.

"Anyone else in this room?"

I told him there wasn't.

"Penny, listen to me." He faced me: a blank mask of tubing and gauze. It took what was left of his strength to rotate his head that few inches. "You can't imagine how ... All I need's a shot. Insulin. One fucking syringeful. You know."

I listened. I let him keep talking. I hated making him wait for my responses, but I had to find out *exactly* what he was asking for. I had to know what he was thinking.

"I lie here, no legs, no ... " He sobbed. "People babbling on ... fucking plastic surgery, fake hands, special fucking wheelchairs ... You said you'd do what I asked, did you not?"

I had not, but I squeezed his hand hard. "Yes," I said. "Yes."

"Penny, I'm really not kidding. You have to." He always said Penny or Pen—never Emma. I was almost surprised that he hadn't misspoken himself. I half expected her to waltz into the room any moment. But I hated myself for obsessing about trivial jealous details when David was fighting for—whatever it was that he wanted.

"I know you're not kidding," I told him. I kissed the bruised wrist. "I've told them that over and over."

"So please, Pen. *You have to!*" He gagged on the respirator. "Don't make me"—still gagging—"beg you."

"I won't." I was panicking. "I never will—"

"Next time they put me out. Then." His voice was exhausted and angry. "Asleep'll be easier."

"David, sweetheart, I just want—"

"I'm already dead, Pen. You know it! Don't make me lie here!"

We faced each other through the glare and the blindness and gauze, holding hands. He was shaking.

I nodded.

"Penny—okay?" He was begging.

I told him I'd do it.

I ate a small meal, walked around, tried to sleep. I ate one more meal after that. Did my shots. Declined to be interviewed by a psychiatrist. Borrowed three Merits from one of the surgeons. Accepted an apology from David's uncle for his sister's behavior. Was asked not to smoke in the hallway.

I sat in the too-bright solarium. The harbor below the hospital was dotted with seagulls and tilting, cerise-colored buoys. An enormous white cruise ship had docked at the end of the street, and some people were playing volleyball inside a floppy mesh cage on the deck. The men all had shorts on, no shirts; two of the women were wearing magenta bikinis. Every few minutes a float plane would taxi through the choppy water out beyond the harbor, giving itself room to take off, or another would land farther out. Sometimes, from where I was sitting, their paths seemed to cross. I wanted to witness a plane crash then refuse to respond to reporters.

There would not be a suicide note, even if he'd wanted to write one. He'd made it entirely clear to the doctors, to his mother and uncle, to me, what he wanted. But I still wanted more time to think about it. He'd never be able to walk, see, make love—either way. There was no possible cure for the physical state he was in, at least none that I could imagine. I tried. I had to assume that once a person's eyes were gouged out, or their legs or penis or hand was torn off and eaten, they could not be replaced. Would the medical state-of-the-art allow these things to be replaced in the future? In time to make a difference for David?

He probably wasn't going to die in this hospital. They could keep him alive either here or in Chicago almost indefinitely. In the meantime he'd suffer but never get better. He'd hate and resent every second. The only real question was whether he might change his mind if I gave him more time to think about it.

I was desperate to get some perspective, to know whether I was seeing all the issues rationally and objectively, but there wasn't anyone I thought I could confide in. I was the only person who might be willing to help David who was also in a position to help him. I had the poison: my insulin. I doubted that anyone would suspect me, but I genuinely didn't care if they did. If I mentioned to anyone else what David had asked me to do, the option would be foreclosed immediately.

I decided what to do—once and for all, that was it, I was ready—and changed my mind completely at least twenty times. I was running out of emotional gas pretty quickly. And then I decided again: I would do it. I'd promised him to, after all.

I would do it.

From following the Von Bülow case, I knew there were procedures that coroners could use to detect insulin poisoning, but I was prepared to accept the consequences for helping David get what he wanted. What I felt much less confident about was whether I could get myself to go through with it. To actually push down the plunger.

For hundreds of reasons, I wished that I'd known David longer. I also had to wonder why I was so sure that I was right about what course to follow and that the woman who'd known him all his life was dead wrong. I wondered what Emma would do.

I wished I could talk to him about it—in private, at length, without him being sedated, in pain . . . But what was I going to say?

One thing I wanted to be absolutely clear about in my mind was that his severed penis wasn't a factor in my decision, even though I suspected it was a rather key factor in his. Perhaps even the deciding factor. I hoped that it wasn't, but I couldn't shake the feeling that it was. That made me cry even harder. Because to me, at that moment, it couldn't have been less relevant.

I paced the beige hallways, walked down to the harbor and back. Would two hundred units of Regular insulin kill him? I couldn't remember how toxic it was supposed to be. (If I'd been able to concentrate normally, it probably would have shocked me to realize how little I knew about the drug I was injecting into my body twice a day.) It depended, of course, on the dosage, the size and condition of his body, how much glucose he had in his system. Since every diabetic's regimen called for subcutaneous—not intravenous—injections, I knew it would make a huge difference if I mainlined an entire two-cc syringeful of fast-acting Regular into a body as torn up and weakened as his. I had to believe it would work. *Finish killing him* was one of the phrases I used while debating with myself. Another was *helping my Saint*. Or, *just do it.*

And then for a while my plan was to nurse him. I wouldn't know how to at first, but I'd learn. Even if I wasn't altogether reliable at maintaining my own regimen, I vowed I'd be perfect at maintaining his, whatever and however many there turned out to be. I imagined procedures for feeding and bathing him. I could read to him, rent books on tape, transcribe his screenplays . . . Then I'd curse and give up and be sure he'd be miserable. Two seconds later we'd be married with three or four kids. Our first would be a daughter named Moira, and she'd be healthy and beautiful; she'd make David terribly happy, satisfied in a way that his body could never provide. Plus, he could always listen to music. I'd help him select which CD's . . . The next thing I knew I was sobbing and trembling, paralyzed by bloodthirsty rage at the sow. I think that I knew I was going to kill something soon—something or someone or anything. Ten seconds later David and I would be married again, two daughters, one son, computer games and Suzuki violin lessons, living in a white stucco house with a slate-shingle roof, far from water or forests or animals and I would be with him and he would be fine and I would be whispering, whispering . . .

Another determining factor was my own plan to kill myself when my symptoms became too severe. There were circumstances under which you wanted, or were willing, to live your life; there were circumstances under which you refused. You lived your life as intelligently as you could, and you decided when it was over. *You* decided. You didn't let some faulty organ or misguided T cells, or a badly funded research program, or some vicious and ignorant sow decide things like that for you. No.

In the end it was not a close call.

When I went back to his room in the ICU, I could tell from his breathing that he was asleep. I checked to see whether anyone else was around. His bed was observable from the nurses' station, but for the moment no one was watching. Plus the nurses all knew me by now.

I took the syringe from my pocket. I'd already loaded the two hundred units of Regular.

I put my mouth to the side of Saint's head. "Sweetheart, it's me."

He didn't respond. I pictured his face underneath all the bandages. His skeptical, marvelous eyes. I was thoroughly cried out by this point. I stood there and watched him and listened, then sat down beside him. I put my lips next to his ear.

"We ready?"

No response. His breathing did not even change.

"Are you sure you're ready?"

I prodded his forehead, his hand. No response. I removed the tube-end stopper from one of his catheters, inserted my needle into the feed line, pushed on the plunger; my thumb had to strain to make it go down all the way. I removed the syringe then, reattached the tube to the catheter, slipped the syringe in my pocket.

Through the freshly wrapped gauze, I kissed David's forehead. I was crying again, but less hard, less out of control than I'd thought I would be.

"Goodbye now, sweetie. I'm sorry. I'll never . . . " I started to go. I had to get out of that room, but I wanted to stay—*had* to stay. "I love you very much." I was whispering.

I turned, took a step.

"Penny, thank you." It was him. It was David. His choked but still wonderful voice. But even before I turned back around I realized I'd only imagined it.

I went to the side of the bed, but I didn't know how to

embrace him. I was desperate not to injure him further, cause him one more second of pain. I held onto him now by his hand and his arms and his face.

"Oh, sweetie, I thought you—"

"I know," David said.

The insulin began to kick in as I held him. His system was already devastated, couldn't take this gigantic new shock. I was feeling and watching him die in slow motion. Was he trying to get out more words? I told him to shush, just to shush, though I wanted to hear what he'd say. If he *had* changed his mind I could still call the nurses and doctors, tell them to give him some glucagon, use their devices and skills to save him again. His voice was still woozy and choked. I told him to try to relax, just be calm. That I loved him. I loved him. I told him *I know* several times, though I couldn't tell what he was saying. I was calling him David, my Saint, feeling him staring at me from the place where his eyes should have been.

His hand gripped my arm at the elbow, but weakly, so weakly. I used my other hand to stroke his gone face through the gauze. I knew he was trying to say something, one or two sounds at a time. His whole torso shuddered as he squeezed my right arm, then tensed as his hand let me go. Spit bubbled out from the hinge of his mouth. His voice wheezed and faded. I watched him and listened, trying to get what he wanted to say. I want to believe he was saying my name, but it could have been anything. Nothing.

Two nurses ran into the room as his hand fell away from my arm and I held on to all I had left of him.

PART 2

The sun is directly above my left earlobe, about seven light minutes away. I can feel each speedy little gamma ray arrive on my skin, bleaching the peach fuzz and cooking the blood in my temple, though my earlobe and temple feel cooler somehow than the rest of that side of my head. I have no idea how this happens. I do know that my hair is a stringy, wet tangle tucked behind my pink ears. The darker pink, flaking left lobe is pierced in four places, but I'm not wearing earrings today.

What I'm doing is riding my bicycle north by northwest through tar and loose gravel on the too-narrow shoulder of County Road 136. My guess is I'm still about thirty miles south of Chequamegon. Officially, as far as my department chair and thesis advisor are concerned, I'm also at work on a dissertation having to do with the novels of Samuel Beckett, but that is not strictly the case. I have lied.

And because I have lied, I ride on. The veins in my hands are upside-down wishbones bulging pale green through my pink, sweaty tan. I've been staring at my hands off and on since I pedaled north out of Chicago six days ago. In addition to sunblock, bananas, and a serious newspaper, I need to pick up a pair of those fingerless gloves, the ones lined with foam, with the mesh on the back to let the air circulate through, since the vibration buzzing up through the frame has been putting my palms and the tips of my fingers to sleep. It's a problem. What's less of a problem—it's really a cosmetic issue—is the fact that silicon sludge from the chain keeps tattooing my calf with pewtery crescents of linked, half-inch-long figure eights. I scrub them away in my pre-dinner showers and smudge myself with fresh ones each morning, usually before ten o'clock. Perhaps if I left them unscrubbed through the evening they'd ward off bad luck: female mosquitoes, insulin reactions, the notorious banshees of Chequamegon County. Whatever. My calves, after all, are among my best features—aside from good noses and cheekbones, they're the last things to go on most women—especially with all of this work I've been making them do. They tend to look best when I have on a short, pleated skirt with my clogs or suede pumps, heel perpendicular to opposite insole, toes lightly tapping . . . Unfortunately, there was no room in my panniers for clogs or suede pumps *or* a skirt. But even in rugby shorts, ankle-high sweat socks, and sneakers they might not look too unintriguing—at departmental functions, in French class, or, more realistically, glimpsed from four tables away as I sit by myself with *Molloy* in McDonald's, Red Lobster, or some chic Chequamegon bistro—crossed at the knees, neatly shaved, with the mark of the chain on the steep inner curve of the right one.

I finally snap to. I've been doing far too much daydreaming, even for a farm road with almost no traffic. I concentrate again on the shoulder. My hands grip the black-rubber handlebars, braking and shifting and steering. My heart, lungs, arteries, kidneys, and most of my capillaries also continue to function. I exhale and inhale, oxygenating my blood, transferring glucagon into my muscles, expelling some carbon monoxide. When a rickety Chevrolet pickup goes by, I inhale some.

I've also begun, after quite a long time, to think fairly often and hard about sex. About actually physically having some. About doing some things, having some other things done to me. Perhaps even some of the same things. It has been, after all, seven years, so who knows what I want by this point? I'm not even sure why I've gone on this trip. I know there are things I'm afraid of, and things I want, that I'll never admit to myself.

In the breeze my momentum creates my nipples are small, hypersensitive thimbles, unpierced but strangely exposed through my heavyweight T-shirt and the damp spandex blend of my bra. My septum and navel and eyebrows are also unpierced, but I've punctured my body in dozens of other locations.

A Honda swings by from behind me, giving me adequate berth, but I still have to lean to my right to compensate for the sudden low suck of its passage. My knuckles are skeleton white.

I've been in a bad mood for a couple three years, so I'm riding my bike to Alaska. To Gustavus, to be more specific, the town at the entrance to Glacier Bay National Park, about sixty miles up the panhandle from Juneau. Three thousand two hundred and eighty-five miles, five sixths of which are still ahead of me. It's either a therapeutic pilgrimage I'm on or a sorely misguided debacle; it's still way to early to tell. My absurdly high-maintenance, rapidly deteriorating renal and cardiovascular systems need the exercise, and my dead brain can use the endorphins. I'm going.

I spent months getting in shape for this, trying out different kinds of tires, applying for credit cards, getting advised not to ride by myself, only to ride west to east . . . I trained hard last winter by riding outside when I could; when it snowed or rained or got much below forty, I propped my bike on rollers and pedaled inside my apartment. There's always plenty to look at when you're riding outside; just to avoid crashing, you have to pay steady attention. Riding inside is so safe and boring I let myself watch CNN or *Mary Tyler Moore*, or I read German monographs on *Endgame*.

So far, the program's paid off. I've been able to ride almost six hours a day, though my plan is to throw in a short day at least once a week, and to take a day off when it rains. My blood sugar levels have been holding steady, usually between 125 and 140 at this time of the afternoon, around 115 just before breakfast. I've never felt leaner or stronger—more "in control," as the pancreatically challenged so like to put it. On this score at least, I feel pretty proud of myself. If I stay on schedule, I'll have two weeks to take care of my business up there before I pack up my bike and fly home to O'Hare. I have to start teaching again the Tuesday after Labor Day, assuming I still have my job.

Aside from one road back in Antioch that turned out to be an extremely long driveway leading to a complex of modernoid offices (one of which was flying the South Korean flag), I haven't gotten lost yet. Two nights ago on *Headline News* there was a story about a man who was found by the California Highway Patrol in San Diego, sitting in his car half a block from the Pacific Ocean, at the very end of Interstate 8. According to the patrolmen, the man had a map in his hand and a "real perplexed look" on his face. He explained that he'd driven from Fort Worth, Texas, and was looking for a town in New Mexico.

A trio of pelicans are flapping along right above me. I've seen about ten since I moved past the Dells into central Wisconsin; before that I'd only seen them in bird books and zoos. Right now I can't help picturing them dropping a baby on my head—although it's storks that bring babies, of course. And yet what's a stork if not a long, narrow pelican in a bow tie and glasses, like an old-fashioned pediatrician?

I'm riding my bike to a place you cannot ride a bike to. Not a single road, paved or otherwise, leads to either Juneau or Gustavus; you have to take a ferry from Prince Rupert, British Columbia. But so far I'm making good time. Wednesday, against a slight headwind, I made seventy-eight miles. Tuesday, between Babcock and Ogema, I made a hundred and five, though not as the pelican flies, since the road is more like a staircase as it wends its way through the farms. On Monday I rested. I wrote a few postcards, lost forty dollars playing video poker, did what laundry I had: both pairs of riding shorts, all three bras, three panties, three bandannas, six T-shirts.

I'm planning to make Chequamegon by early this evening. Chequamegon is the town where I'll finally pick up Route 2, and Route 2 is the key to "Part One" of this trip. It's the northernmost east-west highway in the country, but it hardly gets used since the four-lane interstates like 94, 90, and 80 were built. Since the interstates get most of the car and— especially—truck traffic, Route 2 is much better for riding a bicycle on. It's also the most direct route, according to the various bike magazines. It starts in Houlton, Maine, winds through New Hampshire and Vermont, disappears sporadically (or merges with other roads) between upstate New York and lower Michigan, then firmly reestablishes itself at the north end of the Mackinaw Bridge and maintains an unbroken line from the Upper Peninsula all the way out to Seattle. Once I make Chequamegon I simply turn left and take Route 2 straight west through the rest of Wisconsin, Minnesota, North Dakota, and most of Montana. I cross the Continental Divide just west of Browning, then pick up Route 93 at Kalispell and take it north into Jasper, Alberta, then north and west on the Yellowhead Highway to Prince Rupert, where I catch the *Malaspina* ferry to Juneau. I'll need to average about seventy miles a day, with one day off per week for good behavior, to make it by August 15. (Four time zones in less than nine weeks—not exactly speed-of-sound velocity, but still.) During July and August the ferries depart from Prince Rupert six days a week, so I don't have to time my arrival precisely. The ferry ride takes about forty-eight hours and costs a hundred and twenty-four dollars, twice that much if I want a private cabin. I've called the 800 number and told them approximate dates of departure and asked them to put my name on the waiting list; I've also ascertained they take Visa. If I'm lucky I'll get a cabin; if not I'll sleep on the deck, which is how most people make the trip anyway. There's no charge for bikes on the ferry, and if I could pass for sixty-five I could sail for free myself. By the time I get out there in August, I just may be able to.

A powder pink Mustang convertible with a black plastic bra framing its headlights cruises by, heading south. Six teenaged girls altogether, four in the tiny backseat. One of them shrieks something I can't quite make out, but I gather it's derogatory from the tone of her voice slipstreaming back down the asphalt. Something about my fat ass.

So far this sort of attitude has been very much the exception in northern Illinois and Wisconsin. Most people wave or show me thumbs-up or a peace sign. One little boy—he couldn't have been older than six—called me "Bike Babe" as I clicked past his parents' BMW at a stop sign. A girl at a lemonade stand called me Sweetie. She told me her name was Carol and I told her my name was Penny.

"Is that *really* your name?"

"Yep, it is."

"A *penny?*"

"Weird, ain't it?"

"Yep. Are you thirsty?"

I bought three Dixie cups of warm, "not diet" lemonade from Carol, since they cost only fourteen cents each. Carol and I got along.

But if 197 cars go by of a morning, all of them giving me room, slowing down a few mph, emitting the occasional wolf whistle, wave, or hello, or—most often—simply ignoring me, and a single passenger in the next car shouts, "Why don't you *park* that butt, Bertha," it will be car number 198 I'll remember and obsess about for the rest of the day and half of the following morning. Why is that? There are plenty of things about me one could persuasively mock or impugn, but the truth is, my ass isn't fat.

I pedal and brood and keep going, inching my way up the yellow and blue and white map in my head. I've already been riding for almost six hours today, so I need to think pretty soon about finding a motel, doing my shot, eating dinner. I'm packing a nectarine and two granola bars in my right-rear pannier, just in case my sugar gets low.

When I ride over pebbles or crumbly asphalt—as now—my bike becomes a kind of colossal vibrator, whether I like it or not. I don't like it. And it's probably not a good sign that my crotch has become a bit numb. I'm already wearing a fleece-lined pad liberally smeared with chamois fat along the seam of my riding shorts. Plus the shorts have their own foam padding, so there isn't much more I can do. But I sure don't feel terribly appetizing.

Two minutes later, as I daydream about my sore parts, my front tire catches the edge of a triangular pebble and catapults it sideways; I can feel the twangy little ping all the way to my shoulders.

A hundred yards later it happens again: a pebble pings off to the left. I don't remember this ever happening before, and now twice in one minute. Car tires manage to do this all the time; I've already been personally dinged a half dozen times on this trip, and I'd love to be able to nail a car back. The next one that goes by, I'll aim my front tire at the edge of a pebble appropriately shaped and positioned, making sure it pings left at just the right angle . . .

I've been worried that a bike trip this long might turn me into something of an Ironthighs—not that there's anything wrong with that. I also worry that the friction from all this pedaling might wear down my labia; the image that keeps coming to mind is a dry, ratty baseball mitt. I guess I'm afraid it might make the nerves down there even marginally less sensitive. Although maybe that wouldn't be such an awful idea after all.

Another thing I'd like to know, as the minuscule shock of each little pebble and tread bump keeps wending its way to my vulva, is how a bodily part can be numb and still tingle. It's a different sensation from the stinging numbness you get when your fingers get cold, or the itch when they finally warm up. (I'm already becoming the connoisseur of numbnesses that all diabetics are destined to become.) It's more than a little distracting to have your vulva be almost continually buzzed while your already sensitive nipples get chilled by the breeze you're creating. Already "seismically sensitive," I'd be tempted to say, if that were an adverb-adjective combination that made any sense and I weren't preoccupied with not overstating things, even though that's how they feel. I support myself, barely, teaching freshman composition at the University of Illinois at Chicago, and I can never completely switch off my paper-grading fixations. Which is probably one of the reasons I've made so little progress on my dissertation, which is why I remain ABD: All But Dissertation, A Born Diabetic, Another Beckett Deconstructor . . .

So. What's the difference between having diabetes and riding a bicycle? They both make your crotch and extremities numb, but riding a bicycle doesn't ravage your kidneys or make you go blind.

Pedal and brood, brood and pedal. No pelicans, loons, or coyotes. Not one cloud to get in the way of the sun. No convertibles. Just telephone poles and pine trees and asphalt. The dirt on the side of the road is discernibly more red than it was even five or six miles ago. Iron.

I think I can smell a Great Lake.

Officially I'm still a Ph.D. candidate in the Department of Irish Literature at the University of Illinois at Chicago, although I haven't made much headway on my dissertation in two years, nine months, and counting. I've completed my course work and passed my orals, and I have over three hundred pages of notes, all of it neatly arranged into chapter material under well-chosen titles for the thirty-eight files on my hard drive—all of it backed up, of course, on a floppy I keep in my office at school. I even have twelve lengthy paragraphs—almost seventeen pages of prose, double-spaced—of my dissertation. At the rate I'm proceeding I'll have my degree, and thereby some prospect of full-time employment, in just under fifty-six years.

In the meantime, as long as I'm still working on my dissertation, or until I formally admit that I'm not, or until seven semesters have elapsed since I passed my orals, whichever comes first, I'm eligible to keep my two-thirds-time teaching assistantship and my health insurance. Then I'm out. The tenured, full-time faculty teach two courses a semester for between forty and a hundred and eighty-five thousand dollars a year and have guaranteed health insurance until the second they're pronounced dead, at which point a quintuple-your-salary life insurance policy kicks in. TA's teach two courses a semester—invariably the biggest, most introductory courses, filled with non-volunteers who every two weeks turn a four-inch-high stack of dismal "compositions" that have to be responded to sentence by sentence, graded, turned back, and encouragingly conferred about—for twelve thousand eight hundred dollars a year. The second a TA's contract expires, her health insurance coverage does too. That's the deal.

So what else does ABD stand for? Lots of things, probably. Academically Beleaguered Dupe? Aficionada of Bondage and Discipline? American Boy Desirer? I don't think so. Angry Bull Dyke? Alpha Butch Damsel? Not exactly. American Boy Destroyer? Who knows.

But speaking of which: Where do men keep their dicks and their balls when they're riding a bike?

I don't know.

There's a gas station with a Qwik-Mart coming up on the left. I can taste a cold pint of mango Snapple iced tea going down the back of my throat. But I know that as soon as I stopped I'd get stiff, especially this late in the day. I want to make Route 2 by five o'clock at the latest. This trip is supposed to be about physical discipline, and so far there hasn't been a day when I didn't reach the town I planned to reach when I left in the morning, and twice I've exceeded the target. According to my map, Chequamegon's only another twelve miles, either flat or downhill, to the north. One more easy hour at most.

On the other hand, there *is* a motel about two hundred yards up the road from the Qwik-Mart. The Pine. With its raw-log facade and loons sculpted onto its sign, it looks down-right homey. Cable TV, queen-sized beds, heated pool.

Vacancies. Visa accepted? Three junior-high girls in tube tops and acid-washed Daisy Duke shorts are playing badminton and cursing each other in the yard on the side. Taco Bell half a block away. I have to admit I'm tempted.

When I cruise past the door to the manager's office, there's no Visa decal on the window. No decals, period. In fact, there's actually a sign that says NO CREDIT CARDS. SORRY.

The nerve!

I've been on the lookout for loons, but I'm usually not on the road when they're active, which is right around sunrise and sunset. What I should do is spend a few evenings by the lakes around here or over in Minnesota, or get up earlier and scout around before breakfast.

I've already seen whitetail deer, a coyote, two baby fox, and a porcupine. No bear. Most of the furrier fauna—possum, raccoon, squirrels, skunks, chipmunks—have been wet hanks of roadkill swarming with maggots or flies; it depends, I suppose, on how long they've been lying out here on the pavement. Sometimes all the cars running over the corpse have smushed the maggots down into what's left of the fur. There's often a crow or two picking at entrails. Some crows don't even budge as I cruise slowly past, paying my respects, or they wait till the very last second, making me veer around them. The obscene, awkward hops of armless, contemptuous crows: I don't like them. I've never seen a crow display fear, only anger and hunger and maybe some blatantly reluctant prudence. One even lunged toward my foot, then made a point of flying away extra slowly, flapping its iridescent midnight-blue wings, with a stringy yard of raccoon entrails dangling from its beak.

I personally try to avoid riding over the roadkill, especially animals I can still recognize, like that gray-and-white opossum yesterday morning, with its hideous tail and beady dead eyes staring past me into the sun. But sometimes it's hard to avoid the ones who've been out here too long; all that's left of them is bald, torn-up pieces of unidentifiable pelt ground halfway into the asphalt. Your tires just barely tick over what's left of the creature: not much more than a stain with some texture. Even the maggots and ants are apparently no longer interested.

So far the birds have been the best part of the trip. Hawks, ravens, pelicans, woodpeckers ... This morning I startled some red-winged blackbirds in a cornfield. One of the males flew alongside me for at least forty yards, inadvertently (I assume) maintaining the same speed I was pedaling at and wondering why I hadn't disappeared from his flight plan. Perhaps he was checking *me* out. In any event, I got to see him up close and personal, without the usual distortions you get when they're flying away from you, or you're too far away to begin with. It was like watching one "behave" in a PBS nature special, with the four-foot-long lenses and slow-motion, you-are-there editing. He coasted and flapped alongside me, rising and dipping, a beaked black cigar bisected by a yellow-and-red blur of wing. It was great.

Although some of the roadkill has feathers.

My bike is a black, nineteen-inch Trek 790 with upright granny-style handlebars. They don't make the bike-and-rider profile all that aerodynamic, but they do help me see where I'm going. My admittedly insular theory is that I don't want to ride two thirds of the way across North America hunched halfway over, forearms locked into aero bars or reaching for those low-slung racing handlebars, forced to stare down at the asphalt and my spinning and boring front tire. I also like my bike because it looks like the dictionary-picture definition of a bicycle, like the bike slashed out on no-bicycles signs. But the principal reason is that, except for small details like seventeen extra gears, a quick-release seat post, Dia-Compe brakes fore and aft, and Shimano Hyperglide grip shifters, it's virtually identical to the bike Samuel Beckett rode around Dublin and Wicklow. A Swift, I believe, was his model.

My Trek 790 is a hybrid, a cross between a road bike and a mountain bike. It has seven-hundred-millimeter anodized rims, thirty-six-spoke hubs, nubby forty-millimeter tires, and toe clips so I can use my calf muscles as well as my thigh muscles. I fell in love with it the first time I test-rode it three years ago. It was expensive, but I figured the more I loved it the more miles I'd spend on it and the more fit I'd become, hence the longer I'd be *able* to ride it, and so on. Exactly what the endocrinologist ordered. About a year ago I decided that if I rode back to Alaska, I could create my own traveling health spa on the cheap: no trainers to pay, no dieticians, and, above all, no doctors. I'd have built-in, six-hour workouts five or six days a week, and actually get someplace too. This is the theory, at least.

Only two flats so far, one of which I repaired, in the rain, by myself. That was not pleasant. I was under a Burlington-Northern viaduct for almost two hours, plus I gashed my left pinkie getting the rear wheel back on. But the other flat happened right in downtown Baraboo, a block and a half from a bike shop. The basic rule of thumb is, you need one spare tire for every thousand miles, but my current master plan is to halve that—to stop at a bike shop every five hundred miles and have two brand-new tires put on. I haven't passed a shop yet that didn't take Visa, and I do not expect to. I hope.

For a 3,500-mile trip, I'm not traveling terribly heavy. For one thing, no tent. Keeping my load as light as possible makes it easier to steer and saves wear on the tires. But the main reason I'm cycling tentless across the continent is that I do not camp out. I don't brush my teeth in the lake, bathe in the river, or shit in the woods, though I am packing toilet paper in case I get caught between gas stations. The point is, I don't sleep in tents. I sleep in motels every night, in motel rooms with walls, doors that lock, toilets, showers, towels, individually wrapped bars of soap, miniature bottles of shampoo and conditioner, TV's and reading lamps and ice machines. There aren't always mints on the pillow or cubes in the ice machine, but I've learned to make do. The rest of the items are mandatory.

I do have a waterproof sleeping bag insulated to thirty-two degrees F, in case I have bad luck with weather or vacancies. I eat no-cook meals on the road, mostly sandwiches and fruit and granola bars, mostly while sitting at picnic tables. Breakfast and dinner I eat at a restaurant, so the only cooking utensils I carry are an Irish army knife with a spork, and some matches. I have two panniers on the back, a pump and three water bottles in the middle, a decent-sized handlebar bag clipped to the rack on the front. My tool kit—crescent wrench, tire iron, glue, patches, Allen wrench, Band-Aids— hangs under the saddle. That's it. No extra cables or tubes, no spare tire. No front panniers, no fenders or mudguards, no lights, locks, generators, computers, EKG monitors, defibrillators—even though any or all of these things certainly might come in handy. There's also no Kleenex dispenser attached to the frame. (I've seen bikes that had them.) With all of the pollen up here in Land O Lakes country, I've had to blow my nose guy-style a time or two, pressing down one nostril while snorting backwards through the other: bright strings of translucent caviar. I try to avoid implementing this procedure if there are witnesses in the vicinity, unless they're shirtless road construction workers. Although when gnats fly into my mouth and get stuck in the back of my throat, the hocking maneuver I deploy, out of utter necessity, to dislodge them is not always perfectly ladylike, no matter who might be watching or listening.

If I'd been able to find one—I've searched far and wide in bike shops, garage sales, Ben Franklins—my upright handlebars would be sporting a spiffy rubber horn, like Molloy's old bike had. Toot! Instead I have a small plastic odometer that can also display miles per hour. Right now I'm doing sixteen.

My Visas and cash, what there is of it, I keep in my little green belt pack.

I'm not only riding this bike to a place you cannot ride a bike to, I'm also apparently riding in the wrong direction. I've been told this by experts. Three days ago, back in Plainville, I met a couple of guys riding from Seattle to Toronto who were anxious to narrate their entire life stories. Alex and Tim, I believe. Maybe Tom. They lived in Toronto and had flown to Seattle with their bikes, this in order to be able to ride home with the wind at their backs. They (especially Tim, or Tom) had lengthy and elaborate theories about which route beginning from which direction at which time of year was superior. Not only were they amazed to hear that I was riding east to west, against the wind, by myself, they seemed genuinely affronted to hear it. Why did I not take the scenic route, Interstate 90, which ran through the Badlands, the Black Hills, Yellowstone, Missoula . . . ? On their best day, Alex was anxious to inform me, between Kellogg and Bozeman, with the wind at their backs, they had covered 244 miles. And why was I not camping out?

What could I say? We were standing in the parking lot of a 7-Eleven in Plainville, Wisconsin. They wanted to get to Toronto, I needed to get to Alaska. We had known one another nine minutes.

"Camping's awesome, man," Alex informed me. "You should get a cheap tent and camp out."

I told him I needed a desk every night because I was working on my dissertation. It's a lie I can't stop telling, apparently. I even began to enumerate my reasons for not liking to camp out.

"But don't motels start to get pretty expensive?" asked Tom.

I admitted it.

"Though showers are cool," Alex said. I could tell he was checking me out with suspicious new eyes, looking for and finding a surplus of evidence—Discman, faux Rolex, uprightness of handlebars, tentlessness—of undue or spurious affluence.

I smiled, displaying my imperfect teeth. Didn't help.

"I could go for a shower," said Tom.

Their attitude has not been atypical. Four fifths of the people I told about my trip during the planning stages wanted to know if I was "sure." A woman my age (I'm either too old or too young) alone on the road without pharmacies or a man or WordPerfect 6.0 or a personal endocrinologist? I'm sure, I would tell them. One oft-noted fact was that a plane could get me there in six hours, probably for less money than I'd spend on motels and food. Driving a car I could make it in a week, leaving me the rest of the summer to—what?

I figure that if I'm alone, I may as well *be* alone, especially since going solo is better than not going at all. Plus riding a bike is Der Grune thing to do, is it not? Transporting oneself across most of a very large continent without fossil or nuclear fuels? These days even congressmen and fashion designers ride bikes to and fro' power brunches in Milan and D.C. and Manhattan. But the bottom line is that I never feel better than when I'm humping along on my Trek. On good days, especially after a run of fifty or sixty miles, I really feel *swinging*. My legs are pumping, my knees don't hurt, I'm sweating out soupçons of poison, and my lungs start to feel vaguely sweet. Each half-rotation of the pedals, left foot, then right foot, forces a miniature syringeful of endorphin, maybe .00015 cc's, to be secreted directly into my pons. Plus each surge of blood through my legs, then upward and out through the rest of my system, shores up my rickety, erosion-prone capillaries. Or so I imagine. I hope. In the meantime I'm using up x ergs of energy, y grams of glucose, together with an appropriate measure of insulin. Toot! It's perfect. Regular strenuous exercise actually increases my sensitivity to insulin, lets my muscles use it more efficiently. If I give myself the same doses each morning and evening, eat the same amount of grains, fruits, meats, and vegetables, then ride the same number of miles every day, I will *in theory at least* maintain my blood sugar levels pretty much in the range of a normal person, something I've never in my life been able to accomplish, outside the odd stint in a hospital.

Beckett was obsessed with bicycles. He got the name of his most famous noncharacter while watching the thirteenth leg of the 1948 Tour de France; he apparently overheard a cluster of fans say they were waiting for Godot, who happened to be the oldest competitor in the race.

A man in his story "The Calmative" rides a bicycle while reading the newspaper, using both hands to hold it open in front of him, ringing his bell from time to time to warn drivers and pedestrians of his approach. The only things *I* can read while riding my own bike are road signs and billboards and sections of map, stealing brief glances while steering with a hand and a half. I do read as I move from room to room in my apartment; sometimes I even grade papers. I used to read things while I walked home from high school, except it was *Ada* or *Ariel* or *Lucy* or *Pride and Prejudice* or *Fear and Trembling* or *Rapture* or *Catcher in the Rye* or *Final Exit* or *Exit to Eden* I was reading, instead of an open newspaper; with a book you could still sort of see where the turns were.

Mercier and Camier share a bicycle, but it gets vandalized and all they have left is the pump. Watt never actually owns one, but he fantasizes about them in maniacal detail. Clov, in *Endgame*, pesters Hamm for a bicycle even though he knows there are no bicycles left in the universe. Nagg and Nell, Hamm's parents, both lose their legs falling off a tandem—the quintessential Beckettian moment. That's why I love him, of course.

In the so-called Trilogy, Molloy rides his bicycle everywhere, even though only one of his legs still bends at the knee. He introduces himself to Lousse by running over and killing her dog. Moran *père* rides on the back of his son's bicycle. *I trembled for my testicles which swung a little low. Faster! I cried. He bore down on the pedals. The bicycle swayed, righted itself, gained speed. Bravo! I cried, beside myself with joy. Hurrah! cried my son. How I loathe that exclamation! I can hardly set it down. He was as pleased as I was, I do believe. His heart was beating under my hand and yet my hand was far from his heart.* All that remains of Malone's bicycle is the cap of its bell. The Unnamable, tellingly, does not own a bicycle.

I tend to remember things like Moran Jr.'s pulse points because, in addition to reading and teaching and exegetically accounting for this stuff for a decade, I also did about a quarter of the research (and fact-checked the other three quarters, then proofread the entire eighty-nine pages) for Professor Leona S. Marvin's PEN-award-winning monograph *Terminal Velocipedes*. So.

As Hugh Kenner puts it (and Lee wishes *she* had): "The Cartesian Centaur is a man riding a bicycle, *mens sana in corpore disposito*." His point is that bicycles complement human bodies perfectly, each being indispensable to the other's progress through space. Pedaling one transports you to "an ideal, Newtonian plane of rotary progression and gyroscopic stability."

In my own Kenner file I have him asking his reader to "Consider the cyclist as he passes, the supreme specialist, transfiguring that act of moving from place to place . . . with impenetrable dignity, the sitting posture combined with the walking, *sedendo et ambulando* . . . All the human faculties are called into play, and all the human muscles except perhaps the auricular. Thus is fulfilled the serpent's promise to Eve, *et eritis sicut dii*."

That's me, folks. I wish I had written it. I have, in a sense, if only a limited one: I've entered it into my hard drive, part of a lengthening hodgepodge of items to be seamlessly incorporated into my own "shrewdly luminous appraisal.—Ruby Cohn." Because even though I'm still light days from finishing even a rudimentary first draft, I can't stop myself from concocting endless streams of unattenuated blurbola, each quote to be understatedly reproduced on the back of the Yale University Press and or the Vintage International trade edition (seventeenth printing and counting), all the while doing my best to avoid, in addition to the usual clichés, such inadmissible terms as *potent* and *masterpiece* and *seminal* and *penetrating*. And now that I think of it, if semen is luminous, perhaps it would be better for Ms. Cohn to say . . . But *is* semen luminous? Maybe I'm confusing it with ectoplasm, the come of the dead. It would not be unlike me to do so.

Meandering rondos like this are seductive enough when I'm sitting at home in front of my computer, or working at one of the ten-inch-deep "desks" in my latest motel room, trying to grind out a paragraph, but they can get out of hand as I pedal in a funk down the highway. You'd have to wear sunglasses just to glance at the back of some of the dust jackets I've come up with. "In a stroke, the landscape of Beckett's demesne is altered ineluctably. Penelope Culligan is a necessary critic.—Harold Bloom." "Makes the major novels bloom for a new generation.—Robert Alter." Even Harold Pinter usually has some deadpan but astonishing accolade to add as a kicker, his first blurb in almost five decades. In the meantime my actual dissertation—the degree-clinching thesis, the well-published excerpt, the *book*—never quite manages to get itself written.

Writer's block. I have to strain pretty hard to derive any comfort from reminding myself that only smart people get it, or that I'm avoiding carpal tunnel syndrome by having it. It's much more comforting (and perhaps even relevant) that Beckett himself had a fairly virulent case, from his twenties until his early forties, when he had his famous "siege in the room," switched from English to French, and began writing the warm-up exercises that led to *Godot* and the novels and *Endgame*.

Faulkner and Larkin and Berryman and Lowell and Elizabeth Bishop all had it. Sylvia Plath had it bad for a while, especially while Ted Hughes was getting published and winning the prizes that Sylvia coveted. The thing to remember, of course, is that Plath did get past it, at least for one brief siege in *her* room—a room in Yeats's old flat in London. So for that matter did everyone else whose names might occur to me. Otherwise their names would never occur to me.

How did these writers get past it? Dunno. All I know is, I'm blocked now. Stopped up, it feels like, for good. I'm not only not convinced I can finish this thing, I'm convinced that it might not be worth it.

A billboard announces CHEQUAMEGON 3. As it happens, there are three blue-black crows perched on top, 4-D silhouettes against the pale Lake Superior sky. Below the Chequamegon

3 there's a veritable smorgasbord of lodgings and places to eat. Skunk entrails? Anything. Everything.

I upshift one gear and work harder. At sixteen miles an hour, I'll be there in—what? Fifteen minutes? I've never been real great at math.

What I *can* appreciate is the exquisiteness of my ability to do what I'm doing right now: move down this ironbound road under my own power. I'm out in the air on my own, not strapped aboard some ergocycle in a rehab facility. I stop when I want to, proceed when I feel like proceeding. Twenty-nine years ago I didn't exist, so I wasn't in a position to appreciate physical independence. Twenty-nine months from now I might be strokebound in a wheelchair, blind, minus a few of my toes, shitting into a fitted diaper, drool slanting across my chin as I press some steel button and call out for—what? What could I possibly want?

In the meantime I intend to enjoy myself. It's the principal reason I don't always wear my helmet, since I'd greatly prefer a violent, adventuresome, active sort of death to the one I'm probably headed for. If I happen to get winged by a Maxima, somersault a few times in the air and land on my forehead, I want that to be all she wrote.

Two cars go by, and I veer half a foot to my right. Both give me plenty of leeway. A small red-haired girl in the back of the second car waves a plump hand. I wave back. She's wearing a zebra-striped Bucks cap.

Once again I've been spared; I ride on. There's a breeze coming out of the forest. It's sideways right now, almost directly out of the west, more woodsy than the one I create on my own. When a van with a big blue canoe lashed to the roof whooshes by from behind, I catch whiffs of diesel and even a half dozen aromatic subatomic particles of Velveeta tostitos.

I'm hungry. The sun ricochets off my skin. It feels good. I've worked up a pretty good sweat as I whir along over the asphalt. I've had another good day: seventy-two miles and still counting.

I pedal and pump the endorphins.

I wheel my bike into room number four of the Pick C Motel. Not too great, not too shabby. It's also the only room left, according to the ringletted, gold-necklaced man at the desk. Red Roof Inn and Motel 6 were both booked up solid. There must be a convention of crows.

I lean my bike against the side of the desk, look around. Much knotty, unpixie-ish pine is in evidence: desk, headboard, dresser, the trim. I can smell it, I think, through the vaguely rancid ghosts of six thousand post-coital cigarettes; although maybe that's Pinesol or Mr. Clean I'm smelling, liberally applied to eradicate X-rated fragrances. But I shouldn't complain: it's vacant, I'm about to pass out, they took Visa. The wallpaper, now that I look more closely, features smiling mermaid poodles in a variety of fetching poses. The TV is cabled and new.

I sit on the side of the bed and shift my throbbing butt back and forth. The synthetic threadbare spread is printed with a stain-hiding gray floral pattern that matches the one pair of drapes. I lean my fist into the mattress; it's reasonably firm but has small curdled lumps near the middle, though not so spread out that I won't be able to avoid them. I usually sleep on the left side of the bed, unless there's only one lamp and it's attached to the wall on the right.

Lake Superior is directly across the street, less than a hundred yards away, but a block-long Wal Mart is blocking nine tenths of the view. When I first caught a glimpse of the lake, as I was finally riding west on Route 2 through the town, it looked like Lake Michigan: gray blue and vast enough to change the color of the sky, but too calm to be anything more than a miniature ocean. It's the last body of water I won't be able to see across till I get to Prince Rupert in August.

There isn't too much to unpack, since the panniers make my Trek function as a portable dresser. The handlebar bag detaches with two Velcro stays, and I can use it as a purse if I have to.

I swallow a peppermint Lifesaver to tide me over till dinner, then take out my evening wear: undies, socks, narrow black shorts virtually identical to the ones I have on, only clean, and a new olive T-shirt.

Before I undress I double-lock the door and check the walls and mirrors for peepholes. I look behind both of the paintings of sailboats: just cobwebs and more mermaid poodles. The mirror above the sink in the bathroom doesn't open, but I do my best to pry it back half an inch in order to peek behind it. Doesn't budge. I keep trying anyway, even when it threatens to snap off my nails. The hands-on-hips poodle an inch from my nose winks coquettishly.

Right.

I stare at myself in the mirror. Even after I've checked out the entire surface, I can't shake the suspicion that it isn't some cleverly designed two-way glass. I'm always more suspicious when a mirror is bolted to the wall, especially in the room guaranteed to produce naked strangers in compromising positions. I also try to avoid mirrors on walls I might share with the manager's office—although a cagey manager's custom-designed, impossible-to-detect peephole, around which he and his stoned or vodka'd comrades gather of an evening to watch women pull off their clothes, could just as easily be in the (purposefully) unrented room next to mine. I try to reassure myself by fondly remembering my *Psycho* shower curtain at home: the silhouette of a knife-wielding, bewigged Anthony Perkins looming down over me—a reverse-voodoo

talisman compliments of Jane on my birthday. I also check the
ceilings for cobwebs. I don't want any Spiders of Damocles
dangling over me while I'm naked.

Okay. No spiders or cobwebs or peepholes. I'm exhausted
and hungry and ready for a half-hour shower. I peel off my
sweaty T-shirt and drape it over the mirror, which also happens
to be the best place to dry it, then run the hot water and take
off the rest of my clothes. My tan lines, of course, are absurd.

Inside the four-foot-square stall I lather myself front and
rear while crooning to myself about nothing. I shave my pits
first, then my legs, then scrub off what's left of the smudge
from the chain; it wasn't that interesting anyway. I let the hot
water—which smells like cold iron—pound down on the back
of my neck. It's smashing and scalding and wonderful.

But I can't shake the idea of peepers, though I realize I'm
probably being paranoid. More so than usual, even. And what
would a peeper see anyway? It's not as though I'm actively
participating in exotic or even conventional ménages in these
motel rooms, unless shooting insulin into my naked thigh or
smearing gobs of chamois fat onto my crotch at seven o'clock
in the morning count as peepworthy solo routines. But I have
to take showers, of course. I have to thrash air guitar bar-
chords if Neil Young or Elvis or Hole comes on MTV. I've
also flexed my quadriceps and glutes before mirrors to see
how much (if any) progress I've made in those areas. I admit
it. But I've yet to bungee myself by the throat or left wrist to
the shower curtain rod, gag myself with a quadruple-knotted
pair of black panties, or kneel on the side of the tub while
watching, entranced, as I pierce my own nipples. I haven't
even pinched them with clothespins while wielding a motor-
ized dildo. I do have a pair of midnight-blue panties neatly
folded inside a baggie at the bottom of my left pannier, just in
case. But other than that I am innocent. Chaste. Because that's
what this trip is about, after all: self-control.

As I shampoo my hair, I massage my scalp and my temples
while making my standard inquiry: Am I really a murderer?

Most of the time I'm fairly convinced that I'm not.

In the strict legal sense, according to the relevant state and federal statutes, there isn't much question. There were extenuating circumstances, of course, though it's doubtful they're relevant. Section 11.41.100 of the Alaskan Criminal Code states: "(a) A person commits the crime of murder in the first degree if (1) with intent to cause the death of another person, the person (A) causes the death of any person." Slightly tautological, perhaps, but nonetheless legally binding. Persons so indicted and convicted are subject to a maximum term of ninety-nine years in prison.

However. Among the various "notes to decisions" printed in casebooks along with the statutes are endless collateral references: "Under the common law, murder is the unlawful killing of a human being with malice aforethought." Although a lack of malicious intent would not be considered an affirmative defense by itself. "In many cases the killing itself, if unexplained, was enough to support an inference of malice." That one's from *Gray* v. *State*.

There are also collateral references having specifically to do with aiding and abetting: "one who assists another in committing suicide by perpetrating the act that causes the death of that person is guilty of murder." Some courts have stated that where a person actually performs the overt act resulting in death, such as administering poison, that person is guilty of murder; it's wholly immaterial whether the act is committed pursuant to an agreement with the victim, e.g., a mutual suicide pact.

I've read up on this stuff rather thoroughly. So I know, for example, that in Michigan a man named Roberts mixed a poison called Paris green with water and placed it within reach of his bedridden wife, who drank the poison and died. Mr. Roberts was found guilty of first-degree murder, even though his wife requested him to mix the poison. The appeals court upheld the verdict, arguing that Roberts deliberately placed within her reach the means of taking her own life, which she could have obtained in no other way by reason of her helpless condition. A Texan named Cleaves tied up his lover in such a way that the lover, who was dying of AIDS, could strangle himself. I can picture the tenderly intricate network of clothesline that hog-tied and strangled this man. The judge instructed the jury not to even consider the lesser, related offense of aiding and abetting suicide. Although Mr. Cleaves did not apply pressure to the ligature itself, he admitted having overtly and actively held his lover to keep him from falling off the bed with the intention of helping him complete the strangulation; he therefore was guilty of first-degree murder. Whereas in New York a man named Duffy was found innocent of aiding and abetting, even though he had given his drunk, depressed, known-to-be-suicidal friend a loaded rifle and then goaded him to put the gun in his mouth and blow his head off. Mr. Duffy's only defense was that he was "sick and tired" of hearing his friend complain about his personal situation; he admitted he'd encouraged his friend to kill himself as well as provided the means. It was nonetheless held that Duffy was (1) not guilty of murder, and (2) could not be tried on charges of reckless manslaughter for the same act because that would amount to double jeopardy. He'd apparently acted *too* recklessly to be convicted of aiding and abetting, and not recklessly enough to be guilty of manslaughter. I tend to pronounce this word "man's laughter"; behavior that causes me to snort or cackle derisively I think of as Duffy's Defense. And whatever the charge is, my plea is nolo contendere.

Then there's the old Sixth Commandment. Bless me, father, for I have sinned. My last confession was seventeen years ago, but since this one here is also going to be my *last* confession, you'd better hold onto your seat—unless you want to meet me outside in the pews and molest me, sentence me to thirteen rosaries or to perform some numinous act of contrition on you while wearing only the thirteen rosaries . . .

Speaking of sins, isn't it in the lucky thirteenth canto of the *Inferno* that Virgil takes Dante through the Wood of Suicides? The only ones I can remember are Piero delle Something, a poet and statesman who killed himself in jail by dashing his head against the wall of his cell, and an anonymous trader of Florentine financial instruments (extra-virgin olive oil futures?) who hangs himself at home. All of the suicides have been sentenced directly to Hell. None of them had been suffering beforehand a fiftieth as much as David, but Signor Alighieri doesn't place too much emphasis on motive: in his divinely comedic cosmology, *no* grounds are sufficient for killing yourself. Yet he still gets so choked up by the plight of the suicides, he needs Virgil to ask them the questions. And compared to the gluttons and usurers and the wrathful, the suicide cases don't fare all that badly. They may not get off as lightly as the lustful, who are merely lashed by high winds; a few of them, couples like Francesca and Paolo, get to be lashed and stay naked together forever: that's *their* punishment. Suicides get turned into saplings nibbled on by Harpies, who, depending on whose definition you accept, are either less-than-attractive birdwomen (birds from the navel down, with women's torsos and faces) or beguiling winged maidens. Either way, if all they do is shriek and nibble away at your extremities, how bad can that be? Compared to being frozen in ice upside down or drowning in boiling blood, it seems at least tolerable. No? I would take it.

Dante never even mentions accomplices or accessories before the fact, let alone condemns them. There's nothing like—

> To the right of us appeared two shades, Humphry
> and Kevorkian, who by amoral urging,
> the one with heaping bowlsful of yogurty
> Nembutal, the other with his infernal machine
> dripping potassium chloride, did both of them
> aid and abet me to do my sick self in
> months, even years, before my appointed time. . . .

Nothing like this in all of the thirty-four cantos, and nothing in there about Duffy. There's no special circle of Hell for people who procrastinate in the writing of their dissertations, either. Another aspect of the *Inferno* that strikes me as more than fair is that on the final Day of Judgment everyone else has to reclaim their bodies, but suicides never have to inhabit theirs again.

But I don't think I'm riding to Alaska to try to exonerate myself, or get myself off some Christian or existential hook. I do think it might be useful to implant some fresh memory bytes, or give myself a kind of reverse, after-the-fact vaccination against all the dread I've been feeling. I'd like to rethink some events a little more clearly, or at the very least frame what I remember more—advantageously? No. I don't think so. Knowing me, I'm determined to rub my own nose in it. And I certainly don't think I'm innocent.

In fact, I have dozens of theories about why I'm taking this trip, all about equally serviceable. My imagination has become "diseased" and needs to be healed. I need to be spiritually cleansed. I need to "own" my grief (and or my sorrow or anger or guilt). I need the endorphins. I'm compelled to return to the scene of the crime, hoping to get caught. None of the above. All of the above.

I'm also genuinely curious to see what Juneau and Glacier Bay look like under less melodramatic circumstances; I've heard they're ineffably gorgeous. If I revisit the scenes of a nightmare and find out they're beautiful, maybe I'll have fewer sequels. Maybe I'll meet someone. Maybe I'll crash and get killed. Maybe I'll be forced to acquire some physical discipline. And work habits. Maybe it's a last-ditch effort to draft some sort of truce with what happened up there, or at least a cease-fire. In the meantime, all the fresh air and exercise will bolster my flagging renal and cardiovascular systems, engender a sunnier disposition, help my dissertation get written . . .

My dissertation. I've concocted a dense and sensible outline, taken a few hundred pages of notes from the primary and secondary sources, and scribbled down dozens of thesis-clenching phrases and fatal counterexamples to the objections of my "opponents." What I've so far not managed to do is string together enough of my own pithy observations into anything that resembles a chapter. Yet if I've stayed home and worked on it for almost four years and it's gotten me just about nowhere, is it all that farfetched to imagine that leaving my desk, computer, B-heavy bookshelves, and folders full of articles at home will somehow, somewhere, some *way* be a catalyst? A solo bicycle trip is, after all, the quintessential Beckettian enterprise. And besides: not writing my dissertation can't be any more emotionally debilitating at Super 8 or EconoLodge or Pick C Motel desks than not writing it has been in my book-lined, computerized study. (My "study" is actually a windowless wall in my bedroom along which my desk, corkboard, maps, photo gallery, computer, printer, file cabinet, unpainted bookshelves, and French-English-French dictionary stand/humidifier are arrayed.) I certainly can't get too much *less* work done out here. Or can I? There are, after all, dozens of distractions on the road I wouldn't have to contend with working at home or in a library carrel. The kinds of things that make road trips exciting tend not to be the things that help a large writing project move forward. Sit home for two years and grind the thing out—that's usually the way it gets done.

But Kerouac and Rimbaud and Jan Morris and Susan Sontag and Joan Didion and Melville and William Least Heat-Moon all needed road trips to help them get work done, so it isn't just me. Faulkner needed bourbon, Poe needed opium and very young girls, M.F.K. Fisher needed food, Sade needed sadism. Fitzgerald needed to think that his penis wasn't too small. Joyce had to get out of Dublin. Beckett had to get out of Dublin, shake Joyce's influence, shake Lucia Joyce, shake off his mother, get stabbed through the ribs by a pimp, avoid the Gestapo, wait until World War II got settled, change genres, change languages . . .

As I come out of the bathroom I stub my left baby toe on a bedpost. Goddamn it! I sit on the bed and start rubbing it. Shit! From evening to evening the furniture is never arranged the same way, and I've been stubbing toes and banging hipbones on the corners of dressers more than my fair share of times. And it *oits!*

I gingerly hobble back into the bathroom and take out my toothbrush. I already miss my electric Braun terribly, but I seem to be getting the hang of conventional brushing again: not only the back-and-forth but also the all-important up-and-down strokes, plus the angles I need to achieve with this rakishly contoured red manual.

While I'm gargling I launder my shorts in the sink: first in warm water with Woolite, then rinse them with cold, wring them tight, empty the sink out, and spit.

Back in the bedroom I turn on the desk lamp and drape the wrung shorts over the lampshade. It's one of those rickety old-fashioned shades shaped like an A-line hoopskirt, so it's perfect. If I leave even a forty-watt bulb burning beneath them all night, the shorts should be dry in the morning; if they're not, I'll wear the others and spread the still-damp pair across the panniers, letting them bake in the sun while I ride. Whereas if today's T-shirt hasn't dried on the mirror by the time I'm ready to leave, it just stays here. I figure it's cheaper to buy new T-shirts than to lug my own perspiration over a few hundred miles of highway, especially if I factor in the cost of detergent and feeding quarter after quarter into washers and driers—especially if stores that sell T-shirts take Visa.

I carry my works in a red vinyl purse: four little glass bottles of Regular Humulin, three bottles of Lente, stainless-steel lancets, chem strips, logbook, my Mr. B's Ticket Service pen, and a half dozen hundred-unit syringes; the rest of my supply of syringes is stowed in my right pannier. I've run out of alcohol swabs.

Using a trip-hammer lancet, I prick the tip of my left middle finger, squeeze out a droplet of blood. It shimmers and trembles there, boring or awful or gorgeous. I wipe off the blood with the tip of a chem strip, then insert the tip into the glucometer, which will take sixty seconds to read it. There's a machine on the market that uses a laser to read your sugar level directly through your skin, but it costs four thousand dollars and is about the size of a desktop printer: slightly too bulky to be hauling around on my bike. But when I get back home in September, I'll find out how far the price has come down. I won't be able to afford one, of course, though maybe I'll also find out whether the company that makes them takes Visa. My Citibank card features a holographic dove that flaps its wings quite convincingly when you swivel the card back and forth in the light. Even with the last four digits of my account number poking through it, I can still imagine it soaring majestically up and away from its cheap, plastic, mercenary domain. *Just let the white pigeon fly*—that's my motto.

Okay. Since my smeared blood has registered *beep* a half-decent 136, I download 34 units of Regular Humulin, 52 units of Lente. The doses are based on the assumption that I'll consume about six hundred calories before I do my next shot before breakfast. But no matter how fanatically I test, monitor, exercise, or weigh my meals down to the picogram, it never becomes an exact science; it's more of a clandestine, Talmudic, repulsively *insular* twice-a-day ritual. Stress, menstruation, stray hormones, colds, grouchiness, or exhilaration all affect your sugar levels in ways you can never predict. Even when doctors have you cathetered up to an insulin drip and are doling out hospital food, they can't hit it right on the money. And when your blood sugar spikes up and down, all the little capillaries in your toes and your eyes and your kidneys get subjected to a whole lot more stress than they were designed to put up with, so bad things are going to happen whatever you do to take care of yourself. What I do is basically eyeball things and hope for the best. And so far on this trip it's working.

Once I've loaded the syringe with eighty-five units, I snap my fingernail to dislodge the stubborn little bubble that would keep the insulin from passing through the needle, then push the bubble out through the aperture. I've also been good about alternating injection sites: lower thighs, backs of my arms, left and right sides of my abdomen. Tonight is an arm night—right arm, as it happens, my least favorite place to hit up, since it forces me to use my left hand to stab in the needle and hold it steadily perpendicular while I push down the plunger.

I pull up the sleeve of my shirt with my teeth and press the back of my arm against the bathroom door jamb. This bunches the flesh up and gives me a fairly soft target. I stab into the bulge, then change grips and push down the plunger. The insulin stings as it spreads out under my skin. I rub it in circles, then pat it a few times and slap it.

I bend the needle back against the desk, drop it in the garbage pail, and cover it with Kleenex. I could sell these syringes on the street in Chicago for twenty-five dollars, twice that if they were still sealed in plastic. My prescription allows me to buy them in boxes of a hundred for less than thirty cents apiece, so selling two boxfuls would net me enough to buy the new prickless glucometer. I could even pay cash, though in that case I'd forgo the American Advantage miles. And I'll probably need them if I'm going to make it to Dublin and Paris next summer.

After riding all day, it always feels funny to walk. My thighs want to move along faster than my calves and my feet, which seem to be going so-o-o slo-o-o-wly. As I was crossing the street—Dunker Road—I tried not to tip too far forward. Nobody seemed to be watching me.

The Taco Bell salad bar, as always, was well stocked and cheap. I got two kinds of pasta salad, peaches and cottage cheese, and what looked and smelled like fresh chicken salad for dinner, chocolate pudding as a snack for tonight, plus two sourdough rolls and a banana for breakfast. All this for less than four dollars.

The guy at the table beside mine is also dining alone. He's fortyish, bony, good-looking. But he's off somehow too. He arrived at his table just after I started eating, but before he sat down he moved his food from his tray to the table, picked up *my* empty tray, and carried both trays to the bin. He did it quite matter-of-factly, not flirting or hitting on me, I don't think. I thanked him, he did it, it's over.

He clears his throat while unwrapping his burrito, then coughs, sips his drink. Very nervous. I dab mayonnaise with a napkin. We eat. I wish I had something to read.

As I start on the peaches, I notice that the sleeves of his blue, green, and yellow plaid shirt are folded back to expose the glinting gold hairs on his forearm, and—a few glances later—that the hair on his head is at least two shades darker, less glossy. He does not wear a watch or a ring.

The thing is, his sleeves have been folded back in neat, cuff-sized units instead of the usual bunched, crooked roll job. I've never seen sleeves turned more neatly. There aren't even ridges or bumps where the seams or buttons would be.

He finishes quickly and doesn't nod good-bye or make eye contact as he gets up to leave, failing to even acknowledge that he once bussed my tray. I watch him deposit his wrappers and cup in the trash. Then he's gone.

I sit here alone with the other thirty-odd Taco Bell customers: shrieking blond two-year-olds, adolescent blond banshees, their parents. Everyone has on blue denim.

When peach juice spills onto my wrist, I lick it off daintily, then steal a few glances to see who was watching. Can't tell.

I drink down the rest of the juice, using the small plastic dish as a cup.

A breeze has picked up off the lake, and my room is quite cool. Almost cold. I get under the covers and turn on the television. If a front's blowing in, I'll have to consider not riding tomorrow. But the Weather Channel forecast is for clear skies, low eighties, SSW winds ten to fifteen.

Using the blanket and spread as a shawl, I get up and arrange the banana and rolls on the windowsill, then check my odometer: eighty-one miles since this morning. I get back in bed with my maps and trace the day's progress with a kelly-green marker, green of course standing for GO. Having reached Lake Superior, I'm poised to head west on Route 2. I use my thumb and index finger as a protractor to measure the seventy-five miles I'm hoping to cover tomorrow. This should get me to Floodwood, Minnesota, my third state in less than eight days. I also have a *National Geographic* map of North America from which I've cut everything east and south of Chicago, and I use my green pen on this too. I've finished part one of the trip.

I arrange my notebook and pen to the left of my hip,

where the spread is most flat. I like to know where everything is, in the event inspiration should strike. Not that I'm counting on anything.

I tilt up the lampshade and open the Trilogy. I have the new trade edition, which has much larger print than the original paperback. The three-volume hardcover edition I've been using at home wouldn't travel by bike quite as well.

I'm reading the novels in sequence for the first time in ages. My habit had been to come at them mostly through secondary sources, or by concentrating for weeks at a time on one discrete segment of text. Didn't work. I'm hoping for fresh inspiration by approaching them now more "holistically." And the thing is, I have been inspired, but not in a way that I'd planned. I'm starting to think of them as a single 414-page comic monologue about having your body fuck up, though I also read it for pure, almost forbidden, entertainment. I can seldom get through more than two or three sentences without snorting with laughter. I still dutifully make little notes in the margin, or underline newfound motifs or echoing imagery, but these days I mostly just lie back and dig it: . . . *in winter, under my greatcoat, I wrapped myself in swathes of newspaper, and did not shed them until the earth awoke, for good, in April. The Times Literary Supplement was admirably adapted to this purpose, of a neverfailing toughness and impermeability. Even farts made no impression on it. I can't help it, gas escapes from my fundament on the least pretext, it's hard not to mention it now and then, however great my distaste. One day I counted them. Three hundred and fifteen farts in nineteen hours, or an average of over sixteen farts an hour. After all it's not excessive. Four farts every fifteen minutes. It's nothing. Not even one fart every four minutes. It's unbelievable. Damn it, I hardly fart at all, I should never have mentioned it. Extraordinary how mathematics help you to know yourself.*

I can't get enough of this stuff. I just don't feel like writing a *paper* about it.

I feel myself start to doze off. A woman is laughing, I think, in the room behind mine. A man's voice; then giggles. But I'm too tired to eavesdrop—I have sweet, limb-long aches in both legs—even when the giggles modulate into pleading directives . . .

I wake up at twenty to three in the middle of an anxiety attack. Bedside light still on, Trilogy wedged under me inside the covers, cricket just outside the window. I switch off the light by my bed, but the desk lamp stays on. That's not what woke me. I dig out my notebook and pen, put it on the floor with the book. I can't remember what I was dreaming, but right now I'm scared.

Diagnosis: dialysis: di. Why are the glomeruli inside my kidneys filtering my blood less and less efficiently? Why doesn't my pancreas work? That's the six-dollar question, of course. The answer is *Je ne sais pas*. Not exactly.

When I was four and half years old I was diagnosed with Type I diabetes. Juvenile diabetes, as it is called. The kind where your pancreas stops producing insulin. You can't clean your blood or turn food into energy properly. You poison yourself coming and going. And it keeps getting worse every day. The younger you are when you get it, the sooner the damage occurs and the more extensive it becomes. On the day I was diagnosed my life expectancy went from eighty point nine years to *snap my fingers* thirty-seven point seven *if* I stayed in good control, which basically amounts to taking RN-caliber care of myself around the clock every day of my life, which I haven't been able to do.

My father called the shots "magic bullets." He and all the nice doctors and nurses convinced me that they were good for me. For the first year or so, I didn't even mind taking them. I was a good little girl and I did what I was supposed to.

Since the development of insulin therapy in the thirties, Type I's have tended to live into adulthood, so we're breeding it into the population. There's evidence that it skips generations, especially when passed through the mother. The people who get it tend to have light-colored hair and pale complexions. In my case, beige hair and an "uneven" complexion. I do not intend to have children.

Tuberculosis made Kafka cough his lungs out (and write *The Metamorphosis*) not too long before the cure for tuberculosis got discovered. Half the characters in Dickens had TB and look how cute *they* seem. So what I'd like to know is: in thirty or forty years will diabetes seem as quaintly tragic a malady? How about in fifteen—or three?

Every week that goes by without researchers finding the cure increases my chances of going blind or getting a leg amputated. Half of all Type I's have their kidneys fail, about 20 percent by the time they are thirty. By the time I'm thirty the continual up-and-down pressure will have been ravaging my capillaries for over a quarter of a century. Most renal complications start to kick in after ten to fifteen years, so my luck is about to run out.

I have to accept the fact that I'm losing my health, though I never really had it to begin with. And I cannot accept this. It knocks me off balance with spite and anxiety and rage: night and day, grading papers, annotating tertiary sources, changing my clothes, in the middle of sexual fantasies, riding my bike, eating lunch, watching the news on TV. Doing nothing. Worrying about diabetes is something that *helps* me do nothing. I'm often convinced it's the reason I'm blocked. But any worrying I happen to do about it releases hormones that make the process of deterioration proceed even faster. These days every twinge or buzz I feel in my chest or my head, every little throb in the veins of my neck, I have to wonder if it's the big one, my San Andreas Fault shifting tectonic positions . . .

I used to keep a scrapbook. Every time an article came out in *JAMA* or the "Science" *Times* section or the *JDF Newsletter*, I taped it to one of the powder-blue pages. FK506, an immunosuppressant derived from a Japanese fungus, determined to help prevent the rejection of transplanted pancreatic tissue. Studies show five shots a day control blood sugar levels 80 percent more effectively than two shots a day. Captopril inhibits the production of the hormone angiotensin II, which decreases pressure in the glomeruli.

The problem with these studies is that they're never complete. Follow-up studies are always necessary. Even if you've volunteered to be one of the guinea pigs, you've got a fifty-fifty chance of being put in the control group and given a placebo; in the meantime you've spent another five years losing renal or retinal function. And it usually turns out that the new drugs or procedures are only available for patients whose eyes or kidneys are already seriously damaged. I say, why bother? Because once the doctors start calling you "end-stage," it's definitely time to cash in.

While I wait for the researchers to follow up, irreversible damage is being done to my organs. I know this because the articles don't pull any punches. *Cardiovascular complications including myocardial infarction and amputation due to peripheral vascular disease are frequently seen in those suffering from end-stage renal disease.* They go on to describe how nearly every major organ gets ravaged. Since your kidneys no longer produce enough red blood cells, your bones get soft and you become anemic. Your neuromuscular system breaks down, and you lose your ability to concentrate. You get infections. You have strokes. You go blind. You spend most of your time in the hospital, and that's where you die. In the meantime, in order to "save" you, doctors will amputate things.

But in spite of the confidence-destroying jolts I get from every paragraph or sentence I read about diabetes, and even though 90 percent of the cutting-edge research reports are technically beyond my understanding, and what I do understand makes me worry incessantly, and worrying makes me destroy myself faster, I'm still compelled to find out as much as I can about the likeliest cures and regimens for control. I hate all the nacreous details, but I have to know how to take care of myself in order to delay for as long as possible the onset of complications. That's part of what this trip is about.

I also can't stop reading the articles because one of these days the author is going to say the magic word. The "C" word. He or she isn't going to hedge, equivocate, or emphasize the necessity of further tests. It's going to be something. And then I'll be ABD-C.

If it doesn't happen soon, then I'll have been taking this particular bike trip a ways beyond the middle of the journey of my life—more like the *fine* or *terminé*.

But suicide?

Not now, of course. I'm just not that sick yet, and there's still a half-decent chance a cure will be ready in time. But who knows? I don't want to let the thing that has ruined my life also kill me.

According to the Bible, not to die cheaply and efficiently is to pursue one's own vanity, make an idol of oneself, elevate oneself above communal obligations, and to reject the sovereignty of God. Is it a problem that these happen to include some of the best reasons I've come across in favor of actually doing it?

Life insurance companies refuse to pay off if the insured person commits suicide. But how can their investigators be certain what's happened? And who decides if it's a close call— if a car wings a tree or flies off a cliff, a commuter gets nailed by a train, a jilted little sister slips from the deck of a ship?

In any event, I don't have a sexy big sister or brother. I don't have a car. I don't have life insurance, either. Actuarially speaking, my life is worth about zero dollars. Same as it ever was. Same as it ever was. Same as it always has been.

I don't think I'm terribly afraid of dying, at least not much more than the next person. What I've never been able to tolerate is the hassle of feeling drowsy or sick half the time, of having to monitor every last Grapenut and minute of exercise and unit of insulin. It's the fucking inconvenience that gets me. I'd also like to make this official: I've done my time in hospitals, doctors' offices, and blood-test labs. I've sat on my last too-high examination table in a backless paper smock listening to very bad news from a preoccupied doctor, or getting lectured about the damage I've "let happen" by living like a normal human being.

One of the major last straws was the time I passed out at a dinner party and woke up in Evanston Hospital. It took the nurses eight days to get me stabilized. While I was there I vowed I'd never become an in-patient again—examined by medical students, mocked by the white plastic bracelet, chained by IV's to a starchy little crib ... I understand that MD's understand diabetes, as do the RN's and technicians. I understand most of them mean well. But every last cell of me violently rejects being fingered and punctured and question-naired, prevented from wearing my clothes, fed intravenously, assisted in moving my bowels, being briskly awakened three times between midnight and dawn to have my fingertips punctured with angled spikes, all for my very own good. I just do not find this amusing, however much cheer and efficiency the nurses might bring to their duties. I can't even read with much pleasure in hospitals; I tend to watch television, feel sorry for myself, promise or refuse to turn over new leaves, drift into bleary half-sleep. I also get fierce claustrophobia. I spend most of my energy deciding I cannot and will not toler-ate another second of it—yet I stay there and let it continue for hours and hours and *days*. Until I get better again. Because the thing is, I never get better.

So killing myself is by far the most practical alternative. Now more than ever, in fact. The only real questions are when and how. Having ruminated on the subject for tens of thousands of hours already, I'm convinced that one's death should be elegant, painless if possible, and swift—maybe even heroic and beautiful, like I hope David's was. Maybe even slightly triumphant. It should also be an adventure, and so should occur long before one becomes decrepit, since the decrepit tend to be unadventuresome.

The trick is to figure out a way to schedule it for the day *just before* you reach the point of no return: canes, Seeing Eye dogs, dialysis machines. I don't want to cheat myself out of very much good time, but I still have to err on the side of doing it slightly too soon; if I wait even one day too long, I risk having the stroke that removes all my options.

But I don't want to talk myself into doing it too early, either. One of the scenarios I'm most afraid of is going through with it late of a Monday evening, three or four hours before the cure gets announced in the "Science" *Times* pages of the newspaper down in my hallway, immaculate inside its sapphire-and-black plastic tube, inky fragrance, just waiting for me to *damn* read it and go get my islet-cell implant, my bad genes unspliced or resequenced, then launch about a seventeen-month, one-girl party. Instead, I'd be lying on the floor of my apartment with viscous beige drool caking up on my cheek. Or whatever.

I'd also like to schedule it for when there's nothing I've been looking forward to on the horizon: making it back to Alaska, getting my dissertation approved, or even a tenure-track job.

But the real trick is to somehow make it an act of pure joy. A big-time relief to be sure, but something more sublime or expansive than that: lighting out for another form of consciousness, a form of existence a little more *plain*. Maybe come back as a musical note, like Rahsaan Roland Kirk tried to do. Or maybe turn into a tree: This was, after all, Dante's clear-eyed idea of a suitable punishment, and it's never struck me as a particularly infernal form of existence. I don't think I'd mind spending my time as a spruce, with a couple of finches' nests, say, in the forks of my branches; or maybe a paper-bark maple, with all of those magnificent six-pointed leaves turning amber and gold in the fall. I'd love to just stand near some river or ocean or lake, in the sun or the thunder, get rained on and snowed on, "Go Fishing" notices stapled to the backs of my knees, drip golden sap, pare myself down to twigs every winter and stand out there naked, get waxy new leaves in the spring. Or if not a paper-bark maple, then maybe a paperback novel, getting thumbed and obsessed over, cozied up with on buses and el trains, in beds . . .

The first thing I do in the morning is turn on the Weather Channel. Before I can determine my dosage and draw up my shot, I need to ascertain that I'll be able to ride. If there's a front rolling in, or one is scheduled to arrive before late afternoon, I have to stay put; I'll expend only 30 percent of the energy I'd use if I rode all day, so I give myself maybe five fewer units of Regular, ten fewer Lente. If I gave myself a riding-day dosage, then got rained in, I'd have a major reaction by eleven o'clock. I'm hoping the days I'm rained in will coincide as closely as possible with when I need to rest anyway. A thunderstorm, oh, every Tuesday, when the traffic is heaviest and the libraries and laundromats are open, would be just about perfect.

In any event, the local forecast—"accurate and dependable from the Weather Channel"—is for it to be clear, lower eighties, west-southwest winds five to ten, so a riding-day dosage will work.

No problema.

Michelle Halle, my most recent endocrinologist, has been on my case hard since last summer to go to three shots a day—one before every meal—to control my sugar levels more efficiently. I've promised her I'll try it as soon as I get back from Alaska. To which she replies: Please stop stalling. But even hard-assed Michelle had to accept at least part of my logic:

having to hit myself up while out on the road at lunchtime is an unideal regimen; whatever kidney or cardiovascular damage I'd incur being 33 percent less efficient between now and September would be counterbalanced by the regularity of the exercise I get in the meantime, the weight I'd lose, etc. Regular exercise has always been right at the top of her list of the areas in which I need to improve.

She only half bought it, of course. She made me promise to call her at least once a week to discuss my blood tests and dosages, and she gave me the names of six endocrinologists evenly spaced along my planned route. It seems I also promised her to get a blood and urine workup at the University of North Dakota Hospital in Williston—either there or with her as soon as I got back in September. We'll see.

Breakfast consists of the perfectly ripe, 6-percent-brown-splotches Chiquita, along with two boxettes of Wheaties, skim milk, and a packet of Equal from the spread the Pick C had out in the lobby.

Last night I picked up a postcard for my roommate, Jane Hartley. Four views of downtown Chequamegon. Since Jane's ship is cruising the Russian Far East (she's the associate activities director), I'm sure this little sidewater won't drive her too crazy with jealousy. She always insists she "just must" hear from me three times a week, even though her mail gets delayed by a month; the only way to reach her when she's working is to write to her in care of the company's headquarters in Stockholm—or happen to be home when she calls.

Jane is under the impression that I'm on some sort of slow-motion suicide mission: The trip is too long, I shouldn't be riding alone, what if I had a reaction. What do I hope to accomplish *anyway*. She wants to know why I don't ride to St. Louis or Pittsburgh, where the most promising research is being done; that way I'd be killing two or three birds with one stone—a dubious metaphor to deploy on a person she refers to as Bird Nerd.

So. *Brane Drane, Dissertation completed and mailed off to*

Marvin this morning. No loons so far, at least not up close and personal, but I'm fine. Wish you were here. Only kidding. Where are you, anyway? Slainte, Me. I don't add that killing myself is the last thing I'm going to do. Having been one of my little household jests for the last several months, it's lost a percent of its humor.

I fill my three water bottles, see if the tires are hard, stuff my dry, dirty clothes into the left pannier, pack up my book and red purse, load *Blood Sugar Sex Magik* into my Discman. Okay.

I wheel my bike to the door, slide on the earphones, hit Play, scan the room one more time to make sure I've got all my stuff. I've already forgotten my copy of *How to Cook a Wolf* somewhere in central Wisconsin, and my pink-and-black socks back in Antioch.

When I open the door I'm startled to see a handsome young Federal Express delivery man standing there, his fist getting ready to knock. His purple-and-orange uniform fits quite picturesquely. We look at each other. He lowers his fist and raises his eyebrows. There *is* something about men in uniforms.

"Penelope Culligan?"

I admit it. I've just smeared a goodly portion of my already goofy countenance with chartreuse magnesium sunblock, but still. Who else could I be?

"Sign on this line, please?"

As he holds out a clipboard, his wrist glistens with arching gold hairs. Just like Mr. Neatsleeves last night in the Taco Bell, only more nonchalant. He steadies the clipboard, making it desklike in front of me, and proffers a pen.

"By the X, eh?"

While signing I ask, "You Canadian?"

He grins like I've paid him a compliment. "I was till two years ago, ma'am."

Ma'am? I stand in the doorway, watching him hustle his narrow, Canadian, khaki-clad butt toward his van.

The Letterpack he gave me feels empty: no weight or thickness at all. I look at who sent it: Leona S. Marvin, 5277 S. Dorchester . . . Jesus.

All that's inside is an MCI phone card in her name, with a powder-blue Post-it stuck to the back: *Penny dear, Hope you're well, making much progress on all fronts. Forgot to give you this Friday. Please stay in touch. Love, Lee.*

Lee Marvin is my dissertation advisor. She's also chair of the Department of Irish Literature of the University of Illinois at Chicago. It's to Lee I owe my tuition waiver, my teaching assistantship, and the health insurance that comes with it. My deadline for completing the dissertation was two Septembers ago. I've already been granted two extensions, and the chances are "somewhat remote" that I'll be granted "a turd," as Marvin is wont to pronounce it. She insists that I finish before this November, which is one reason she's so anal about my keeping in touch. If I happen to be canceled by the university's medical plan, walking preexisting condition that I am, I won't be able to get other insurance. It will basically be all that she wrote because of all that I haven't. Lee knows this. She sympathizes. I've told her I'm "maybe half done" but refused her incessant requests to see drafts. She'll do just about anything to help me, even turn herself into my very own personal Fury.

How did she know where to send this? It's addressed to me in care of the Pick C Motel in Chequamegon. Mailed at 6:00 P.M. yesterday. The last time we talked was the evening before I took off, and all I gave her—all I *could* give her—was my approximate itinerary for the first week or so. By yesterday afternoon I could've been almost anywhere in northern Wisconsin or Minnesota; and even if she hit the town right— it *is* on Route 2, I suppose—I could've ended up in any one of half a dozen different motels. If she knew my credit card number and my mother's maiden name—though I can't recall giving her either—she could call in and track my last charge. Maybe she's having me followed.

*　　　*　　　*

I pedal along in the sunshine. West of Chequamegon, Route 2 is two lanes of deteriorating asphalt with little or no ridable shoulder. I did hit a stretch when it spread into four lanes of gleaming new blacktop, but that lasted less than a mile. What shoulder there is at the moment is littered with cigarette filters, rust-colored gravel, helical strips of black tread. Some of the cracks in the asphalt are patched with a syrupy tar; others have weeds sprouting up from them: *boing!* I'm doing my best not to roll straight down into the deeper ones. The trick is to take them at least slightly sideways. You do not want to hit these guys parallel.

I'm riding through what's been designated the Chequamegon National Forest. The name makes it sound densely woodsy, but most of the foliage is widely spaced aspen and fir trees clinging to low, rolling hills not quite sandy enough to be dunes. You can tell you're still close to the lake. Most of the houses are tiny, not much bigger than the satellite dishes beside them. One trailer propped up on blocks had a spanking-new concrete basketball court alongside it, complete with two see-through backboards. There are also some gorgeous log cabins. A few of the tilted, unpainted gray shacks have portions of walls or roofs missing, but nonetheless seem to be occupied: curtains in windows, laundry on clotheslines, large dogs. The smaller the shack, the larger the dog tends to be. I haven't been attacked yet, knock wood or chromoly. If a yammering pit bull takes a run at me and its tail isn't wagging, I've been told just to talk to it soothingly; I should not pedal faster or stop. I haven't decided yet exactly what I'll say, soothingly or otherwise, but I doubt I'll be tempted to stop.

I've pedaled past Moquah and Roeder and Kindt. Delta Mason smelled fiercely of cows, made me foreswear eating burgers. Instead I had a tuna-salad sandwich and fresh apple cider for lunch, then circled south of Superior and Duluth and pedaled uphill for three miles into Proctor, Minnesota, home of Dis Restaurant and Starvin Marvins. I couldn't help picturing Proctor's dozens of malnourished Marvins lined up outside the Restaurant of Lower Hell, the last dining establishment to survive in the Town Without Apostrophes.

A trailer swings by bearing two Appaloosas as I cross the St. Louis River. The sun's blasting down, but the breeze in my face keeps me cool. The Burlington Northern tracks are now on my right; I can follow them out through Montana or catch a ride back to Chicago. A squadron of redwings takes off from the field between me and the tracks. I shift up one gear and push harder, taking advantage of this smooth stretch of blacktop. The shoulder's at least five feet wide.

In the last half hour I've been feeling less riled by Lee and her antics. And yet am I supposed to feel *encouraged* to have watching over me the anal retentive dissertation advisor? The Lee Marvin—literally—of dissertation advisors? The dissertation advisor from Hades? This phone card is only her latest effort to keep track of the progress she knows I haven't made. Exactly how such tentacled fosterage might help me overcome my writer's block and get on with the thing is not clear. Lee's little stunts seldom are.

Though she's come to doubt the soundness of my mind, I believe Professor Marvin is fond of the sound of my voice. She apparently finds me photogenic, as well. Two years ago she proposed that I pose shooting up while wearing some lacy silk lingerie, the occasion being a "serious photo-essay" she was collaborating on for an anthology called *Illness as Metaphor in Beckett*. Samuel Beckett and lingerie? To paraphrase Descartes, who was, after all, Mr. Beckett's favorite Cartesian philosopher: I don't *think* so.

The unnaked fact is that Lee has told me two times, neither time drunk, that she loves me. When she first started buying me books, taking me to dinner and plays and then conferences, insisting that "everything's research," my impression was that one more horny professor wanted to lick one more grad student. Fair enough. Lee wasn't gonna lick *me*, but as long as she didn't push things too hard, I suppose I was flattered. Plus there were usually ways to construe her behavior simply as the practical and emotional encouragement she'd be expected to give a young protégée. Not that at twenty-nine I'm terribly young anymore.

Maybe I'm kidding myself. It certainly would not be the first time. Maybe Lee just wants me to make it through the program, get a job, and go out into the world; in fact, I *know* she wants that to happen. And maybe she really does love me.

Two and a half years ago we both attended the MLA convention in New York. Lee maneuvered to have the department pick up my airfare and registration fee, then offered to let me stay with her in a double room at the Paramount. I was tempted—more than Lee realized, I'll bet—but I had to decline. I saved eighty-five dollars by taking the train (which cost me about forty extra hours of travel time) and stayed in Stuyvesant Town with my chain-smoking, light-libretti-composing Uncle Joseph, who turned out to be vastly more trouble than Lee would've been.

The time I came closest to making myself clear was two Christmas Eves ago, when Lee took me to lunch at Le Nomads. After her pro forma ten-minute discourse on how brilliant but neurotic her bone-surgeon husband was, she gave me a box wrapped in iridescent green paper. Was this a "Christmas" color, or somehow a reference to Irish literature? I was tense. The wrapping reminded me of the head of a deranged, buzzing fly. Inside was a Discman and the complete six-disc set of Chopin recorded by Claudio Arrau. Problem two: I had no gift for Lee. I'd thought of picking up a bottle of wine or a paperback—it was Christmas, after all—but I was afraid of giving her the wrong impression. I also didn't have an extra thirteen dollars. (My father likes to talk about how he and his brother Don wanted to go to the movies in the early 1930s, when admission was five cents apiece, but their mother was unable to provide them with a dime; she went through her purse, her pockets, all seven drawers of her bureau, but she couldn't come up with one. In my version I'll have to stagger people with my inability to scrounge together thirteen bucks.)

I tried to tell Lee that I couldn't accept her gifts.

"At least keep the Arrau," she said, knowing full well I didn't have a CD player. She'd been in my apartment three times.

When I mentioned having no gift for her, she ignored me.

"I was wondering," she said, quite blasé, "if you'd be interested in having Hyatt Reese take your picture."

"Why would he want to do that?" Even in those days, Reese was considered a young though still major photographer: big shows in San Francisco, New York, and Venice; still doing a lot of his quasi-kinky fashion stuff too.

"I think he wants to shoot you, you know, injecting yourself with insulin."

This was a subject, I knew, that had riveted Lee's attention since she'd found out that I was diabetic. She'd spied a syringe in my purse once as we primped side by side in the eighteenth-floor john and cheerfully asked if I had "a habit." I told her I wished; that it was nothing so glamorous as that. There was no being coy with her though; she was going to make me come clean, so I told her what habit I did have. After that it was something we didn't discuss much. It was, at least, something *I* didn't discuss much.

So as we sat in the little back room of Le Nomads, I dared her with my eyes to continue, knowing she was just getting started. I have to admit she had nerve.

"Hyatt supplies all the props and the costumes," she said.

She returned my stare frankly.

"The costumes?" Too shocked, ostensibly, to object to the general premise, I quibbled instead about details. In retrospect I suppose it may have indicated that, dismayed and offended though I was, I was also a little intrigued.

"Something tasteful, of course, but also disturbing and—*puissant*. He told me he knows it will work."

"You've discussed this with Reese?"

She glanced at the table and blushed. "I assumed we both knew Hyatt has been doing this series of . . . " She did not want to say it.

"Diseases?"

"You saw his last show."

I had. I'd seen it with Lee, as a matter of fact. It consisted of gorgeous but harrowing black-and-white prints of beautiful, stoic, very sick young men and women. Nudes with mastectomies, bald chemotherapy patients, hospice nurses who had AIDS themselves. The one of a blonde with MS dragging herself up a staircase made the cover of *Artforum*. The show had just traveled to Lisbon.

"Why does Reese shoot only good-looking women?"

"That's a good question," said Lee. "Would you like me to ask him?"

"I think I'd like to ask him myself."

"I believe it can be arranged."

"Oh, I'm sure it can."

"Shall I?"

I shrugged, sipped some four-dollar water. I'm still not sure why, but I suddenly felt—what? Defeated? Humiliated? Pissed. And diseased.

"I'll have him get in touch with you," said Lee.

"I thought he was done with that series."

I had now made my teacher blush twice. "Guess not," she said finally. "Penny, what can I tell you?"

That's what I wanted to know. Would prints of me shooting up be . . . changing hands? Would I be asked to wear special lingerie to make my plight seem more poignant—the alluring but doomed Beckett scholar? I was willing to bet tenure and decades of salary and health benefits that Reese would supply Lee with prints. Wasn't that what was up? Allow Hyatt Reese to aestheticize my disease, my dis-ease, my unease with my body, in exchange for my gratitude to the woman who'd set up the shoot? I suddenly felt as though I'd been asked to perform in some sort of one-frame, NC-17 snuff film.

My brain was racing ahead of confirmable evidence. A legitimate and famous photographer wanted to capture the daily routine of a diabetic. If I weren't the proposed subject, I'd probably think that was good. But I couldn't help wondering if there was some physical flaw he'd focus on or exaggerate. The spongy flesh on my arm where I shot up the most, for example. And what were these "costumes" and "props" Lee was talking about? I was dying to know, but I didn't want to give Lee the satisfaction of asking.

I excused myself, went to the john. I stood by the fireplace and stared at the arrangement of dried flowers down where the fire would be. For five or ten minutes I considered walking out on her. I understood how this might complicate my academic career. I understood that I wanted the Discman. I decided I wasn't in sleek enough shape to have photographs of me in my scanties exhibited in galleries or reviewed in the "Living Arts" section.

I went back to the table, but I didn't sit down. "I'm sorry we've misunderstood each other," I said.

"Penny, please sit." She patted the table.

"I'm not feeling very well at the moment. I have to go home."

She stood up, reached out, took my elbow. It was the second time we'd touched.

"Penny, I'm terribly sorry." I could tell that she meant it.

"I believe you," I said. "I forgive you." It was strange to be saying that too.

"If only—"

"I really do have to go home now."

I left.

It was shamefully melodramatic behavior, and I knew I'd overreacted before I was even out the door of the restaurant. But, I mean, diabetes—isn't that an excuse?

In any event, Lee forgave me.

Jane isn't terribly fond of Lee Marvin. It is, in fact, her unswerving opinion that she's a womanizing hypocrite, a meretricious academic bureaucrat, a thoroughgoing non-scholar without clue number two as to the literary, let alone the human value of Samuel Beckett's prose, verse, or drama. She is using me. Her interest in my thesis has exclusively to do with her campaign to fetishistically possess me. I am bought and sold both academically and morally if I don't immediately—

"What? Change dissertation advisors in the middle of my thesis?"

"People have done that before. People a lot farther along than you are, my dear."

"Misguided, self-defeating self-defeatists maybe. Not me."

"Carrie whatshername did it. People do it all the *time*, Penny Bird. People, in fact, who actually *are* in the middle of their dissertations."

In Jane's relentless calculus, even the fact that Lee's husband, Jack, isn't executive director of the Samuel Beckett Fan Club counts for points against Lee. I once made the mistake of passing along to Jane Lee's account of how her husband had groaned and shifted his weight during the first act of *Happy Days* at the Coyote Theater, then claimed he had a migraine during the intermission and took a cab home. Jane immediately deployed her high-powered weird-sister alchemy to transmogrify Jack's early exit into a transgression against Beckett on *Lee's* part. "That play requires a two-thirds-empty theater to work, and you know it. The more walkouts there were, the happier Sam always was; rest in peace. Certainly Herr Professor should know that."

What could I say?

"And besides," Jane went on, "it gave her the perfect excuse to sneak off and have yet another in a suspiciously lengthy series of 'drinks' with her prize student."

The more Jane attacks Lee, the more I want to defend her—if not quite jump into bed with her. It does make me want to have drinks.

When I muster the gumption to suggest that Jane's line of argument seeks to have things both ways, she claims my response is "just so incredibly *typical*."

"And yours is ass backward."

"It's *your* ass that's the issue here, girl."

I pat it and nod, waiting for her to continue. I never have to wait very long.

"You complain about how this woman is undermining your integrity, fucking with your thesis quote unquote, but when push comes to shove, you've never failed once to defend her."

Jane goes on.

"Because letting this weenie dyke pant up your skirt ain't gonna get you the—"

"I haven't worn a skirt in her presence in over two years. Since the time—"

"That's beside the point, girl. *Duh?* I was speaking figuratively? And besides, you have *too* worn a skirt for her. Your green-and-blue men's tartan kilt to that party she threw for . . . "

Oh. Right. Forgot.

Jane's central thesis is that my extreme abhorrence and guilt, which I pathetically deny, about having let my advisor breathe down my neck, in my ear, over my shoulder, up my men's kilt—exactly where she breathes on me depends on Jane's current level of vituperativeness—has rendered me incapable of confidently and objectively assessing my own work as a critic and a scholar. (This conclusion is principally based on the *one* time I let slip a reference to a paper I'd written as "amateur-hour exegesis.") Furthermore, my anxiety over this state of affairs, and my perfectly justifiable anger, which I also insist on denying, are the reasons I'm currently blocked. Instead of being the person who's keeping me *in* the Ph.D. program, Lee is actually causing me to flunk out—or at least to remain ABD.

Jane so distrusts her that she uses *marv* as a transitive verb meaning "to simultaneously help and fuck over." Lately she's come just short of demanding that I file sexual harassment charges with the university; if I don't, she implies, she'll have little choice but to file them herself, since she's legally culpable as a non-reporting accessory after the fact to a crime. She'll be happy to put me in touch with an ass-whupping lawyer who'll represent me pro bono.

First off, I don't think Lee Marvin is technically guilty of sexual harassment. There's been no forced physical contact, though there have been unwanted advances. My sense is that Lee wouldn't press things once I actually said no. Instead I've just smiled, shaken my head, pretended to be more or less innocent: Lee, what's got into you? Really!

The first time we spent time together—an end-of-semester dinner party at my apartment—Lee's good-night kiss on the cheek turned into a briefly moist smooch on the lips. Her breath smelled like cognac and coffee—delicious. One of her hands on the small of my back, the other one brushing my throat.

I turned my face, stiffened.

"You don't want me to kiss you like that?"

"I'd rather not, you know, complicate our academic rapport."

"You sure?" she said, holding me.

I pulled back and mumbled something about her husband. I never told her I was still in love with David. I never said no, or forget it, or that I was strictly a heterosexual. So I'm afraid that in the aggregate I've given Lee to infer that if she'd just be slightly more persistent, I might acquiesce. This is more than a little my fault. Because I don't want to lose her support, I'm probably guilty of subtly leading her on.

The real question is whether any quid pro quo has been threatened or implied: Does our friendship and what it might lead to confer upon me unfair advantages within the department? Probably. Would it be to my disadvantage to suddenly not be her protégée? Definitely.

But even if she were technically liable, it would be stupendously time- and emotion-consuming (not to mention the damage all the stress could do to my capillaries) to make the charge stick. In the meantime, of course, Lee and her colleagues would remain in a position to make my life slightly difficult, a fact that I've tried to make Jane appreciate.

"That's precisely the point," Jane insists. "That's how harassment *works*."

"But it's only the point if you assume she's guilty in either the letter or the spirit, before I even bring up the charges.

Anyone's gonna get a tad pissed off if you accuse them of a crime, especially when they've been trying to help you."

Round and round we go. Where we stop depends a lot on when Jane pulls her next assignment to Alaska, Antarctica, Mozambique, or wherever. I do know I love my roommate dearly. I'd be roommateless without her. I trust her opinion, even though sometimes I think she lacks perspective. Because the point I'm not ever quite able to make has to do with what an astonishing luxury it is—with what I wouldn't give to have some *harassment* as the overriding concern of my life. People are in agony all over the planet from cancer or flamethrowers, getting chased through the countryside by maniacs with machetes, so I can't always get comprehensively enraged each time some middle-aged professor lets me know she has a crush on me. Sorry.

At least this is what I tell myself when Jane gets in my face about Lee, my dissertation, my "aggressive passiveness." When she's *not*, when she's out of town or the hemisphere, out of phone contact, and I'm back to spending most of my hours and minutes and days more or less by myself in Lee's creepy force field, I often feel, well, somewhat differently.

So this is another reason to ride to Alaska: to put some distance between myself and Lee Marvin. To wit: 632 miles and still counting.

In the weeks before I left, I tried to become more direct. "Lee, our relationship . . . " But I haven't come up with what I'm supposed to say, exactly. Please don't ask me to participate in your personal life? Thanks, but I prefer bi-gender encounters myself? I haven't had a serious smooch or caress in seven years, but please keep your lizard hands off me? Because except for that first night at my apartment, she never has put her hands *on* me. No one has. I haven't even done it myself. It's not that I don't get the urge, it's just that . . .

Another good question: Why haven't I had a boyfriend since David? It's a very long story, of course, but to summarize, I'd have to say that men make me nervous. So do women for that matter, but that's another story.

After riding through switchgrass and bluestem and scrubby little forest-service pine trees for almost two hours, I feel a tad bleary as I approach a railroad crossing outside a hamlet called Dobie—just as the bells and crossing lights start to go off. As the long red-and-white wooden barrier bounces into place I swing to the left and slow down, trying to see if I'd make it. Unless it's absolutely necessary, I don't want to get caught here for forty-five minutes watching eight miles of ore trundle by. I balance myself with one foot, then hop and roll forward another few yards, craning my neck to see past the station.

Goddamn! A blue train blasts into the intersection going twelve times as fast as an ore train. The ground clacks and rattles. I realize that the horn has been blaring, but so piercingly loud I can't hear it. I'm engulfed. The engine disappears to my left while the noise of its horn breaks laterally across me, in the opposite direction the rest of the monster is headed. I shiver, lean back, with nothing to hold but my bike.

It's an express, not a local, apparently. I'd figured the barriers and lights would be calibrated to afford one more notice— an excess of notice, erring substantially in favor of the lame or incautious. Not in the case of *this* train, which seems to pick up speed as it keeps smashing by. The air roiling up from the wheels feels violent enough by itself to separate an arm from a shoulder, an eye from a socket. I've never felt anything like it. My only real basis of comparison is silver-and-glass CTA express trains, which will wake you up quick from the foggiest of reveries as you drowse on a platform in rush hour, but are of an entirely different order of magnitude—flimsier—than this million-ton tantrum of suction and noise and big steel going on five feet in front of me, tugging me in toward its maw. I had no idea. Two, three more hops and I would've been sucked in and blendered into tart, vaguely splintery salsa before I knew what hit me.

Which would not be a bad way to go: sudden and semi-involuntary, every last pain-sensing, consciousness-generating component instantaneously obliterated. Still.

Now I know.

I ride on through more scrubby forest, past round ponds and narrow gray lakes rimmed with cattails and black slime and reeds. The farther west I go, the sparser the traffic gets: about a car every ten, fifteen minutes. I relish the road and the sun, the breathable air and the solitude.

A green Toyota pickup goes by, heading east. Three teenage boys with Anthrax or some such metallica grinding from the window, from which one of them whistles. At me. No one else out here, unfortunately. I pretend to ignore it but keep a close eye on the truck in my mirror till it disappears round a bend. I take swigs of water, sprinkle some onto my face.

Ten minutes later a perky blue Beetle comes sputtering up behind me, swings out into the middle of the left lane, zooms by. The driver waits till he's a hundred yards past me before drifting back over again.

There are five or six ways for a driver to pass you out here. The politest way for the operator of a two-hundred-horse-power, four-thousand-pound vehicle to slip past a girl on a thirty-pound bicycle trying to negotiate a strip of asphalt maybe ten inches wide—on shoulderless stretches I'm often forced to straddle the white, slightly convex painted line, bracing myself for the impact—is to slow down and bear as far to the left as possible. If there are four lanes or no oncoming traffic, beneficent drivers will use the next lane, as the guy in the Beetle did. Most cars are at least five feet narrower than a lane of Route 2, so drivers have plenty of latitude. Even when they can't move very far over, they can always slow down; and most of them do, bless their hearts. I also get peace signs, thumbs-ups, wiggled fingers, and various other forms of digital encouragement. Go, Penny!

Less friendly folk, especially when oncoming cars have forced them to stay in their lane, at least give me a beep to let me know to move over. Only one guy has leaned on his horn. A small percentage of drivers, one or two out of a hundred, just blast right on by me, practically winging my elbow, letting their wake drag me sideways and come about yea close to killing me. These morons clearly don't give it a thought; either that or they outright enjoy it. It's hard to be sure when you can't see their faces, but there are certain ways of accelerating that I associate with purposeful bike haters.

There's also the occasional oblivious geezette, barely able to see over the steering wheel of her twelve-foot-wide boat of a Buick and who'll run you right into a ditch quite inadvertently. Whoops! These tiny dames seem to prefer the early A.M. for their self-absorbed sojourns, I've noticed.

Fortunately, aggressive or unfriendly drivers are very much the exception in Wisconsin and Minnesota. A lot of the people up here ride bikes themselves (my Trek was made in Waterloo, Wisconsin), which I think must incline them to give me some space as they pass, if not always to—

Erupting from out of a splash and a black-and-white whir on my right, there's a loon. I squeeze both brakes hard, swerve to a stop. It's a big loon—a common, I think. I squint, shade my eyes, trying to follow its path as its skims the bright water. Its beak is dipped lower than the rest of its body amid much frantic flapping. I'm *glad* that it's such a bad flier; it gives me an extra two or three seconds to watch it. I love it! It does not make a sound as it settles among some tall reeds on the opposite side of the lake, disappears.

What's a loon doing this close to a highway? They're supposed to feed much farther north in the summer, and never at this time of day, plus they assiduously avoid human habitat. This guy must be a stray adolescent on the prowl for a mate in exotic, off-limits locales like Route 2. Yet it had mature plumage: black neck and head, zebra-striped throat, black-and-white pot-holder pattern across the wings and the back. It was just so lovely! I feel like my week has been made. To have spotted one anywhere, let alone close enough to actually *see* it: a ghost-spooky bird of the north, of wetness and silence and coolth, where I'm going.

I feel like it's made the whole trip.

Bad news, I think. An acid-green pickup truck is tailing me. It's hard to be certain in my shaky rearview mirror, but it looks like the same dickhead teenagers I saw coming *toward* me twenty minutes ago. If I'm right, and they've doubled back to follow me, then I definitely have some serious trouble on my hands.

Here they come.

They slow way down as they approach but stay in their lane, then veer to the right as they pull alongside me, maintaining the same speed I'm doing.

The guy riding shotgun says, "Hah." I believe it's his version of "hi."

I pretend he's not there and say nothing. I glance up the road, then down in my mirror. No cars in either direction.

They maintain my pace for another few seconds—as long as I can stand it. I stop. They keep going.

So now what?

The TO and TA of TOYOTA on the tailgate have been neatly painted over. A fiberglass bow and some nasty-looking hunting arrows hang crookedly from a gun rack in back.

When they get twenty feet ahead of me, I can still hear their cackles and whoops. Then they stop.

I slow down as much as I can without tipping over, and check in my mirror again. Not a soul.

I put on a "bored" face, staying behind them as I memorize the Wisconsin license plate—DJP 240—trying Dweeb Jism Punks and Dickhead Jerkoff Punks as mnemonic devices. Two-forty, two-forty, two-forty, which is also the number of days, the number of hours per day . . . Doesn't work. Dumb Jerkoff Punks two four oh.

As I pull alongside, the pickup moves forward again. I notice them checking *their* mirrors to find out if anyone's on the horizon.

The driver suddenly guns it and pulls away fast, spraying gravel. I almost cry out with relief. But they stop less than fifty yards ahead of me. That they must have resolved whatever issue was making them flee I take as a very bad sign.

To maintain my pride, I ride slowly toward them. The guy in the middle has on a backward Bulls cap, the kind with the red-and-white zebra-skin bill. The driver has a matted blond crew cut with long fringe in back. The guy riding shotgun is wearing a Magic cap. He's watching me in the long side-view mirror, the kind with the convex mirrored ball at the bottom. I can see him in both of them too.

The shoulder is just about wide enough to allow me to ease past the truck on the right, but if I give it too wide a birth, I'll risk sliding into the ditch. I hold on and pedal and steer. The truck burps and grumbles in neutral as I pull alongside it again.

"Excuse us, miss, but we're gettin' kinda lost?" says the guy riding shotgun. Snaps his gum. The driver unclutches, and the truck lurches forward.

I stare straight ahead and keep pedaling, hoping to spot a convoy of highway patrol cars. I'd settle for a spacey geezette in a Buick.

"Where you from?"

This as the rearview mirror very slightly grazes my elbow. The driver is edging me off the shoulder. I slow down, then speed up a little. The truck groans and lurches.

"He said, where you from!"

Definitely the driver this time. I turn and stare hard at the guy riding shotgun. He looks back in my general direction but does not meet my eyes. The guy in the middle looks nervous.

"Where mah from?" I drawl, directing my voice toward the driver. I feel my eyes bulge—rage and fear—which makes it much harder to steer. I try to stay cool, or at least to sound as though I haven't quite lost it. "I'm from Kiss My Butt, Kentucky. Where *you* from?"

This succeeds in cracking up the middle and shotgun cheeseheads for a second or two. Then there's silence. We roll on in tandem. I can tell the driver is pissed, at me *and* his partners. They're simply not holding their end up.

"You *want* us to kiss your butt?" he says, veering the truck farther right.

My front wheel slides into the weeds and coarse gravel. I let out a weak little groan.

"Is that what you're saying?" says the guy riding shotgun.

I stop, and the truck rumbles forward. All three cheeseheads are hooting and barking about what they're gonna do to my butt.

Their brake lights go on, and they stop. The driver's door opens. I glance at the bow in the gun rack.

"Do you want us to kiss your butt?" shouts the driver. "Maybe we should just kill your butt."

Much more hooting.

The marsh on my right is too wet and clumpy, too deep, to ride through. On the other side of the road is a pine forest. Either way, they'd catch me on foot in two seconds. Plus, if I ran, I'd be prey.

As the driver gets out, the other door opens. The arrows and bow all stay put as the other two assholes climb out. I don't see any guns or knives either, but I also understand they don't need them. I try to stay calm, think this through. Standing up I'd be taller, more mobile, more stable, but I also might seem more aggressive, which could induce an attack. Plus while getting off the bike, I'd be vulnerable.

They pause near the back of the truck, glaring and whispering. Shorts, high-top sneakers, T-shirts that say things.

They're sixteen or eighteen years old. The driver has major acne boils on his forehead and cheeks. The kid in the Magic cap looks like his brother: same bad skin, reddish-blond hair, ropy build. Backward Bulls Cap is taller than both of them; he also looks younger, more nervous, much less interested in seeing through whatever's about to go down.

"What did you say?" says the driver.

Okay. Defenseless-girl tears or fuck you? I'm willing to go with whatever will work. But I have to think fast, and I can't. At least not in time to come up with a plan. The YO in TOY-OTA peeks through their shit-eating ranks, makes me grin, shake my head. I can't help it.

I blurt, "What's your problem?" and glare at the driver.

"Wad you say?"

"You heard what I said. What's your problem?"

"What's my problem?" he says. When he steals a glance toward his brother, it looks like they might have a plan. They advance and spread out.

Since I'm still on my bike and cannot move backward, they effectively have me surrounded. I stare over their heads up the road, as though a squad car's about to arrive. Magic Cap turns around and looks, but the driver just takes a step closer.

"Tell you what. You can kiss *my* butt, you cunt."

I stare at him hard, and for what turns out to be longer than he was prepared to stare back. "Lemme guess," I say. "You can't help it, correct?"

"What?"

"Acting this way? Like, it just isn't really your fault?"

"You hear me?" he says, coming closer. His right hand is balled in a fist, and his cheeks are bright pink. It dawns on me now: they've been drinking. His comrades have moved forward too, but say nothing; no way would they make the first move. The driver glances at each of them in turn, urging them to do *something*. When they finally look at each other, the bills of their caps point in the same direction, even though they're facing each other. Absurd.

"Real big tough fuckin' bitch now aren't you." Driver talking. His brother is cursing me too. I can't see Bulls Cap, but I hear someone screaming for them to leave me alone. Unless I'm imagining that.

"Maybe we'll just fuckin' kill you, cunt. Yeah!"

Bulls Cap runs toward the pickup. The bow!

The other pair turns and runs too.

"Let's fuckin' *go*, man!" the brother is screaming. "Just move it!"

I turn.

A blue car is rounding the bend a few hundred yards back down the road.

The right door slams shut as the pickup spits gravel, pinging a stone off my bike. It swings a hard U. They could still run me over, I guess, but none of the cheeseheads will look at me. I want to shout something ferocious, proclaim their disgrace, but I can't catch my breath.

The blue car keeps coming, gets larger. I watch as the pickup drives past it. I wave with both arms while trying to think what I'll say.

A middle-aged woman is driving. As she surveys the scene, she doesn't look terribly happy. I try to make eye contact, but she won't let it happen. She shakes her cocked head, waves with two fingers, drives by. Do I look like a dangerous person or simply too much of a bother? I feel more like telling her—

I feel something stuck to my forehead, almost dead center. I reach up and pluck out a shiny black cinder.

I roll it back and forth between my thumb and index finger, but it's even more satisfying to rotate it clockwise in bumpy but regular ovals. Some of its surfaces are concave, and that makes the corners much sharper. I pick out the point where it probably lodged itself into me.

I don't think it drew any blood, though I don't want to check yet. It glints on my finger, set off by the slashes and whorls of the print: irregular, chipped, like a gritty black diamond.

It's perfect.

* * *

I pedal through more scenic lake country. It's a veritable vaca-
tionland paradise around here. Postcard city.

According to my Super 8 map of Minnesota, I'm now
about five miles from Enok, which features an outlet with
pool, cable, pets (with permission), and laundry facilities. Ten
miles beyond that the Mississippi River loops north for a couple of miles before heading south to the Gulf. But so what.

To go, or not to go, to the police. I should, of course, but I
haven't. I've got the license plate number—DJP 240—and
could identify all three of them down to their blackheads. If
I'd called the police, they would probably have been arrested
by now; indicted eventually, maybe even convicted. Of what,
was the question. Certainly not of rape, though it's definitely
what they had in mind. Assault? Aggravated assault? They
might've even done time in jail, though I doubt it. My word
against theirs. Three clean-cut boys in nice suits and ties,
fresh haircuts, halfway decent lawyers, sobbing mothers and
stern, responsible fathers: the whuppings they'd get if only the
judge would be reasonable. Trying to abduct, rape, and kill
me—not our Andrew and Ryan and Brad! Even if the local
DA stuck to her or his guns and managed to put them away,
the process would take months, maybe years: the lineups,
hearings, lie-detector tests, plea bargains, jury-selection ques-
tionnaires, continuances, assaults on my credibility, inquiries
into my past . . . What was I supposed to do in the meantime,
camp out in Enok?

What I'm tempted to do now is ride to the nearest Amtrak
station and decide when I get there whether to go back to
Chicago or keep heading west; I'd base the decision on which
way the first train was headed.

I want to nail those three cheeseheads and I want to ride my
bike to Alaska, and I really don't think I can do both. Life is too
short; mine is, at least. Because just the idea of getting further
caught up with those pimply nowhere little boluses makes me
even angrier and more tired than the idea of them getting away
with it. But so that's what they did, I suppose. Got away with it.

I'm riding. There's that. I'm not being raped on the floor of a shed. I haven't been trussed up with wire and pierced from close range with those arrows. I'm also not confined to some police station or DA's office, repeating myself in quadruplicate. I'm out in the sunshine, pumping fresh surges of blood to my feet and my brain and my kidneys. That's the plus side, I guess.

Something must've convinced me they're not coming back, but I could always be wrong about that. Usually these straight, open stretches of road are my favorite kind of riding, especially this late in the day, when I'm almost to the next motel and I have that sweet muscular tiredness and can just lean down and mindlessly pump. But not now. I have to keep checking my mirror. I have to fucking *think* about those guys coming after me.

So I have, in effect, become prey.

I put up in Enok, ate dinner, slept maybe three or four hours all told, rode out at 8:10 this morning. I called Michelle Halle last night and slightly adjusted my dosage: two fewer units of Lente each evening, since I've tended to wake up too low. I also called Citibank and checked my balance: 2,457 dollars, and counting. I didn't call Lee or the cops.

I'm now in an Amoco minimart just outside Bagley. I need to buy apple juice, yogurt, and some sort of sandwich for lunch. They also have bananas and apples, asbestos gloves, chewing tobacco, a rotating stand of romance novels, two racks of ancient cassettes: Gary Puckett and the Union Gap, Cher, Herman's Hermits . . . The cashier is listening to KFC Minneapolis—"We put the lite in polite," chirps the deejay—and has the AC cranked up. It can't be much more than fifty in here, so I'm hugging myself as I shop.

I've been introducing "my husband" into conversations since yesterday. I scan the restaurant or motel lobby and look at my watch, as though he's due to arrive any moment. I'm hoping people will infer that he's kinda big and he's awful strong, hey la, hey la, my husband's due back any second . . . The folks I've run into so far have either been neutral or exceedingly friendly. I don't want to let the Très Cheeseheads poison my mind against everyone else on the road.

Most of these gas station minimarts carry a decent variety of juices, canned fruit, iced tea, and more or less edible sandwiches. They always have granola bars, bread, peanut butter, toothpaste, canned tuna, Fig Newtons, and Tampax, and they usually have T-shirts and undies. What they tend not to have is fresh fruit or vegetables; for these I need to find towns with a Kohl's or a Safeway, or get them as takeout from restaurants.

Two little girls, six or seven, are staring at me—at my nubby-nibbed chest, to be slightly more specific. I smile and then shiver, by way of explanation. In response, they just stare. I assume they are sisters: same flaxen hair, same round brown eyes. Similar enough to be twins, except that one of them is six inches taller. They even have identical sunburns.

The shorter one finally makes very brief eye contact with me; she's shy but too curious not to. We grin. The taller one has on a powder-blue T-shirt with big purple ironed-on letters: REAL WOMEN LOVE JESUS. Okay . . . I just need to pick up some groceries.

They continue to spy as I move around a corner, change aisles; I'm now in the boxes of cereal. When I suddenly turn and look at them sideways, they duck behind a shelf of Rice Krispies.

As I scan other shelves for some unsalted cashews, I hear them both chanting:

> Milk, milk, and lemonade.
> Around the corner fudge is made.

And giggling. I assume Jesus hears this as well. If He can also see my cold nipples, or—even better—can touch them without my knowledge or permission, I certainly hope He approves.

Munching an apple, I stow the rest of the groceries in my pannier, then squeeze-check my tires. According to the map, I'm twenty miles southeast of Fosston. Two hours, tops.

An overcrowded station wagon moves slowly away from the pumps. A teenage boy looks out from the middle seat. From the far backseat the two girls are pointing at me, and their brother is nodding. I look at them cross-eyed; then, as nonchalantly as possible, I shoot the core of the apple at a big rusty garbage can twelve feet away. It bangs against the back of the can and rattles around on the bottom. Feels good.

No response from big brother. The two squealing girls have ducked down, but almost immediately—first one, then the other—they peek out the back of the wagon. I shoot them an upside-down peace sign as the wagon pulls out of the station.

My routine when I arrive in the town I've been aiming for is to check into the first motel that has a vacancy and takes Visa. By this point in the day I want things to be as automatic as possible. I'm tired, I need to do my shot and have dinner, and I don't want to have to employ an elaborate calculus to determine whether the $49.90 room at Best Western that includes an all-you-can-eat breakfast of cereal and juice is a more economical deal than $46.66 for a room at Motel 6 that doesn't include breakfast but is directly across the road from a Charlie T.'s that has a $3.99 breakfast special.

This evening I'm staying at a Super 8 with 122 rooms. It makes me feel like I'm part of a cozy little hamlet of wanderers. Everyone above, behind, and to the left and right of me is headed somewhere east or west in the morning; if locals have rented a room for a liaison dangereuse, they've probably cleared out already, gone home to their husbands or girlfriends.

My bed, desk, and chairs all have stained walnut trim. There's a La-Z-Boy parked in front of the TV, with a remote control panel and a reading lamp next to it. Luxe! Even the trio of almost identical lithographs of pink-and-mauve orchids aren't excessively hideous. Plus the vending machines off the lobby have aspirin and tampons and rubbers and nail-polish remover; not that I'll be needing any of those items tonight, but it's still nice to know they're available. Another of the machines would, for two dollars, dispense a cheese sandwich on pita. But the Toast Bar in the lobby itself is the pièce de résistance. In addition to cereal and milk in the morning, there will also be bananas, three kinds of bread, jams, complimentary *USA Today*. In the meantime there's a microwave, a serious coffee machine, gratis tea bags: Apple Spice, Cranapple, Original Herb, Lemon Lift. All I'll need to add after breakfast is my little jar of Skippy and I'll be able to assemble my ten o'clock snack *and* my lunch.

In addition to my hatred of camping, I simply love staying in motels, even by myself. Forty-two dollars a night doesn't seem exorbitant, not in exchange for a firm queen-sized bed, telephone, cable TV, soap, water, iced coffee, shampoo, towels, breakfast, and part of my lunch. I also appreciate the way everything, especially the bathrooms, is impeccably maintained by professional staffs of *other people*. I don't like to have to be neat.

My first night in Wisconsin it never got much cooler than eighty, and the air conditioner in my room at the Black Stallion Inn was pumping warm air. One phone call to the desk produced a knock on my door three minutes later. A six-tyish, German-accented gentleman introduced himself as Peter and promptly inspected the unit. His verdict was that it would have to be replaced. Ten minutes later he wheeled an identical but functional unit in on a dolly, removed the faulty one from its rectangular cavity, singlehandedly hoisted the new unit into position, plugged it in, and voilà: paroxysms of coolth. And I slept. If only such service were available for broken-down pancreae.

I do not much like to maintain things, myself. I don't mind rinsing out a sink from time to time, doing some dishes, vacuuming a carpet or two, but the idea of marshalling specialized cleansers or equipment or disinfectants I find quite abhorrent. I do not relish cleansing soap scum or mold spores or mung from behind, around, underneath, or inside used toilet bowls. At all. When I was in high school, lilac and chromium-yellow fungi were known to flourish during the summer in the vicinity of my bathtub. Soap scum accreted year-round, sometimes to depths of three fourths of an inch (my father measured), while I remained sanguine, unfazed, seventeen. How many times had I been specifically asked to clean up my bathroom? Countless dozens of times, I supposed. Had I done it? I hadn't. Why not? I was a spiteful, unfit, thoughtless slob with no sense of shame or responsibility or self-respect. I was grounded until the bathroom was thoroughly cleansed, and if it ever got into that state again, I could count on unpleasant ramifications befalling me. I can count on two fingers, I think, the times that I thoroughly cleansed it.

Why did I refuse to maintain my physical premises? Why did I always put it off, or do it half-heartedly, warped by a white-hot resentment? In retrospect I think I'd semiconsciously decided I already had enough to maintain, thank you very much. Having to monitor my blood sugar levels twenty-four hours a day every week, every year, every day, when other people's pancreases did this work *for* them seemed more than a little inequitable. Requests that I do any further monitoring I considered as class-X offenses. My position with respect to my bathroom was that, maintenancewise, enough was enough. Ditto for my closet, my bedroom, the kitchen, my locker at school . . . Why I never bothered barking this rationale up my father's shaggy nostrils remains a mystery to me. Maybe I was hoping he would reach that conclusion on his own. I now understand that if I had explained how I felt, he would have sympathized with and forgiven me. He may not have hired me a personal maid, or cleaned it himself, but at least he would have heard me out, and stopped thinking I was being purposelessly recalcitrant; I didn't realize it at the time, but it was important to me that he knew that.

In the past decade I've matured somewhat in my thinking on this issue. I understand that bathrooms and kitchens and "common areas," even rooms of one's own, must be maintained to reasonable standards of order and cleanliness. I know now to do my fair share. I still resent, insanely, ragefully, sometimes even tearfully, having to do it, but usually in the end it gets done.

But still. Given an opportunity to avoid custodial effort, I take it in a heartbeat. The idea of trekking across the continent from professionally maintained motel room to motel room, every last one of them with a spic-and-span bathtub and toilet bowl (some with a paper band stretched tautly across the seat, like an autographed novel, to stipulate as to its disinfectedness), all of it executed by someone-not-me, is such a stark and simple luxury that it just about floors me, bicycle and all, every time I roll my old Trek across a new threshold. I love it.

Letterman and Barbara Bush. Rerun. She talks about her dogs, her books, her terrific relationship with Boris Yeltsin. Dave drops his jaw and says, "Whoooaaa," implying Bar's sleeping with Boris. She doesn't play along, but she takes it in stride. She has a not-bad sense of humor. She talks about her children, two of whom are apparently running for governor of large southern states. Did that really happen? I seem to recall now that one of them actually won.

Later I reread the end of *Molloy*, the part where Moran Sr. is preparing to make his report:

> They were the longest, loveliest days of all the year. I lived in the garden. I have spoken of a voice telling me things. I was getting to know it better now, to understand what it wanted. It did not use the words that Moran had been taught when he was little and that he in turn had taught to his little one. So that at first I did not know what it wanted. But in the end I understood this language. I understood it, I understood it, all wrong perhaps. This is not what matters. It told me to write the report. Does this mean I am freer now than I was? I do not know. I shall learn. Then I went back into the house and wrote, It is midnight. The rain is beating on the windows. It was not midnight. It was not raining.

Someone is being spanked in the room next to mine. And spanked hard, it sounds like. It seems to be going on right behind my bed. Several loud smacks, unmistakable, each of them followed by low, muffled cries. Then it stops.

I kneel up in bed, put my ear against the wall. A voice, or two voices, in fierce husky whispers. "That's right! This Kevlar." Kiss liar? Miss Kevlar? . . . It sounds like two men. The wallpaper's cool, waffled grain presses against my warm cheek.

Should I call the front desk or lie back and masturbate? There's a long whining moan, two more smacks, and much groaning. I imagine the person receiving the spanking elaborately bound with white clothesline: wrists crossed behind him, yanked cruelly far up his back by lines around his neck. Couldn't excess clothesline be doubled over and deployed as a whip? I wonder whether they've smoked any grass, or had a few glasses of whiskey. Maybe they're drinking right now, the person in charge allowing the bound one small sips. I haven't heard glass clink, or anything that sounded like whipping.

I get back down under the covers. Without reinserting my bookmark, I close the Trilogy and turn out the light. I can still hear the smacks, though more faintly. I lie on my stomach. I imagine the person bound up is a beautiful red-haired woman: thin, with very white skin stretched across delicate bones. My nose pushes into the pillow. I imagine severe penetration, not against her will exactly, but vigorous, hard, from behind; she's tied up so tightly, expertly, there's nothing she can do to prevent it.

The couple next door seem to have moved nearer my wall—right up against it, in fact. I turn on my side. Loud exhalations, small muffled cries, and more panting. The woman's pretending to struggle. She isn't tied up anymore.

I double up one of my pillows and hold it between my knees. There's panting and more violent spanks. I keep my head raised a full inch to be able to use both my ears.

I just listen.

I ride into Knutson on pebbly blacktop, a stretch strewn with cellophane, fur, shredded beige Styrofoam, and lipstick-kissed filters. There's even a waterlogged paperback. I'm still pumping major endorphins and shoring up capillaries, doing eighteen or nineteen in spite of the pocky conditions.

Route 2 zigs and zags past car washes, kennels, and strip malls, while the trucks and the cars in a hurry get to detour around on 2A. In addition to the absence of belching diesel semis, the town sits in the middle of the Chippewa National Forest, so it smells pretty good around here. A lot of the houses have dusty-gray ponderosa pines in the yards, along with white aspen and spruce. Except for the malls, it's quite gorgeous.

The Burlington-Northern tracks are now on my left, though I don't remember crossing under or over them. There are plenty of places to eat or buy food to go, but I'm already packing a sandwich and five cartons of AJ. I don't have to think about stopping for another three hours.

Two girls on mountain bikes pop little wheelies as they prolong figure eights through a Texaco station manned by a ponytailed boy deftly wielding a nozzle; there isn't a mountain for 865 miles in any direction, of course. Bob Dylan was born not too far from here, and the Mississippi River flows north the next place I cross it, I'm told. Everyone up here is blond. There's also a bunting-draped lot selling BOAT'S   CAR'S

HOME'S, which reminds me of all the "NO" SMOKING and "COLOR" TV signs I've seen around here. I want to whip out my red paper-grading pencil and nail them.

What makes me slow down are some squiggly, undulating lines on the side of a galvanized shed at the west end of town. Someone has spray-painted BOOK over four other letters. My guess is, a local elder decided that the tainted corrugated surface was unscrubbable; short of sandblasting, or painting the entire shed black, the original word would have to remain there: a rude, clichéd stet, a scandal, I'm sure, in these parts, a virtual crime wave in fact, yet another example of sick Scandinavian-American hooliganism. "GANGSTA NORWEGIANS TAG VILLAGE! WILDSTYLE A NUISANCE IN KNUTSON!" In any event, the second writer has done a fair job of camouflaging the previous letters. She even retraced the "K" in order to be stylistically consistent, the better to *tromp* my *oeil*. When I squint and slow down, the lines of black paint don't match exactly the style or shade of the glyphs underneath them, but still. It's close enough, at least from this distance, moving along at this speed. On the other hand, it seems rather doubtful that too many folks will be fooled. Either way, I agree. And I'm booking.

In the formation of a memory, what you feel and what you repeat to yourself and believe about an event often turns out to be more important that what actually happened. I read that in my book-lined, computerized study, in the introduction to a collection of critical essays about Victorian horror fiction—I think. Or wherever. What happened in Glacier and Juneau isn't a horror story, but I can't make myself not remember it. I don't even think I want to forget anymore.

When we went to Alaska, David was almost twenty-three. I was twenty-two. I'd had diabetes for almost eighteen years already, and the most obvious way it was a factor was that it placed me in legal possession of a controlled substance in a supply sufficient to kill him. But I can't shake the feeling that it changed things in other ways too. It made me more amenable, I think, to doing what he asked me to do.

It wasn't until I was thirteen or fourteen that the kinds of things that were actually going to happen to me began to sink in. Before that the focus had been on gram scales and blood tests and Equal; I'd learned to load a syringe and do my own shot every morning, and my life didn't seem all that difficult. I was a cute and innocent little girl, and my father wanted to keep it that way. I went to the same sleepovers and played on the same softball teams as everyone else, and after the games I went out with the coach for ice cream (one scoop) at Homer's. I had to turn in most of my candy at Halloween, but my father always paid me good money for it, and it happened only once a year. When I snuck Baby Ruths or Cokes at sleepover parties, or even at home, the only effects I suffered were a high blood test or two, for which I was firmly but sensitively remonstrated. I'd been duly informed about the dangers of not maintaining good control by Dr. Ardholder and my father, but the message had been soft-pedaled: The bad things would only happen to diabetics who didn't maintain good control for a very long time, and I'd never be one of those persons. The emphasis was always on what a good job I was doing with my diet and blood tests and exercise. And besides: the Cure was probably going to come "within a few years," so if I just hung in there and maintained control of my sugars, nothing too terrible was going to happen to me.

Whatever anxiety I felt in those days was like a summertime cricket: persistent but impossible to locate, not quite annoying enough to keep me awake for very long. By the time I was twelve, it was more like the pre-fertilized version of the hydra in *Alien*, before it had a warm human body to turn inside out and obliterate. In the meantime I had more practical issues to deal with. I was now doing two shots a day, and I'd learned to adjust my dosage if I was going to be eating some special dessert or playing softball all day in the sun. I was still Dr. Ardholder's star little patient, or so I was given to infer, even if I was getting too old for sugar-free lollipops. I'd never liked those too much.

I started to blow off my regimen around the same time I began to see evidence that the Cure might arrive too late to save me. My hormones had kicked in by then, too, so I'd become thoroughly nutso in other ways, but there was more to it than that. Through reading about it, through the unofficial network of diabetics anonymous, through osmosis—however it arrived in my brain, I finally started to actually process what was in store for me.

Once I knew what to listen and look for, I began to hear stories. About a thirty-one-year-old woman having a stroke—Linda Baumgartner, a friend of a friend of my father's who lived two blocks away; I'd met her a couple of times. When I asked to visit her in the hospital, my father claimed that no visitors were being allowed on that day—or was it all week?—and took me downtown to a Sox game.

There were pieces on the news about an insurance company refusing to pay for an experimental pancreas transplant, then episodes on similar subjects on *L.A. Law* and *Murder, She Wrote*. I saw *Steel Magnolias*. I read about things in the paper.

My friend Katy Wisniewski's uncle had one of his feet amputated. And everyone knew that Mr. Alt, one of the math teachers at New Trier, was a juvenile diabetic, ABD all the way, who had recently, at age thirty-eight, turned legally blind. My father took care to casually point out that Mr. Alt had grown up in the days when the regimens for control weren't very sophisticated. He brought out some charts and reports demonstrating beyond a shadow of a doubt that the new synthetic human insulins I was using were dramatically more effective, and that even in worst-case scenarios, laser surgery could inhibit the progress of most forms of retinopathy, especially if the ophthalmologist detected it early enough, which was why it was crucial that I kept my appointments every six months, etc., etc. "Most forms?" I asked him. He blinked and turned pale. (Most people blush when they hedge on the truth; my father turns pale—although maybe he only does that when he fibs to his daughter about complications.) His point was that diabetics didn't have to go blind—they *didn't* go blind anymore. "Didn't ever?" I asked him. "Not if we stay on top of the situation," he told me. Besides, the Cure was "just around the corner," whatever that meant. At school I watched students wave to Mr. Alt, or flash him a peace sign, as he shuffled and tapped down the hallways with his red-and-white cane, or held the arm of one of the other teachers. He even held the arms of his students, who always went out of their way to demonstrate how much they respected him. Boy, that logarithms test was *so* hard, Mr. Alt. Stairs coming up on your left, sir. Right here. Everyone loved Mr. Alt. And so wasn't what happened a shame? But hadn't he stayed just amazingly independent? He always wore stylish brown tortoise-shell sunglasses.

During my junior year my new ophthalmologist, Bruce Brody, informed me that I'd developed the initial stages of retinopathy. He told me that he had reason to believe there were parallel levels of capillary damage in my kidneys and liver. If I didn't maintain better control, I might lose some vision or kidney function before I was thirty. According to Dr. Brody, the Cure might be just as far over the horizon as it was when I'd been diagnosed. Even if it weren't, I'd be much better off taking care of myself as though I would have diabetes for another ten, fifteen years. Maybe more.

That made me angry. No one had ever explicitly promised me I'd be cured by the time I was twenty, but my father had certainly given me to infer that. My working premise had always been that if I could just hold out on my own a bit longer, the research geniuses in Pittsburgh and St. Louis and elsewhere would come to the rescue with functional, rejection-proof islets ex machina before the complications began to get serious. But now—maybe not.

My response to this news was three years of unfocused rage. Faced with the clearly delineated medical requirement that I take better care of myself, I went out of way to take none. I made a point of it. I was going blind, dying young *any-way*, so fuck doctors' orders. Fuck doctors. Fuck nurses. Fuck orders. I slept until two in the afternoon, did my shot at three-thirty or skipped it altogether. I did not test my blood. Not wanting to hear what I knew would be bad news, I began to skip doctor appointments; when the receptionists called to reschedule (and gently berate me), I stopped making them at all. About the only appointment I made voluntarily and actually kept was with a gynecologist to get a prescription for Lo Ovril. I sometimes drank ten rum and Cokes of an evening, making sure I kept up with the roqueros or poets or pot smokers or drinkers or soccer players—whoever I happened to be drinking with. I smoked roughly twelve thousand cigarettes.

Why would a person who'd been told in no uncertain terms that they had to take care of themselves behave in this way? Was I trying to do myself in? I think it had something to do with being *told* to take care of myself. I also resented the reward-to-sacrifice ratio. Why get up at the same time every morning, prick my fingers four times a day, and put myself through ridiculous aerobics routines when I was only marginally forestalling the inevitable? I'd only put up with a rigorous maintenance program if someone guaranteed me a pardon or a commutation of sentence within a reasonable number of years—say, two or three. Otherwise, I didn't really think it was worth it.

At some point I read in my biology textbook that the human body regenerates itself, replaces each cell with a new one, every seven years, in which case . . . I got rather excited, in an adolescent sort of way: tears, screaming, dancing around in the bathroom. I also went to the library and did a little research, and I read through my JDF literature. I called Dr. Ardholder. And as it turned out, what the biology book said was true: the human body did regenerate all new cells every seven years. The only exceptions were brain cells and islets of Langerhans.

I spent a lot of time, and hundreds of millions of ergs of emotional energy, wanting to kill someone: classmates, doctors, nutritionists, actors relieved that their abdominal pains weren't caused by perforated ulcers but only required

Mylanta, girlfriends, friends who were boys, teachers, actual boyfriends, myself . . .

And it worked.

When Yeats wrote that virginity renews itself like the moon, I believe he meant female virginity; there was only one kind in those days. But I'd like to believe it could also be true for some men.

I believe I was the second woman David made love with. I may have been the third or the fifteenth, but he told me I was the second. I believe him.

Simenon claimed he'd had ten thousand lovers, and some too-tall basketball player recently claimed over twenty thousand. Maria Callas had seven, I think. Gretta Conroy had two if you count Michael Furey; I do. Sade had a hefty number, although probably fewer than is widely assumed, since he spent all those years in the Charenton prison. Sylvia Plath had either three or four or seven, depending on which biography you find most convincing. Billie Holiday had about twenty, Sarah Vaughan eight. Anne Rice admits of only six or seven to her authorized biographer, whereas John Cheever seems to have had over fifty, of pretty much all stripes and sizes. Anne Sexton had a few dozen, including her daughter and one of her psychiatrists; another of her psychiatrists wrote about it, and did not change the names. Her daughter wrote about it too. I no longer find this amazing.

In spite of her scars and the pain she was in, Frida Kahlo had Diego Rivera and Trotsky, no less, in addition to fifteen or twenty less eminent lovers. Elizabeth I seems to have had three, not including England herself. Rosalynn Carter and Barbara Bush, uno. Ditto for Elizabeth II. But Elizabeth's bishop and Roosevelt apparently managed to explore a few boundaries. And then there was always H.D.

I'd love to reread the biographies and letters, do some lite research, double-check all of these numbers. Sounds like a custom-made project for me when I finally get back, something I wouldn't have to sumo wrestle with myself to get busy on each morning. Not too much writing, just scanning the texts for the good parts, counting the lovers both proven and conjectural, annotating the lists, convincing myself that it was somehow worthwhile, getting horny. Padded with photos and footnotes, with the right sort of publisher, it would probably sell like espresso in the frozen ninth circle of Hell.

James Joyce had only one *tangible* lover, that being Nora, and Nora had only her Jim. With Beckett the number continues to be up in the air; he seems to have frequented untold numbers of prostitutes in Dublin and Paris, and the Bair biography is vague on the question of his relationships with women he didn't have to pay—somewhere between ten and twenty before he finally married Suzanne, and none besides her after that.

Most of the non-famous women I know have had four or five by the time they are my age, most of the guys about twice that many. As far as I'm able to tell. That Saint has claimed only the one before me is nonetheless small consolation, even smaller than knowing I was the last one. I want to have been the first *and* the last, and I wasn't.

The first was Emma Pitt. Emma Pitt is also one of the most immaculate women I've ever laid eyes on. She has reddish-brown hair, green eyes that curve outward like sine waves, flawless skin—though a dozen pale-brown freckles do garnish the bridge of her nose. This to go with her flawless bosom, her flawless pancreas, her demure breathy whisper, her tallness. I think she was taller than Saint; even worse, I don't think something like that would've bothered him, any more than it would've bothered him that she managed to look both exotic and cute, relaxed and intelligent—even, I dare say, affectionate. Saint never commented, though I certainly— and, I hope, subtly—urged him to.

At his funeral, Emma wore steel-colored stretch pants, setting off her weensy and numinous buttocks to remarkable advantage, and a black satin camisole with narrow black ribbons for straps, counterpointing the fragility of her collarbone with the taut musculature of her shoulders. As though she could still tempt him back.

She wept a great deal and was comforted by all and sundry while managing to convey the distinct impression of being unescorted. She lingered on her knees for three or four minutes alongside the casket, which matched her stretch pants in both color and sheen. As she transferred her weight from one fragile knee to the other, her buttocks flexed pertly—fourteen times, one for each Station of the Cross. A pious and slow bump and grind. The rest of the mourners were only too happy to gawk while they waited their turns, wanting to know who he loved at the end, doubting it wasn't their Emma.

She and I caught each other stealing glances and exchanged one good stare, but no one introduced us, and we never did speak. I perforce remained very much in the background. I had on my frumpy gray knee-length cotton dress, the single funereal garment I owned that wasn't triple-ply wool. It was only the third week of June, but by ten in the morning it was already ninety degrees, with standard Chicago humidity. Even under the cheeriest circumstances, weather like that makes me nauseous.

I wasn't accorded anything even vaguely resembling the status of grieving widow—just the opposite, in fact, as far as Mrs. St. Germaine was concerned. She'd reserved that role for herself. And technically, of course, I wasn't a widow. I also don't think I appeared overwhelmed with grief: I still hadn't cried—I barely could speak for another six months—but the look on my face apparently gave a number of people to believe that I was "doing okay."

Mrs. St. Germaine was running her only son's funeral, and she went out of her way to make me unwelcome. It was her considered and public opinion that I'd "voted" to accede to David's "sacrilegious" request to be taken off life support. So what was it, exactly, that kept me from announcing to the assembled congregation that I had, in fact, killed her son with my very own hands? I don't know. I certainly didn't respect her, wasn't afraid of going to prison, wasn't embarrassed I'd done it. I was convinced David would've wanted his family, his friends, even Emma—especially Emma—to know what he

wanted. Plus *I* wanted Emma to know. Shouldn't Emma Pitt
have been aware that David had asked me to kill him? It
seemed to me then that she should. And I wanted his mother
to know. As much as I hated her, she still had the right to the
facts. As his mother. In spite of the way she'd been ready to
prolong his agony. Maybe I'll be able to tell her when I get
back from Alaska. I doubt it, but maybe. I hope. Or even give
Emma a call . . .

In any event, I was relieved to be able to stay in the back
of the church. The priest led the congregation in prayers the
deceased would not have approved of: The Lord is my shepherd, now enter the kingdom of heaven, etc. Two cherubic
altar boys (one with a shaved-above-the-ears hip-hop haircut)
swung thuribles smoking with incense toward the priest and
the casket. Emma Pitt sobbed and coughed. Her apple-esque
cheeks were further inflamed by the tears streaming down
them, then lit from below when she tried to smile bravely. In
their entire lives, women seldom become more alluring than
this, and she knew it.

David's sisters, Hanna and Page, wept quietly while their
mother beat her breast (literally) and cried out to various
powers. David's uncle cried too. When our eyes happened to
meet, he seemed to acknowledge the things that had happened in Juneau, to let me know he secretly agreed with his
nephew's decision and respected my willingness to allow the
doctors to carry it out. That he understood how much I loved
him.

I may be imagining some of this.

I left the church early, as soon as the priest told me to go, I
was dismissed. I'm going, I thought. Don't you worry. Not
that I need your permission.

I'd already decided to skip the whole scene at the ceme-
tery. My father's car was too hot to touch, and I'd neglected to
spread out his cardboard White Sox sunshade; it was accor-
dioned on the passenger seat, right under his copies of
Penthouse and *Paris Review*. I left the door open, got in. My

plan was to drive out to Interstate 294 and keep going north till the north and south lanes weren't separated by concrete, then plow into oncoming traffic. Either that or go run down the crowd at the grave site. Or maybe just sit in the heat and not breathe. I couldn't stop sweating, even after the air-conditioning finally kicked in, but I did understand that the heat wasn't going to kill me.

Since I hadn't been invited back to the house, I've never even seen David's bedroom—never seen any room in the only house he ever lived in. (I stopped driving by the place three or four years ago.) My memories of the thirty-six days we spent together are fading. They started to fade almost immediately after he died, but the rate at which they're fading seems to get faster every week. And I don't have much access to new information about him.

I believe this is one of the reasons that being the last woman David made love to, and loved—if he loved me—hasn't been the consolation it's often supposed to be.

So. Am I riding my bike to Alaska to get new information? To figure out how things might've been if we hadn't gone up there in the first place?

No. I don't know. I don't think so.

I spent last night at the Motel 6 in Wanzer. My second-floor room overlooked a huge bunting-bedecked gravel lot called Used Arnie's on which were parked acres of tractors, threshers, rototillers (or whatever they're called), a dozen yellow school buses, and four long neat rows of garbage trucks. The trucks were parked right alongside the motel. There must have been fifty or sixty of them, and they certainly *smelled* used. A gigantic bright pink one had its motto emblazoned across its rear bumper: SATISFACTION GUARANTEED OR DOUBLE YOUR GARBAGE BACK. I wanted this big pink truck desperately, having concluded it was the ideal vehicle in which to transport myself west. I could sleep at night in the cab, and during the day on the road no one would try to edge me onto the shoulder. If I got a flat tire or the engine broke down, my Trek would be stowed in the compactor. I'd just have to be careful not to hit the wrong lever or button.

Later on, around two, as I stood behind the drape and stared out the window, the trucks looked like squads of crustaceans swimming in watery moonlight. They didn't seem big anymore. I wiped my fogged breath from the glass and squinted at them through the crescent my fingers had made.

Just before dawn I dreamed about them in their rows, a flash cut of hundreds of garbage trucks bearing down hard from behind me, all of them neatly lined up, waiting their turn to demolish me. Then it turned to a dream about *rows* . . .

This morning I left the motel before eight, and I'm now about twenty miles west of it. There are almost no cars along here, no menacing squadrons of garbage trucks, and, so far, no cheeseheads.

In the last forty minutes the forest has given way to bean fields and pastures of fly-swatting cows. The pastures have wet spots one might call small ponds, but nothing a loon could take off from. More like large mud holes. Burlington-Northern tracks still on my left, faded gray contrail above them. That's all.

I just pedal.

Exactly what happened between Emma and David I never found out, but I've inferred it was Emma's decision that they "see other people." Emma was almost two years older than David. When David and I started seeing each other, she was already in her first year of grad school at Brown; like everyone else in this country not trying to be an actor or a doctor or a roquero, she was getting her MFA in creative writing. About three years ago, one of her stories came out in *The Atlantic*. It was about a young couple in Delaware whose daughter has scoliosis; the husband has just lost his job, they don't have insurance . . . I only read the first column and a half.

Emma Pitt. Maybe one day she'll write a tragic well-made little short story about it: my lover was mauled by a bear, but didn't we still love one another? I'll probably never find out, since his next female friend took it upon herself to put Donald out of his misery. . . . I'm surprised that she hasn't already. Maybe she has. I can't put it past her. Not Emma.

The facts are that Emma moved to Providence in August, and David and I started seeing each other the following May. The first time in almost five years she and David weren't together. I don't know how closely they stayed in touch, but I gathered that during those ten months David wasn't terribly happy.

I've always assumed Emma met someone else: another grad student, say, or some semi-famous married writing professor. It was never too difficult picturing slews of either of these types queuing up to help Emma Pitt move her well-made short stories from draft to draft, or place them in high-profile magazines.

David never brought her up voluntarily, and I decided not to ask him about her. My strategy was based on a number of admittedly dubious assumptions: that no news was good news, that if he wasn't talking about her he wouldn't be thinking about her, that I was sufficiently confident in my ability to hold his attention, that he and I could fill each other in on our respective pasts all in good time. There may have been two or three others.

The shoulder along here is strewn with six-pack rings and cigarette filters, from which I deduce that civilization—in the form of, oh, say, a Qwik-Mart or 7-Eleven—is approaching. If it is, I can't see it.

According to my odometer, I've covered thirty-one miles since I left Wanzer this morning, so I still have at least forty more to go before I get to Crookston. It's also the case that I've been known to miscalculate slightly when I add or subtract mileage numbers. Who knows where I am. I've been a bit lazy for the last half hour or so, just cruising along in thirteenth. I shift up two gears and work harder.

A hawk drifts on the thermals a few hundred feet above the oak trees and pond on my right. As it scans the ground for some lunch, I try to imagine what a field mouse would look like from that far up in the air, especially if it were camouflaged by leaves, dirt, and mouse-colored twigs. A trifle on the tiny side? Somewhat indistinct? An electron-microscopic speck? Yet hawks have no problem, of course. This guy has probably spotted *several* mice by now and is up there coolly deciding which one looks the most succulent. He's picking out *characteristics*, perusing a menu of heart-smart, low-cholesterol specials. With eyes that can spot things that small, what would my face look like from up close? (I obsess about eyes all the time.) Would the pores in the pores of my nose have their own little personal pores? How finely would you be able to differentiate between one broken capillary and the one alongside it? What about the one underneath it? I literally shudder to think.

While David and I were pitching our tent on Tarr Inlet, we spotted an eagle flying along while clutching in its talons a salmon that must have weighed fifteen or twenty pounds. Except for its wingspan, the eagle wasn't any bigger than its cargo. The salmon was swaying and flopping, alive, and the eagle was straining to maintain its rhythm. We stood there and watched it, amazed, and for several long seconds the eagle watched us. "I wonder what she thinks of tourists like us," David said. I told him that was exactly what I'd been wondering, and I made him clench pinkies. Two tourists; I liked that. We breathed the crisp air, gawked at the mountains and looked out for eagles, went back to pitching the tent.

My greatest fear, the more I fell in love with him during that trip, the more plans and assumptions I made about our future, was that I'd lose him by getting sick and dying on him. I was so comprehensively desperate not to disappoint him, I loved him and love him so much . . .

Two cars swing by me, giving me plenty of room. Both have blue-and-white Michigan plates and are cram-packed with what looks to be middle-aged women, from which I deduce that the passengers of both cars must be together. The driver of the second car taps her horn, and one of the women in the backseat swings around and waves. I wave back and wish I was with them.

As soon as they're gone, I start missing them—their cozy and wonderful caravan making its way across the north woods at seventy miles an hour. Sitting back telling stories, drinking tea from thermoses, playing gin or the license plate game, waving at arduous cyclists. *Gossiping.* I could've told them about my problems with Marvin, and I know that they'd know what to do.

In spite of the fact that there are probably five thousand lakes within half a day's drive of here, I can't help believing those women from Michigan are driving all the way to Alaska. That they wouldn't mind having me with them.

Riding a bike seems too hard.

The glaciers David took me to see in Alaska are retreating about a thousand feet a year up the valley between those two mountain ranges. They've been retreating so fast that the ground we were camped on that night wasn't there when we were in grammar school; it was buried under three thousand feet of glacier. I try to imagine what it would be like to be caught, like the traitors in the ninth circle of the *Inferno*, under billions of tons of blue ice. And to stay there for hundreds of thousands of decades. Forever. Because before I was born I was nowhere, unconscious, neither frozen nor unfrozen. Blank. So the idea of "cold" wouldn't mean anything. Yet you never would age or deteriorate.

To be painlessly, blissfully dead, so cold the concept of cold would be meaningless, perhaps even pleasant. In any event, *not alive*. I'd like to know how that would feel.

A month from now, when I get back to the campsite, that blue wall of ice will be more than a mile farther north than it was the last time I saw it. As I approach from the bay, the left side of the landscape will be entirely different. New plants and trees will have grown in the raw, exposed earth. Under those circumstances, it might be difficult to get my bearings.

But still. I'm convinced I'll be able to recognize exactly where I am when I get there. I won't need a marker or guide. I won't need a radio.

Even now, homing in, I can feel those coordinates deep in my brain.

I will know.

As I cross the iron cage of a bridge above the manicured banks of the Red River, I'm accompanied by several thousand persons on motorcycles. Word is, there's a Harley convention tomorrow down in Sturgis, South Dakota. Wherever these bikers are going, the roar from their tailpipes is astoundingly loud, but otherwise they seem perfectly civilized. I keep catching sweet whiffs of grass. It's like I've picked up a stoned, ragged, absurdly large personal convoy. Am *I* stoned? Maybe all the action and racket seems strange because I'm so used to having Route 2 pretty much to myself.

At the center of the bridge there's a sign overhead featuring a picture of the governor and his wife: WELCOME TO NORTH DAKOTA, GEORGE A. SINNER, GOVERNOR. I feel pretty proud of myself. It took me exactly a week, including a rain-enforced rest day, to cross Minnesota. My fourth state in fifteen days, and the states around here aren't small.

The Harleys started passing me about fifteen miles back, as I was leaving West Fisher. It seemed like the entire population of each little hamlet I rode through had turned out to watch the parade. Some of the spectators looked as if they'd camped out for days just to get a good angle to wave from. Lawn chairs and babies and coolers, forty-foot motor homes, Polaroids and Kodaks and minicams. A lot of the bikers are wielding American flags, so it looks like the Fourth of July.

When the bikers ride by two across, they give me less

room than a car does, but they don't cause a tenth of the draft. Colorful, undersized license plates from Illinois, Michigan, Ontario, Rhode Island, D.C. Also a lot of tattoos—weeping Jesuses, voluptuous pirates, Harley wing logos like pink lipstick kisses—these to go with acres of armpit hair, ponytails, two-foot-long beards, and thrice-pierced appendages. Much exposed flesh in general, and precious few helmets. The whole miles-long crew is rowdy and friendly. A few honk or wave as they pass, and I usually wave back. They've been waving at me for the last ninety minutes, so it's starting to get out of hand.

And now how's this for timing? Just as the traffic up ahead in Grand Forks makes the convoy slow down to my speed, a woman with tangled black hair pulls beside me. She reminds me of Juliette Binoche, but with attitude and muscles; she even has that vein along the top of her biceps. The sisterhood is indeed looking powerful. And more than a little self-confident. All she has on are black boots, denim cutoffs with the pockets extending below the frayed hems, and a way-too-small black leather vest. She guns her red Harley and grins. She looks to be about thirty-five, and is flaunting how well she's preserved. Her vest is designed to reveal the gold ring laterally piercing her pert maroon nipple—at least it's maroon in this light. It's her left one. I'm assuming the right is pierced too, but who knows? Maybe left but not right signifies something utterly beyond the limits of my imagination. That's what this vest is about, after all: uncertainty, tension, a tease and a glance, sideways angles, a code designed not to be cracked—at least not just yet. I smile and keep pedaling, *clunk clunk ca-chunk, click-click-click*, feeling awfully naive and low-tech.

She nods—meaning *what*, for God's sake?—then dallies beside me for another long block while I keep pretending she isn't. I do have to look to my left a few times to maintain a suitable distance, but otherwise I stare straight ahead. When her chromium tailpipe savagely backfires, I cringe like a shaved-armpit wuss. I know that she did it on purpose.

"Later, amiga!" she shouts—with no Spanish accent—then zooms up ahead, wending her way through the pack.

Adios.

Ten seconds later a couple goes by wearing twelve yards of quilted baby blue leather between them. They're snuggled up close, ass to crotch, talking to each other through what must be an intercom system wired into their red sunburst helmets—in love, head to head, looking like a cross between bowling balls and electric guitars.

Then, right behind them, a covey of identical Harleys, all fifteen riders in matching white helmets, white gas tanks, white gloves—everything matches, down to the two-foot-long fringe streaming behind their red, white, and blue leather jackets.

I pedal.

"Nice panniers!" some guy shouts, then guns his chopped hog. He means mine. I briefly, reluctantly, turn. I figure it's safe in a crowd of five thousand. But—hello! The guy is absurdly good-looking: a John Ford Apache with narrow green eyes. He looks like that last mama's brother. Black jeans and sleeveless red shirt. Dress him *up*. Tattoos of swords on his biceps. Oh boy.

"Nice guns," I tell him, trying to get into the spirit of the rally. Mistake?

He flexes his arms for me, posing, raising both fists and rotating his torso to give me more angles. Not bad. He cruises beside me, maybe four feet away, effortlessly keeping his balance. No sweat. Armpits not terribly hairy. I'm tempted to flex now myself, but I don't.

We finally salute one another. Bye-bye! He guns it and slingshots ahead. I pedal and watch him get smaller, his back now a muscular V with a dark swath of sweat down the middle. Flirtation officially over.

Route 2 through downtown Grand Forks was a near-lethal circus of Harleys and piggybacked semis and cars. I've had to take side streets, trying not to get lost by staying more or less parallel. It isn't a bad change of pace.

I've been in this state half an hour, but I've already noticed a pattern, amateur sleuth that I am. All North Dakota license plates begin with either a B, a C, or a D, followed by two other letters, followed by a space and three numbers. How do they decide who gets the D plates and who gets the C's and the B's? Are drivers being graded somehow? No A's in the whole goddamn state?

The only exceptions are the vanity plates, which can apparently begin with any letter but are still restricted to the six-unit limit, a limit that's apparently taxing the ingenuity of those North Dakotans willing to pay for the privilege of succinctly proclaiming their mottoes or nicknames. Some folks, of course, have no problem: TUCHIT, GIDYUP, TOTALY, UWANNA. I do. No problem either for IT IS I, MS WHIZ, or COWBOY. But is NDBUFF a nudist or a North Dakota—or Notre Dame—enthusiast? You've gotta feel sorry for PLABOY and SERIUS, too.

Another thing about North Dakotans: If their bumper stickers are to be taken seriusly, a goodly percentage of them are in favor of life, despite having been born more than once. This is not Beckett country for sure.

When I get back on Route 2 at the far end of town, it feels like I'm finally Out West. The flora is different, for one thing. It's prairie, with no pine or fir trees at all. And since everything's low to the ground, the sky seems enormous. The only thing impinging on my nascent western big-sky experience is the unnamed establishment on my right: acre after acre of junked cars, tens of thousands of them, though a goodly percentage are hidden behind a long wall of corrugated iron. A *very* long wall, as it happens.

Five minutes later I ride past a sign: GRAND FORKS INTERNATIONAL AIRPORT. But the airport at the end of its own little road, a quarter mile north of Route 2, could hardly look less international: three or four hangars, some prop planes, a terminal that looks like a seven-store, one-story mall.

A few hundred yards beyond the road to the airport is a shack with a hand-lettered sign: BAITSHOP/SALE/MEDIUM

LEECHES. Because who would want large or small leeches when the mediums were on sale?

I'm not in a very good mood.

An hour west of Grand Forks the traffic has thinned out considerably. The shoulder is bumpy and narrow, pocked with ruts and loose gravel, which makes me feel harried and shook. Most of the time I'm forced to ride out on the road.

Yellow-headed blackbirds dart in small squadrons across the highway. Except for their yellow heads and throats, they look pretty much just like redwings; they may also be fractionally larger. Their song is much croakier, too, and they apparently hang out in flocks. I've never seen or heard even one until now, so the fauna is also quite different. I don't expect to see any loons.

A semi blasts up from behind me just as the first eastbound car in ten minutes happens to be approaching. Nice timing. Since the truck can't swing over, I have to bounce off the asphalt and into the gravel and weeds and around two small boulders, then actually stop and wait till the suck and stench of the truck has gone by. Pyoo! Tyson Foods. If I get bit by a snake, now I'll know who to sue, I decide, as a blade of tall grass whip-stings the back of my calf.

I pull back onto the asphalt, stand on the pedals to regain momentum, ride on. To cool off a little I empty a water bottle onto my forehead, my temples, then down the back of my neck, like one of those professional cyclists with the numbers and ads on their shirt. Day One of my Tour de Dakota.

Later a pickup goes by with bumper sticker: NORTH DAKOTA, MOUNTAIN REMOVAL PROJECT COMPLETED. At least it isn't one of those fundamentalist mullah types with no sense of humor. Right on, I say, raising my fist at the pickup's rear end shimmering up through the heat waves. Damn straight. Although I have to add that NORTH DAKOTA HILL REMOVAL PROJECT COMPLETED might be more accurate, since the landscape out here is almost preternaturally flat. And but what about North Dakota, Abortion Clinic Removal-By-Firebombing Project Completed?

Or North Dakota, Highway 2 Shoulder Improvement Project *Not* Completed?

I don't mean to pick on North Dakota. There's plenty of room in the world, as far as this girl is concerned, for places like this. I chose this route specifically because I wanted some flat highways and wide-open vistas. I've also got nothing against affordable leeches or grand international airports. I've only been in it for a couple of hours, but right now I'd have to declare North Dakota to be an outstanding place to ride a bicycle across every so often. Plus any state with a Governor and Mrs. Sinner welcoming you at the border can't be entirely boring.

I space out and think about Saint. I think about what a good kisser he was, about all his strange hats, but it never takes long for the scene to shift back up to Juneau.

I can't say for sure why there wasn't an autopsy. I'm not even sure there wasn't one. Who would have told me? I was not next of kin, not his wife, and his mother would have taken great pleasure in refusing to pass on the word.

Plus how would a coroner know where to start? There were so many things that were about to kill him anyway: infections, shock, despair, loss of blood. The grizzly sow had killed him; no one was looking for an additional culprit. I heard nurses say that it was a miracle he lived for four days. In any event, no one ever accused me. Not even his twat of a mother.

There were lawsuits, of course. Four years ago I got a letter from an Eleanor Vloda, a Chicago attorney who was representing the state of Alaska. Before I'd read the first two sentences—all I needed to see was "Alaska" and "attorney"—I'd concluded I was being investigated for murder. But all Ms. Vloda wanted to know was whether I would voluntarily participate in a discovery deposition involving the assumption of liability for camping that night in Glacier Bay National Park. When I called her office, she explained to me that Mrs. St. Germaine was suing the state of Alaska, as well as the U.S.

Park Service, the hospital, and the outfitter. Wrongful death, negligence, reckless endangerment ... The deposition took place on the forty-fifth floor of the Mies IBM Building in a posh, less-is-more conference room with a view of the bend in the river. Mrs. St. Germaine didn't show. Vloda had told me she wouldn't but I'd steeled myself anyway. I was definitely in the mood to tell her some things.

Events at the hospital never came up. The only issue openly on the table was who was responsible for David being attacked at the campsite, although at a discovery deposition anything could have been raised. I admitted that David and I had signed the outfitter's waiver, identified both our signatures, admitted that we'd seen the warning signs and read the brochures. It was over in eight or ten minutes and never became even slightly unfriendly. The court reporter looked like Aretha Franklin. The only words she spoke were "no," "yes," and "hold it," and she never sang a note. She stared straight ahead while her gleaming mauve fingernails fluttered above her adding machine of a typewriter.

Within the next month I got calls from two lawyers in Juneau and one in Chicago; all three encouraged me to sue the Park Service and or the outfitter for either endangering my own life or the trauma I suffered witnessing David being eaten alive. All three would be happy to represent me on a contingency basis: two thirds for me, one third for them. I declined. I wanted it over and done with.

That was four years ago. Mrs. St. Germaine must have settled her various lawsuits because I was never invited to testify. I can only infer this, of course, since we haven't been in touch since the funeral. I did call her once to ask about getting a photo of David; I left a message on her machine, and she never called me back. Which is probably just as well. If I'd been in a truth-telling mode, either on the witness stand or over the telephone, and someone had asked me, especially if I was under oath, what I knew about the death of Mrs. St. Germaine's son, I might have said something unfortunate.

*　　　*　　　*

I ride on and on, fingering sweat from my forehead. I eat a granola bar and suck down two boxes of AJ, fastidiously depositing the wrapper and boxes in my handlebar bag. DO NOT LITTER. Lick some sweet crumbs from the corners of my mouth while brushing the rest from my T-shirt.

The best place to stop will probably be Emerado or Block. I'll make Block by three-thirty or four, and I'll see what it looks like; Emerado is seven miles farther. The Burlington tracks run as straight as Route 2, about a quarter mile off to my left. The flat prairie landscape extends from horizon to horizon, with a slightly overcast sky. It's really a great day to ride.

I put Clifford Brown and Sarah Vaughan into the Discman. Nothing overtly sexual or hypnotic, just those exquisite soprano pipes and superfine trumpet. I've always found it easy to get lost in this disc, just become mindless and swing.

But I'm also trying to decide whether to cut my hair. I wash it each night in the shower, just before I go out for dinner, which allows me to make a faster getaway in the morning and not have to ride with wet hair. During dinner, even when I'm out on the town, I still wear it wet, in a braid. (I want to look at least reasonably presentable as I stroll about Knutson or Antioch.) But I'm not altogether convinced I'm accomplishing much by keeping it clean, especially since it's frizzy and sweaty all over again by ten the next morning. And except for the tool kit and my extra pair of shoes, it's probably the heaviest thing I'm carrying.

Which leads to some difficult ancillary questions. *How* would I have it cut? Like Audrey Hepburn's in *Wait Until Dark*? Sinead O'Connor's? O'Connell's on *Northern Exposure*? Who'd do the cutting out here?

Which leads me to: What in the heck am I doing riding a bicycle in the northeast quadrant, the far northeast corner, of North Dakota, or for that matter any Dakota? Questions like these seldom stop percolating through my brain, trickling sideways and down through my hypothalamus, anally and forever submitting themselves for revision, as if their syntax or rhythm or structural elegance made a punt's worth of difference as I pedal my butt down the road, writing it down in my head.

The prairie is spread out in every direction, green and brown and gray, mostly flat. Except for some low rolling hills to the north, the earth looks convex, with good old Route 2 cutting straight through the bottom of pale, imperturbable sky. I feel like I'm getting somewhere.

A small reddish hawk is cruising the thermals off to my right. Butterflies, honeybees, squadrons of blackbirds hover and dart in wild figure sevens and eights while pink-and-yellow torch flowers sway in what slight breeze there is. Other than that it's just mile after mile of big sky and grass and my 2. I feel opened up, optimistic almost. I also feel kind of exposed. I'm out in the middle of nowhere.

The shoulder here isn't terrifically smooth, but I'm still in a physical groove, pumping briskly, eating the miles up while singing along—a little off-key but with gusto—with Sassy. My sweat has saturated the foam-rubber pads of the earphones. It tickles and chills as it leaks down my neck, but I just let it leak for a while, trying to get off on the Zen of the drip. Doesn't work. Steering with one hand, I squeegee each pad between my index finger and thumb. In the process, I almost tip over.

I steer with two hands, pay attention, deciding to cut off seven eighths of my hair—or at least get the ends trimmed. After that I decide I'd look *interesting* and feel much more comfortable if I had it buzzed down to a crew cut, and that any of the local cowboy barbers could do it for five or six bucks. I decide not to cut it at all. In the meantime I'm singing and sweating and pedaling. No cars in either direction. Okay. The sun's out for now, but there's not too much glare off the blacktop. The temperature's just about perfect. The next thing I know I am flying.

PART 3

I landed. Was not on my bike anymore. Was hurting in five or six places. What happened?

What happened was that headlong and precipitously, in very slow motion, I crashed. Before that? Three measures into Clifford Brown's solo on "April in Paris" my front tire entered a four-inch-deep rut running parallel to the highway, about ten inches onto the shoulder. Almost immediately the narrowing width of the rut became identical to the width of my tire: thirty-five millimeters. Then it became slightly narrower. Gripped by the vise of the rut, the tire stopped rotating, while the rest of the bike maintained its forward momentum. Me too. The bike bucked down into a backward semi-wheelie that launched me headfirst over the handlebars. My right foot got briefly caught up in the stirrup, which shortened my plunge by yanking me sideways and down.

At least this is how I reconstructed things afterward, as I lay bleeding and stunned in the gravel, and then, several minutes later, retraced my skid marks and looked at the rut. I figure I was doing eleven or twelve miles an hour; if I'd really been pumping, or had the wind at my back, I would've probably broken my neck and solved all my problems.

I remember going over the handlebars. I squawked: a hasty amalgam of *what*, *shit*, and *help!* Then I landed. I broke part of the fall with my elbows and knees but took most of the brunt with my palms. Not my face.

There was vast and immediate silence, and I didn't feel pain. I thought I was deaf, knocked unconscious, or dead. It gradually dawned on me that the earphones had been ripped from my head.

I began to feel rage that I'd crashed, that I hadn't been paying sufficient attention, that my body and bike had been damaged—and I *needed* these things to keep going. Having squawked made me feel like a chicken. I lay on my side, semi-fetal, trying to establish whether I'd broken any bones, deciding how elated I was to still be alive. On a scale of one to ten, about nine.

The droplets of blood bubbling up around the pebbles embedded in my kneecaps and palms made me feel faintly nauseous. I groaned.

A bird chirped behind me somewhere—*chip-chip-chip-chip*, low and hoarse—and I actually wondered what kind. Rosy finch? Did orioles stray this far west?

It calmed me down further to discover the headphones dangling down my back. My spine might be damaged, my trip might be over, but all wasn't lost if my Discman still worked. Sassy's voice soothed me as she crooned—albeit faintly—from the headphones, which were down near my butt. Brownie was back there as well, sounding tinny but still pretty mellow.

I lean on an elbow, sit up. My right wrist has started to throb something fierce. Even the wispiest of hairline fractures would force me to cancel the rest of the trip. I wouldn't even be able to make it home on the train very easily, or exercise for several weeks once I got there. If it had to be casted I wouldn't be able to button my pants, write legible comments on student papers, load syringes, zip zippers, type, do my makeup . . .

My first inane plan is to try to dislodge a few cinders by rubbing my palms together *exceedingly* gently. The pain makes me swoon, even as I sit on the ground. To keep from tipping over, I brace myself with tentative karate-style chops with the side of my left hand. My right hand could not take the pressure.

When a gray car goes by I shout "Hey—" but my voice

doesn't carry. I raise my right hand, then pull it back quickly, tucking it next to my ribs. "Hey, *stop!*" But I'm squawking again. Is it possible the driver didn't see me? Or that he did and just *chose* not to stop?

One by one, wincing, I pick out the pebbles and cinders, prying them up as gently as possible with a fingernail, then tweezing them out with my fingertips. There must be forty or fifty of them, ranging from rounded-off pebbles to glassy black nuggets with edges. I have to keep licking the blood off to see what I'm plucking. I hope that I'm getting them all, that some aren't buried too deep. I imagine a small razor-sharp one—an off-center BB—getting sucked into a vein and wending its way through my carotid artery and into the pristine left lobe of my brain.

In the meantime another Bad Samaritan whizzes by, heading west in a crowded green minivan. Again I can't tell whether or not they saw me. Maybe someone noted that I was sitting up, not unconscious, not trying to flag them down, and thereby concluded that I didn't require assistance.

My God . . . A two-inch-long grasshopper almost gives me a heart attack by arriving out of nowhere and landing on my forearm. I thought I'd been bitten by a snake. The dusty beige bug proceeds to deposit a quarter-inch slime trail of tobacco juice before launching itself from my arm. As I wipe off the juice on my pants, there's a flurry of shaking and scraping in the sage bushes—isn't that what they're called?—near the spot where the grasshopper landed. Again I assume it's a snake—a snake that has eaten the grasshopper. From where I'm sitting I can't actually see it, but snakes tend to understand camouflage. I pluck two more cinders and listen.

There's nothing.

I put one of the larger pebbles onto the front of my tongue, tasting blood, then roll it around in my mouth to help keep my gorge down. My spit tastes like battery acid.

By the time I've removed all the cinders from my hand, two other cars have gone by. Neither one even slowed down.

Creakily, one aching joint at a time, I stand up, testing to see how much weight my ankles and knees want to bear. The knot in the small of my back loosens up when I stretch it a little, and the throb in my left knee seems to have more to do with the bloody contusions than a fracture—but what do I know? I could've broken a leg or a wrist or my spine and still be in shock and not notice.

I discover I can walk, fortunate girl that I am, at least the six ginger, tilted, baby-sized steps it takes me to reach my poor bike. It's splayed out on its right side, but all things considered, it looks amazingly undamaged. The right-rear pannier, the one I stow my works in, got knocked partway off and mashed rather thoroughly. But so fuck it, I decide, refusing to investigate further on the grounds that enough is enough as far as bad news is concerned.

I pull the bike upright and shake it as hard as a sixty-pound object can be shaken with a sprained wrist and hamburger palms. It seems solid. Chain still on the derailleur? Check. On the chainwheel and freewheel? Check, check. The saddle and handlebars also look straight. The right-brake lever has been munched near the tip and looks slightly crooked. Squeezing it makes my wrist throb ferociously, but it also makes the rear brakes engage. So okay. Finally, left-handed, I adjust the panniers, hoping—even though I've warned myself not to—that everything inside is intact.

Another small van whizzes by. When I step out onto the asphalt to investigate, I realize that between me and a car heading east there are tall sage and wolfberry shrubs; between me and the cars heading west there's a rise in the asphalt, and, about sixty yards up, the back of a road sign. I'm hidden. By the time anyone gets close enough to see me, they've already pretty much passed me.

Not that anyone's about to get a chance to slow down and come to my rescue. There's no car on either horizon.

I feel the first wobble as I roll the bike forward. I even have to smile when I see it. Oh *good*. The front wheel is shaped like a potato chip and two spokes are sprung—neither more than half an inch, but they no longer function as spokes. Even if they did, the wheel won't make half a rotation. I also understand that, even with two good hands and a bikeshopful of vise grips and spoke wrenches, I could never get the thing back in true.

The first strategy that occurs to me is hitchhiking to the nearest bike dealership, which I figure is either due west in Devil's Lake or back in Grand Forks. I'll need to have someone in a van or a truck pick me up, since the Trek wouldn't fit in most cars and I don't want to leave it out here. If I hid it well enough, then hitchhiked to town with the wheel ... although why would I take the old wheel if I'm simply in town to replace it?

What about rolling the bike to the nearest Amtrak station and taking the train on to Minot or back to Grand Forks? I'd get on whichever train came first. I can't see them from here, but the tracks have been running pretty much parallel to Route 2 since I got to North Dakota. Two questions, then. In which direction is the closest station? And, less important but still of some interest: How far away is it?

I let the bike rest on its front fork and take out my four-color map of the state, compliments of Governor Sinner. Where was I? Ah, yes—northeast quadrant. Okay. If I'm still ten miles east of Niagara, then the closest town big enough to probably have a bike shop is ... either Grand Forks or Devil's Lake. I seem to be right in between them—unable to walk, though, to either. The good news is that both sit directly on the Burlington tracks, though I can't tell for sure whether the train actually stops at either or both. I decide to head west, out of habit.

I release the front wheel, disconnect the brake, bungee the wheel to the seat tube. Okay. I hold up the front by the handlebars and roll the bike forward. No cars go by or approach. I take a few steps, rest for five seconds, proceed for another few steps. No cars on either horizon. I take ten more steps. As Al Neri told Michael after Tom Hagen concluded that it would be impossible to assassinate Hyman Roth while he was under federal protection, conveying myself and my bike in this manner is *difficult, not impossible*. I even manage to make it to the top of the rise before it starts to sink in that this isn't necessarily the right direction, and that going in the wrong direction might make a big difference.

A van whizzes by, heading east. I put up my left hand and wave it politely, imploringly. I even manage to make eye contact with the driver, a pink, crew-cut guy with a mustache. The van doesn't even slow down.

Is it me? Have I passed so far out of young-babehood that even when viewed from a distance and at a velocity that should be flattering, I still can't attract some attention? I suppose it wouldn't necessarily be the most evolved act on the planet for a man to pull over simply because he took me for a damsel in distress, but it bothers me that the notion of damsel wouldn't cross the guy's mind at least long enough to make him slow down. And what about simply *in distress?* Even for someone driving by at seventy, it has to be clear that I require assistance. Maybe the broken-bike prop makes me look a little *too* helpless, like bait in a carjacking trap. Maybe the guy in the van's just an asshole.

I'm feeling so pissed off and desperate that I almost start laughing, especially when I step back and get a good look at my bike. My poor little stalwart *does* seem pathetic, kneeling forward like that on its elbows like some scared, fragile antelope, with its overloaded butt thrust abjectly in the air. I'm sorry, but that's what it looks like. Handlebar antlers, water-bottle udders, tool kit and chain and panniers all part of its exotic biker lingerie, nubby black rubber spoke heels. I can even imagine it . . .

Boom!

The air churns and crackles around me. I shudder. Two more vast booms. Then another. Between booms the whole sky stays charged with a rackety silence, the hairs on my arms at attention. *Achtung!* It reminds me of supercharged thunder, or a blue calving glacier across the Tarr Inlet, only seven or eight times as loud.

A huge shadow flashes across the highway, then ripples out over the prairie. I look up and turn. I'll be darned! It's one of those slate-colored cubist Batman-cape things—stealth planes, I think, is what they're called—slanting along through the clouds almost directly over my head, dipping down to one side and then gone.

Was it dipping its wings to signal the imminent arrival of a rescue party? I don't think so. Can its crew members identify things like ABD's with warped bike wheels at that speed from up there? Maybe I've just had the honor, not being all that stealthy myself, of appearing as a blip on their radar. Maybe the pilot was saluting my stylish crash landing.

I hear brakes engage, tires squeal, a powerful engine rev down. It sounds like a jet on the highway—like the stealth plane has doubled back double-quick and then landed in order to save me; I'm actually convinced for a third of a second that my wish for the delivery of a new unbent wheel has somehow been spontaneously fulfilled. Who knows what a stealth plane can do? If only because . . .

I must be more dazed from the crash than I thought. A mean-looking black convertible has pulled onto the shoulder thirty yards ahead of me. The cloth top is up, so I can't see inside. It's a 500 SL with the Mercedes three-quarter peace sign centered above the red brake light.

The engine revs up, rumbles a little, then idles back down. The brake light goes off, but the Mercedes just sits there. It doesn't have a license plate, either, just four shiny screw heads where it *would* be affixed. If there were one.

The top of the car opens up. The part with the clear plastic window pivots away from me, and a hatch swivels open; the front half of the top stands straight up in the air, then slowly articulates downward and disappears into the trunk. The maneuver reminds me of something a Bond car would do—as though krypton lasers were about to open fire at me through trim, recessed turrets.

The driver regards me in his rearview mirror. I regard back. He looks to be an extremely young black guy in a neon-green shirt and Wayfarer sunglasses. He swings his arm behind the passenger seat, rotates his big D-shaped head, and backs up.

He does not back up slowly. Pebbles get spit toward the front of his car. Is he nuts? He looks too young to be driving this car in any direction, let alone backward. He certainly looks too young to own it. He stops when the right rear tire is a foot from my bike. I tried not to flinch. Didn't work.

This is the first time I've seen a Mercedes two-seater up close. The paint has the density and sheen of a sheet of black coral. The driver is gorgeous as well. Cheekbones like ledges, with little freckles under his eyes and along the wide bridge of his nose. From this distance he looks about twenty, but he might be much younger. A swirling design—it looks like a black rose or tulip—is etched into the bristle on the side of his head. His scary, flared nostrils remind me of someone I know.

"Yo," he says. "Hey."

"Hey." I smile noncommittally but try to look grateful. I'm scared. "Thanks for stopping."

"You okay?" His voice arrives from the lower registers, and has a smoky, provocative grain. Makes him sound like he's from a big eastern city.

"I think so." I glance at my bloody right palm, then back at his face. At his freckles. His shades. I want to look into his eyes.

He nods and keeps staring. We nod at each other a while. I can tell that he senses I'm scared, and I wish that it weren't so obvious. He finally turns up an enormous beige palm: Can we talk? There are no sonic booms overhead. No cars go by on Route 2.

"You sure?"

"Just had a slight crash on my bike."

"I guess."

I have to think fast, since he's about to offer me a lift and several things tell me I shouldn't accept it. I always and forever want not to be racist. My problem is that this young man just looks too much like a carjacker: nineteen years old, hip-hop haircut, wearing five-hundred dollars' worth of sweat clothes, Rolex watch, and driving this *car* that he stole. He is, in fact, straight out of a CNN special on carjackers that I saw less than a month ago, its central thesis being that they were thoroughly cunning and vicious, using guns, crowbars, screwdrivers, mace, razors, bricks, or whatever instrument was handy to force drivers out of their cars, then get in and blithely drive off—if the owner was lucky. One woman got her arm caught somehow in the seat belt, and they dragged her up Riverside Drive doing eighty; by the time the ambulance got to her, she had a dozen compound fractures and no right arm; she died on the way to the hospital. Granted, the northeast quadrant of North Dakota isn't the likeliest place in the country to cross paths with a carjacker; it's also the last place the cops would start looking. (Didn't a lot of the higher-end cars get driven to L.A. or Seattle, to be smuggled onto Chinese container ships? Where had I heard that?) On the other hand, just because my friend here happens to fit some generic description of a certain criminal type—I remind myself impatiently—doesn't prove he's dangerous. It's also a fact that I can genuinely use some assistance right now. But so where did this kid come up with the kind of money it would take to legally acquire this car? A friend of a friend of Jane's brother who works at the Board of Trade has one of these cars, and according to Jane it set the guy back 135,000 dollars. Maybe this fellow's daddy's a movie star or a musician—maybe he's rich and famous himself and I'm too unhep to recognize him. Not that I personally give a red-throated hummingbird's dropping how he came by the money. It's just that—

"Wanna ride?"

I half-nod and shrug noncommittally. The explicit conclusion of the CNN piece was that if confronted by a carjacker one shouldn't try to resist. Although there's been nothing—I remind myself impatiently—so far *to* resist. But why does he not have a license plate?

"Nice ride," I tell him. It is.

He gets out of it, letting his door click Germanly shut. He

walks around the side of the car, in no particular hurry, stretching as though he's been driving a while. He's enormous. Not bulky or barrel-chested or even tremendously muscular. But *large*—at least six-four or six-five, with boulder-type shoulders and very long arms. Sinews and veins stand out even in his legs, which emerge from a loose pair of yellow-and-black baggy shorts. There can be no question in either of our minds that he could effortlessly kill me in eight or ten seconds, which seems to render moot my anxiety as to whether he's a gun-toting criminal. He is weaponry unto himself.

"Nice *bike*," he says. Shakes his head. "Leastways it used to be."

"You think so?" I manage to say. I'm finding it hard to articulate. To choose the right words and form sentences. I suppose I'm out of practice these days. To make things simpler for myself, I point toward the damaged front wheel.

He turns his head sideways and mimics the shape with his hand, describing a warped, wheel-sized circle. He smiles, shakes his head. A very faint afterimage hangs in the air; the arc is uncannily accurate.

"Friend a mine rides one of these 790's."

"Oh really?" I say. It's really the best I can do.

"His is sapphire."

Oh. I just nod.

He looks back and forth between me and the bike. Into my eyes for a second, then lower down, sizing me up. *For what* is the question.

The harder I try to calm myself down, the faster my crazed brain is racing. One second I'm convinced that he's hijacked this car and is therefore capable of physical violence; the only other explanation for the Mercedes is that he paid cash for it, an inch-thick stack of C notes he made selling drugs, women, protection, whatever. Probably drugs, I decide. Probably that new kind of cheaper, more concentrated heroin; he just doesn't look like a pimp. The next second I concoct a scenario in which he's saved up his paychecks for a decent down payment and is now making monthly installments on a car that cost an eighth of a million dollars by working at Kinko's or selling gym shoes or teaching high school geology . . . He's probably still *going* to high school. Although weren't all gang-banging carjackers dropouts? He hasn't yet claimed to be making monthly payments, but what does that prove? Rolex, no license plates . . .

I'm already three-fifths hysterical when he suddenly takes two big steps toward me. I inhale. Another step. Jesus. I freeze. His head blocks the sun.

"My name's Ndele," he says. He offers his hand. It's beige on the inside and under the fingernails; on the back it's the color of coffee. It's also gigantic.

I stare.

"Ndele Rimes."

"Penelope," I say. Way too stiff. "Penny Culligan."

When I put out my own hand, he pauses, then takes it inside his quite gently. Awkward silence. He holds it more tightly and shakes it two times, up and down. It feels like I've inserted it into a piece of machinery lined with cool skin.

"Pleased to meet you."

"I'm real pleased to meet you, Ndele."

He lets my hand go. I concentrate on not withdrawing it too quickly; I err, in fact, too far in the other direction. My wrist throbs again; it hadn't five seconds ago, while he was holding my hand. The sweat I'd like to wipe off on my shorts is my own. But I don't.

"How 'bout a lift to the local Trek store, wherever that turn out to be." He gestures around at the farcical vastness of the bikeshopless territory we've found ourselves in. "Nome sayin'?"

"I do."

It's almost as though he's flirting with me. Or softening me up for the kill. My hand is still clammy, still trembling. *I'm* trembling. But I'm not quite as scared anymore. Bouncing off the ground must've shaken me up more than I realized. Plus I probably need to eat lunch. I'm starting to feel kind of dizzy.

"I really appreciate this. Thanks a lot."

"No problem."

He reaches back into his car and plucks out some Kleenex. Pink Kleenex. He tells me to clean off my wounds, then suggests we remove my panniers so he can stick the bike into his car. With fresh Kleenex wadded in my palm, I help him unstrap the panniers.

He picks up the bike as though it were made of bamboo and tentatively tries three or four angles of insertion, never once letting any part of it touch any part of the car. Personally, I would've put it in the trunk, then bungeed it closed over whatever part was left sticking out. It's his car, however, however he came by it, so he is in charge. Though I can't help wondering if there's something in the trunk he prefers I don't see.

On the fifth try he flips the bike upside down and fits it saddle first into the slot behind the seats. Voilà. Perfect fit. Neither the dusty tires nor the greasy chain is touching the slate-blue, immaculate leather. I hand him the panniers and the wheel, and he slides them in too. So okay. The rear tire and naked front fork stick up above the headrests, destroying the lines of his beautiful car, but it doesn't seem to bother Ndele. I'm glad.

He holds the door for me while I climb in the passenger seat. It feels like I'm sitting in a custom leather cockpit surrounded by metal and glass and more yards of buttery leather. I exhale nervously, relieved to be no longer stranded. I may have just sealed my fate, guaranteed I'll be raped and then murdered, but for the time being my lumbar feels quite well supported.

Green-black-and-yellow sneakers first (and no socks), followed by long veiny thoroughbred knees, then the shorts, Ndele maneuvers down next to me. He pulls his door closed, clears his throat. If his legs were a quarter inch longer, he would never have fit.

He shifts into Drive and pulls back out onto Route 2. "Must be a bike shop up here somewhere."

"Probably in Devil's Lake, I was thinking." It's also the direction in which he was heading.

He nods.

"You know, I really appreciate this."

"Hey, it's no big one. Is that where you was walking just now? Devil's Lake?"

"As a matter of fact . . ."

He laughs, shakes his head, and accelerates.

We cruise toward a line of low clouds. A sign says DEVIL'S LAKE 26, MINOT 125—I think. At eighty miles an hour, the road signs look smaller, and you get much less time to peruse them.

In the meantime I'm sunk back in comfort, watching the mileage zoom by. Many young cows have been flayed for this seat to be able to caress me with such supple creaminess—and God bless them for it!

"If you wanna adjust that," says Ndele, "go lower . . . " He avoids—barely—touching my thighs as he reaches across my lap to point out the seat-adjustment buttons on my door. Above the gold Rolex he's wearing a pair of orange-and-black braided leather wristlets. I wait for his hand to accidentally on purpose graze my sunburned and bloody right knee, but as he pulls back his hand he gives my poor flesh a wide berth.

"Thanks. This is perfect." I smile, trying to show him how much I appreciate both the seat and his gentlemanly comportment.

He drives with two hands, says, "You're welcome."

"You'd really have to straddle a two-inch-wide saddle for a couple three weeks to appreciate how great this here seat is."

"Straddle a saddle. That's cool."

I notice what looks to be a registration form taped inside the lower-left corner of the windshield. I feel a lot better already. "Your whole car, in fact."

"It's a slammin' ride, ain't it?"

"It is."

"'Cause a Ferrari *look* cool, but it's a fucked-up ride. This is a luxe ride. It's like, fo'get about it."

"Definitely."

I've never been in a Ferrari, but I've been in my share of convertibles—Mustangs, MG Midgets, Lee's little Alfa-

Romeo (her "Graduate" car), plus Fiats, Miatas, del Sols. This car is of an entirely different order of magnitude, a whole other caliber bullet. We're doing about eighty-five, but I can't feel anything even resembling a vibration. Ndele drives aggressively, but he doesn't seem reckless. Plus the road here is straight, with no traffic. The car actually *hums* as we rocket along, eating up every few minutes the kind of mileage it would've taken me hours to cover on my bike—the rest of the month if I was walking the current one-wheeled incarnation. Compared to the velocity I'm used to, it feels like we're literally flying. No rattling along over gravel or ruts, no wind in my face, no bracing for semis' foul suction. It's like riding in a sleek, low-slung tank with jet-propelled wings and no roof, snugly encased by the leather—like *buddah*—and polished burl walnut, air bag poised right here in front of me too, just in case. Everything about it is high tech but understated, recessed and tidy and wonderful. I haven't been in it ten minutes and I'm already terribly used to it.

As though he were reading my thoughts, Ndele has begun describing his car in highly technical terms. What's stranger is the mock-German accent he's using: ". . . zee handling ov zee 600SL iss ass precise ass its rote handling iss tenacious." He stares straight ahead, watching the road as he talks. "Under zee hoot iss a vor-camshaft, thirty-two-valfe light-alloy fife-liter fee-aid vit wariable inlet timing, qvik enuv to propel zee 600 from zero to vun hundred-zixty in two point two secunts, unt profiding deep reserfs ov power unt torque—"

Amazed, I blurt out "Ya vol" just to get him to stop, or slow down, for a second.

He holds out his palm in a Nazi salute, then seems to think better of this gesture. There's no trace of Deutsch when he asks, "Where you headed?"

"Alaska. I started in Chicago a couple of weeks ago, and—"

He whistles and shakes his large head. "Alaska!"

"Alaska." It does sound a little preposterous.

"Damn!" He's still shaking his head. "Why you wanna ride to Alaska?"

"Good question." I wish I had a good answer. "You know, 'How I spent my summer vacation.' What about you? Where are you driving to?"

He looks over at me, seriously offended by my question. I mean, truly *aghast*. I don't understand what I've said.

"I mean—"

His right hand flies back off the steering wheel and hovers between us. It looks like he's going to hit me. "You're bleedin' bleedin' on me fookin' lehvuh uphoolstery, loov." He points with his nose toward my hip.

I look down. My left palm has produced three nearly identical intaglio blood prints on the edge of the blue leather seat.

"Oh shit! Oh my God! I'm so sorry!" But why is he talking like that? I dab at the prints with the hem of my shirt. Is he one of those split-personality psychotics? It's as though he's undergone another sea change, mainly expressed with his voice but also with finger and wrist movement: looser, more daft. In the meantime I'm licking my fingers and rubbing the blood marks with spit. Doesn't work.

"I'm really so sorry . . . " I scrape at the stains with my bitten-down fingernails. Shit! I'm a bleeding, perspiring nincompoop. I'm used to leaving blood stains on tablecloths, napkins, the sleeves of my dining companions, but never on leather upholstery belonging to handsome but menacing strangers.

Ndele keeps driving. We go by a sign that says DEVIL'S LAKE, such-and-such number of miles; another one heralds the Turtle River State Park. Ndele says nothing. I want him to talk cockney or German again, just say anything. He glances back down at the gray virgin leather smeared with my blood and saliva. He winces.

For the sixteenth or seventeenth time, I apologize.

"No problema," he says, exhaling slowly.

I continue to work on the stains.

"Might make more sense if you clean off your *hand*. Nome sayin'? Your knee's bleedin' too."

This time when he points he does graze my leg. I excuse this by reminding myself that, one, he's right, I am bleeding—

I'm bleeding, in fact, on his car; and two, the space we're shar-
ing (by his invitation) is so limited, and his arms are so long,
and his hands are so big, that unless we both remain perfectly
rigid we're bound to make physical contact.

"So it is."

He pats my leg twice, both times just above my knee, first
with the flat of his hand, then with the side of his pinkie. Like
a consoling karate chop—*damn* you; there there. I bring my
legs closer together as his ring finger grazes the blood. What's
he doing? Both of us freeze for a second, but his hand stays
right there. He's tracing the shape of the wound.

He brings his hand up near his face. A truck thunders by,
heading east, as Ndele examines the blood on the tip of his
finger. My blood. He keeps driving.

I exhale and gasp, a deeply pathetic half-wheeze, as he
reaches behind me and—*shit!* what's he . . . —plucks three more
Kleenex from the dispenser between the two seats. He presents
the pink Kleenex to me as a stemless geranium, even bowing his
head half an inch, then puts his hand back on the wheel.

"Thank you."

"You're welcome."

I dab at my cuts with the Kleenex, then pull out two more
on my own. It's beginning to dawn on me now that I owe him.
I've accepted a ride in his valuable car and stained the upholstery. I am in this young man's jurisdiction, inhabiting his
high-powered kingdom. He can take me pretty much wherever he wants to. For the moment it seems that he's anxious to
help me. I have no way of knowing what his further intentions
might be.

He turns to me, eyes still hidden by the Wayfarers, both of
his hands on the wheel. There are two small gold loops in his
earlobe. He's smiling. "Doncha think it's probably safe now,"
he says, letting his big straight white teeth blaze themselves
into my consciousness, "to take off your helmet?"

I do.

Ten minutes later, fifteen more miles down the road, we have a specific destination and approximate time of arrival. Using his speakerphone, Mr. Rimes has ascertained that there's a bike shop at 601 12th Street in Minot—Hi-Line Cycles—that it carries seven-hundred-millimeter wheels, thirty-five-millimeter Kevlar tires, and is open till seven. They'll be looking for me around five.

He also informed me—without too much prodding—that he was driving the car from Norfolk, Virginia, to Seattle. He'd planned to take Interstate 94 straight across, but he got bored going through Minnesota. He cut north at Fargo and took Route 29 up to 2.

"Change of scenery, you know. Wanted to see how she'd handle on a bumpier road. Maybe swing north up to Canada." He also volunteered that he and his brother used to drive cars across the country between dealerships. "So we're used to long distances."

"But that's not what you're doing—" I stopped myself. I didn't want to sound too much like a district attorney. "You know, driving for one of those . . . "

"What?" He gave me the look again too, like I was making more prints on the seat. I was actually eating my lunch. I hadn't explained why I had to, but I was being exceptionally careful not to spill any crumbs. I unpeeled my banana and offered him half. He declined.

"Transporting a car for a dealership?" I asked. *A* car, not this one.

He shook his head no. "This baby's mine. Blood stains and all."

Apologies nineteen and twenty as I finish the banana. We ride on in silence. I roll up the peel, stuff it into my brown paper bag. I'm much more alert, having eaten, but it's still hard to know what to say.

"Goin' home," Ndele volunteers.

Oh. "So, to where? You live in Seattle?"

Tiny—almost imperceptible—nods. Especially tiny for such a large head. "To Seattle."

"So you must've just bought this." Took nerve, I admit, but I had to get the subject on the table. Impatience is a virtue, I always say. At least sometimes.

"Brand new," he says. He bounces his lengthy right thumb across his other four fingers; he's counting. "Just got it six days ago. Not even fifteen hundred miles on it yet." He gestures toward the odometer to confirm this assertion. "Fo'teen fitty-nine." It must've been obvious I doubted some parts of his story, which makes me feel awful. His story is none of my business.

"In Norfolk?" I say.

Normal-sized nods.

"Is that where you live?"

He nods, shakes his head. As though he's forgotten. As though he's still thinking. *You just asked me that, bitch!*

His story is *genuinely* none of my business, but I can't not continue to press him. It's horrible, being this way.

"Used to live?"

Damn! He speeds up a little. The broken white line down the center of the road gets more blurred.

He finally says, "Went to school there."

"You did? You mean, at Old Dominion?"

He yawns now, then suddenly reaches behind me and grabs my warped wheel. "Blessed are the flexible," he enunciates melodramatically, then takes on a preacherly aspect as he awaits my response.

I don't really have one, unfortunately. *Blessed are the flexible?* Was this a biblical aphorism I wasn't familiar with? Something "J" had composed in all of her Bloomian wisdom? Or was Ndele, as he called himself, about to deliver a homily on bicycle safety or conjugal open-mindedness? On how unclassy it was to hassle one's rescuer with too many questions? But so where had all his accents and personae been coming from?

"How so?" I venture.

Keeping one eye on the road, he shakes my warped wheel. "For they won't get bent outta shape!"

Oh. It's a joke. So I smile. Make sure my nods are substantial enough to express my appreciation.

Ndele puts both his hands on the steering wheel, shows me his teeth one more time. He looks pretty proud of himself. The interview about who he is and where he went to school, I have gathered, is over.

Over what? I don't manage to say.

We stop for gas in Devil's Lake. I've already offered—I practically begged him—to use my credit card to fill up his tank, but each time Ndele turned me down, gallantly pointing out that he'd have to cover this territory whether or not I was with him.

He gets out and turns on the pump. When I ask him if he wants anything to drink or eat, he pats his flat belly.

"Just ate. Hey, but thanks."

As I pass in front of the bug-spattered Mercedes, I sneak a quick peek at the registration slip taped inside the windshield. What I see in one glance looks legitimate: a multi-digit serial number, two dates, a round embossed seal, someone's signature. Interesting fact number two about the front of the car: each headlight has its own wiper.

The minimart is crowded with kids playing video games, three of whom have stopped to stare out the window at Ndele. With all of the pickups and vans and normal-sized white people using the station, Ndele and his sleek black Mercedes stick out pretty far. They look good.

I pick up a two-pack of oatmeal cookies and a bottle of Gatorade. The selection of T-shirts seems to include only horrible polyester jobs with truck stop, Big Johnson humor emblazoned across them. HOW ARE WOMEN LIKE DOGSHIT? above a not-bad depiction of two shriveled turds, then THE OLDER THEY GET, THE EASIER THEY ARE TO PICK UP. I have to find something I can plausibly wear, since the shirt I have on is clammy and smeared with my blood. The least tasteless thing I come up with says ON VACATION below a sappy pastel of two moony oldsters fishing cheek to cheek in a red constellation of hearts. I'd much rather wear the two turds, but I don't want to give Ndele the wrong impression. I also buy a box of Band-Aids and pick up the key to the women's room.

I pee, amateurishly dress my various abrasions, rinse off my face and my pits, change my shirt. I look like I've been in a fight. The front of the asinine shirt brings out the red in my wounds and my sunburn; it couldn't be too much less cool. I rebraid my hair, throw the stained shirt in the trash. My right wrist is throbbing again. I wish it would be more consistent.

If I'm going to ditch this Ndele, make my big getaway, this is probably my best and last chance. Even if the local phone book didn't reveal there to be a bike shop in Devil's Lake, I could tell him I'd talked to someone inside the store who told me there's one down the road. As long as I had access to telephones, food, a motel, I knew I could get a new wheel. Even if I had to take the train, or a bus, or a cab, or hitch a ride to Minot from someone slightly less suspicious. If I came up with a story about a mechanic or bike shop nearby, thanked him profusely as I took back my bike and panniers, what could he say? I wouldn't seem terribly grateful, of course. Only scared. But even if he had a knife or a gun, he wouldn't be able to stop me. Not in broad daylight in a gas station crowded with witnesses.

When I return the key to the cashier, she pinches the tip of its chain between two lacquered fingernails and makes a production of holding it at arm's length as she hangs it on its peg. It must have just registered on her who was driving the car I arrived in. She turns now and stares at me—as though I've just administered fellatio to a battalion of Zulu guerrillas. This woman is not unattractive: tall, big green eyes, clear complexion. She has on a green floral sundress that accents her eyes and flatters her figure. So there's nothing about her physical person to focus my contempt on. But I still want to bark something withering up her nostrils, then unscrew her head and spit down her foul, scabrous cortex.

"Well, I'm off . . ." I tell her pleasantly enough, but I don't turn to leave. I stand here and waggle my tongue as lewdly as I know how.

It gets to her for a couple of seconds, but she fully recovers—and then some. She picks up a towel and makes a big show of wiping her fingertips.

". . . like a prom dress," I say. She nods and smiles as though she *knows*. We watch each other levelly, even though she's five inches taller. Two weeks from now, or even two hours, when I'm hundreds or dozens of miles from here, I'll hit on a thoroughly devastating comeback. For the moment the best I can do is moisten my upper lip and give her a quick little wink before I walk out.

As I head toward the pumps there are three fourteen- or fifteen-year-old boys staring at Ndele and furiously debating some issue. One kid even points at the Mercedes as he illustrates his point. About what? The sides of his head have been shaved and he has on expensive gym clothes, as do both his comrades. They don't look like locals. More likely they're on vacation with their parents from Kenilworth and belong to one of the minivans alongside the pumps.

Ndele doesn't seem to have noticed them. He's in his car reading a map. As I get back in next to him, he slides an Amex gold card into his wallet, then folds the receipt into quarters and puts it down inside his door.

"Feel better?" he asks.

"Way. Thanks for waiting."

"That's good," he says, laughing. "'Cause you sure as heck *look* a lot better."

"Oh yeah? That a compliment?"

"Hey," he says, raising one hand in surrender as he pulls from the pump. "Absolutely."

"Well, then thank you."

"You got it goin' *on*, nome sayin'?"

"In a sense."

"Yeah, you do. Yo' bad self look righteous."

I blush.

As we circle the pumps and pull back out onto 2, I can see the cashier furiously dialing the telephone. Was Ndele's golden credit suddenly not in order? Have we violated some Devil's Lake miscegenation statute? Has she recognized his face on a wanted poster?

The three teenage boys are still standing there, speechlessly gawking.

"We gonna make it?" I say.

Ndele has to think. "It's a hundred and thirty miles to that Hi-Line place in Minot. Shouldn't take more than a couple hours." He looks at the Rolex. "Should make it by five at the latest."

My watch says 3:04. The clock on the dashboard says 2:59.

"So," I say. "Should take you about—what? Ten, fifteen minutes?"

"Fifteen tops."

"You don't have to risk getting pulled over just to get me there. I can always stay over and wait till they open tomorrow."

"Not on no Sunday," says Ndele, accelerating. "We be there by five at the latest."

I settle back into the leather. It's been a while since I kept real close track of what day of the week it was. Is that a good sign or a bad sign?

"Just don't risk getting a ticket for my sake," I tell him. As if.

We zoom west on 2, which angles slightly north as we leave Devil's Lake. We won't get to Minot for another hour and a half. I wonder if my works are intact. Even if they're not, I assume there will still be pharmacies open. I hope.

There's a mark on the side of Ndele's thick neck, a brownish-red circle about the size of a nickel. I can't tell whether it's a birthmark, a bruise, or a hickey. I have no idea what to make of the rest of him either. He avoids certain personal questions, but he isn't unfriendly. He saved me. He's taking me speedily and in comfort to where I need to get. He doesn't ask questions, which makes me feel even more guilty and grateful. What's so weird (and uncanny) is his chameleon routine. When he pretended to quote the Bible, his gestures and facial expressions were downright evangelical. He also does pretty good Nazi.

We nose up behind an old Buick with a red-white-and-blue license plate. The plate also features a figure on horseback. The motto across the bottom says DEVIL'S LAKE SIOUX.

"I didn't know Indians got their own license plates."

"It's the least we could give them, I guess," says Ndele.

"I guess."

He swings out alongside the Buick, then punches it, slingshots ahead. The women in the Buick ignore us.

The song on the stereo now is vaguely familiar. It sounds like a cello or bass accompanied by moody, Asian-sounding drums. Isn't this . . .

"Isn't this 'Summertime'?"

"Well, I be dammed by beavers," says Ndele. Then, as Ed McMahon: "You are correct, sir!" He wets a fingertip and marks one up for me on an imaginary scoreboard above the mirror. "As covered by Elvin Jones and Richard Davis," he adds in the smoky whisper of a late-night jazz deejay. "Mister John Coltrane's rhythm section makin' their *own* heavy sounds."

Maintaining this whisper, he annotates the eleven other discs on his changer. *A Love Supreme, Lift to the Scaffold, Aretha's Gold, Rhythm Nation,* plus things by Niggaz With Attitude, Bill Frisell, some ensembles called Baron Down, Miniature, the Decoding Society . . . The changer is mounted in the trunk—along with what else?—but controlled from the console between us.

"I could use one of these on my bike."

"Yup," says Ndele. "You could." He laughs, nods his head up and down—mockingly oversized nods. It seems he's no longer a deejay. "You definitely could."

The Burlington-Northern tracks are now on the right; as usual, I don't recall crossing them. Beyond the tracks is an endless plain of blue gramma grass and wolfberry shrubs, the occasional boulder or hillock. On our left, pretty much the same picture. Yellow-headed blackbirds (no redwings) flit back and forth across the road. I hear their hoarse creaks as we blow past their chaotic squadrons. One or two of them usually insist on pushing their luck by pecking and hopping around till the last possible second, seemingly daring us to pulverize them into pie. I wince because this time I'm sure it will happen—but no. The stragglers have dodged us again.

A storm's blowing in from the west. With all the other distractions, it seems I've missed the big sky getting darker. Charcoal-black cumulonimbus are stacked now at least a mile high, marbled by capillaries of lightning. Squalls angle down to the prairie. I've read somewhere that the horizon is so low in this part of the country you can see a front rolling in from a hundred miles off. This one looks quite a bit closer, although it's still far enough away to be able to see the top and both sides of it. It's spread out across the west-northwest edge of the prairie, slightly off to our right, and coming right at us. I haven't heard thunder, but I can feel the air getting humid and gusty. The sun blazes through the mostly blue sky on our left.

Ndele so far hasn't commented, but he's started to drive a bit faster. Fifteen minutes ago the only things we passed were threshers and Buicks and cattle trailers. Now we are swinging past cars. We also pass a leather-clad couple on a Harley. They wave as we pass them, and Ndele waves back. So do I.

MINOT 100 announces a sign—intentionally mocking us. It's gotten dramatically darker. Ndele takes off his sunglasses, concentrates on driving responsibly. Disc three, track five—first piano, then trumpet, then sax—pulses and bops through the speakers. Ndele does saxophone fingering on the steering wheel, squints in the relative glare. His short, glossy lashes curl back up over the lids. He looks vaguely Asian. When he finally stops squinting, his eyes stay elongated, large, slightly hooded. Pupils the same mocha color as his skin. Without the sunglasses his nose becomes more a hooked beak above wide convex nostrils. He looks way too menacing to think of as cute, but if someone insisted, I'd have to admit he was beautiful.

"So when did you go to Old Dominion?"

"Like two years ago," he tells me, then takes a deep breath. "Smell all that ozone?"

As I inhale through my nose, I realize I've been smelling it for five or ten minutes. "I do."

His nostrils flare wider as he savors the aroma. "Gone rain like a muthafucka."

I cannot disagree.

There's a *thwack* on the windshield in front of him; it sounds like a hailstone or pebble.

"Whoa, dude!" says Ndele.

"What the . . . "

In the meantime the ding in the glass is oozing, expanding. Ndele is squinting again. We lean our heads forward and stare.

"It's—"

Small chunks of dull yellow fur tremble near the center of the glass. It *couldn't* be fur, though. It's—

"But isn't it—"

"Yes," says Ndele.

It's the remains of a jumbo honeybee oozing golden and jittery up the windshield, a slo-mo translucent explosion of grainy, all-natural phlegm. Ndele is fascinated, turning his head to get better angles, but he doesn't slow down.

I ask, "Can you see?"

"Can I see? I can see that that's one very dead bug on my windshield."

"I guess she was slightly overmatched in this particular collision."

"Amen to that, fella," he tells me. John Wayne? "Only question is whether the North Dakota Highway Patrol has equipped themselves yet with radar."

In the meantime the speedometer is edging past ninety, though the ride is so smooth it doesn't really feel like we're speeding. I focus down onto the shoulder, imagine myself humping and rattling along through all of those stunted gray weeds and deep cracks.

It's a blur.

After cutting through Penn and Churchs Ferry, Route 2 angles left just beyond a road marked Lake Alice. The storm is directly in front of us. I believe we're now headed straight west. The sun has disappeared behind pink-and-gray cotton-ball clouds being pushed by the edge of the front.

The problem is obvious. If we don't find a place to pull over, the inside of the car will be soaked, and it's going to be all my fault. Because as long as my bike remains wedged behind the seats, Ndele can't put up the top. The faster he drives in order to make it to Minot, the closer we get to the storm. Minot is still eighty miles west, and it's going to pour any second.

There's a thunderclap in the middle distance as we fly over a ridge in the road. Gravity tugs at my bowels. It's scary but kind of exhilarating. Ndele is hunched over the steering wheel with exaggerated concentration. He enunciates Frankenstein style: "Must—make—Mi-not."

The sky in that direction is charcoal and rose for the most part; black at the horizon, pale smoky yellow up near the top. Gray sheets of rain are slanted in the opposite direction of the bright shafts of sun that plow their way through. One shaft has fashioned a parallelogram sliding across a small hill, lighting it up like a diva. A lone red-winged blackbird swoops up across, then below us. *Ka-ree!* Must've missed him.

"Looks like we just gone sneak through," says Ndele.

"So what are you, *aiming?*"

"You bet," he says, gripping the wheel and knitting his brows—as though with expert steering and intense concentration he can wend our way through all the squalls. I can't tell whether he's kidding. For the moment he seems perfectly serious.

"Mi-not."

A raindrop wings the tip of my nose, sprays my cheek. Tickles. "Whatever," I say, suppressing a giggle as I'm wiping it off. This is crazy. Another drop splashes my arm. But it's great that Ndele is so optimistic, that he seems to be both kind and . . . kind of funny. He also seems smart. Weirdo smart maybe, but smart. On the other hand, he does seem to be unrealistically convinced that he can deliver his passenger to her appointed destination *and* keep the interior of his convertible dry, so what does that tell me? Even though it's clear we won't make it, I'm touched. I also feel guilty—especially when a trio of raindrops explodes off the console between us.

Ndele keeps going. There isn't a building, an overpass, a house or a shed or a barn or a trailer in sight. The only alternative to getting drenched that I can imagine (besides Ndele regretfully inviting me and my bike and panniers back out onto the shoulder, putting his top up and booking) is hanging a U-turn, heading back to Churchs Ferry and waiting it out in a diner. (Wasn't there a diner? Maybe not. Can't remember. The town was so small—ten or twelve houses—I wasn't paying too much attention. I suppose we could wait in a church, though I don't recall one of them, either.) Or else we could skip Churchs Ferry *and* Penn and just keep going east. This car could outrun a thunderstorm almost indefinitely—an idea that's a little bit startling, especially since I'm accustomed to bike speed and for the last three weeks I've needed hours of advance notice to stay out of the rain. But I assume that no cloud can do ninety. I'd be back in Chicago by midnight. If only the storm was blowing in out of the east . . .

Raindrops are slapping our faces, our laps, the walnut veneer, the upholstery. Big ones. It lets up for fifteen or twenty seconds, continues.

Ndele's right cheekbone gets splashed. Sheets of rain whip all around us, but so far the inside of the car has only been sprinkled—because of our speed, I assume, along with the aerodynamical tilt of the windshield. The drops that do make it in here are grape-sized and chilly.

When Ndele hits a button to turn on the wipers, there turns out to be only one: a single elaborately articulated metal arm wielding a two-foot-long wiper that scrapes every drop in its path (and eleven twelfths of the honey), then disappears under the hood. Four seconds later it pops up and does it again. The honeybee is history.

And now it is pouring. Ndele speeds up the wiper and turns on the lights. His drenched neon shirt clings to his shoulders and chest. The wiper does its job quite superbly, but in order to see we still have to flick the rain from our eyes. An eastbound semi whips past, honking its horn and spraying my forehead with road water, trying to outrun the storm.

Ndele fingers rain from his eyes, glances over at me. He's shaking and snorting with mirth. I must look ridiculous. Whereas he has a haircut *designed* for such eventualities.

"Gettin' *wet* over there?" More snorts and shakes.

I look up and scream—and catch a cold spoonful of rain. I splutter and cough and start laughing.

Ndele holds onto the wheel with both hands as another huge semi roars by, sucking us slightly off course and winging cold spray past our heads. We both holler "Shit!" at the top of our lungs. We start yelling other things too.

I almost start crying. The puddle in the seam of the seat near my crotch squishes and tickles me each time I shift my position. Big cold hard raindrops keep slapping my face; they're massive and speedy enough that each of them stuns me a little. My nipples stand up—as is their wont—through my T-shirt and bra, so I cross my arms over them. (Ndele is driving, so he can't cover his.) The Discman is still in the pack in my lap, and I try to protect that as well. I can only hope that my panniers turn out to be waterproof, since the glucometer shouldn't get wet. Gore-Tex panniers are what I could use, at the moment, plus a Gore-Tex glucometer, Gore-Tex socks, Gore-Tex panties, a Gore-Tex foam-padded brassiere . . .

Ndele keeps squinting and cursing and driving one-handed, pants and shirt plastered against him, flicking the rain from his eyes with the tip of his right index finger. Everything smells now like ozone and worms and wet leather. The front tires splash through huge puddles as Ndele speeds up. He says nothing. I'm too embarrassed to yell anymore, but I'm screaming my head off inside as we skate on a glaze of cold rain.

Finally, as the downpour gets fiercer, we spot what looks to be a garage or large shed on the right side of the road. When Ndele hits the brakes we fishtail a little, then bounce up and down as he pulls up alongside the shed. The building is on the perimeter of a golf course, fenced in with rusty barbed wire. Its doors, if it has any, must be on the other side, facing in toward the course. Two hundred yards beyond the fence I can make out some brightly dressed twosomes on powder-blue carts scampering west—the direction, I presume, of the clubhouse. I can't keep from hoping that, as just retribution for denying us shelter, lightning will strike and just miss them, singeing the little wool pompons they keep on the ends of their clubs. Ndele and I look at the scrambling golfers, then back at each other—both of us dripping, ridiculous. I'm amazed that he doesn't seem angry.

"Must be something open round here. Some fuckin' clubhouse or something."

I agree, though it is hard to picture us strolling into the pro shop and getting much sanctuary. . . .

Rain pours down harder as we bounce and splash back onto 2. Out over the golf course thunder cracks stunningly, and three seconds later there's lightning, then a lot more of both right behind us. Maybe I've gotten my wish.

We drive another few hundred yards before spotting a sign to the left of the road: J & J MOTEL in blue cursive neon. Underneath in red letters: VACANCIES. The "NO" has been covered by plywood.

Ndele waits for two eastbound cars to go by—patiently, casually, *dum de-dum de-dum*, like we're out for a spin in the country on Sunday—then turns into the potholed lot and pulls up under the canopy connecting the sign to the manager's office.

Okay. The rain's pouring off the forest-green canopy in almost unbroken streams in front and in back of us, but at least it's no longer falling inside the car. Not that it makes much difference anymore. The leather and carpets are thoroughly soaked. I open the door and get out to unload my damn bike. I feel awful.

Ndele sits still for a moment, probably trying to think of the best way to ditch me, then quickly gets out of the car.

I take hold of the frame of my bike, but it's hard to get the right sort of angle to lift it. My back won't—

"I got that," he says.

"*I've* got it. Don't worry. Just get—"

He takes hold of the frame and lifts the bike out of the car, swings it around right side up, sets it down next to the door. "I'll meet you inside in a minute."

I grab the panniers, say, "Okay."

But what else? I'm convinced I'm forgetting something, something I can't be without. I'm thoroughly soaked with cold rain. I can't think. "But so, are we staying . . . "

Ndele is already back in the car and the black two-piece top is rising up into the air. More motors whir as the top subdivides itself: the longer, horizontal section slides forward and fits itself to the top of the windshield while the diagonal rear-window section tilts and swings back toward the trunk.

"Just go inside!" he calls out.

I hold my panniers. Are we staying?

"Go on! I'll park it and meet you inside!"

There are only three cars in the lot, two of them backed up to the red-painted doors of the rooms. Rain slashes into the puddles. I watch the Mercedes bump slowly across the gravel and into an extra-wide space.

I wheel my bike into the lobby. The AC has blasted the room into a chlorofluorocarbonized gelidness, a climate I normally relish. But not dripping wet. Is it necessary for a room to be quite this cold on a day like today?

The woman behind the counter is petting a tan-and-black kitten. The woman's hair has been dyed a pale blond, and not all that recently. A TV is on in the corner. Stuffed bass and antelope heads adorn knotty paneling. One of the antelope looks especially unhappy to be here.

"You ride in through all that rain on *that*?" asks the woman. She smiles. She's husky but pretty, with clear skin and anxious blue eyes. And tall. Very tall. Her too-tight, blue-checkered sweatshirt has BLUE CHECKER CAB/UNALASKA, ALASKA stretched across her full breasts. Unalaska, Alaska? I admit it's an interesting concept.

"Yep," I tell her. "Made pretty decent time, I must say."

She hands me a little white towel, but I can tell she doesn't appreciate the sarcasm. And she's right. It was stupid, uncalled for. It's just that I'm freezing!

"My God," I say. "Thanks." Should I start my apologetic routine with this person too? I don't think so. Whether or not it's called for, I don't have the energy. I rub my hair hard with the towel. "This is just what I needed."

"Are you with that man in the *cawr*?"

As I tell her I am, I notice the towel is mottled with beige-yellow stains. I use it to dry off my hip. We smile at each other. I tell her we might need a couple of rooms, depending on how much longer it rains.

"A couple."

"Depends on when this business lets up." I gesture outside toward the rain. Was she mimicking me?

She looks at me now as though I'm terribly confused. I suppose it is true that I am.

"Two single rooms." If she insists on more forthright or specific information, I'll just have to improvise.

She repeats what I've said in a "midwestern" accent.

I hold up two fingers, using my left arm to cover my chest for some warmth.

"Oka-a-a-ay . . . " She peers long and hard at the logbook in front of her, carefully tracing one sheet, then another, with an inch-long blue fingernail. No checks on her nails to go with the sweatshirt, but she's certainly color coordinated. I place the used—the twice used or thrice used—towel along-side her logbook. And shiver. She continues to study the columns. Her motel only *has* seven rooms.

The kitten meows and arches its back as it stares at me, frankly skeptical. When I stare back, it sniffs the damp towel, meows more insistently. I nest my crossed hands in my armpits, try to stop shivering. Can't.

Where's Ndele?

"Two rooms, you say?"

I shiver and nod. "If you have two. They don't have to be adjoining or anything."

"For you and Mr.—?"

How to explain this? The answer is: don't. "Does there happen to be a bike shop in town, by the way?"

She stares over my head out the door. When she finally speaks, it's like she's reciting her multiplication tables: "Bowling alley, tennis courts, putt-putt golf, regular golf, swimming pool, the monument, the Frontier Museum. No bike shop." She sounds as though she's from the south—not South Dakota, either. More like Memphis or Houston or Selma.

"Looks like you need a new wheel."

"Or a decent mechanic," I say.

She thinks about that, holds up one finger, stares at the ceiling.

"What town is this, anyway?" I say, trying to make the question sound friendly.

Ndele comes in. He's carrying my handlebar bag and a fluffy green terrycloth towel festooned with Gatorade logos. He looks around at the trophies, the TV, the tall woman. I'm terribly happy to see him.

"Well," says the woman. "Would you just look at *you*. Where's *your* broken bike?"

She's brash, this old girl, and she isn't even that old. Under thirty, I'd guess. But a thoroughly shameless blond hussy. Probably no man in town quite her size till Ndele strolled in, so now she can barely contain herself.

"My bike?" says Ndele.

"Don't *you* have a broken bike *too?*"

He shakes his head no.

"Well *that's* good, I guess."

Awkward pause.

"How you livin', homegirl?" says Ndele. He hands me the towel.

I thank him and wrap it around my shoulders. "I think we're okay. I'm okay."

"Hello there yourself," says the woman.

He tells her hello, then looks back at me. His wild Nike shirt doesn't look wet anymore. I can't tell whether he's changed into an identical dry one or this one is cut from one of those miraculous new water-shirking materials. Maybe it's just the strange light. He also seems taller. He doesn't have to actually duck, but he makes the tile ceiling look low.

"What you think," he asks me.

You're making the ceiling look low. "About whether it's gonna keep raining?"

He shrugs. The ceiling has beige-yellow stains on it too. What's the story?

The kitten leaps from the counter and lands near Ndele. It circles him, purring. He stiffens and shuffles his feet.

"See?" says the woman. "She likes you!"

"Where we at?" says Ndele. It appears that he doesn't like cats.

"Man, you're in Rugby, North Dakota, the Geographical Center of North America!"

"That a fact?"

"One thing we could do," I say, but I can't think of what to say next. I watch the cat boxing and hugging Ndele's elaborate sneakers. He shifts their position minutely. "You could just drop me off here, and—"

"Where you folks all coming from?"

"Back east," says Ndele.

I point.

"Where did you get that sweet cawr?" she says, apparently forgetting she told us she thought he was riding.

Ndele looks irked, exactly by what I can't tell. "Norfolk," he mumbles.

"From—*what?*"

"Nor-foke, Virginia," he enunciates. "My friend here's fr—"

"Paris!" says the woman.

Baffled, embarrassed, I stare at the kitten, which is stalking Ndele like he's a mile-high scratching post. I need to eat something.

"Paris?" I ask.

Ndele shoots me a look: You're from Paris?

I shrug, shake my head. It helps warm me up. His towel is made of silky, spectacular terrycloth.

"Paris West, the *mechanic*," the woman blurts out. "Mr. Goodwrench, whatever you call him. Maybe *he* could have a look at your bike."

"There a bike shop in town?" says Ndele.

"Paris *West*. He works on the combines and stuff. Fixes bikes all the *time*." She stretches and looks at the ceiling. Her breasts are quite ample and shapely. Her navel peeks from under the bottom of the sweatshirt: an innee. "Though isn't he still down in Bismarck this week?"

I don't know.

Ndele turns up his palms, winces sharply. The kitten is climbing his ankle, hooking its claws in his sock. He gently shakes the foot, but the kitten's claws are firmly embedded in his socks.

"Owww!"

In his flesh.

"Cakers!" shouts the woman. "Now you just leave this nice boy alone!"

She sashays around the counter, modeling her voluptuous bod for Ndele. She has on gold sweatpants three or four sizes too small; they fit her like baseball pants. Her buttocks and calves are substantial.

"When were you up in Alaska?"

"No! Me? Never!" She pats the checked shirt, nods toward the door. "Jim got me this thing just there in Minot."

She squats in front of Ndele, revealing (to me, at least) the tan and violet crack of her butt. Baby got back. She slides her hand under the kitten, tries to lift it. It clings to Ndele's white sock and meows.

"*You* are a very bad *pussy!*"

Ndele's sock pulls away from his leg as she scoops up the kitten. I watch as he tries not to wince.

The woman stands up with the kitten. "This is Carmella B. Cakers. Yes! There! Isn't she the pussenest little puttytat ever? She is!"

She holds up the kitten in front of Ndele. Their hands and arms are practically touching—this woman makes sure of it.

When Ndele leans back, she gets up on tiptoe. The kitten meows, unamused. Baby got back *and* some balls.

"I guess," says Ndele.

Behind Every Pretty Face There's a Bitch, I decide, and *Behind Every Pretty Behind There's a Pussy to Fuck You Around*, and other lame T-shirtiana. But true. I make a mental note to try to remember these things.

Ndele takes hold of my elbow. "Would you excuse us a second?" he says to the woman. His hand feels raptorial.

She carries Carmella B. Cakers back around the counter, swinging her golden behind and waving a hand in magnanimous dismissal. "A course!"

Ndele gently leads me toward the door by my elbow. The room is too small to get more than fifteen feet away from her.

I wipe away the fog and we peer through the finger-smeared oval—first me, then Ndele, who has to bend sideways. The sky's even darker than when we arrived. Sheets of rain slash through the parking lot.

"What's that theory—big drops don't last long?"

"Something like that," says Ndele.

"Supposed to rain all night," says the woman.

I ignore her. "How's the inside of your car?"

"Nothin' a little badass ceramic replacement hip-hop air retroactive *mink* oil wouldn't clear up."

"Oh gosh." Gosh? I catch myself starting to giggle again, even though I'm mortified about the damage I've caused. "It's entirely my fault. Really. I really should pay you or something."

Ndele raises his hand and shakes his head, disagreeing—I think. "Listen, you wanna just crash here? We both need to put on dry clothes." He nods toward the woman. His eyes do a strange little dance, then refocus. "They got any rooms?"

I shiver and hug myself, nodding. We're staying? I've already covered my quota of mileage three or four times, and it's not even three forty-five. If the storm blows over in the next two hours, we could still reach Minot by sundown, although by then the bike shop would probably be closed. But at least I would be there, in a town with motels and a bike shop, ready to go as soon as they opened—in the morning, on Monday, whenever.

"I'm sorry, sir," says the woman, "but we do only have the one vacancy. My name's Debbie, by the way." She holds out her hand toward Ndele, who is standing not only on the other side of the counter but across the entire, albeit diminutive, room from her.

"I thought you said . . ."

Ndele crosses the room in three strides and shakes Debbie's hand. He tells her his name.

"N-deli." She pronounces it three or four times to herself,

mulling it over. "Hmmm. Ndele." Like she knows him from somewhere, perhaps.

"That's right," he says.

I too step forward and introduce *my*self. Hmmm— Debbie? That's *Debbie*, you say? On the TV behind her, turned low, Rob and Laura Petrie are bickering. My sympathies immediately gravitate, as always, toward Rob. What the laugh track registers is more evenhanded. I hate that. I need some fruit juice or Lifesavers, soon.

"Would you mind calling another motel or two," I say. "See if they have any vacancies?"

"I certainly wouldn't," chirps Debbie. "Though I doubt that anyone *does*, what with this great big huge softball tournament in town. We've all been booked up for just *weeks*."

I look at Ndele, who turns toward the fogged-up glass door. The oval I cleared has fogged over again, with my breath and his—and this Debbie's. There are ghostly white traces of handprint. My smears. Red taillights radiate sideways behind them, then gone. It would've been more considerate if I'd made the oval at least a foot higher, even though I would've had to stand up on tiptoe to see what the weather was doing.

Ndele's still thinking. His height, as I watch him, his almost preposterous tallness, makes him seem somewhat older. He no longer looks eighteen or nineteen.

I'm suddenly anxious to be back outside, in the moist and dark air, on my bike. On my bike, on the road, by myself. And out of this blasting AC.

"I guess you could just drop me off here and keep going." I'm whispering—pointlessly, pointlessly. Whatever this woman is telling us, I'd sort of like for *him* to decide, since he's the one who's been forced to pull over and had his upholstery ruined. I feel that I owe him a vote, or two votes, or at the very least a thorough sounding out, on how long we should stay here. Or not.

"You know, with the top up," I add.

"I suppose we could do that."

"I mean, are *you* staying here?"

He shakes his head, nods. "I suppose." Then he shrugs.

His utter neutrality both relieves and disappoints me. It gets me off the hook as far as spending any more time with him, but what am I anyway? Dirt?

"Or you could just keep going without, you know, with the top up. Or else we could . . . " I'm speaking to him, for what little it's worth, sotto voce. I can feel Little Debbie and Carmella B. Cakers tuning right in to every false note and pleading syllable.

"I suppose we can do that," he says.

"I suppose" pretty much exhausts his reservoir of opinions on the subject, but I decide that it's better this way. I can't keep riding today, but he can keep driving; so I will stay here. Ten minutes ago I had far too little control of the situation. Now I can call ahead to Minot, pick up the train or the bus schedule, maybe get a new wheel here in Rugby.

I put my hand on Ndele's arm to announce my decision. "If you wouldn't mind my taking this room—"

"No, wait!" Debbie shouts. She looks up from the logbook, brushes her bangs from her eyes. "I just remembered! That couple from Ottawa just checked out of seven this morning! I can give you two folks six and seven!"

I'm giddy and dazed. It's hard to say whether it's the weird situation or I'm having an insulin reaction. Either way, I can't quite parse all of these second-by-second decisions.

I look at Ndele. His gleaming black eyebrows move farther apart. He inhales.

And we take them. Rooms six and seven of the J & J Motel, Rugby, North Dakota. Side by side at the counter, without any more hawing or hemming, we take pens in hand and fill out the forms we are given. My handwriting's shaky. For several long seconds I can't remember my street address in Chicago, so I begin to make one up; when I suddenly recall the correct one, I cross out and start over. I know it looks pretty suspicious. Fuck Debbie. Halfway into the most delicate negotiation I've had to conduct with a man in the last seven years and our sleeping arrangements wind up getting brokered by the Giant Motel Clerk from the Geographical Center of the Frozen Ninth Circle of Hell. I can also imagine, as I hand over my Visa, that if worse comes to worst, Ndele and Cakers will save me.

The shower of room number seven is a wobbly fiberglass stand-up affair with sunburst rust stains and whip marks of royal-blue paint by the drain. The curtain is opaque yellow plastic. I run the hot water and suck down two cartons of AJ.

It smarts when I yank off the Band-Aids, exposing the three-inch-long scrapes on both knees. A cinder is still embedded in the moist, sticky scab on the left one. (How did I miss it in my preliminary roadside exam?) Damp, scabby gore on my palms.

My right wrist is swollen. It throbs when I peel off my clothes, though nothing quite painful enough to convince me it's broken. If it's throbbing tomorrow, I'll get myself X-rayed in Minot.

Ndele and I have a date to eat dinner at six in the diner across the highway, and he's promised to let me pay. It's still raining hard, so our plan is to spend the whole night here. It's too late to make Minot anyway.

I rinse off my wounds in the shower, lather them gently with soap. They sting but don't bleed. I scrub the gray silicon sludge from my calf, then shave both my legs and my pits. After I shampoo my hair, I let the limp jets of almost hot water beat on the back of my neck. As the water gets cooler I direct it onto my temples and forehead. I shiver. It's soothing and chilly and wonderful.

*   *   *

The warped beige linoleum floor feels strange in bare feet: the smooth and cool stretches, the coarse grain of cracks and old grit. I watch myself dance in the mirror, a dumb little jig I learned in sixth grade from Ms. Lin-Matthews. Each step I execute counts as physical research into the Hibernian spirit of Beckett, of course, although Sam never jigged in his life.

I stand still and squint at myself. I contract a few muscles, toss Ndele's green towel onto the bed. My legs are the first place I look, since they're probably the best things about me: *reasonable* is the word that now comes to mind. I jig myself sideways and stare. My ass, too, is reasonable. Just. If pedaling a bicycle happened to involve one's chest and or abdomen, I might be in fairly good shape. But it doesn't. And then there are my preposterous tan lines: little white anklets, brownish-pink formal gloves past the elbow, pasty white T-shirt complete with a pussy and ribs and small erect rose-colored nipples— but no banal mottoes, at least. My neck by itself must be seven or eight different colors. Plus my hair . . .

The room smells of Lysol and smoke. I was probably too dazed and grateful to notice when I first staggered in, but it *reeks*. Cigarette burns on the floor, along the bed's gray wood headboard, the edge of the mismatched blond dresser. Both windows have aqua-maroon floral curtains, but they're not the same length. Close, but not quite. There's also a faint maroon stain—it actually goes with the curtains—centered exactly between them. It's shaped like an old-fashioned woman's shoe—like New York. It even has a kind of Long Island deal going on right in the place where it should be. It must be Chianti or burgundy, or one of those vodka and Jell-O concoctions. Or blood. Or whatever. People have partied in here.

My lame bike is parked in the corner, but it no longer looks like an antelope. Probably never did, really. I dig out my works, check for damage. Two vials of Regular, three vials of Lente: intact.

I open my fresh pair of panties. They're a little too small, but that's good. The cut's pretty racy, as well. Brevity is, after all, the soul of lingerie, even with my gut hanging over the lacy elastic.

Now an outfit. I have three clean T-shirts on hand, two white and one navy. It's cooled off because of the rain, but my blue jeans—my only long pants—aren't exactly immaculate; they haven't been washed in two weeks. I shimmy down into their rankness.

The only option for my hair is to braid it. (I don't know about the other six rooms, but room seven of the J & J happens not to be equipped with a hair drier.) I use the mottled dresser mirror to put on some makeup, reminding myself to go easy. Charcoal eyeliner halfway across the tops, maybe two thirds of the way across the bottoms, then smudged so it looks less severe. A few flicks of charcoal mascara. I decide not to use any lipstick.

Through the wall behind my bed I hear grunts and hard breathing. I dash across the room with unbecoming swiftness and stand with my back to the wall. I hear rhythmic exhalations and occasional out-of-time sniffs. The breathing's that loud, the walls are that thin. So I have to assume Ndele heard *me* banging around in the shower, doing my deeply pathetic Maria Callas impression, not to mention my . . .

Debbie!

I press my left ear against the paneling, plugging the right with my pinkie. The breathing gets hoarser and louder, then abruptly changes rhythm—to raspy, less regular, but more relaxed gasping. Below me. I crouch to get closer to the floor—to his floor, that is—cupping both hands around my ear.

I gradually understand that it couldn't be Debbie. She's too déclassé. Not his type. There is only one voice to the grunting. Ndele's alone in his room, doing push-ups or sit-ups or some such. I'm able to picture it clearly. It sounds like he's slapping the floor between push-ups. Stripped to the waist, I decide. *From which direction* is the only real question. I wonder.

Then *thwack!* and I jump. While straining to listen, I heard something bang right behind me—at my door or else outside my window. I glance toward the windows, the door, guilty for eavesdropping and scared I've been caught, trying to catch back my breath. Someone coughs. My blood's pounding up through my temples.

Nothing there. Both drapes are pulled closed. So's the door. I stealthily pad to the window and pry back the drape half an inch. A sixtyish couple wearing identical straw cowboy hats is standing alongside their big blue American car. The woman takes off her hat and presses her palm against the top of her hair as she gets in the passenger seat. The man picks his nose, slams the trunk, stares at Ndele's convertible. He's smoking a dark cigarillo.

Ndele's toilet flushes, then his shower goes on. I pull the drape closed and dash back to the wall, but I don't put my ear to it. No. I'm under control, after all. Dignity before curiosity.

Maybe I have too much dignity. Maybe that's been part of my problem the last three, four years. Because would it be too appallingly undignified to tap on door number six as soon as the shower goes off and to ask, when Ndele arrived at the door in his towel, whether he had an extra box of Band-Aids or map of North Dakota or canister of retroactive mink oil? What harm could possibly come of it?

I sit on the corner of the bed and rotate my wrist back and forth, doing my best not to picture him taking his clothes off, testing the temperature of the water before he steps in, jerking his hand back and shaking it when the backs of his fingers get scalded. And cursing. I refuse to let myself get carried away. I stay on the edge of the bed and stare at the speckled linoleum, massaging the throb in my wrist, and just listen.

Five fifty-seven, assuming we're still on Central Daylight Time. Mountain Time begins somewhere in the middle of the state, but I don't think we've reached it yet. Although, since this *is* the center of the continent, it seems as likely a place as any to draw the line. I'm definitely in the mood to change zones.

I've already done my shot and eaten a sixth of a Power Bar to tide me over till dinner. All I need now is my date.

I sit at the desk and push back my cuticles with the eraser of my complimentary pencil. There's also a pad of powder-blue notepaper. The top sheet is catching the light at an angle that reveals quick, slashing marks etched through the previous sheet—by the alleged couple from Ottawa, perhaps. When I shade in the marks with the side of the pencil, all that emerges are three indecipherable figures. SIS? I don't think so. I stare at the marks while I push back a cuticle. ZIP? Ndele is due any minute, assuming he'll show up at all.

Then voilà! As soon as I turn the pad upside down, there it is: 212. Which is what? Miles to go? Three days of riding for me, two or three hours by car . . . I look at the telephone an inch from my pinkie and put 2 and 212 together: the couple from Ottawa . . . while staying in Rugby . . . had been calling Manhattan. It seems like a clue of some sort.

I'm hungry and jumpy. My watch says six-o-one but could easily be fast. I usually have it set between five and ten minutes ahead, but right now I sense it's on time.

I put my lips against the network of soft little scabs across my left palm, doing my best to relax. Blessed, after all, are the flexible, for they shall not have a reaction. Will Also Make Minot in Morning.

I want to know what happens next.

Six-o-seven and twenty-five seconds. I sprawl on the bed, watch my old pals on the Weather Channel, peruse a brochure about Rugby. It turns out that Debbie was right: the place where the rain has deposited me is the exact geographical center of North America, at least according to the brochures fanned neatly on my desktop. The site was officially so declared in a geological survey conducted by the United States Department of the Interior. It's hard to say why, but I'm kind of impressed. Two thousand miles from the Arctic Ocean, two thousand miles from the southernmost tip of Mexico, fifteen hundred miles from the Atlantic Ocean, fifteen hundred miles from the Pacific—though it sure doesn't feel like I'm right in the center of things. More like out in the middle of nowhere.

Rugby, as it happens, is also the hometown of the world's tallest salesman. Eight feet seven inches, four hundred sixty-five pounds. Are any *non*-salesmen that big? The brochure has a picture: Cliff Thompson, right hand stuffed awkwardly into his suit-coat pocket, and bearing more than a passing resemblance to Karl Malden. What the picture fails to include is a normal-sized salesman standing beside Mr. Thompson to give some perspective. I wouldn't mind taking three or four of Cliff's inches as leg length, especially for dinner this evening.

Ndele knocks on the door, *dat da da dah dah*, leaving the familiar tattoo unresolved, at sixteen after six. It's within, I suppose, if just barely, the acceptable limits of lateness.

I tell him "Just a second" as I check myself out in the mirror. Nothing to be done, I decide.

When I open the door I'm flattered to see that he has spruced himself up. I've also forgotten (again) how tall he is. I have to tilt my face upward; moving my eyes isn't good enough: my eyebrows remain in the way, cutting him off at the throat. He's wearing black jeans and a fresh gold-and-black zebra-striped sports shirt below his freshly shaved chin. Very pretty.

"You ready?"

"You hungry?"

"I'm starving."

"Let's go."

It's misty and drizzling, but clear enough to walk fifty yards to The Hub. A hyperreal rainbow arcs through the smoky black sky above the golf course; I've never seen one focused so sharply. The sleeves of Ndele's shirt get inflated by gusts of damp wind. They settle back down against his arm, then fill up again like gold-and-black sails. The muscles inside them remind me of knotted-up cables.

"You look a lot better," he tells me.

What's *that* supposed to mean? I sidestep a puddle and thank him, then I tell him he looks a lot drier.

"Your braid," he says, miming its helical mesh with his fingers. He makes it seem seven feet long.

I reach back and touch it. Still wet. Does he like it?

A car hisses east on Route 2.

*   *   *

As we approach it, skirting each putty-colored puddle, The Hub is a typical fifties-style glass-walled diner, nondescript in every way but one. Protruding from the parking lot is a twelve-foot-high four-sided pillar of fieldstones topped with a shiny brass ball. Alongside the pillar are a pair of fifteen-foot poles with the U.S. and Canadian flags flapping at the top. Placards on the sides of the pillar say:

GEOGRAPHICAL

CENTER OF

NORTH AMERICA

RUGBY, N.D.

"Oh, *si—dos*," says Ndele. At least I think that's what he said. We both paused to read the four placards, but now he has hustled ahead and is holding The Hub's glass door open for me. The door is covered with little square decals with stars in the middle. Two larger decals inform us that the *Grand Forks Herald* and *Minot Daily News* are sold here. They also take Diners and Visa.

I squint in the fluorescent glare near the entrance. Ndele's behind me with one of his hands on my shoulder, steering me, letting me lead him. I don't want to look too conspicuous as we check out the room. There are fifteen or twenty tables, some booths, a long m-shaped counter with round, backless stools. One empty booth by the window. The others are filled with what looks to be farm families. Men with triangular sideburns spreading out below two-tone Styrofoam feed caps; others with orange or camouflage hunting caps next to their coffee cups. Women with hairstyles straight out of Mayberry next to nieces and daughters in heavy-metal fringe, frosted corkscrews. Two girls have looked up and are checking us out. Other diners either ignore us or smile up politely. There's neither a particularly friendly nor unfriendly vibe. Everyone here is just folks, including Ndele and me. Right? I hope.

A perky high school–age girl in a pink waitress uniform

appears out of nowhere beside us. Her teased, stiffened hair is three shades of blond. She raises her eyebrows and grins.

"Hey. Just the two of you?"

"Hey," I say. "Just the two of us. Do you think we could have that booth right over there?" I point to a booth by the window.

"Sure thing," she says, fanning herself with two menus. She couldn't be friendlier. Even the hairless nickel-sized mole on the side of her chin seems somehow *convivial*. It's pale grayish brown and shaped like the head of a mushroom, though the girl couldn't look much less witchlike. But I can't shake the feeling that something unconvivial is about to go down.

We follow the girl to the booth. Two pink-clad waitresses hustle to serve all the dinners. A busboy with long straight black hair clears the tables. His green beaded earrings swing from his ponytail to his jaw as he circles a table and disappears into the kitchen.

As he had at the gas station in Devil's Lake, not to mention the J & J lobby, Ndele turns heads. A ten-year-old boy in a crew cut nudges his mother and points. His mother exhales, slaps his finger, but he gawks and keeps pointing. His younger sister, too, is openly staring. There's no way Ndele has missed this.

"You're famous," I tell him.

"More like notorious these days."

These days? "I hope not," I say.

He nods blankly, waiting for me to take the seat facing the highway, then slides in across from me. His shin knocks hard against my knee, and both of us apologize. The waitress hands us menus and flashes her XXL grin. "I'll be right back with your water and the specials."

Ndele fingers the little glass salt shaker. Smiles. Brushes invisible dust from the top of the pepper, clicks the two shakers together. "You don't know who I am, do you?"

I admit I do not. I don't even think that I know what he means.

"Not that it's any big deal."

"Don't tell me. You're a famous basketball player, and all of these kids want your autograph."

He nods, looks surprised.

I suddenly get it. I'm *right*. Which explains—

"Remember that Nike commercial?" he says. He touches the gold thread *swoosh* logo on his shirt. He looks at me sideways and raises his eyebrows. "Them three ugly dudes in black hats?"

He doesn't seem overly disappointed when I tell him I don't watch much television. Seems relieved, as a matter of fact. He tells me he played two years ago for Old Dominion and now plays for the Seattle Supersonics. As the waitress comes back with two waters, Ndele informs me that he "works with" Michael Jordan, that he missed all but a week of last season because of an injury to his knee, that his team's pre-training camp begins in ten days in Seattle. "So it's do or die now for me and my knee."

It fits. His story, his car, the gawking teenagers at the Devil's Lake gas station. He probably makes two or three million dollars a year. Plus his body makes sense in this context. I watch parts of ten or twelve Bulls games a year, though I don't know the names or faces of many of the players from the other teams. But I actually think I believe him. He certainly looks like a professional athlete. At least he conforms to my limited sense of what a professional athlete might look like up close. I believe him.

"And Seattle's pretty good these days, aren't they?"

"We the world champs, baby," he says, making a fist.

"I heard that." But don't the world champions in big sports like football and baseball and basketball all wear enormous platinum diamond-studded rings? Both of his hands are right here in front of me: one still balled in a fist, the other resting flat on the table. No ring of any sort on any of his fingers. But still. I decide to forgive him for lying because he said *baby*.

I ask him, "Are *you* any good?"

"Was," he says matter-of-factly. "Was before I blew out my knee."

I ask him what happened, even though sports injuries are things I tend to have minimal sympathy for; I want to advise injured athletes (and the sportscasters who incessantly analyze them) that they have to stay focused, just take it a game at a time, try to stay healthy, win one for God or the Gipper. But for the purposes of dinner conversation with the person who's chauffeuring me to Minot, I try to keep what I understand to be a distinctly minority bias out of my voice. And he certainly doesn't *look* injured.

"Ain't no big deal," he is saying, though he gives me the impression that it is. "And it's healed." He looks at his menu and concentrates. "It's healed," he repeats, to himself.

It's darker outside than when we walked over here. The huge sheet of glass reflects the back of Ndele's head and the side of my face peeking past him. In the hazier plane beyond that are the pillar and flagpoles wetly streaked with green neon tracers. *Dos* flagpoles. Mexico apparently doesn't count.

I realize again that I'm hungry, that I could really go for some—what? It seems I've had chicken about forty-nine nights in a row. The fluorescent lighting explodes off the white plastic menu.

Ndele keeps nudging my toes with his flashy green sneakers. He doesn't apologize, but I know that he's not playing footsie. His legs are too long for the booth.

I take sips of water. Is he going to volunteer any more information about his basketball career or his injured knee? While he looks at his menu he plays with the pepper and salt shakers, rotating them in his jumbo left hand, making the glass grind and click. I can't tell whether he wants me to inquire further about his fame as a championship-caliber athlete or let a sore subject stay changed.

"What I wanna know is—" I blurt this without really deciding what to say next— "is, you know, what happened to Mexico?" I'm kicking myself, getting kicked.

Ndele looks out at the flagpoles, shading his eyes to be able to focus through the various angles and glares. There's that etching again in his stubble. It definitely looks like a rose.

Didn't guys on the New York Knicks sport similar designs on their heads—and didn't one of their players dye his hair blond and green? The guy who went out with Madonna.

Ndele has his nose pressed against the plate glass. It doesn't do much for his profile: there's no nose to speak of right now, and his chin's something less than heroic. It's the first time he's looked so . . . exposed, even with the thick cords of muscle connecting his neck to his shoulder. I feel almost guilty for making him turn, though I hadn't been trying to trick him.

"I mean, if it weren't for Mexico, this wouldn't be the 'exact geographical center,' now would it?" It's the best follow-up I can muster.

The waitress returns with her grin and her pad. Ndele turns back to his menu without having answered my question. We both order whitefish—grilled, with potatoes and zucchini. The viability of his knee or the absence of Mexico's flag doesn't come up. For a minute or two, nothing does.

As we anxiously fiddle with condiments, a family is finishing their dinner at the table across the aisle. It's actually three smaller tables pushed together, surrounded by eight or nine chairs. A ten-year-old girl who's been threatening to smack her six-year-old brother since we sat down finally makes good on her threats. And again. The brother for some reason looks right at me instead of at his parents or sisters; then he looks at Ndele and screams. The father sips coffee, impassive, while the mother makes halfhearted efforts to calm the hysterical son. No reprimand from either of them for the daughter, who sits there and gloats—then suddenly smacks him *again*.

"Manda hitted me!"

Ndele behaves as though it's not happening, but I can't keep from staring. Maybe it will give us something to talk about.

The youngest child drops his plastic action figure on the floor, climbs down to get it, gets up, bangs his head, and starts shrieking.

Our food comes. We eat. The whitefish tastes as fresh and well-prepared—oregano, lemon, white wine—as anything I've eaten in Chicago. I haven't had a good piece of fish in months, since my dad took me out for my birthday.

Ndele says something unintelligible.

"Didn't quite catch that."

He holds up a finger and chews. His hand is an abstract mahogany sculpture that reconfigures itself into a fist as he finally swallows: ". . . so even though this is gonna be my second year with the team, technically I'm still a rookie, since I didn't play a minute last season."

"Because of your knee."

His Adam's apple stays down for a while, then clambers back up. "I still don't know *for sure* if I can play on it this year, and since the last two years of my contract ain't guaranteed—" He forks some zucchini into his mouth.

"You mean, you're saying that if you can't play because of the injury, you don't get paid at all?"

"I don't make the team in October, that's it. I'm history."

"Even though you injured yourself during one of the team's practice sessions."

"That's what my agent been telling me. It was during a pre-season game."

I don't know the rules or conventions of this. I don't know what to tell him. He eats, and I eat. We swallow.

"Well, you certainly *look* like you're in cyborgian shape."

"Hey, girl. I am. Except for this one little tear in my anterior cruciate ligament." He's holding his thumb and index finger a quarter inch apart. "Doctor Luce sewed it back together with these fibers from my patellar tendon." He blinks, shakes his head. "I been ready to play for six months."

The waitress brings two plastic cuplets containing a tangerine-colored substance neither of us ordered. She tells us it comes with our dinner. There's a sprig-squirt of processed whipped cream in the center. I taste it—a tart, spongy, room-temperature cross between pudding and sherbet; funky but edible. Ndele pushes his to the side and takes up the shakers again.

"So what about you?" he says. "Think you're gonna finish your dissertation?"

I empty a packet of Equal into my coffee, snapping the last few granules from the corner. I've already told him about school in the car; now I wish I'd told him I was a salesperson, a waitress, an heiress—something that didn't require an elaborate explanation. I shrug, nod my head. It's a perfectly fair question, of course.

Ndele sips coffee and watches me. Arteries of lightning zigzag crazily off to the south; Ndele blinks twice as they ricochet off the wet glass and catch in the vertical droplets. He looks very good in this light.

"You know, now that you ask, if I don't get *my* act together big time in the next two or three months, I'm gonna get axed from my program too. Out of my job, no paychecks, no health insurance . . . "

The look on his face makes me think he's convinced I am fibbing—that I've concocted a friendly coincidence. What he says is less skeptical: "Hey, you'll get it done. I know *I'm* gonna. Workin' hard, comin' back, every day. *Every* day. Plus you look like you're in some kinda shape your own self. Nome sayin'?"

What's this, a pep talk? I love it. I semi-immodestly shrug. It especially pleases me that his normal self seems to be doing the talking.

"Gee, thanks."

He opens his hands: he's only reporting the facts.

"Yeah," I say finally, "except for this one tiny little—" I hold my fingers a quarter inch apart, just as he had. I decide it can't hurt now to break the news to him, partly because it isn't that far out of context. And I must've decided I trust him. "There's this glandular thing that just sort of decided to malfunction on me a while back. Called a reverse transcriptase, I think. Like my grades didn't transfer or something." I leave it at that for the moment.

I can see that he's puzzled. What else is he feeling? Revolted? Intrigued? Either way, I don't entirely regret what I've said, even though it isn't the can of medium leeches I'd planned to open in the middle of our romantic Hub dinner. If that is, in fact, what we're having.

Ndele holds his thumb and index finger a half inch apart, trying to follow my drift. Even eager.

"My islets of Langerhans." When Ndele leans forward I realize I'm whispering. But I can't get myself to say this much louder. "These minuscule miserable fucking little beta cells down in my—"

"Right. In your pancreas, right? Diabetes?"

I nod. I feel myself blush or get pale. I can't tell.

"My sister has that," he announces. He makes it sound almost like bragging.

"I'm sorry to hear that. How long?"

"You got diabetes and you're riding your bike to Alaska?"

"And a sorry-ass bike it is too. But your sister—"

"Least at this stage of things." He looks at me now like he's dealing with a whole different animal. I suppose that he is.

"Actually, at this stage of things I'm effortlessly averaging about eighty-five miles an hour in a hundred-thousand-dollar convertible."

"Hundred thirty."

I can't decide whether I want to change the subject just yet. "Tell me how your sister is doing."

"Francie?"

Ndele and *Francie?* "Yeah. Tell me."

"You really wanna know about Francie?"

"I do. Very much."

He sighs. "I guess she's doing okay. She works for these lawyers in Baltimore, just typing stuff. 'Briefs.'" He picks up the bottle of ketchup. "It's tough sometimes—you know. She has to go see her endocrinologist every three or four months. Then there's all that damn business with the ophthalmologist . . . "

"What kind of control is she in?"

He seesaws his hand back and forth: just so-so.

"How old is she?"

"Thirty," he says, then looks up and thinks. "Just turned thirty. It's extra hard for Francie sometimes, 'cause she got this weird metabolism. You know better than me how all that shit works."

"When was she diagnosed?"

He has to think again. "I wasn't born yet. I think she was six. Six or seven. I worry about Francie a lot. Her boyfriend is kind of an assh—he isn't too cool about the diabetes and all. You got a boyfriend?"

Awkward silence, though I feel that a bond has been established. I look out the window at the fieldstone pillar and the two—not three—flagpoles. A piggybacked trailer blasts by behind them, slinging a wake of white spray.

"Actually, no. I don't have a boyfriend."

He angles his head, looks away.

"Not at this moment," I add. Just to clarify.

The waitress arrives with the coffeepot. "Can I warm these guys up for you?"

Ndele yawns, shakes his head. He looks to see whether I want some. When I shake my head no, he tells her, "No thanks. Just the—" Nods toward the check in her hand. I hadn't spotted it soon enough.

"I'll take that," I tell her.

She hesitates, turns up the volume on her smile, flattens the check in the middle of the table. Both of us reach for it, but Ndele is quicker and his arms are much longer.

"Hey, man. C'mon . . . "

He pulls a gold MasterCard from his wallet (it really goes well with his shirt) and hands it to the waitress along with the check. She thanks him and heads toward the register.

I can't decide whether I'm pissed. Ndele is grinning and shaking his finger at me, displaying his gums above perfect white teeth.

"You promised me, man. Gave me your word."

"Word," he says, mimicking the way I complained. He puts up a finger, then stops himself from saying something else; he looks out, instead, at the flags. "Maybe they thought Mexico wasn't part of North America."

"Didn't you promise?"

"Word," says Ndele.

"In which case," I say. I gather my thoughts, try to transpose them to words. Doesn't work. "We're not really *in* the exact geographical center. Good heavens!"

"Dang," says Ndele. "That's right. Or maybe they remembered when they was doing the measuring, but *then* they forgot. Nome sayin'?"

"Or something like that. Either way, we don't really know *where* we are."

He takes in The Hub with his spooky brown eyes. "That's for damn sure."

He keeps grinning and jiving me until the waitress returns with the check and his card.

"I'm awful sorry, Mr. Rimes, but the people we call, um, they told us—they said to say 'charges denied.'" She turns to her right, toward the register. I turn and look too. A thin crew-cut gentleman—the manager, I assume—is peering suspiciously at Ndele and wiping his hands on an apron. He catches my eye, looks away.

The waitress repeats that she's sorry. It begins to seem likely that she's going to cry.

Ndele takes out his wallet again. "That's okay, that's okay." He smiles but looks dazed. "My accountant just must've forgotten to pay that damn bill." He gives her his gold Amex card.

The waitress bites her lower lip. Her cerulean eyes start to glisten.

"I'm so sorry, sir, but we only—"

"And They Don't Take American Express," I chime in.

Two tiny nods; intensified blushing and glistening.

I open my wallet and take out my Visa, overjoyed to be able to back up Ndele a little. But he's already proffered a twenty-dollar bill, confounding the waitress again.

I flash open my wallet, then close it, pretending to show her a badge. "Miss, I work for the United States Information Agency." I hold out my Visa. "If you don't accept this card, I'm afraid you'll be in violation of Article 1099, Section ABD of the 1966 Civil Rights Act."

She takes my card and hurries toward the register.

Ndele snorts derisively, but I can tell he's impressed. "Yo, man, you shouldn't a did that." He snorts again, shaking his head.

"Hey, I owe you *at least* a cheap dinner. Besides, it's a well-known fact that carjackers are chronically short of credit—" I watch as his eyes get much rounder— "but they've always got plenty of cash."

Ndele looks embarrassed, then affronted; I realize it wasn't entirely clear that I was kidding. I grin, raise my eyebrows, trying to show that I was.

Doesn't work.

As we wend our way back through the puddles, the full orange moon peeks through the tail end of storm clouds. A coyote starts howling. I gnaw on a mint-flavored toothpick.

"Is it *co*yotes or co*yotes*?" I say.

Ndele pronounces both versions to himself as he chews on his toothpick. "*Co*yotes?" He shrugs. "I don't know. Ain't it Wiley Co*yote*?"

I hold up one finger and lick it: good point.

"So you thought I was a carjacker, huh?"

"I was kidding, Ndele." His elbow keeps brushing the front of my shoulder. Unless one of us alters our course, it's gonna continue to do so. "Besides—did I say that?"

"You thought it."

"Don't you ever think things you wanna keep secret? That you realize you're wrong about later?"

He makes his hand into a pistol and points it at my nose. We keep walking and brushing each other.

"Either that or one of those El Rukn guys with a stash of stolen plastic." I try to make sure it's clear that I'm kidding. "Plus you *said* I could take you to dinner."

"We *say* a lot of things, lady," he growls, then puts the muzzle of his finger against my temple. When his left hand grabs my shoulder, it's like being snatched in a vise. "Okay, get out the fuckin' ride, muthafuck!"

I'm too startled to react for a second—to indicate that I understand *he* is kidding. He's holding my shoulder too tightly.

"You already dead, fuckin' bitch! Just you *do* it!"

He's very convincing.

"Dat what you thought I was, girl?" Lets me go.

We keep walking. To show him I wasn't afraid, I edge even closer as we stroll through the gravel and mud. Ndele has holstered his pistol; made his point. (What was his point, anyway? That he *could* be a carjacker? That my thinking he might be was racist and rude to the point of absurdity?) He's also developed a very slight old-knee-injury-style limp I hadn't noticed before. Is he putting it on to corroborate his story? Maybe it's the puddles, or the irregular stones in the gravel.

His finger comes up near my face. It isn't a gun anymore, just an extra-long finger. "If you collected last year's rookie bubble-gum cards you'd've known right away who I was."

"Yeah, and if you kept track of ABD Beckett scholars, you'd've known right away who *I* was—" I lower my voice, even though no one can hear me but him: "motherfucker." I believe it's the first time I've called someone that, even jiving around. It feels strange.

He blows himself away with his pistol, blows smoke off the end of the barrel: touché.

"Sounds like maybe both our rookie cards gonna be hot someday."

"Damn straight," I say, then can't keep from asking, "Do you really have an accountant?" I know it sounds like I'm changing the subject, but he takes it—still limping—in stride.

"Lawyer, accountant—same guy. Bobby Newman. Shithead forgets stuff like that *all* the muthafuckin' time, 'scuse my Lithuanian."

"It's excused." I'm touched that he thinks R-rated language—when he's in his serious, "normal" persona—might actually bother me. I appreciate that he doesn't presume.

And now he is singing: "'Scuse me while I kiss this guy," bashing left-handed chords on an air guitar, bending the "Purple Haze" notes from the back of his throat, complete with fierce reverb and feedback. And then, just as suddenly, stops. No gun, no guitar. Back to normal.

"You're excused, I suppose. 'Kiss this *guy?*'"

"What guy?" he says. Looks around. "You show me a guy and I'll kiss him."

We stroll. Moonlight pours down past his shoulder. I'm starting to feel slightly spacey.

"Do you know what Helen Hayes said just before she died?"

Ndele shakes his head, apparently about as surprised as I am by the question. "What she say?"

I find myself staring, entranced. Is it lust or just too little insulin? Did I dose myself with too much extra Regular? Maybe it's that little dessert treat. Ndele looks like a dessert treat. Actually, he doesn't look at all like a dessert treat. He looks like a scary Adonis. The side of his neck is particularly intriguing, just the way that it . . .

"Do *you?*" he says.

Oh. Yeah. Where was I? I concentrate hard, forcing myself to snap out of it: right. Helen Hayes. "She was ninety-three years old, long 'healthy' life, lotsa money, all this success as an actress from the time she was five—you know what she said?"

He shakes his head briskly. He's waiting. At least I now have his attention.

"She said, 'I never rode a bicycle.'"

Step. Puddle. Step. Puddlestep-puddlestep-puddlestep. I haven't felt this giddily spaced since I had coffee with David in Starbucks.

"You love riding that bike of yours, don't you?"

"I have to, you know, to maintain my sugar levels, so I actually hate it a little. But basically, yeah, I do love it. How could you tell?"

"I can tell . . . Shit. I mean, I love playing *ball*. I love playing defense. You know what I mean? Beating my man to a spot, fightin' through screens, doublin' some other guy from *just* the right angle, *stealin'* the muthafuckin' pill . . . "

He's just warming up on what's clearly a favorite topic when we come across Debbie. She's sitting outside her office on a white plastic lawn chair. Smoking a cigarette with one hand, fanning the smoke from her face with the other.

"How was dinner?" she asks, addressing Ndele.

He tilts his flat, face-down hand back and forth: only fair. I like that he doesn't use words.

"I'm sirprahzed."

I tell her that dinner was fine. We've slowed down a bit—almost stopped. I try to keep both of us moving.

"You two go to The Hub?"

"Yes, we did."

"Well, but isn't that place just the—" There's a sudden commotion behind and above her. She flinches and shrieks. "Jesus *Christ!*" A bat or a swallow rockets away from her head, wheeling above the motel and into the navy-blue sky, and then gone.

"What was *that?!*"

"That," says Ndele, "I believe, was a bat."

"Oh my God!"

"Good night, now," I tell her. Keep strolling.

"'Night," Debbie mumbles. She's checking her hairdo for bats. "Jesus Christ."

"Good night," says Ndele.

We stroll. What little light is still left in the sky is reflected back up off the puddles. Ndele looks down, doesn't comment. We step past the miniature water-filled craters in tandem, leaning against one another.

I hear Debbie shouting from back in her lawn chair. It sounds like she's singing some bad New Age country lament:

> You get e-nough to eat
> from those Hub folks, or what?

"Sure did," I shout back. Ndele and I don't break stride. I fight the temptation to groan, roll my eyes, or say something withering; it helps to know that I wouldn't come up with the perfect kiss-off for another three hours, at least. If I could mimic voices I'd do it, even though we're still within earshot. *Or wha-a-at?*

Ndele starts to say something too, then sniffs and yawns into his fist.

"Long day?"

He nods, shakes his head. Yes or no? We're arriving at door number 6. "Yo, so Penny . . ."

Cocking my thumb, I cover him with my straightened-out index finger. "What's up?"

"So what you call an Irishman you keep outside in the summertime but you take him back in in the winter?"

Say what? Is this a preamble to more jiving encouragement to finish my dissertation? Was Hendrix or Helen Hayes Irish?

"Think," says Ndele.

"I'm thinking. An Irishman that you—"

"Keep him outside in the summer, take him back in in the winter."

I have no idea. Both Beckett and Joyce *died* during winter, but—leprechauns?

"Leprechauns?"

"Nope."

I can't think what else it might be.

"You give up?"

"I give up."

He stares, makes me wait. Then, with a drunken Mick flourish, he tells me. It's: "Paddy . . . O'Furniture."

I snort. "Yup. That's what you'd call him. You know what you call a Polack in a two-hundred-dollar hat?"

He shakes his head no.

Even as I'm telling him "Pope" I realize two hundred was low. Plus my timing was awful—too quick.

He looks sort of blank, finally gets it. "But who's Helen Hayes?"

"Just some actress," I tell him. "Some pampered and fortunate woman who in ninety-three years just never quite happened to ride a bicycle. Do you know Samuel Beckett?"

"He's your writer dude, right? Waiting for something?"

"For Godot." Did I tell him that? No. I don't think so. Either way, I stand there and mumble something to the effect that I'd take *him* inside—meaning Beckett—whatever season it happened to be, but my timing's all wrong once again. What I manage to say more emphatically is, "Now *he* rode a bicycle."

Ndele's look tells me he thinks I might be crazy—or ill. And yet I keep babbling; Ndele keeps nodding and staring. Some moments later, I stop. I take some deep breaths and try smiling, fighting to regather my concentration. I'm convinced it won't do any good to simply wait for my wooziness to pass; I must *act*.

In the meantime I'm apparently giving Ndele the two-minute version of my spiel about Beckett and bicycles. He actually seems to be interested, though I know he's quite good at pretending. He doesn't even allow himself to appear all that skeptical about Beckett being my main inspiration for riding my bike to Alaska.

"Now he rode a bicycle," I repeat, but without much control over the emphasis.

"Any of his books in particular you think I should read?"

"You serious?"

"*Shit*, yeah. My coach is real big into these serious-ass types of books anyway. Passes 'em out before road trips."

"As a matter of fact—have you got a piece of paper?"

He checks his pants pockets: no paper. Pats his shirt pocket: no pen. Unlocks his door, holds it open.

Okay. What to do. The small of my back and the backs of my knees are all damp. My left heel is holding the door open.

Ndele leaves me standing like this while he goes to his dresser. He opens the middle drawer and lifts out a small leather pouch. I survey his room: the dresser, two single beds, a desk even smaller than mine is. The expensive-looking gym bag on the floor features the same white swoosh logo his shirts do. A conventional suitcase is open on one of the beds, revealing more shirts, a copy of *Sports Illustrated* with a baseball player on the cover, two more big Gatorade towels—one green and one white—and a gun. It's half covered up by the towels. Maybe it's one of those new-fangled fold-out telephones that look like small pistols. I wish. This thing is thicker than a telephone—denser and more metallic. Gunnier. When I move to the other side of the doorway to get a better angle, it definitely looks like a gun.

Ndele has picked up a pad, but he can't find a pencil or pen. He goes through the stuff on the bed, covering—on purpose?—the gun thing without missing a beat. I stand there. He eventually finds a new Bic in his duffel.

"There's this monster bookstore in Seattle," he says. Where's the gun? "They got absolutely everything." He hands me the pad and the pen.

My hand doesn't shake; I feel like I'm back in control. I write *Endgame, Three Novels, First Love*. I could go on and on, but I don't. I decide that it wasn't a gun.

"Phil Jackson goes there whenever the Bulls come in town."

"He does?" He's the coach, unless I'm mistaken. "Check these out." I hand him the pad back. "The first one's a play."

"I heard of this one. About some guy's parents living in garbage cans?"

"Right." I'm impressed. I gnaw on the pen and say, "Hamm."

"What?"

"The guy."

"Who? Puts his parents . . . ?"

"They crashed their bicycle too. They were cruising along on a tandem."

He looks at me evenly. "Gone get me these three, check 'em out."

"I'll be anxious to hear what you think." Whatever that could possibly mean. What was I babbling about? Am I scared? I don't think so. Ndele is no more dangerous to my person with a gun than he is without one. He is either absolutely lethal or thoroughly ingenuous. Or both. In no sense does this man seem harmless.

I realize I'm gnawing his pen—have been for a while from the looks of it. I dry off the end on my jeans, hand it back.

"Well, good night. And thank you again for the ride. You definitely rescued my butt."

"Then it was most definitely my pleasure."

"Okay . . ."

"And hey, thanks for dinner. Sorry 'bout that shit with the card."

"Thanks for letting me *take* you to dinner."

He uses his Ed McMahon voice to tell me, "He-e-ey, thank you for the thank you."

"So I'll see you again—when? Around eight o'clock?"

"Eight sharp." He makes two fists in front of his chin and starts squinting, pretending he's steering through rain. "Must Make Minot. But I buy the breakfast. That fair?"

"You got it."

He puts out his hand and I take it. He places his left hand over the top of my right.

"Good night, Ndele."

"Good night, almost-a-professor Penelope Culligan. I wish you sweet dreams."

I bring up my left hand to cover the other three. "I wish the same to you, Mr. Rimes."

We shake our four hands up and down a few times. Then it's over. We're still holding on, but it's over.

I let him let go of me. He looks strangely solemn, but I don't know what to tell him. I try to look wicked but demure. I don't know what he wants, or what I want. Is it possible to be coy with oneself? What would be the point, after all? Not that I doubt for a second that I'm capable of deceiving myself . . .

I start walking backward the five or six steps to my door. The last three steps I take sideways. I make it; I do not fall over. What would be the point, after all? I want to put my hand under this young man's loose, silky, boisterous clothes and move it around just a little. Both my hands, actually. But this is not going to happen.

As I dig the key out of my pocket, I bring up some lint and a penny. I slide the dark penny back into my pocket and unlock the door, push it open.

From the opposite end of what looks like a hundred-foot-long titanium corridor, Ndele salutes me. I wave with two fingers.

Good night.

I lie on my back on the bed, massaging my temple and cheek with the corduroy spread. *Raindogs* on the headphones, not loud. It's probably the five- or six-hundredth time I've listened to it all the way through. My opinion right now is that there's way too much growling and grouchiness, although "Downtown Train" might still be my all-time fave rock song. Maybe this is the time I get sick of it once and for all.

Headline News glimmers from the set on the dresser. The sports is about to begin. I can almost hear the stupid fanfare, and I'm suddenly . . . interested. A player slides into home plate.

My headboard vibrates minutely: a truck hitting gravel as it barrels through Rugby. I can also imagine Ndele tapping on the other side of the wall, unable to resist some temptation.

And then: *oooo*. And then: *ow!* What the heck? Something is nipping my crotch. It feels like I've impetuously grown a new tooth, a miniature rogue bicuspid on the lower-right side of my labia. My body's done *much* stranger things . . .

I unzip my jeans, push them down a few inches, make sure the drapes are drawn all the way, then reach down as far as I can, feel around down by the . . . *Ow!*

I tilt up my pelvis to get a better angle. Whatever is nipping me is pretty far back, on the right. Another sharp pinch as I reach farther back, feel around; and then beyond that, back there inside the elastic . . . Ah. Okay. Got it. I fish out a small slip of paper. One of the corners is wrinkled, producing three separate hazardous edges.

My panties, I'm pleased to discover, were INSPECTED BY CYNTHIA. At least someone did. But what flaw could panties have? Seams not symmetrical? Only one leg hole? What about sharply creased inspected-by fortunes wedged in the crotch? Someone should inspect them for *that*.

It's just what I needed, of course: paper cuts on my labia, the ultimate feminist academic tribulation.

Another tinny bang from Ndele's room. I take off the headphones. It sounded like he—or someone—tossed a watch or a can against the wall. What's going on over there?

Is it possible Ndele doesn't have a girlfriend? That he's never had sex? That he's gay? People talked about Magic Johnson and Isiah Thomas . . .

I lie back again and massage both my temples. When a truck buzzes by on Route 2, it sounds like it's five feet away.

Seven years.

It's not that I want or expect to feel virginal; it's just that I no longer trust either my physical or emotional impulses. My inclinations since David have been so consistently negative or skeptical, often just blank, though sometimes I catch myself thinking *just who are you trying to kid?* That I'm repulsed by the idea of sexual contact because I associate it with David's mutilation—this is pretty much Jane's opinion, as well as Tracy Fox's, the psychologist I was seeing for the three years after the accident. Fox also persuaded me to admit that the attentions of other men made me feel less than loyal to David. The attentions of women did not.

Aside from my scrapes with Lee Marvin, the closest call I've had probably came with Billy McIntyre. He entered the program two years after I did and got his Ph.D. last May, so of course I was insanely jealous, although that's not the reason we didn't sleep together. Billy's a sweet, skinny, hyperactive, wonderful guy, and he has the sort of teeth that seem to snaggle so prolifically along the jawlines of very smart men.

Meaning what? His teeth weren't straight, he didn't have much of a chin, and he reeked of tobacco and three-day-old perspiration; whereas my pancreas didn't work, I had puncture marks all over my body, my hair was beige, I was fifteen or twenty pounds overweight. Neither of us dressed very fashionably. So I figured we were just about even. The point is—could I get any more hypocritical? If physical splendor and hygiene and health were to remain the principal criteria, what chance do I have in this world?

Billy's comp class met in room 201 of Stevenson Hall and mine met in room 205, right next door. I could hear him hassling students who arrived late, or without their assignments. "Unacceptable!" he'd tell them. "Imagine your tuition money, thick piles of green and gray twenties and hundreds, being torn into expensive confetti and flushed down the toilet, spinning wetly and clockwise right out of your life!" My own students would groan or cackle derisively, but I tended to appreciate Billy's proclivity for striking imagery. After class I would walk with him to the library while he chain-smoked Merit Ultra Lights and sarcastically characterized the syntactical competence of UIC freshmen, the mayor, the editor of *The Atlantic*, or waxed exegetical about *Play* or part one of *Molloy* or *Catastrophe*, often within the same sentence. It always impressed me that he never pretended not to be trying to impress me. "You *are* gorgeous today," he would tell me. When I showed him a précis of my latest hypothesis, he'd arrive the next morning with three or four single-spaced pages of lucid—even quite plagiarizable—commentary. Maybe he simply felt sorry for me. He talked very fast and walked very slowly—sideways a lot of the time—exhaling long plumes of smoke. He was almost as tall as Ndele, though his aggregate mass was distributed quite a bit differently. His most overt flirtation consisted of the sentence "Anyone who has read this far will be taken to dinner at Le Nomads and will receive a fifteen-minute hand job," which he had inserted into page 226 of his 280-page dissertation. No member of his committee claimed either part of the prize, although I've never been

exactly sure what that proved. Personally, I read every word of
the copy he gave me (on eight-cents-a-page, three-hole paper
in a snazzy red binder for extra-easy reading) and found it
amazingly good—but wasn't ever tempted to claim the prize,
either. When I asked Billy about the sentence, he insisted on
making good on the offer, including my fifteen minutes of
"fame," as he called it. I reminded him that I wasn't a member
of his committee. "Be that as it may," he said, coughing and
lighting a Merit. I demurred: a friend had arrived from St.
Louis; he'd be staying with me for two weeks; we were more
than just friends, I implied. I was fairly well practiced at such
insinuations, having honed my skills in the face of Lee's fre-
quent proposals.

I did persuade Billy to let me take him to dinner at Tommy
Nevin's to celebrate his degree. Hand job or no, Le Nomads
would have cost him about two months' salary, a salary he was
about to forfeit anyway, having been impertinent enough to
actually finish his course work and write his dissertation; he'd
thus lost his eligibility for an assistantship and entered the job
market—a white male Ph.D. in literature. Good luck. He had
something like seventeen interviews at last December's MLA
convention but got kooshed in the end every time—a pattern
that both of us knew would continue.

I found Billy charming and brilliant, but I didn't want to
have sex with him. At all. And it wasn't just that he wasn't my
Saint. The bottom line was that nothing ever clicked or
hummed when I walked alongside him. I didn't have day-
dreams about him. He didn't come up in my conversations
with other people. He always wore a stylish navy-blue blazer
with gold-plated buttons—thoroughly incongruous on a man
who changed clothes about three times a month.

Then there was my beautiful student, Rawley Richley. I'd
be much more convinced I'd made a "looksist" decision about
Billy were it not for my forbearance concerning Mr. Richley.

Rawley had gone to Evanston Township High School and
taken honors English courses; he could write up a storm,
especially compared to the rest of my class, and he knew it.

He'd read his Joan Didion and Oliver Sacks and Lewis Thomas; and so, there was that. He was nineteen and I was twenty-six; the gap didn't *seem* obscenely indecorous. He twice rode his bike to my office; we talked about bicycles, about trips to Peru and Nepal he had taken. He showed me his pearl-handled Allen wrench; the hairs on his fingers were blond. Even his muscles were blond. I was thrilled every time I saw him sitting in front of me. And I was tempted—sorely, sorely—when he asked me if I wanted to ride down to Starved Rock with him. I told him I had to grade papers that weekend; to prove it I held up a stack of them. But I wanted him to know that I wanted to go on a trip with him too. He shrugged and said, "Some other time." I was really quite taken with him. He turned and waved back—caught me watching, half my head out the door—as he wheeled his blue bike toward the elevator. That he never got pushy about it intensified my interest by an order of magnitude. Just seeing his name on my roster always perked me right up. Richley, Rawley. Around the middle of April he began to arrive in class wearing a frayed maroon T-shirt and unit-revealing bike shorts, and he made it quite clear he was interested (if I was) whenever we talked after class. I demurred.

So what was I? "Good"? I was probably scared. Not of losing my job or breaking some unwritten rule about teachers riding bikes with their students. His blond, robust healthiness intimidated the hell out of me, I think. I don't know. If only Billy had bathed or quit smoking or done a few push-ups, or offered to go on a road trip . . .

I've almost forgotten my lone date with Theodore H. V. Gufzys, the quasi-notorious Slavic Jewish New Yeatsian—"the Beav," as we referred to him around the department the semester he was in residence. One ferociously intelligent guy, and a guy who can write. He took me to see *Last of the Mohicans*, paid for the taxi back to my apartment, invited himself up for coffee, mumbled about C. Day Lewis while inviting himself into my study, which is also my bedroom, informing me that he "of course *must* inspect" my books. We somehow wound up sitting side by side on my bed, paging through *his* two. The Beav smoked a cigarette, further fouling the atmosphere, as he inscribed my paperback copy of *A Sligo Intensity*: "Penelope, You ask me"—I hadn't—"who is the future. I say that *you* are. Compose it. Compose yourself." Signed it "Theo" and dated it, all this with violent green splashes and embellishments from his black Mont Blanc pen. I thanked him. I coughed. I said I was honored—I was. I gave him a shot glass with paper clips in it to use as an ashtray. He thanked me and asked if he could kiss me. Said, "I've not brought a condom, my dear." Somehow, his pants were unbuttoned. I stood up. I couldn't stop coughing. The Beav stood up too, asking again for "one kiss." After eight or ten seconds of squirmingly fended-off clutching caresses and exactly one one-way kiss—I stupidly gave him permission with the firm proviso that once it was over he'd pull up his pants—he groaned, spun around, and ejaculated onto my key-pad. It's an evening I've repressed with some energy. Unfortunately, neither the semen nor the critical acumen ever completely rubbed off. The cigarette ashes are still in the shot glass, mostly at the bottom by now, having sifted their way through the clips.

I've never been very good at figuring out how to respond to the wanted attentions I do get, or to act on my own lustful impulses. E.g., right now. I want to make love with Ndele, I think, but I'm afraid the feeling might not be mutual. I'm afraid of some other things too. I'm as good as a virgin as far as my experience is concerned: fourteen acts of lovemaking followed by seven years of abstinence. So I may be about as horny as a girl gets to be. It's not as though I'll turn inside out and start foaming at the crotch if I don't get an erect penis inserted into my vagina in the next fifteen seconds. The feeling is more all over, totally proceptive from my baby toes' tips to my scalp, with various points of heightened receptivity in between. My nipples, for example, ever since we got caught in that downpour. Even my wounds feel responsive. And each of these pulsing, localized aches is definitely specific to Ndele. It's *his* legs I want to see naked, his fingers I want to feel soothing my wounds. I'm also disinterestedly curious about what it would feel like to run my mouth over whatever parts of him (if any) that happen to be experiencing heightened receptivity.

What I want right now is to go over and knock on his door and reintroduce myself, since he might just need More Information. *Well, hello there again. 'Member me? The woman whose butt you were rescuing? Um . . .* I've already decided thirty-four times to get up and go do it. The farthest I've made it is turning on my side and propping my head up, causing my elbow to press against the corduroy bedspread. I could go over and show him the pattern that's etched on my skin.

I think I'm too used to having to monitor and make adjustments to my various electrochemical apparati to trust what they're trying to tell me. I had a great chance and I blew it.

I massage my left socket and cheekbone. My eyeball rotates and clicks as I crush six or seven more capillaries.

Good.

I hear a noise—creaking. A suspicious noise actually, but also a noise that I recognize. It's door number six swinging open. And footsteps.

I dash to the bathroom and gargle, arrange my beige hair. Ndele was apparently lying on *his* bed on the same wavelength I was, and this turns me on something fierce.

As I wait for his knock, I use the sleeve of my T-shirt to de-slick the tip of my nose, then spit out the last of my blue Listerine in the sink. A car starts up outside my window. I spit one more time, then dash to the window and pull back the drape. A black Mercedes convertible is bumping sleekly through the puddles and gravel. Ndele? The space where he'd parked is now empty. I can even make out the side of his big D-shaped head. He doesn't look back as he pulls from the lot and goes west.

I draw a short line through my breath on the glass. Then another. An X. A fly bounces into the pane, buzzes off. The shriveled-up husk of another fly lies overturned on the sill. Spider fare.

I move to the center of the room and stare at my bike. The stumps, all the miles I've put on it, the way I crashed, the idea of antelope lingerie. The idea of antelope, period. It seems like I crashed about six or eight weeks ago. Longer. I sort of have to laugh about this.

I sit on the side of the bed and breathe in and out. Tilt back my head and try to pretend I don't care. Try to pretend I'm relieved. The guy had a gun, after all. Stolen car, stolen credit cards, gun. I could've been killed if he'd stayed.

But that's not what's happened. I'm safe. I still have my bike, my panniers, my money, my Visa, my works. Ndele Rimes knows that. He has met with flying colors his responsibility to deliver me from roadside peril, causing his leather upholstery to be stained in the process. He's lost several hours of driving time. He's flirted with me, and I've flirted back. So we're square. I've covered my allotment of miles for almost two days, so I'm even ahead of the game.

I yank the corduroy bedspread up past my chin. I try to get in underneath it, but I'm holding it down with my weight. The spread reeks of cigarettes, sex, disinfectant . . .

I'm shivering. Floaters go by when I blink: worms and syringes and rings. I also can smell human shit. Hundreds of people have fucked and drooled and shat in this room! Into this bedspread! Exactly what the fuck does sex smell like anyway? All of this, everyone, fucking!

I try not to breathe anymore to keep out the horrible odors and suddenly find myself screaming. Coughing and shrieking. Oh Jesus. A shriek rises up, then gets caught in the back of my throat and just sticks there.

I sob for a while, catch my breath. I don't want to deal with policemen or nurses or Debbie. I wouldn't be able to. I wouldn't know where to begin.

I'd like to be dead. I'd take dead right now in a second. To be able to just let that happen, I'd happily turn over everything. Anything. Any last fucking thing I have.

In a second.

I unfold my Amtrak schedule, look up the times for the Empire Builder. The next westbound train stops in Rugby at 8:32 in the morning; next eastbound at 9:47 at night. I must've just missed it—although maybe it's late. Since most Amtrak trains run behind schedule, there's still a good chance I could make it.

I'll have to call a cab to get my bike and the rest of my gear to the station. And I may have to pick up a cardboard box big enough to fit the bike into, since I distinctly remember hearing somewhere that you can't transport a bike on Amtrak unless it's packed in a box. Which means I'll have to take it apart. Maybe Paris West can break it down for me. For that matter, maybe he can straighten my wheel, or at least get it sufficiently unwarped to transport me to Minot. Maybe Paris could unwarp *me* a rotation or two while he's at it. Assuming he's back from Bismarck, of course. Assuming he's not flown to Paris. Maybe I should head back to the Grand Forks International Airport, hand them my Visa, and get on the next flight connecting with Paris.

Ow! Shit. Goddamn it. Strands of my hair are snagged in some splintered-off wood grain. I try to unsnag them, gingerly tugging from three different angles, but I finally grab them down near my scalp and yank them away from the headboard.

I prop up my neck on a pillow. Paris, after all, is the place

Samuel Beckett is buried . . . It's only 10:10. Should I call the police to see if there's a price on Ndele's big head? Since I didn't get the ride out to Minot he promised, I might be eligible for a large enough reward—for information leading to his capture and conviction—to pay off my Visa. Because that's what my balance must be as of now: about seven pieces of silver.

He may have told Debbie where he was going, or why he was leaving, when he turned in his key, but I'm certainly not gonna ask her. I blame her whoroics, in fact, for making him feel so uncomfortable. A female Norman Bates in her little motel on the prairie, sufficiently pathological to pull any stunt I could imagine. Maybe she persuaded him to go kill a spider in her bathtub at home, or check out her collection of too-tight Unalaskan T-shirts. I wouldn't mind having one that said UNALASKA myself about now. I'd like to unalaska my life.

I take out the Callas CD and look at my face in its silvery blank side, the side that contains her sad voice. But where is her voice now, exactly? I imagine CD's as hollow magnesium needles spun out centripetally, like single-serving pizzas, into ultrathin mirrors with pinkie-sized holes in the middle—through which I can now see the top of my bent left knee. I can see only two of the dark maroon scabs; the rest are beyond the horizon, over my knee, toward my shin.

I stare at my not sightly features. From this close up I look rather fish-eyed and gray. Am I really that puffy and pocky? Good Lord. I tilt the disc back and look at my hair. In some lights it can accurately be described as bronze-colored. My father has a snapshot of me with a mustache and devil's goatee drawn above my lips and onto my chin; the picture was taken a few months after I came home from the hospital, and my hair was still flaxen and white. My first driver's license said blond; the current one doesn't force me to declare, since there's a color photo of my head cut into the shape of the state of Illinois, this to go with a holograph of the Lincoln's head side of a penny embossed over my birth date, so I never forget who I am. Lee Xavier Marvin once, after downing three snifters of grappa, referred to it as my gilded locks. In this light, however, even though I shampooed it five hours ago and used my fancy Body Shop seaweed conditioner, it looks distinctly beige. There's also a strip of what appears to be spinach or lettuce—seaweed perhaps?—adhering to my top-left incisor. Attractive! I can only hope that Ndele was too tall to spot it. My complexion looks ten years more crinkled and leathery than it did in the (admittedly underlit) bathroom mirror just before dinner. The pores on my nose are medium-sized craters, with what looks like an active volcano where my nostril connects with my cheek. How *alluring*, especially with that soupçon of green stuff. Who was I kidding with those self-aggrandizing appraisals? Not Ndele, apparently. Nope.

I turn the disc over. Instead of a spread-out version of one of the hollow and stainlessly vicious steel needles that puncture and scar and humiliate me while saving my life every morning and evening and pretty soon every morning noon and night, there *I* am, just me, along with some red-and-black ink: the EMI logo with a naked angel of uncertain gender lounging serenely on its own little lily pad of a long-playing record. There's also a lot of small numbers and extremely fine print informing me in no uncertain terms who owns what and since when and what sorts of things are prohibited. *Kein Verleih! Vervielfaltigung, Vermietung, Auffuhrung, Sendung!* Such a sonorous language, this Deutsch. The tone's so humane and seductive. Maybe that's been my problem: I've been living my whole life in plain old American English, a tongue well designed to languish alone but in love by . . .

When I focus three inches into the mirror, beyond the miniature letters and pictures, there I am again, languishing. Gah! With my goofy face and rheumy blue eyes staring me down. Who *wouldn't* steal away at the first opportunity?

I would.

I turn the disc sideways and hold it perpendicular to my nose, nestling it between the bridge and my forehead. So now it's a circle—or a spherical plane—turned into a bisecting line. I'm trying to make the needle and what's in the mirror be gone. I close one eye, then the other; the disc and my fingers shift back and forth. In roughly this manner does my ground-breaking, job-enabling dissertation not quite get written.

Am *I* gone? Is this room, this no-tell, sucked-dry-by-spiders motel in the middle, or at least on the outskirts, of the geographical center of North America, at least of its two whitest, northernmost countries—still here? And, if so, is *that* where I am?

I wonder this, therefore I'm here. On the local to nowhere, as Billy McIntyre used to say, referring to his job prospects. I can see my left palm in the wedge of the disc, so I'm forced to conclude I am here, on this bed, bisecting my tangential schnoz. I close one eye, then the other, dividing the room into two mirrored halves with a hole in the left side, the right side, the left . . . When I rub the silvery music-laden side with the sensitive pad of my pinkie, I can hear Ms. Callas sing Gounod's "Waltz Song," I think; I don't have the jewel box with the liner notes, so I'm seldom sure which track I'm hearing.

I do know I hate and love the fact that she had to diet almost constantly—starving herself, just about—in order to even approximate the look she wanted. She was a natural beauty all along, but she never understood that. She was already Maria Callas, but she wanted to be Audrey Hepburn. Go figure. Her anxiety about how much she weighed drove her almost insane. You can hear all that in her voice, in every little tone change and quaver. My warped brain has also decided it's terribly consequential that these arias are sung by a dead woman, a dead woman who when she was alive slept with Aristotle Onassis, who slept with Jackie Kennedy, who slept with one of the first dead guys I ever had a crush on, who slept with . . .

I grab my personal GEOGRAPHICAL CENTER OF NORTH AMERICA ashtray and fire it against the far wall, the wall with the windows. It does not hit a window. It bounces and clanks on the floor. I didn't hear it shatter, but I don't go to check. I set my alarm clock for seven.

I'm okay. I'll be ready. The trick in this situation is not to get bitter. Stay focused. Move on. Just get my bike fixed and keep going.

Am I okay? I guess I'm a little surprised by how disappointed I feel. How humiliated. But at least I'm out of danger. Even so, I thought that it might've been interesting.

Traffic goes by on Route 2. Usually I can tell in which direction it's headed from the hum and whoosh as it approaches, slips past. Not tonight.

A car slows down on the gravel lot outside my room. It splashes through five or six puddles, then stops. It crunches through more of the gravel, then stops. The engine shuts off. A car door swings open, clicks shut. A few seconds later I hear the door of Ndele's room open and close, then somebody moving around over there.

I bounce off my bed to the window, peek past the side of the drape. This is getting to be a regular little motif—woman pulls back drape, expecting to find . . . —but this time I'm shaking. Ndele's car is parked where it had been, not five feet away, except that he's backed it in. Has he? Who else could've parked it? The three-quarter peace sign on the grill seems like a numinous signal, something straight out of Nietzsche or Kiefer. It also seems cruel, or unholy. I don't really know *what* to make of it. Maybe he's returned and backed in to facilitate the loading of a body he's stashed in his room, someone he's killed and chopped up, wrapped in garbage pail liners. Anselm Kiefer, Mercedes? A peace sign and Nietzsche? Does that even make sense? Maybe Ndele's come back to stash *my* body into his trunk. Or maybe he's *un*loading something . . .

I let go of the drape and just stand here. I have to monitor each stupid, achy breath to avoid hyperventilating. Is this how it feels to be drowning? I only can hope I'm succeeding. It's not a good time to pass out.

Has Ndele forgotten something? I can't for the life of me decode this fresh text. But I try. I peek out the window again. Penelope Culligan, All But Detective. There are fans of gray mud behind both of the wheels I can see: left front, left rear. Meaning what? As I stare at the rain beaded up on the hood, I start to go more or less blank.

*   *   *

I find myself standing outside room number six, convinced that Ndele is in there. Two lights are on in his window. His car's right behind me. He's in there.

I stand in front of his door for what feels like a very long time. The red paint has bubbled and chipped near the bottom, and one of the tacks holding down the brass six needs to be hammered again; I wish I could hammer it now. Pink light leaks out near my toes.

I knock. My knuckles are itchy and throbbing, on fire, though my fist barely touches the door. I hope I don't pee in my pants. I try to push down the loose little tack with my thumb.

The drape gets pulled aside and Ndele looks out the window. When he sees me, he raises his eyebrows. I wave. He holds up one finger and grins, disappears.

He is gone for a suspiciously long time. Thirty seconds? Two minutes? I can't decide whether to knock again or stand here and wait like a doofus.

When he finally opens the door, he looks sort of happy to see me.

"Yo, Penny. What's up?"

"I'm sorry to—it's just that, I thought . . . " Standing before the closed door, I'd come up with a dozen of what I thought were convincing excuses for knocking, but I don't recall *one* at the moment. I try to look Abashed But Demure while I think.

Ndele saves me by saying, "I thought you went to bed." He squints, checks his watch. "Shit, 'bout an hour ago."

"I thought you *left*," I blurt out. My attempt at an ameliorating follow-up doesn't cut it, but I plow staunchly onward. No choice. "I mean, I saw you drive off, so I figured—"

"Left?" He smiles, but it's clear he's offended. "Now ain't that a bitch. I just went into town, man, to pick up some munchies and beer. C'mon in."

"Where's town?"

He points past my head. "Half a mile up that road. I mean, 'left'?"

"I saw you pull out. Then you were gone, and . . . " Oh God.

"Ain't a lot open in the Geographical Center of North America, I'm afraid." Sweet tinge of beer on his breath. "C'mon in," he repeats.

"I really . . . " I've already pushed this demure thing too far. I'm totally out of my mind. "It's so late."

Now he looks genuinely offended. As who wouldn't be? I finally go in. The way the situation keeps changing has thrown me way off, so I hardly feel confident about my decisions or the feelings I'm trying to base them on. He pushes the door closed behind me.

The TV is on: CNN. Four silver cans from a six-pack of Coors on the bed. Pistol, of course, not in evidence.

He proffers a Coors and I take it.

"All they had."

"Oh."

I pop the sharp tab, take a sip. He pops open another one for himself.

"First you think I'm a carjacker, then you think I'd just drive off and leave you." He's shaking his head. I can't blame him.

"Actually, I really didn't think you'd exactly—"

"Yo, Penny, that's a direct quote." He manages to look extremely menacing as he puts his huge hand on my arm. Coors sweet and cool on his breath. Is he drunk?

"You're bustin' a Barkley on me now, huh? Sayin' you were misquoted in your own fuckin' autobiography?"

"Um . . . " I'm amazed to discover him holding my hand.

"What your man Sam gotta say about that?"

"I think you'd be surprised. We'd probably both be surprised by what Sam *or* this Barkley guy . . . "

"Your man Sam got an opinion on misquoting yourself?" He pulls up my hand and kisses the wounds on my palm. His attitude is very *there, there.* Nothing too hot or lascivious. Still.

"I don't know."

"What's your dissertation got to say on that subject?" He grazes the side of my wrist with his sandpaper chin.

"Let me think." I kiss him on the mouth, letting my tongue brush his thick lower lip.

"That's right—you think."

"Hmm ... " I kiss him again and pull back. "Actually, nothing."

He touches my cheek with his lips, then lightly brushes my lips. The slower he goes now, the faster I want things to happen.

"Nothing?" he says.

I kiss him. He kisses me back. His lips are so tasty. Our tongues ...

He pulls back his head and we look at each other. I'm up on my toes and Ndele is holding my shoulders. His teeth are so white and enormous.

"Nothing?" he says.

"Not one thing ... " I press my cheek, then my chin, against his hard chest. ". . . not one word . . . not nothing."

Still standing up, in the light from a CNN business report, we begin to undress one another. I can't reach high enough to pull off his shirt, so Ndele takes care of it for me. I hold up my arms while he pulls off my T-shirt. He drops it. We look at each other. He yanks down his little white underpants, dances sideways a little, steps out of them. Jesus. I take off my own jeans and panties, exposing my ridiculous tan, my proportions . . . Ndele's proportions are startling.

We kiss standing still. His cock bounces against my ribs, and I shiver. I touch it. It's heavy and warm and enormous. When my legs start to tremble and buckle, Ndele holds me up by my nipples. I'm mortified by all of my cooing, my shudders, my awful and general noisiness. Oh . . .

I run my forearms back and forth across his wide chest. I've never seen anything like it: brutally sinewy, no hair except for a few glossy curlicues between two slabs of muscle. I rub both my hands up and down, digging in, trying not to scratch him too much. I can't help it.

He puts me facedown on the bed, holds me like that while he nuzzles my buttocks and squeezes the backs of my thighs. His yellow bedspread smells like cigarettes, sweat. I don't care. And now things are happening fast. I don't think I'm scared, but I'd rather be facing him. Much. To be able to see what he's doing, to watch it all happen. To touch him. I want things to happen more slowly.

He's licking the backs of my knees, running his teeth up and down while squeezing my ass with his hands; he's crushing the muscles together, lifting me up off the bed, short whiskers burning my skin. I want to turn over, but I like how he's holding me down. What should I do with my hands?

Things bounce and clatter as he kneels behind me. A beer can. A bedspring. A belt. Where's the gun?

Bracing myself against the wall, with Ndele behind me, I picture my room through the wall: my maps, my wet clothes, my bike leaning forward . . .

When I tell him I want to turn over, he pauses, then lets me. I grab him by his wrist and his leg and guide him down onto his back, on the floor.

"Lemme just slide on a jimmy."

I gingerly ease myself onto him. It hurts and it hurts and it doesn't.

"Lemme just get a jimmy!"

As I lower and turn myself onto him, down, can't go down, I'm shivering, can't catch my breath, but whoa baby. Oh Jesus! I can't close my eyes. I can't stop.

"Jesus, girl! Penny! You sure?"

He rolls on his side and maneuvers me onto the floor on my back. Gets on top. Holds my arms over my head. He slides his wet teeth across my hipbone and ribs and my pits. Bites my nipples—too hard and then even harder, but not too hard, either. Then harder. I need for these things to keep happening, to not ever stop, to never stop happening, Christ! . . .

He angles himself above me, forcing back my right leg with his chest. My kneecap is grazing my cheek—a position I've never been in. But it works. He lets my arms go while he guides himself in, oh good *God*, then grabs them again and yanks them back over my head. In the meantime he jams himself into me, hard. He already has this *momentum* that sears me and tears me—I really don't think I can take it or ever allow it to stop.

I picture the rest of our lives: a curly-haired daughter, gray stucco bungalow along the Pacific, dark bedroom furniture, an awkward parent-teacher conference in her second-grade classroom, at night, her rounded and excellent cursive on lined paper tacked to the long strip of cork above a minty-green chalkboard. My kneecap is brushing my shoulder. I'm broken, torn open, can't budge. His rhythm has three little unholy hitches: it burns, jags, and jams me all up. My leg is beginning to cramp but I cannot, could never, resist him. Noises escape from the back of my throat I never approved of or planned and I'm telling him secrets and crying as he keeps banging into my bladder: over and over and over and over and over. My pussy convulses against him, all over him, over . . .

He releases my leg, changes angles, pushes my other leg all the way back, continues to fuck me like that. He holds me down hard on the floor and he fucks me. I'm helplessly licking my own bony shin, gasping and shivering, laughing almost, trying to tell him what good and how terribly good he is doing me, all this without using words. I do not have words. I don't have the strength or the words.

Later we lie perpendicular to one another, face-up on wrinkled linoleum, sweating and catching our breath. I'm having these sweet little spasms, then every few seconds a big one. I can't predict when they'll come next, or where. My upper lip and my eyelids are trembling. The side of Ndele's forehead presses against my left hip. His torso is twitching and heaving. He coughs. My right knee is up in the air, avoiding the wet spot beneath my right calf. A clump of warm shirt and some undies digs into my shoulder blade, so I shift my head sideways and use the bunched clothes as a pillow. The flutters won't stop in my cunt.

Ndele reaches up, grabs my hand. Just the fingers. His left hand, my left hand. Mmm. We lie here like this without talking. I can't make a fist, but my fingers slide over his thumb.

He says, "Hey."

I wake up alone in one of his beds: that much I know right away. It's raining again, but it's light out. In spite of the rain, a couple of finches are cheeping.

He's gone. I'm much more surprised to discover that I'm naked. I reach down to double-check. Yes. Eyes two-thirds closed, I peer around the room, get my bearings. The suitcase and gym bag are gone. He's left me again, but I still have my bike and my Visa. Much beyond that I'm really too cozy and sleepy to form a considered opinion. He is gone gone gone gone and gone.

I decide there's no reason to panic. The sheet and thin blanket come up to my chin, and it's snuggly. I *never* feel this way in the summer—cozy and groggy and tender, like I've slept for twelve hours. A pearly and buzzed sort of tender.

When I got up to pee last night it was dark and Ndele was sleeping beside me. We had not kissed good night. We were both on the single bed, this one, the one without his suitcase and bag on it. I remember the fucking, then peeing, then nothing. I'd looked for the gun, hadn't found it. I also decided that it simply could not be the last time Ndele and I would make love—or he fucked me—like that. I didn't think about my glomeruli, about how much protein there might be in my urine, as I usually do while I pee; I concentrated instead on the semen oozing out of me, like an octuple wad of shampoo. I also nunnishly reminded myself that I don't normally have sex with a person the first evening we spend together. Only the last.

A door opens near me. I hear water running. Not rain. Ndele strolls out of the bathroom; he's brushing his teeth. He has on a blue-and-white sleeveless sweatshirt and narrow black shorts. His limbs are so splendid I can't be surprised he is here. His face makes me even less logical.

"Get outta that bed with your bad self," he tells me through blue toothpaste bubbles. "S'already a quarter to nine!"

"Good morning," I tell him. My voice is still tiny. I yawn and stretch involuntarily. I cannot contain—I'm so happy and sleepy and tenderized. I must've been dreaming before.

He goes back in the bathroom and spits.

A different blond waitress brings us our pancakes. Debbie sits three booths away, drinking coffee with another large woman, quasi-surreptitiously spying. I wave. She puts out her cigarette, looks at her friend, and waves back.

I pour on the syrup, smear a half pat of butter onto each of my four perfect buttermilks. Yum. Ndele is bopping his head up and down, like he's hearing a tune on invisible headphones. He insists for the eighth or tenth time that he's paying for breakfast. I nod. He looks pretty proud of himself as he sips from his small glass of OJ.

A North Dakota babe—she looks like our waitress's dewy kid sister—sashays past our booth, making sad-happy cow eyes in Ndele's direction. But even though she's gorgeous and is wearing antique skintight denim cut off above the ends of the pockets and frayed beyond the point of meaningful ass coverage, she appears to not even have registered. Ndele's with me now, it seems, at least till we make it to Minot.

We stop at a cash station eighty yards west of The Hub. It's attached to the side of the First Rugby Bank. There are two other cars in the lot—both red Le Sabres, parked side by side like two old valentines. One plate says SPLITM. The other's a B plate, followed by five random numbers.

Ndele inserts a platinum MasterCard into the slot, presses four buttons: the three, then the six, then two others. "Goddamn Newman better've paid *this* fuckin' bill . . . "

Alongside the bank is R.J. Hartley's Rugby John Deere, with several neat rows of John Deere–green threshers and sowers and reapers arrayed in the sunshine. A few of the tractors have six-foot-high tires, radio antennas, and glass-enclosed cabs with two seats. You'd reap what you'd sown in considerable opulence in one of these bubbies. Yes, sir.

As Ndele is pressing more buttons, I notice three mud spots on the side-view mirror, and beyond them a huge orange water tower. RUGBY spelled backward is nothing, unless . . . So but why not stay here, in this radically central location? Wouldn't something like *that* work? Location location location . . .

A sudden explosion of curses. When I look past Ndele's shoulder, the cash machine is spitting out his card—neatly shredded. He bangs the steering wheel with the side of his hand. I'm surprised that the wheel—or his hand—doesn't break. He punches the door with his fist.

"Hey, it's okay." I massage his tense shoulder. "Relax."

Doesn't work. He presses a button alongside his seat. "Be right back." He gets out of the car, looks around, takes something out of the trunk, slams it shut. "Muthafuckin' shyster prick!" He maneuvers back down in his seat, slams the door. "What's he been doin' with all my damn money?!"

"Blessed are the flexible," I remind him, using both hands on his shoulder and neck. As I do I remember: the gun. That's what he got from the trunk. I want to massage near his lap, find out if it's tucked in his shorts.

"Flexible my butt," he says. "Baby, I'm so broke I can't spend the night."

"Flexible *my* butt, okay? Just chill for a second or two. Count to eleven or something."

"Out here, fuckin' middle a nowhere. Goddamn."

"Plus I've got some money. Don't worry."

"Penny, I got my *own* money."

Oh. Back to "Penny" already. I tell him again to relax.

"I just need to talk to his office." He looks at his Rolex—which he could always pawn. I don't say this. "Still fuckin' lunchtime in New York. Always fuckin' lunchtime out there . . . How much money you got?"

Surprise me, why don't you. "In cash, about a hundred and fifty," I say. "Plus my Visa."

"Okay, you just hang on to all that." He pulls from the parking lot, turning left onto 2. "Muthafuck!"

We cruise along with the sun on the backs of our heads. Neither of us says very much. Route 2 runs dead straight west. A sign says MINOT 52, and I have to remind myself that it's forty-five minutes away, instead of five hours. The shoulder has all but disappeared, so I couldn't be riding here anyway. Farther off, at the edge of the flat field of oats on my right, some grackles are pecking and bobbing their iridescent green heads. It's quite a spectacular day—not a cloud, not a contrail. No chance the weather will keep us from reaching the bike shop.

A lot of this part of North Dakota looks like a sprawling construction site on which nothing's getting built. Cement-mixing trucks, Port-O-Lets, mounds of fresh gravel, oddly shaped pieces of steel. We pass an abandoned motel, four pastel cabins with boarded-up windows, then zoom through a small town called Towner, which does have a dinky but apparently functional motel. I want to check in and make love.

Ndele punches in CD number twelve. Twangy guitar, clarinet, saxophone, bass, and some drums. Dense and complex country jazz.

There is far too much sex in the world, I decide. Either that or there's much much too little.

"Who's this?"

"Bill Frisell," he informs me. "The Thelonious Monk of electric guitar. Plays some serious shit with these guys."

I listen. The mood of the music keeps shifting between melancholy and slapstick, with the clarinet and the guitar doubling crazed, loopy melodies. I'm convinced that the drummer is nuts.

In his black-musician voice, Ndele declares, "I'm down fo' this blues, but he gots to cycle-analyze dese chord progressions way mo' better."

I can't laugh at jokes at this moment; in the state that I'm in, I can't even tell if he's joking. When he suddenly takes hold of my hand, I start crying. We may not be in love, he may have no credit or cash, and he's probably going to shoot someone in the next half an hour or so, but I haven't been happier. Ever. I love being next to him, here in this snug leather bucket I've stained with my blood. I can't stand the thought that he's dropping me off at some bike shop. I want to make love to him *bad*.

He lets go of my hand and points to the square plastic button I have pinned to my sweatshirt.

"What's this?"

"This?" I sniff. I feel so damn silly and out of control. "This is my Nutt button, honey."

"Sounds sexy."

"It's very sexy. It's deceptively sexy, as a matter of fact, but it's also—"

"But what? But nuttin', honey. Let's see."

He keeps his eyes on the road but coaxes me to hand over the button, wiggling his upturned fingers.

I unpin the button and hand it over.

He drives and examines the button. It's a two-inch-square reproduction of a Jim Nutt portrait of a woman with dark, lacquered hair done up in a lopsided cubist braid. Her eyes are impatient, intense; one is narrow and orange, the other much rounder and green. Her nose is a brown, highly distorted, not unphallic protuberance.

"Juicy," he says. "This Nutt guy has it goin' on."

I agree, but I can't really say anything because all of a sudden a very loud horn begins blasting.

"Jesus!" I scream.

We've drifted across the median into the path of a big silver truck. Ndele swings back to the right as the truck whooshes toward us. Its horn and the suction are deafening and it's almost on top of us now. I close my eyes, hope for the best. Is this it? There are worse ways to go, I suppose . . .

When I open my eyes, Ndele is looking at the button again.

"Are you kidding me?! Gimme that thing!" I snatch it away from him. "Jesus!" I'm laughing. "You shithead!"

"Damn!" he says, shaking his finger. The pin must've pricked him. He's bleeding. "What *is* this?"

"What's with you? You just about got us both killed!"

He snatches it back from me—tries to.

"Ohhh, no-no-no," I tell him, holding the button more tightly. "Just drive."

"Do *you* want to drive?" he says scoffingly, as if I'd never in a million years, or in twenty-five minutes, say yes.

I move the seat forward a foot, tilt it up twelve degrees, shift into drive, pull the car back onto 2. I already have on his Wayfarers. I check myself out in the mirror: quite snazzy. I thought I was happy *before* . . .

Ndele's in the passenger seat wearing the Nutt button, sucking his pricked baby piggy.

"Hurts, don't it?"

"I'll give you a Hertz doughnut." He mock-threatens a karate chop, then winces and sucks on his finger again.

I accelerate past a sign that says MINOT 35. I'd like to add two or three zeros. Ndele keeps sucking his finger.

"Oh, c'mon, you big baby."

"It oits!"

"Yeah? Try doing it four times a day." As I pat his long thigh, there's an ache in the back of my throat.

"Okay. I'll be brave."

But he isn't, at least not about getting pricked. Some people just aren't. "Just make sure you don't bleed on the bleedin' upholstery, baby."

He nods. My sunglasses are too small for his head, and he has them on crooked. They ride too far up on his nose.

I pat him again, slightly higher.

"Just drive."

"I could certainly drive this here *car* four times a day," I say, changing the subject.

"Oh, you could?"

"Yes, I could."

He's checking himself in the side view. "Whatever."

I'd forgotten how much I love speed. The Demon and the Eagle at Great America, zooming downhill on my ten-speed, cruising 294 in my father's old Stanza. I'd tell him I was retaking the PSAT test or visiting a U. of C. clinic down in Hyde Park—anything to get access to a car for five or six hours . . .

I've arrived rather suddenly behind an enormous irrigation tractor, and I have to hit the brakes pretty hard. They respond. Ndele and I both lurch forward.

"Are you kidding me?!" he says shrilly; he's mocking me. (Is *that* how I sound?) My shades look ridiculous on him, whereas I look way cool in his big ones. "Would you please drive more carefully. Damn."

"Yes, sir," I tell him, saluting.

Even with its arms tucked in, the tractor is almost two lanes wide. It's doing about twenty-five. The arms are a pair of infolded skeletal towers, like a gangly biplane festooned with nozzles and hoses. It finally veers to the right and lets me swing past. Ndele squeezes my shoulder as I carefully angle back into the right lane. Then I step on the gas and we *surge* . . .

We flash past a sign that says YES! BINGO RAMA, HIGH WINS AHEAD. The road has more curves around here than it had outside Rugby and Towner. I try to take each of them without slowing down. The car makes it easy to do.

Another sign says DENBIGH EXPERIMENTAL FOREST, with an arrow pointing north. What could that be—trees with irregular syntax, foliage with jarring transitions disrupting the stifling narrative orderliness of the so-called Enlightenment? Maybe the rangers were supervised by Kathy Acker and Raymond Federman . . .

Apropos—or not—of the experimental forest, Ndele gives me a nudge. "You heard this one yet?"

"Uh, dunno."

"There's this pump jockey works at a lonely gas station on Route 2 in the middle of North Dakota. Smack in the geographical center, in fact. Sees about six cars a week. One day a customer pulls in driving an elaborate Italian sports car—Ferrari, Lamborghini, something along those lines. Pump jockey's never seen anything like it. Customer has to explain to him the various high-tech devices: CD player, gas-tank release, cruise control, no-hands carphone, *all* of that shit. On the console between the seats there's some toll money, car keys, nail clippers, two or three golf tees. Pump jockey's never seen none of this shit, so the driver has to explain everything to him. Pump jockey's like, 'What about those?' 'These tees?' says the driver. 'Tees? What're those?' 'You've never seen tees before?' says the driver. Pump jockey shakes his head no. The driver picks up two tees, holds them in front of the pump jockey, says, 'Well, you know, you rest your balls on them when you're driving.'" Ndele lowers my sunglasses an inch, gives me a sly little grin. "'Hot *damn*,' goes the pump jockey. 'This *is* a fancy car!'"

I finally get it.

"Most people tell that joke, the car's a big Cadillac and it's a niggah who's pumping the gas."

"Why not have the car be like this one?"

"Krautwagon, you mean? A Hitlermobile?"

"Absolutely. A Hitlermobile with bloodstained upholstery, of course. You could have the guy ask—"

"Oh, man," says Ndele. He's looking into his side-view again.

I look in the rearview. A patrolcar has appeared behind us with its row of rooftop lights flashing full tilt.

"Was I speeding?"

"Just pull over," he says. "Just don't get excited or nothing."

I slow down, put on the turn signal, pull over onto the shoulder. I believe that the speed limit is sixty-five, but it may be fifty-five. I was doing about eighty, I think. Maybe faster. You didn't feel speed in this car.

The squad car pulls over behind us.

"What does he think, I was speeding?"

Ndele stares down at his knees, shakes his head. "If you listen up, you'll hear what's goin' down." He sounds nervous.

I look in the rearview and watch the cop getting out of the squad car. Brown Smokey hat, unmirrored aviator sunglasses. And then he is standing beside me, adjusting his holster and belt.

"May I please see your driver's license, ma'am."

I'm already digging through the handlebar bag for my wallet. "Yes, sir, it's here—in here somewhere. Here it is." I take out my license and hand it up to him. "Was I going too fast?"

"Yes, ma'am, you were. Does this vehicle belong to you?"

"Belongs to me," says Ndele. "There a problem?"

Shouldn't his tone of voice be a bit more respectful? Obsequious, even?

The cop asks to see the registration, and Ndele pops open the glove compartment. Where's the gun? Wherever it is, I don't want Ndele to touch it. I don't want Ndele to *have* it.

The cop keeps glancing down into the car as he copies information from the "License Applied For" sticker in front of me. Ndele hands what I hope are the registration papers over the top of the windshield.

"Please wait here," says the cop, addressing me as much as Ndele. His boots crunch the gravel as he slowly returns to the squad car.

Ndele stares straight ahead. Twenty yards beyond where I've stopped is a reflective green sign. MOUSE RIVER. It's exactly like the other signs along the highway, only now it looks huge. I follow my mind working "logically"—the sign was designed to be legible to the drivers and passengers of cars whipping past, not those parked in front of it, waiting.

We wait without speaking. What a ridiculous name for a river, I decide. Why put a sign up at all? Thirty yards beyond the sign is the river itself, hidden by tall grass and bushes. A hawk glides and shifts through the thermals above a small stand of oaks. Looking for mice, I presume.

This is bad.

Ndele keeps staring in front of him. I put my hand onto his, knead his tensed knuckles. He clenches, relaxes, reclenches; I didn't expect much response. I can tell he's afraid, and it makes me feel nauseous, enraged. It seems like I've already known him a very long time, several years, when in fact it has only been— what? Nineteen hours?

"Too long," he says. Just like that.

"Sweetie—what?"

"It don't take no fifteen minutes to call in the damn registration."

It hasn't really been fifteen minutes—three or four, maybe five—but I don't want to contradict him.

"Maybe the computer is down."

Ndele is not in the mood for irony or optimism. Had he known I was wondering how long I'd known him? It was like we were on the same wavelength, but our moods were somehow distorting each other's. He's in major despair about *something*. Plus it's my fault the cop pulled us over.

I find myself staring at the wood on the dashboard, picking out figures in the gold-and-black grain: an ear, a jittery W, a molar with three perfect roots. I'd never noticed any before. The organically abstract grain of the walnut had mesmerized me a few times already this morning, but in this seat I have a new angle. Plus the light off the walnut seems different— more intense—now that we've stopped, even though given how rapidly light tends to move, I don't see how going from eighty miles an hour to zero could make that much difference. But still. There now seems to be a miniature violinist in three-quarter profile just below the Dolby button; another burl looks like Jimi Hendrix's—or is it Einstein's?—wild, shaggy head. I can't tell. When I squint, look again, it's just a dark knot in the wood.

I turn around in my seat and look back through the glare.

The cop's lips are moving. I assume he's talking to somebody over the radio.

"Can they give you a ticket for driving someone else's car?"

"I don't know," says Ndele.

Boots crunch the gravel again. "Ma'am, would you please step out of the vehicle."

His gun isn't drawn, but from the sound of his voice I can tell he means business. "Could you tell me what the problem is, officer?"

"Please just step out of the car."

I look at Ndele and shrug. "Be right back."

"Okay. You be cool."

It takes me a while to locate the door opener. I get out and almost tip over. There's a gap in the asphalt three times as wide as the one that knocked me down yesterday. Yesterday? I regain my balance and follow the cop toward his car. The black metal butt of his revolver tilts back and forth as he walks. His boots, belt, and holster are creaking.

Getting in first, he motions me toward the passenger side. Grasping for straws, I take it as a tremendously positive sign that he hasn't ordered me to sit in the back. He reaches across and unlocks the door. I get in.

The front seat is littered with clipboards, a carton of Merits, several rolls of Lifesavers, a clear little packet of Kleenex, a couple of thick three-ring binders. A shotgun. A keypad and color PC screen are bolted to the dashboard between us. The screen is angled away from me, but I can see things obliquely: a long list of numbers and names. The car reeks of cigarette smoke.

The officer takes off his sunglasses. He has doelike brown eyes under his big round brown hat. The collar of his shirt is brown too, as are the epaulets on the shoulders. The nameplate above his left pocket says E. MACKEY. He looks at me, squinting. He might be around my age; might be forty. He taps his pen against the side of a clipboard. He seems neither friendly nor vicious. If I smile or am friendly, will my fine be much lower? Any chance he'll just give me a warning?

"Miss Culligan, has this man abducted you?"

I'm too stunned to speak right away. I look directly into his eyes and hold his cool gaze.

"You're safe now, you know. It's okay to say so."

"It's okay to say that I'm safe."

Solemn nod.

"It's safe to say that I'm safe." I want to laugh in his face, but I know it will behoove me, not to mention Ndele, to filter the contempt from my voice. "What you've got to understand is, I never was *not* safe, at least not till you—"

"Miss Culligan—"

"Yes, I am safe. And no, he hasn't 'abducted' me. He's *helping* me. Officer Mackey, please understand. This man has come to my *aid*."

Ndele turns around, looks back this way through the frame of my bike. Can he hear us from there? The windows of the squad car are rolled halfway down.

Officer Mackey deploys a small microphone: "Please remain in the car, sir." His voice booms outside toward Ndele, who swings back around in his seat. My old seat.

I snort my contempt, shake my head. "He gave me a ride when my bike's wheel got bent on these roads of yours." I point to the wheel sticking out the top of the Mercedes. "You can see it right there."

"What is that gentleman's name?"

I can't really think of a reason not to tell him, unless it's that he doesn't deserve *any* answer. He asks me again and I tell him.

"When did Mr. Rimes pick you up?"

"Yesterday. About two o'clock yesterday. About twenty miles west of Grand Forks."

He writes these things down on a pad. Over the radio, a calm female voice cuts through a staticky haze: "Indiana, no, Indiana. So it's Rimes, yes, yes, Andale, yes, that's a niner." More static.

Officer Mackey is talking to me. "And so where did you two—do you know where Mr. Rimes spent last night?"

"We both spent the night back in Rugby. At the J & J Motel. Would you like to see my receipt?"

"Separate rooms?"

He waits for my response. Tap tap. Tap tap.

"Yes, separate rooms."

"Are you able to say whether Mr. Rimes spent the entire evening in his room?"

On the radio: "That's Rimes—" An explosion of static— "with Rimes."

"We're only asking, of course," says Officer Mackey, "for your own safety and protection."

"So what are you guys now, like rubbers or something?"

Suddenly three other squad cars roar past the car we are in, two skidding sideways to a stop in front of the Mercedes, while the third dents the driver's side door. Cops piling out of both cars, shouting and waving large guns. Pistols and a shotgun all aimed at Ndele.

"Put your hands behind your head! I said, put them behind your fucking head!"

Ndele obeys. Two cops with pistols edge closer. One presses the barrel of his pistol against Ndele's neck. When Ndele angles his head away from it, the cop presses harder.

"Listen, sir, Officer Mackey, you've got to understand: this is really insane. That man was helping me."

"Oh, we understand you, Miss Culligan."

I watch as Ndele is removed from the Mercedes at gunpoint. His hands and legs are spread as he's splayed on the trunk of the car. He looks toward where I'm sitting, but our eyes never meet; because of the glare off the windshield, I doubt he can see me. All the cops seem to be yelling or barking instructions, but one voice stands out in particular: "Your forefathers defended their villages two hundred years ago, you wouldn't be in this mess, son." Another cop uses a white plastic handcuff to bind Ndele's wrists behind his back. They hustle him into a squad car.

"We definitely understand you," Officer Mackey is saying. "Believe me."

We were driven to Minot in two separate squad cars, then taken to separate sections of the headquarters of the North Dakota Highway Patrol. The room they finally sat me down in was crowded with desks and police and technicians. Most of the desks were piled high with boxes; a new computer or phone system was being installed, so the place was chaotic: toolboxes, bags of fast food, foam chips all over the floor. Ndele was off in some other part of the building, apparently to enable them to interrogate us separately, then compare our stories. I only knew he was in the building when I caught a brief glimpse of him being walked down the corridor about two minutes after I finally sat down. That was the last time I saw him.

A large female deputy—J. J. Ruttoni—took my finger-prints and asked me to empty my pockets. I wasn't subjected to a cavity search but was given to infer that she might change her mind. When I explained to Ms. Ruttoni why I had to eat lunch right away, I was given a desk, a ginger ale, a chicken salad sandwich, and my own two detectives.

Timothy Urtagh introduced himself and his partner, Allison Truckenbrod. Urtagh had a New England accent but was wearing a string tie, a tan western-cut suit, black-and-tan cowboy boots. Whereas Urtagh was a well-preserved sixty, Truckenbrod was my age or younger. She had pale, pocky skin, orange-blond hair, a no-nonsense white blouse with a crucifix displayed where her cleavage would be, and a neat khaki skirt.

Though she never became outright abusive, she seemed quite pissed off about something. I had no idea to what extent her attitude was part of some good cop-bad cop routine, but while Tim Urtagh went out of his way to make me feel comfortable while I ate my lunch, and even to give me the impression that I had the benefit of whatever doubts he might have about what I was telling him, Detective Truckenbrod never pretended for a second that she didn't dislike me.

They wanted to know where I was coming from, where I was going, and why. I admitted these were excellent questions and answered as well as I could. I informed them at length as to the circumstances of my meeting Ndele, where we had spent the night, how I had come to be driving his car. They requested and received explanations of the syringes they found in my pannier, the bloodstains on the upholstery of the Mercedes, the traces of a powdery white substance under my fingernails. At first I thought Ruttoni had planted something on me, but when I looked under the nail of my pinkie I saw several white grains of what I assumed they were talking about. It was Equal.

Officer Mackey hands Urtagh a printout, then exits the area we're sitting in without making eye contact with me. As Urtagh peruses it, the printout, Truckenbrod slides her chair a couple feet closer to mine.

"What were you all planning to do with that gun?"

I've presumed all along that this is the central-most issue. I tilt my head, look surprised, and say, "Gun?"

"Ma'am, we're talking about a nine-millimeter SIG pistol with Ndele Rimes's fingerprints all over it."

"He doesn't have to carry a gun."

"Why do you say that?"

I shrug. "I certainly never saw him with one."

"Could you clarify that?"

"Clarify it? I never saw Ndele with a gun."

She glances at Urtagh.

"You haven't?" he asks me.

"No, I haven't." I haven't—I've never seen what was clearly

a gun in the hands of Ndele. But I sense that Urtagh knows I'm fudging. He smiles.

Truckenbrod: "You've never seen Mr. Rimes with a gun."

I stare back into her pearly gray eyes and shake my head no as coolly as I am capable of. By lying about this—or not telling the whole truth and nothing but—I'm probably getting myself into unfortunate legal territory.

"C'mon, Penelope," says Urtagh. "Chicago girl like yourself? You must be used to all of this Al Capone gang-banger stuff." He mimes firing a machine gun. "No?"

"Afraid not." Is he kidding?

Truckenbrod: "You sure?"

"About what? About whether I'm used to machine guns? Is Mr. Rimes under arrest, by the way?"

Blank stares from both of them: the old blank cop-blank cop routine.

I look up at Urtagh. "Am I?" It seems like a relevant question.

"Ma'am," says Truckenbrod, "you are currently subject to arrest on charges of"—she reads from the printout—"driving eighty-six mph in a sixty-five zone, operating a motor vehicle with improper registration, suspicion of receiving stolen property, and conspiring to transport that property across state lines."

"Subject to arrest?"

"Yes, ma'am."

"For transporting *what* stolen property?"

"Currently subject, yes, ma'am." She looks pretty sure of herself, but she apparently felt forced to add, "At this time."

"Ma'am, am I under arrest, or, ma'am, am I not?"

"Not . . ." says Urtagh. He takes back the printout, adjusts his gray trifocals.

Truckenbrod: "Not at this time."

"So I can leave, then. Right now."

"Not at this time," she repeats.

"Then I think I'd better get a lawyer," I tell her.

"Why would you want to call a lawyer if you haven't been arrested or charged with a crime?"

"Let me explain it to you this way. I'm *going* to get a lawyer. One still has that right, I presume? Just west, as we are, of the Geographical Center of North America." I hope that'll scald her perineum.

If it has, she certainly doesn't let on.

"Is it fair to presume that?" I ask Urtagh.

Blank cop, blank cop.

"Hasn't Ndele called *his* lawyer?" Amazingly enough, this thought has just now occurred to me.

"Mr. Rimes has a lawyer?" says Truckenbrod, crossing her legs. She leans back a little, awaiting my answer. It's clear she is curious, and that she's working quite hard to conceal it. I make her work longer and harder.

Urtagh just stares at me.

"I believe that he does," I eventually admit. "I also believe he'd call him if he were under arrest—or when you and your friends point a shotgun at his head and put him in handcuffs does that mean he's only 'subject' to arrest?"

Truckenbrod: "Is his lawyer your lawyer?"

"No, he is not."

"He isn't," says Urtagh. "So they're two different people."

"What I mean is—"

Truckenbrod: "Yes?"

"Are we, either of us, Mr. Rimes or myself, are we under arrest? Yes or no."

"Do *you* have a lawyer?" asks Urtagh, just as Truckenbrod is asking, "Do you *have* a lawyer?"

A moment of levity? No. Truckenbrod, in fact, seems impatient with her elder partner for interrupting her; almost imperceptibly, she is shaking her head, shooting him looks that say *please!*

"I assume that one would be assigned to me," I say, directing my remark right at Urtagh.

It's his young, pissed-off partner who answers: "Not till you're under arrest."

They ordered me dinner from a Chinese restaurant, let me do my shot, made me wait. "Detained for further questioning" was how Truckenbrod explained it, officially. A lawyer is being sought to represent me in the event I'm arrested, a condition which in the meantime I remain only "subject to." They wouldn't let me speak to Ndele. Can't do that right now, Miss Culligan. Forget it.

I haven't stolen a car or touched a gun, and I'm convinced they must know that. Urtagh especially has gone out of his way to suggest he believes me. He even let me in on what he said was *his* theory: It was all a mistake. When I asked, astounded, how could that be, he explained to me how every car's serial number contains seventeen digits—seventeen letters and numerals—from which can be determined who owns the car, who sold it to him, where and when the transaction took place, in which state the license was applied for. But if even *one* of these seventeen digits happens to be mis-recorded—an "8" gets copied down as a "B" by an over-worked car salesman, by a clerk in a vehicle registration office, by a highway patrol officer on a mission to rescue a potential hostage—then the car in question will appear on computers as missing, improperly registered, or stolen. It was a felony and a federal offense for a stolen car to be transported across state lines. It was also a felony and a federal offense to *conspire* to transport a stolen car across state lines. That's what I am sus-pected of—unless Urtagh's theory was right. He told me he hoped that it was.

Through some cucumber plants on the windowsill, I can see the Mercedes being dismantled by two men with power tools. I assume they are searching for drugs—but weren't dogs used to sniff those things out? In any event, the two men are not being gentle about it. My bike has been placed beside two metal sawhorses, leaning forward on its empty front fork, emphatically unlike any antelope.

Around six-thirty a trio of lawyer types with extremely thin briefcases and slouchy Italian suits were ushered past me down the corridor, in the direction Ndele had been headed the last time I saw him. I assumed that one of these guys was

Bob Newman, but I didn't want to venture a guess as to whether this was a positive or a negative development as far as Ndele was concerned.

At eight forty-five I was released on my own recognizance. I still hadn't been allowed to talk to Ndele, though I'd insisted ad nauseam that I had every right to, etc. I was scared to death about what might be happening to him at the end of that corridor. Also, I missed him.

I walked to the Minot Hotel, got a room. As soon as I figured out how to work the TV I flipped through the channels, looking for us on the news. Various local stations had rain and crop reports, commercials for tractors and fertilizers. Another was showing *Bewitched*. Then, on *CNN Sports*, there it is: a photo of a handsome young basketball player in a green-and-gold uniform perched above Fred Hickman's shoulder. The caption says "RIMES," but the guy in the picture doesn't look like Ndele, at least not exactly. When was this picture taken? With a little less hair it *could* be Ndele, plus the color of the set is way off, although . . .

Fred Hickman is talking. ". . . Ndele Rimes, the troubled young Seattle Supersonics point guard, has been arrested in, of all places, Minot, North Dakota, on charges of resisting arrest, possession of an unregistered firearm, and improper vehicle registration, although Rimes wasn't driving the car when the arrest was made. Rimes has already returned to Seattle with his attorney and team officials. No date has been set for the arraignment yet, but team officials have told CNN—"

I run the two blocks to the station. There must've been a shift change, because I don't recognize either of the sergeants on duty behind the counter. But one of them—a young guy with enormous pink ears—recognizes me.

"You again." He looks like an albino bat with a negligible, lopsided mustache.

When I tell him I want to speak with Ndele Rimes, he smirks toward his partner, a tall guy with beige crew-cut hair. Who shrugs.

Sergeant Ears removes half his smirk. "Mr. Rimes has been released."

"When was this? Why wasn't I—"

"Mr. Rimes was released over two hours ago."

"Did he leave any messages?"

Ears shakes his head.

"Could you check?"

"He didn't leave any messages."

"But you're absolutely certain that he—"

"Mr. Rimes didn't leave any messages."

"Actually, there *was* one message," pipes in Sergeant Beige, grabbing his pants at the crotch. "I got it right here for you."

"I'm sorry," I tell him, "I thought you understood. I asked whether Mr. Rimes left any full-scale, man-sized, hearty-appetite-type *messages*. He obviously could've stuck *that*—" I hold my index finger and thumb a quarter inch apart—"on a Post-it and mailed it to me with a seven-cent stamp."

It's not at all pretty to watch Ears snort with laughter, but it is somewhat satisfying. Beige directs a feeble jerk-me-off sign in my direction. I turn and head back toward the door.

"Except that it wasn't Andale Rimes you were shackin' up with in Rugby," calls Beige, "by the way."

"Right." But it does slow me down.

"That was someone enti-i-i-rely different."

That stops me.

"All he's telling you, Miss," allows Ears, "is the man you were arrested with this afternoon is not Ndele Rimes."

"Who was he?"

"Some sailor gone AWOL from his ship in Norfolk, Virginia. Lee Morgan—somebody."

Lee Morgan? I'm sure now he's fucking with me. "You're sure it wasn't Lee Marvin?"

"Actually," says Ears. He picks up a printout and reads. "It was Seaman Second Class Lee Morgan Rimes, some basketball player's kid brother."

*   *   *

At the hotel I call directory assistance for Seattle. I enunciate clearly as I spell out Ndele, then Rimes, but I have to admit to the operator that I don't have the address. He tells me it isn't a problem—that it doesn't make a difference. I say that I don't understand. He explains: There's an Ndele Rimes in that area code, but his number is unlisted. Can I have his address? I cannot.

On TV, a man in a feed cap promotes improved feed. I watch for a while in a daze. Huge bewhiskered hogs loom toward the camera, snuffling down into a trough. I fire the telephone against the mint-colored wallpaper, cringe and half-sob when it dings.

Somebody knocks on my door just after eight. I've already done my shot, repacked my panniers, eaten breakfast in the cafeteria downstairs, and checked out; I'm all set to pick up my bike and head out of Minot.

It's Lee.

"How're you doing?"

"Okay . . . " I don't even try to pretend I'm not shocked to see her.

"Are you sure?"

She's tanner than usual and has on spiffy new wire-rim glasses. When she reaches to hug me, I freeze. But we hug. Chanel, Scope, shampoo—she smells good. She kisses my cheek, pats the side of my head, keeps on hugging—buzzing, as always, with mutinous, precipitate energy.

When she finally lets go, I manage to ask her what she's doing in North Dakota.

"You were in trouble. I thought I could help."

How could she know what had happened? "In trouble?"

"Penny, now listen to me." She suddenly seems both thrilled and supremely annoyed to be here with me. "Why didn't you call me?"

"I'm sorry. Things kept coming up and coming up. It's a little bizarre sometimes, being out on the road every day."

"No doubt," she says, more than a little sarcastically. "But I'm talking about a two-minute call."

I nod in a studently manner to show her I recognize the validity of her observation.

"My God! What happened to your knees?"

"Had a little accident outside Grand Forks."

"Are you okay? It looks like it just happened."

"I'm—"

"And so this black fellow picked you up *after* you crashed?"

"Of course. I mean, how . . . " It was Lee, after all, who helped teach me the difference between asking good questions and asking a lot of questions. Which MO was she taking?

"How what?" she asks me.

"How do you know about this, anyway?"

"Sweet Jesus, Penny. Are you kidding me? It was all over the local news. Every station."

I consider this scenario. What picture of me had they used? Probably the one on my driver's license. Oy. Plus I'd have to get in touch with my father.

"What did they say was the name of the basketball player?"

"Basketball player?"

"From Seattle," I say. "You know. He plays *for* Seattle."

Lee peers at me strangely, as though I'm deranged, then adjusts her new glasses. I can see from the side that they're bifocals.

"From Virginia *going* to Seattle," I say. "Or whatever. Ndele Rimes. The guy who picked me up."

She has started her breathing routine—pointed exhalations to gloss what she thinks of the position I'm developing. "Penny, the man who was arrested with you is wanted for attempted murder."

"Murder?"

"Attempted murder during a carjacking."

"Seems like something the police would've brought up during the interrogation. Wouldn't you say?"

"Didn't they?"

"No."

"But he—"

"In the second place, I wasn't arrested. I was taken into the station for questioning yesterday, but they released me last night."

"Channel Five said you'd been arrested."

"And none of the cops said a word about murder. There was just some mistake with the serial numbers."

"Serial numbers." Exhaling succinctly, she takes off the glasses. "Please listen to me for a second. I really don't think this person was who he told you he was. Do you mean an actual professional basketball player?"

"*Yes* an actual professional player."

"Except that two reporters in Chicago confirmed that the man who picked you up was AWOL from the navy; he'd stolen a car in Indianapolis and was driving it . . . Who told you he was a basketball player?"

"He *is* a basketball player." I like myself least when I start to get shrill, even slightly. "I mean, if you need corroboration, they said just last night on CNN that he played basketball." I point at the television set behind Lee, as though this might clinch my assertion.

"Be that as it may," says Lee; her breathing says, *You naive, stubborn bitch*. "This guy, this young man, he may have played basketball. I'm *sure* he plays basketball. He also has hijacked a car in Indianapolis, and he shot the man who happened to be driving it. In the face. Almost killed him. May as *well* have killed him."

I'm trying to take all this in, not knowing what to believe. It's odd to be discussing such things with Lee Marvin in a hotel room in the middle of North Dakota; we were usually—forever—discussing much different issues.

"What kind of car was it?" I ask her.

"What kind of car?" An impertinent question, apparently. "You mean, the car the man was driving?"

"Right. At the time he was shot in the face. Was it a Mercedes convertible?"

"I really don't know," she admits.

The phone rings.

"I'd assumed that you knew all of this," Lee informs me.

The phone rings again.

"There's been some confusion," I tell her.

She's holding me now by my wrists: fingers underneath, lifting them slightly, thumbs on top moving in circles. She's making my knuckles brush her wrists. "Of course."

After the fourth or fifth ring, she proposes that I answer it. She even lets go of me. Breathing.

It's Stephen, her husband. We both say hello. We've spoken only briefly, maybe a half dozen times—in person at functions, more often over the telephone, but never long distance. He manages not to be too perfunctory when he asks how I'm doing.

I give Lee the phone. She's supremely annoyed that he's called; the breathing gloss he receives is harsher than any I've garnered, and there's some satisfaction in that.

I get up and look out the window, doing my best not to eavesdrop. Two blocks in front of me, three stories down, is the highway patrol headquarters. A block and a half to my left, Hi-Line Cycles, to which my bike has been dispatched by the cops for a new wheel and tune-up; I have the receipt in my pocket. Route 2 is several blocks south—about a mile, I've been told at the desk.

A woman with braided gray pigtails is walking a pair of Great Danes. As I stare at the huge, gorgeous dogs—mostly white heads, piebald flanks, almost as tall as their owner—the woman looks up at me. I return her incurious gaze for ten or fifteen seconds before she shakes her head—in disgust? resignation? she's unhappy with me about *something*—and quickly turns a corner, allowing herself to be yanked by the leashes. I realize that this hotel room is the farthest I've strayed from Route 2 since I first picked it up in Wisconsin.

Lee is all business again when she gets off the phone. She doesn't explain how Stephen had known where to call; nor do I ask her to. She informs me instead how arduous and expensive it was to fly from Chicago to Minot on a half-hour's notice, especially with no Saturday night layover, and in so doing makes the history of her trip here seem almost relevant, in that one of the flight attendants on the leg from Minneapolis had studied with Paul Muldoon at Princeton. She also explains at great length how fortunate I am to be rid of Ndele; how lucky that he hadn't raped and then killed me, or been in a position to take me hostage when the police were about to arrest him. When I tell her he had been very *much* in such a position, she exhales testily but says, "Well, good for him."

In the meantime I've brought out a map, the better to retrace my route from Chicago in response to her queries. I show her where I crossed the Red River with the Harley convention, where my bike crashed and Ndele picked me up, where the storm hit us just east of Rugby. We're sitting on the side of the bed, rotating the map between us. Lee has gradually swung around beside, then behind, me. I'm not overwhelmed with surprise when she takes hold of my shoulders and starts kneading my back with her thumbs. Nor do I think to object. I stretch and rotate my shoulders as her thumbs work the top of my spine, then move down my back inch by inch, a vertebra or so at a time. When she gets to the base, she works her way up again, slowly. She's already told me three or four times to lay back.

"Go ahead. Just relax."

I lay back, resting my head against her crossed legs. I keep my eyes closed as she works on my temples and neck. She makes little noises way back in her throat. I try not to make any noises myself, and I keep my left foot on the floor.

When she kisses me on the forehead, I begin to sit up. Her hands hold my shoulders, unsubtly pressing me down.

"I think I should tell you this, Lee . . . "

"Just try and lie still for a while. You're lucky to be alive, you poor thing."

"Lee, listen to me." I turn halfway over and lean on my elbow. I look in her eyes for a moment, then down toward her leg. Then at nothing. "I lost all my notes. All my pages. I'd already finished—"

She still has one hand on my neck. "For your dissertation?"

I feel myself blush as I nod.

"All of them?"

Still nodding. It's awful.

"My God," she says, stroking my hair. "I mean, how?"

"I don't know exactly. When the cops gave me back my panniers, my blue notebooks and all hundred and eighty-two handwritten pages were missing. Just gone. I've already filed two complaints."

"That's—horrible."

I agree that it is.

"And a little astonishing. Was anything else missing?"

"Just my notebooks, the pages, and a couple of changes of underwear."

"The cops stole your clothes?"

At this point I say something downright nonsensical: "Just till I hit the next laundromat."

"That's incredible," says Lee. She slides a pale finger behind her new glasses, starts rubbing her eye. Then she sighs. My non sequitur seems not to have registered. But I've never known Lee not to choose her words scrupulously: she's stated that what I told her wasn't credible. "Maybe they thought they would find something they could use against this carjacker person." Again, the big sigh.

"That's what they gave me to infer."

She noses my hair off my neck, and I feel her cool mouth near my temple. "You'll have to start again almost from scratch . . . " She nuzzles the side of my throat, but without getting sloppy about it, scraping long lines with her lips and her teeth. I cannot help shivering, though I know it will encourage her. When she puts her lips against mine, I turn my face to the side. I try not to do it contemptuously.

"Lee." I keep my tone flat and straightforward.

She moves her mouth back to my neck, apparently satisfied that my no-kissing edict is final. I'm expecting a hand on a breast or a leg any second. As I try to decide what to say, or let happen, she bites down lightly on my earlobe, tugs back and forth, lets it go. She's breathing in codes I don't understand.

There's a coppery taste on the back of my tongue. Stalling for time, I just sigh.

Her breathing is warm, vaguely minty, on the side of my face.

"I might need more time to—okay, Lee? To think about this?" More Time. It used to be my middle name, but I think it should now be my first. No one's more aware of this fact than poor Lee.

"You know?" I am pleading.

"Sure, sure. Of course." She leans back and breathes at me: Damn you! Her cheeks are vermilion. Goddamn you!

My bike is all ready: new front wheel, two new Kevlar tires, tuned up, greased bearings, new chain. A hundred and eighty-nine dollars. My stealthy white pigeon takes wing and just *flaps*. The manager helps me secure my panniers. Did I know, he asks, that Kevlar was invented by a woman who worked for Du Pont? I did not.

Lee buys a T-shirt, holds it in front of herself for my approval: NORTH DAKOTA, MOUNTAIN REMOVAL PROJECT COMPLETED.

"Tell me about it," I say.

I roll my bike out of the shop, delighted to have it again in one piece.

"And you're sure you don't want to fly back to Chicago?" Lee is asking. "Rest up, wait till you feel a bit stronger, maybe try reconstructing your notes?"

Is she kidding? Apparently not. "You know, physically, the farther I ride, the stronger I feel. And the sooner I get out of *this* place, this whole blasted state, I'll probably feel even better."

"You mean, the farther you get from Chicago."

"The harder I work myself. Not 'from Chicago,' Lee. Jesus. The closer I get to Alaska. You know this is something I still have to do."

Lee rolls her eyes, mouths *Alaska*—but with humor, accepting my decision. "But this time, will you please stay in touch?"

"Definitely."

"I'm sorry about this morning. I just get so carried away when you're—"

"Hey. Not a problem."

Her brown eyes are glistening. She riffles her bag for a tissue, dabs behind her glasses, blows her nose daintily. Twice.

"Not even a very small problem."

She kisses my cheekbone, my temple. I kiss her moist cheek. We kiss on the lips for a second, then bring back our heads. The man in the bike shop looks on.

"And you're sure you'll be back by September?"

I raise my right hand, swearing to tell the whole truth. "August twenty-ninth at the latest."

"Your glucometer's working?"

"Check."

"Extra syringes and insulin?"

I pat my pannier.

"Penny, please just be careful out there. Alaska! My God." Shakes her head. "Although a fresh start might be just what the doctor—might be just what you need."

"Listen, I know what you're thinking—I've caught myself thinking it too. But don't worry. Killing myself is the last thing I'm going to do."

She's crying again. "Was I thinking that?"

"I don't know. But I'm definitely coming back. I've got my classes to teach, the re-deconstruction of my dissertation to procrastinate over, the nefarious affair with my dissertation advisor to assiduously avoid. It's a pretty full plate."

"I suppose."

I leave her like that, with a wet, sheepish grin on her face, adjusting her fancy new glasses.

PART 4

In the last thirteen days I've ridden four hundred and twenty-four miles, from Minot to Stemmings, Montana. I've passed through Ray, North Dakota (featuring Ray Sub, Club Ray, the three-store Ray MiniMall) but have yet to pass through Joe, Montana. I haven't been in touch with Jane or Lee, but I did call my dad from Minot to tell him I was okay; by the end of the conversation, I think he believed me. I hope. He told me the White Sox were winning, that Frank Thomas was leading the league in three "separate" categories. Have not heard word one from Ndele, or whatever his name is. Whoever he actually was.

My main problem is, I seem to have less and less stamina. I also blank out much more often, losing myself in the physical effort to propel myself forward, grinding the miles out rotation by rotation, foot pound by thigh pump by erg. Not much else registers—either that or my mind is racing too fast to keep track. And it isn't all bad, I don't think—not to think. How many hours and ergs can one spend, after all, rehashing the future and the past? I want to get lost in the present. Isn't that "healthy?" That's why I chose to spend my summer vacation this way, and that's why I chose this here route: a straight shot, no tourists (aside from myself), just a clean open artery west, and also *because* I heard it was boring and desolate. I want things as mindless as possible.

Desolate? I'm currently surrounded in every direction by

gold, rolling wheat fields crosshatched by back-and-forth stripes. The sky, as they say, is big. The impression I have is that the horizon extends more than 180 degrees—about 195 or 200. It is *large*, as they say in films about drug deals, referring to bills of impressive denomination. The first and last baggie of pot I ever personally purchased cost five dollars: a nickel. Today if a hit man charges 50,000 dollars to kill someone, that's a nickel too. Apparently anything even quasi-illegal that costs something beginning with 5 is a nickel.

Would hit men give discounts if hired to kill their own client? Two thirds up front but none later, something along those lines? How much would a nickel job cost me—five hundred? Five thousand? Are hit men equipped to take Visa?

A herd of pronghorn antelope are grazing a few hundred yards from the highway, under thousands of miniature white-and-gray clouds serrated with blueness, all just about the same size, except for the ones with—

I'm suddenly clapped in the eardrums by a thunderous boom-crack. In the semi-delirious state I've been in, I'm convinced I have crashed; it's the same sound I heard just after I actually crashed outside Grand Forks. And when I look up, there they are—*two* of those Darth Vader Stealth planes booming through the sound barrier a quarter mile over my head. There must be a base around here. The pilots must be practicing for their dangerous runs under the Korean or Japanese or Siberian radar systems, the better to deliver their payloads of Levi's and Equal and stealthy, invisible Pepsi.

The almost continual wind in my face makes me work a lot harder than I'm used to. The faster I pedal, the harder the wind blows against me. Sometimes I amuse myself by tilting my head a few degrees, making the wind hit my ears at different angles, changing the pitch of its whoosh. But even when I'm feeling energetic, it's been hard to average more than seven or eight miles an hour. Montana is a rather long state, and the wind makes it seem a lot longer. Everyone told me I was going in the wrong direction for a transcontinental bike trip, but before I got to Minot the wind wasn't much of a factor.

After five or six hours of trying to pedal into an almost continual gale, you do go a little bit nuts. Sometimes I have to stand up on the pedals to make any progress at all. Since the towns along here big enough to have a motel are at least twenty miles apart, that's my daily minimum. On Thursday— perhaps it was Wednesday—it took me five hours just to make the twenty-six miles from Fort Kipp to Brockton. Farther back, I got caught in a thunderstorm between Epping and Williston; the Weather Channel had given me the all-clear that morning, but the storm just blew in out of nowhere. I had to sit out the worst of it in a shed for two hours, then ride back to Epping. That doubling back was the worst.

After I crossed the North Dakota border at Wolf Point, I followed the Missouri River for almost three days, although 2 seldom runs close enough to the river that you can actually see it. As the signs and obelisks back in Rugby had under- scored, you can't get much farther from the sea than when you're in North Dakota. So when I first saw enormous white gulls wheeling like M's above the river at Williston, my first dumb idea was that I was making much better time than I'd thought. The river was spotted with mostly naked teenagers drifting along in black tubes. I still had a few states to go.

The novelty of the road trip has begun to wear off. Having to pay for every meal I eat, the room I stay in each night, making sure I have enough water and food to make it to the next little dot on the map—it's taking too much concentra- tion. I'll never again take for granted having a refrigerator and stove down the hall from my bedroom. And I miss all my CD's and books.

Bainville, Culbertson, Fort Kipp, then Brockton, then Poplar, then Stemmings—Montana keeps going and going. In the lobby of Lee Ann's Motel in Poplar, a sixtyish Native American gentleman gave me the eye, then winked when his wife wasn't looking. I smiled. He had on bright yellow golf pants, and his wife wore a short denim skirt. Nothing else happened, but I did get a lift from his horny attention—a sure sign a woman is desperate.

On the road between these gnarled and minuscule towns I'm invited quite often to adopt a highway. And do what with it? The signs never say. The state of Montana also puts up little white crosses to mark the sites of fatal accidents. There were four a mile back: no bend in the road, no intersection, no stop sign to run—just dead straight highway to negotiate. There are also brown-and-beige signs every few miles along here, reminding travelers that they're following the original Lewis and Clark Trail. Either Clark or Lewis wears a tricorn and points self-assuredly westward; his partner stands beside him in a coonskin hat and fringed buckskin coat, holding a musket. At the border with North Dakota the plaque said they camped on April 27 (my birthday), 1805. It took them four months to cross Montana. Four months! A sign outside Culberston marked the spot where they killed their first grizzly. There'd be no signs at all if it was the other way around.

But the world worships bears. Book after book, article after article, nature special after nature special. Football teams, baseball teams. Trinkets and teddy bears and four-color coffee-table extravaganzas. The basketball team in Vancouver. One brown bear's gall bladder is worth 125,000 dollars in Hong Kong, to men concerned about their potency. They dry it out, grind it up, mix it with bean curd or sushi or something. Maybe it would work more effectively if they ground it into powder and snorted it, or cooked it in a spoon and fired it directly into their flagging penises.

I've never laid eyes on the ranger who shot the sow grizzly, but I can picture the person quite clearly. I'm not even sure it was a ranger who did the big deed, though I've read in several places that the task of destroying problem bears—primarily bears addicted to garbage, or those who have tasted human flesh—usually does fall to rangers. It's possible that the Department of Fish and Wildlife hired a local hunter to harvest the sow, and it's virtually certain that the hunter, or the ranger, was male. My ranger's female. Thirty-six, thirty-seven, scraggly brown ponytail, substantial red pores on the side of her nose. And no makeup. She has on the same brown base-ball-style cap I'd seen other rangers wear in Alaska. I seldom picture more than her arms, head, and shoulders, but I know she is not very tall. The rifle she wields therefore appears even bigger, more lethal—a sleek, well-oiled, viciously effectual cannon. She raises it up to her shoulder, shuts her left eye, squints through the scope with her right. The enormous blond head of the sow appears in the crosshairs. My ranger, who does not have a name, is an excellent shot; otherwise she'd never be given this crucial assignment. The sow stares right back at her, sniffs the wind, roars ferociously. My ranger doesn't flinch, doesn't hesitate. We both feel a warm, even sexual, horror as she squeezes the trigger. There's a kick and a very loud *crack* as the three-inch-long copper-jacketed bullet explodes through the teeth and the throat and into the brain of the sow. The impact flips her backward and sideways as the rifle's report rockets hard off the Margerie Glacier, then wafts back out over the inlet. It's done. I wish I had been there to see it. I've seen it and heard it and felt it by now so many hun-dreds of thousands of times, watching that blond fucking sow start to tremble and cough up her blood, choke on her pain and confusion and rage. And then die. I wish I had squeezed that warm trigger.

My bike needs a lube job, but shops around here are rather few and far between. *I* need a lube job, plus I'm running out of gas. I ride on. But Amtrak looks more and more tempting.

Something is wrong with me. The cashier at the Motel 6 in Vandalia wore latex gloves as she ran my bruised card through the Visa machine. The raised-plastic E, P, and C from my name are all cracked, as well as a few of the sacred, indispensable numbers. I'm afraid to call in for a new one.

Last night I dreamed I was standing in a crowded Amtrak station with my face pressed up against the glass. I was ready. Then I saw it. A thing that was shivering, wet. It was me.

Three or four nights ago I watched a documentary in

which Jane and Stephen Hawking decided to get divorced. Apparently, Stephen had fallen in love with his nurse. I think I'd like to try that some time. Although, maybe not. I don't know. I wonder what it's like with Sir Stephen.

Magic bullets still pierce my skin, but less and less often these days. I let myself run out of Lente in Buckhorn, a town without a pharmacy; I got so pissed off at myself (even after I finally found an open pharmacy fifteen miles up the road) that I didn't give myself *any* insulin that day. Or the next, as a matter of fact.

This morning I heard on the news that the United States spends a trillion dollars a year on medical care. And Jack Kevorkian's suicide machine has been declared again not to be legal.

If Manhattan Island were populated as densely as the state of Alaska, seventeen people would live there. The population of Mexico City, which is smaller in size than Jacksonville, Florida, is something like seventeen million. Ballygorman, in the Republic of Ireland (County Donegal, to be more specific, from whence my one genuinely professorial gray herringbone tweed jacket, currently being shredded by moths in the back of my closet and befouled by Chicago humidity, though at least in November it won't smell like mothballs), lies farther north than any part of Northern Ireland. The exact geographical center of North America, including Mexico, lies just south of Rugby, North Dakota, population 3,500.

It takes me another two days to make it to Diamond, Montana. There are many more trucks along here, trucks that weigh thirty tons and have eighteen wheels and go *rrr-r-r-r-r*. Peterbilts. Macks. Clunky Internationals. Piggybacked Fruehaufs. Many tons, many tons. Driven by men, every one. No Mercedes convertibles have made an appearance. No Mustangs. No mountains yet, either. Nothing in a black plastic bra.

A truck is getting ready to pass me right now, roaring and backfiring, zinging gravel out sideways like bullets. If I veer half a yard to my left I'll be sucked in and under, which would certainly make things more mindless. Then again, maybe not. Maybe swerving accidentally on purpose in front of a semi transfers you directly to a place where you spend all your time testing your blood, getting whipped by exhaust fumes, being dunned for your overdue bills by that trumpet-assed devil from the *bolgia* of swindlers and barrators.

As one truck eases back into the right lane ahead of me, another one looms in my mirror. The driver of this truck is apparently unwilling to concede me an extra half inch of his road. I watch him get closer and closer. He doesn't veer left one degree. I understand that there's a principle involved here, but I don't know what it is. He won't sound his horn because he knows he doesn't have to. He's got me over-matched pretty dramatically and seems determined to press his advantage.

I'd certainly love to surprise him. Instead of retreating to my right like a proper little cyclist, I could maintain my ground, perhaps even veer to my left . . .

There's a war going on around here.

I'm forced to consider some facts. Lee is in love with me. Nobody else is, apparently. When she massages my head, it feels good.

What would my life be like, being with her? At this point I feel no desire to put my mouth, or even my hands, on her body. When she put her hands on me, I was able to feel a weird, humiliating sort of pleasure, braided together with streaks of revulsion. But even if I was crazy about the idea of having sex with women, with Lee it would be like having my aunt going down on me. And very different from the throbs of pure lust I felt with Ndele or David. With Lee I'd been acting a bit—enjoying the physical attention, but half the time fighting the urge to get up off the bed. Having actual sex with a woman would take getting used to, though I don't find it unimaginable that I'd gradually become less uncomfortable. I could certainly stand to be loved.

Would Lee get divorced? Would we live together? In one fell swoop I'd become a person of means: car, house in Oak Park—an orderly, even affluent, life. I could spend much more time taking care of my health, and maybe even getting some writing done.

Jane would have a cow. Jane would have a fucking bull-elephant seal. She'd assume I was joking at first—exactly what I would assume if I was my roommate and had heard all my Lee Marvin sob stories. Jane's next step would be to reason with me, explain how this was simply a reaction to going to Alaska again; to missing David; to what happened with Ndele; to what hadn't happened. She'd shout me down, sulk, try the silent treatment. If I stuck to my guns, though, and told her I was happy, that I'd made up my mind, I know she'd support me. So would my father, I think. So would Stephen Marvin, probably, now that I think of it—although, maybe not.

Jane will stand behind me, whatever I decide. She's proven in eighty different ways that she wants me to be happy in the time I've got left. And it's not like I'd be giving up the chance to have children, or to run off with Kazuo Ishiguro or Joshua Redman or Daniel Day-Lewis.

Assuming that's what I decide.

From my Motel 6 window in downtown Vandalia, I watch a fifteen- or sixteen-year-old girl chatting up one of the mailmen. The guy's about my age, perhaps early thirties, and pretty good-looking; he even looks vaguely intelligent. My angle onto the street is oblique, but I can see that the girl is exactly the type that a person like me could never compete with: gold-yellow hair, ninety-three pounds, giggle giggle. She has on white ankle socks, white deck shoes, green-and-white soccer shorts, a too-big white T-shirt. She's pacing, gesticulating, tugging on the hem of the shirt. I can't make out actual words, just the odd tinkly syllable: -id! She sits on the hood of the mailman's white Jeep, pulls her knees up in front of her, covers her feet with the shirt. The mailman's profile reminds me of Frank O'Hara, but I can tell he's not gay. So can the girl. He minutely adjusts his aviator sunglasses. I can tell he's completely absorbed.

Five seconds later the girl has hopped off the Jeep, and it looks like they're arguing. The girl claps her hands, shakes her head, tiptoes along the curb as though it were a balance beam. Posing. Wringing the end of the shirt. She also keeps talking, a hundred words (at least) to his two. Hands on her hips, she bends at the waist, inspects what might be a scab or a mosquito bite on her shin, then stretches and yawns. The mailman nods at a guy in a pickup truck going through the intersection, then waves at someone else I can't see. Is this some sort of explicitly unsecret rendezvous? Are he and the girl kissing cousins, old friends, coach and third baseman—or father and daughter? That I can't read the signs really irks me.

I jot a couple of words on the postcard to my father, trying to phrase how terrific I feel, how well the trip's going and all; I'll also need to further explain the misunderstanding involving Ndele, though I have no idea how to begin.

When I look up from my labors, the mailman is back in his Jeep. What happened? I'd only had my eyes on the postcard for ten or twelve seconds. The mailman adjusts his sunglasses, shifts into gear. The girl is still talking as the Jeep pulls away. She's stretched out the T-shirt so much that it covers the backs of her knees.

I write: *Diagnosis: dialysis: di. Dithering re-re-re-researchers. Dying to, going to. Dying not to, but still. Or the hithering thithering djinn. So don't worry, Dad. Because killing myself is the last thing I'm going to do.*

Even though I've already stamped it, I tear up this postcard and take out another. I begin more congenially: *Hey . . .*

With the wind and late start, I could only make Elder today, barely twenty-five miles west of Vandalia. The town is little more than a 4B's, a Stop-N-Shop Exxon, the Lonesome Star Bar, Bud Terry's Tacos, and the Nordwick Motel, where I'm staying. I didn't check in until seven.

I went to the Exxon station for a new supply of AJ boxes, two raisin bagels and a strawberry yogurt for breakfast, then across to Bud Terry's to pick up my dinner. Walking the fifty yards there and back, I didn't see a house in any direction. The Lonesome Star Bar is a long flat building that resembles a trailer, in the middle of a huge empty parking lot.

A headline of a three-day-old *USA Today* says "HELP FOR SOME DIABETICS." I scan the article for news about a cure. Could it possibly be old news already?

I hope.

The article turns out to be just another rehash: how the

islet cells get separated out from the rest of a donor's pancreatic tissue in a device called a centrifuge, yielding a drip bag full of "what looks like pink grapefruit juice," which in turn gets fed through a catheter into the patient's liver. Then the inevitable kicker: the procedure will not be available for three to five years for persons not already needing a transplant of other organs: kidneys, livers, eyeballs, whatever—the usual Catch-23 for "healthy" diabetics: we can cure the diabetes, but the other stuff that happens to you is much worse, and you're not even eligible for the partial cure till you're three-fifths dead anyway. Wonderful.

It's time to test my blood, do my shot, have some dinner: guacamole, two steak burritos, two diet IBC root beers. As I twist off the first dark blue cap, I imperiously decide to get naked. My islets don't work, so I'll not eat tonight with my clothes on! After stowing my precious utensils, I put on MTV, use the remote to turn up the sound of Sinead singing "Thief of Your Heart." I spin myself round like a centrifuge, this on the theory that maybe I'll dislodge a few old dead beta cells, or, better, transmogrify them into functional ones. That way I wouldn't have to worry about rejecting them, would I?

I do dumb little jigs while I lip-sync, then stand still and listen. Blood churns and gurgles from deep in my gut to the tip of my left middle finger, which now I must prick. But I won't! I use it to say "Fuck you all!"

I spin myself around maybe six, seven times, then kick off my panties and catch them. I twirl them around on my finger.

By the time that the fiddles kick in I am spinning again, breathing and shivering hard, getting dizzy.

Loud whoops and shrieks from the parking lot startle me awake. I look at my watch: five to ten. Almost dark out. I feel like it's ten in the morning. I must have dozed off after dinner, since both the burritos are gone. Loud country music blasts through my closed window. I needed a solid night's sleep.

I stalk through the vast, crowded lot—past cars, fancy pickups and choppers, young men and women in cowboy hats and feed caps. My plan is to threaten the manager or blow the place up.

When a pink-shirted cowboy says "Howdy" and opens the door for me, the music gets three times as loud. A live band on a slightly raised stage is pumping out "Cinnamon Girl." The singer does not play guitar or sound very much like Neil Young.

I'm gazed upon curiously by several tall women and men; they'd be tall even without their heeled boots. When one of the guys says, "Say, lady," I gesture to indicate that I'm meeting someone up ahead. Squeezing sideways and leading with my elbows, I make my way through further throngs of young western women and men—mostly the latter. What's more fun, after all, than a hundred drunk cowboys? Lots of things, actually. Three novels by Samuel Beckett, blood sugar sex magic, the Pogues, not getting stood up by a gun-toting carjacking basketball player, not testing my blood anymore. But—than a hundred drunk cowboys? How's about . . . what about . . . *one?*

One handsome, semi-drunk cowboy materializes alongside, then in front of me, just as I reach the varnished black bar. He seems rather happy to see me.

"Ma'am, darlin', would you please please please dance with me once 'fore I die?"

His breath's sweet and sour with beer; his chin is a prickly gold golf ball. He's cute.

I dance with him, hard. People back up to make room. There isn't much room, but so what. He shuffles around in his aqua suede boots at the end of his very long legs. The song's almost over, so I don't need to conserve any energy. People are watching us. I know that I'm not a good dancer.

When the song ends I'm puffing and sweating. My partner says, "Thank you."

"You bet."

How are women like dogshit? The older they get, the easier they are to pick up. The band tunes and noodles, entertains several requests, then crashes the thundersome opening chord of "Cowgirl in the Sand."

My partner is trying to speak to me, but the reverb is deafening. He winces. I smile. He smiles back while wincing again.

Then he's shouting.

I'm not sure I've heard him correctly. It looks like he's saying Penny, there's a seat at the bar, but how could he know what my name is?

"Say what?" I shout.

Handsome Cowboy leans closer. "I said, let me know if you want a margarita."

"Oh." I nod. "Si."

Big thunder cracks from the amps.

"You mind running that by me again?"

I get up on tiptoe, put my mouth by his ear. I can tell that he likes it. A lot, as a matter of fact. "Yes, I would."

"Comin' up."

He yells to the bartender, then turns back around. "My name's Steve."

"Evening, Steve. My name's Penny."

When we're done shaking hands, I take a five-dollar bill from my pocket and flatten it out on the bar. Handsome Steve gives me a look. I give him one back, since I want him to know I'll be paying. Someone whoops near the front of the room.

Handsome Steve picks up my bill and folds it in quarters, creasing it sharply each time. Making darn sure I'm watching, he shows me the little green square, then slaps his right palm against his left fist. When he opens both hands, they are empty.

"There's not a lot more where that old boy came from," I tell him, impressed. But why am I using such cowgirlish grammar?

In the meantime Handsome Steve has reached behind my left ear, making sure he brushes the lobe with his thumb. It feels good. When he pulls back his hand, there's the five: square, neatly folded, the same. I don't feel his fingers as he slides the bill into the hip pocket of my jeans.

"You from Canada or something?" he says.

I shake my head. Canada? Why would he think that?

"Missoula?"

I shake my head no, realize I'm being too coy. Ask myself, Why not cooperate?

When the drinks arrive, I allow Steve to pay. I lick two tongue widths of salt from the rim of my glass, then sip. Margarita! I savor the burn of tequila cutting through all the sugar and fruit. Three more sips. I'm already feeling the bug-mellow buzz. Es delicious.

"Where you from then?" Steve asks me.

I swallow some more margarita and look him in the eye. He meets my gaze for six or eight seconds, then takes a long pull on his Coors, pretending that's the reason he's looking away. I don't buy it.

"Last time somebody asked me that, you know what I told him?"

"I hope you told him the truth."

"You know what I told him?" I repeat more aggressively.

We stare at each other. Steve looks confused. As who would not be, confronted by such unalloyed, thoroughly unmotivated bitchery. I stare at his crystalline irises. He reminds me of someone I know.

I bring him outside, promoting his butt and the small of his back through the lot to the door of my room. I won't let him kiss me. I won't let him know where I'm from.

Inside, with the light on, I unsnap the front of his shirt, popping each pearly button all the way down to his navel. He lets me. When he reaches for the hem of my T-shirt I brush away his hand. Then I strip him.

His torso reminds me of Michelangelo's *David*: off-white, coolly chiselled, convex. I've never laid eyes on the actual sculpture, but Jane keeps a magnetized version of him on our refrigerator, complete with four outfits. Jane likes to dress him up in his little white briefs and black leather jacket. I put his blue paisley boxer shorts on upside down, making a very tight, very short skirt slit up both sides, this to go with his clunky mid-calf lace-up Wellingtons. Sometimes we just leave him naked.

I've put Cowboy Steve on his back on the side of the bed. His hard-on is warped to the left, but I straighten it out in my fist. I inch up his chest, shimmy myself past his chin, rock back and forth as his mouth goes to town on my cunt. When his teeth nip or graze me, I shout down at him to be careful.

Later I let him get up. When I kiss him, I taste myself. Hmm. But his mustache is scratching me. I pull back and lean on the dresser. I tell him to stand there. "Don't move!" I gulp down the rest of his beer.

We fuck with each other a while. He wants to flip me around, bend me over. I let him. When I feel his hard-on start pulsing, I shake myself loose. "I'm directing this skin flick, goddamn it!"

I bend at the waist, brace my hands on the headboard. He drives in and fucks me. He fucks me. He pulls out and teases me, then fucks me so hard, almost viciously, faster and faster and harder.

We see Steve on top, from behind, fucking Penny. Her face is turned sideways. In the light from the parking lot, we can make out her glassy expression. In spite of Steve's furious efforts, she's plainly distracted by something.

Steve grinds his white concave ass, doing his best to enthrall her.

From two hundred yards away, the neon sign of the Lonesome Star flickers—cut off by trees, reappearing—as Steve and I stroll through a forest of pines. Smells like Christmas. A half-moon breaks through the branches overhead as a stream gurgles off to our right.

Suddenly: a pair of red-yellow eyes and low growls fifteen feet in front of us. I freeze. I hear myself breathe, feel my pulse pounding back through my temples, as the animal charges—an immense female husky. It sends me sprawling backward and slashes at me with its teeth. When I try to turn over, it tears at my shoulder and shakes me. The bones in my spine come apart. I see stars. I scream, but my voice doesn't work anymore. The bitch bites my face, snapping and splintering bone, crunching down into my brain. I keep screaming.

I wake up still struggling, hugging myself, slick with sweat. The light is on next to my bed, but it's morning.

Dreaming all this, I've outslept a thunderstorm. It's almost nine-thirty when I get up and look out the window. The pavement is steaming and glistening around small shallow puddles, but the sun's beating down on it, uninterrupted by clouds. By the time I eat breakfast and roll out my bike, the road will be as dry as a bone.

I swing through the now empty lot on my way back to 2, swerving to avoid a smashed amber bottle. Two songbirds warble and whistle—mountain bluebirds? As I try to pick them out in the bushes, I roll through a puddle of navy-blue puke: someone was having some blueberry pie with his Coors. I slow down to keep it from spraying up off my tire, but a chunk neatly lodged in the tread still appears every rotation, mocking me with its disgustingness.

At the exit of the lot there's an official-looking red hexagonal sign that says WHOA. I pedal right past it, heading west out of Elder, singing out loud and off-key in a bad imitation of Neil:

> Well, hello, bear-ded cowboy,
> Won't you tell me your name?
> When nobody loves you
> Is it the same?
> It's tequila in you
> That makes you wanna play—this—game—

The patch of blue puke has worn off by the time I have played the first solo.

Two evenings later I find myself ensconced in the Diamond Willow Inn near the outskirts of Havre. Last no-smoking room the man had. Last room, period. Sixty-two dollars, no breakfast. Tourists, he told me. And hunters. On top of the car wash next door is a larger-than-life plaster statue of a snarling blue grizzly—bristling, ridiculous, the color of cornflowers. Stupid.

My glucometer beeps and I read it. Four twelve. I throw it as hard as I can against the far wall. It clatters down into the sink.

Four hours later I'm lying faceup on the bed, fingering my J & J matchbook, staring at the white acoustic tiles on the ceiling, the shadows of curtains and fixtures. Even the dumb angry fly bouncing along upside down casts a shadow. It has much more energy than I do.

Headlights go by, horizontal, causing the shadows to rotate. Patterns on the ceiling resolve into moonscape. So now *I'm* upside down and the ceiling is the moon's pocky surface. The fly bounces by like Neil Armstrong, petulantly buzzing its staticky pronunciamento: *One small step for man* . . . Quite headstrong, this fly, although not very smart in its choice of possible escape routes. Ndele F. Headstrong, number-one guy on the moon. I can just hear him sometimes, remembering me to his homeboys: *Yeah, man, I just left the sick bitch lying there, quivering in a slick of her own come.*

Steady now. Exhale.

That's better.

I blink and breathe in. Much much better.

I keep making lists of what his real story might be. He could be a professional basketball player: He seemed to be telling the truth when he told me he was, plus I saw several people react to him as though he were famous. He sure has the body of one. But there also seems to be circumstantial evidence that he's a carjacker, that he has even attempted to kill someone. He could be a drug-dealing gang member who purchased the car with his proceeds. Maybe Ndele Rimes is a famous basketball player, and the guy I was with was his brother, who was simply too embarrassed to admit he was Nobody Rimes. He told me his brother was a car courier, but maybe it's the other way around. Did I hear on the news he was AWOL from the navy, or am I only imagining that?

In any event, this fly doesn't like it in here. It wants to go outside and play, find some more putrid garbage to suck on, roadkill to rub its greedy little stick hands together over, oh boy. Like a frantic hungry prayer before supper. Grace, we used to call it. Before.

Mr Leopold Bloom, after all, ate with relish the outer organs of fifteen-year-old girls. He liked thick giblet soup, islets of Langerhans tucked inside pellets of seaweed, the entangling Velcro of wrecked glomeruli, a stuffed roast heart, nutty gizzards. Most of all he liked FK506, which derived from a Japanese fungus and gave to his palate a fine tang of faintly scented urine.

Kidneys were on his mind as he moved about the kitchen softly, righting her breakfast things on the humpy tray as stately, plump Penelope Culligan pedaled west against the wind on Route 2. She'd never been humped by a woman.

I also have windburn and sunburn and unsightly rings around my collar, salt stains from sweat at my pits. I feel sort of dazed, uncoordinated.

I almost got killed this afternoon. I wasn't paying sufficient attention as a piggybacked semi went past. I believe that I swerved the wrong way. But I knew I'd survived when the truck burped internal combustion back at me. My lungs both seized up for a second, revolted.

I also believe that I may have slightly miscalculated as far as my ability to ride from Chicago to Alaska in eighty-six days is concerned. My plan to be back by September may have to be altered somewhat.

May have to be radically altered.

Ten hours later I'm alounge on a firm queen-sized bed, dunking Fig Newtons into 2-percent milk and watching myself in the mirror attached to the door of the closet. The Trilogy is open beside my left thigh, along with my notepad and pen. Working hard.

The Comedy Channel has a rerun of Seinfeld, the episode in which—or *where*, as they say—George and Jerry get writer's block attempting to compose a sitcom pilot. They sit on couches perpendicular to one another, dutifully brandishing notepads and pens, thinking hard.

Glazed by a week of insomnia, I'm also over-invigorated from riding against the wind and uphill, and exhausted from thinking too much. I even *look* like a freshly glazed doughnut. Holding the torn-open carton of milk in one hand, I shamelessly dunk and scarf Newtons with the other, then suck on my sweet, sticky fingers. Good thing I smashed the glucometer.

Meryl Wilde, a psychiatrist my father arranged for me to see the month after Saint died, asked me whether I thought my taciturnity, my somber visage, my undemonstrative manner was because I was sad or depressed. I told her I thought I was sad, not depressed. Perhaps it was just my "natural motor style," she suggested. Motor style, I told her, relishing the term. I'd never heard it before. And because what, after all, did I have to be sad about? I told her that this was the way I'd always comported myself; it had been my motor style for as long as I could remember. She ended up prescribing the Zoloft anyway. I took it sporadically for three or four weeks, and when the prescription ran out I didn't renew it. By that time I'd reached the maximum number of psychiatric appointments allowed by my father's insurance.

Seinfeld says, "You come in, and you say . . . 'How's it going?'"

Hoots on the laugh track as I bite off two thirds of a milk-laden Newton. It's chewy and succulent, like a small, fruity cake, just like it says on the package. But the milk's magic enzymes have somehow released, then intensified, the natural inner sweetness of the figs. It's amazing.

George says, "'How's it going?' That's *brilliant!*"

The laugh track explodes. I scarf down the rest of the Newton and take out another one. Dunk it. Kramer makes one of his patented hipster-doofus entrances: stumbling coolth betrayed by antic motor style and irrepressible passion.

Applause.

I stop at a sporting-goods store in downtown Americus.

Binoculars, fishing lures, tackle boxes, wading boots designed for extremely tall fishermen. I check out the ice chests, but even the smallest one wouldn't be portable. Most of the clothing is cut from one of three camouflage patterns: old-fashioned green-tan-brown-black, a beige-gray-and-black pattern, or Desert Storm sand pebbles. Most of the rest of the clothing is a Day-Glo orange you couldn't *miss* seeing, even through two miles of woods. Some of the clothes want it both ways: fashioned from camouflage, then adorned with strips of Day-Glo orange tape. Do the people who wear this stuff want to be hidden or noticed?

In the back of the store are the guns. There must be five hundred for sale here, including some beautiful double-barreled shotguns. No Bosses, however—the make Ernest Hemingway used. They remind me nonetheless of that famous last sentence of the Carlos Baker biography: "He slipped in two shells, lowered the gun butt carefully to the floor, leaned forward, pressed the twin barrels against his forehead just above the eyebrows, and tripped both triggers." That was just over the mountains, in Idaho, the next state I'll hit on this trip—three days from now if the wind doesn't kick up again. I don't know what make Kurt Cobain used.

When you're that far in extremis, do you notice things like what gunmetal feels like against your forehead—or tastes like?

The guns in this store gleam with clear oil. They'd probably taste hard and bitterly oily and cold, a jolt to your most recent fillings. Cold blue-black steel just before the white-hot explosion.

They also have pistols and semiautomatic rifles—machine guns, basically. I ask the clerk what the rules are for buying a gun.

"No wait for the rifles," he tells me. His shaggy white eyebrows get crooked. "Not yet, anyway. If that's what you mean."

"Would that stop a grizzly?" I ask, pointing to a gorgeous walnut-stocked shotgun behind him.

"Depends on where you hit him."

"Suppose I hit her right in the mouth."

The eyebrows get higher and farther apart. "Now, Miss, I don't think you really wanna get close enough to a grizzly to where a shotgun would do you much good. What you'd probably want is a rifle, at least thirty gauge."

"Oh."

He shows me three rifles, each of which he guarantees will drop any grizzly I'm likely to come across. He converses with me as though women came in and bought high-powered guns every day. There's a Visa decal on the counter.

He shows me a .357-magnum pistol. Using two hands, I straighten my arms, raise it up, and sight the stuffed deer head mounted to the wall at the opposite end of the store. After two or three seconds, my arms start to tremble.

"That's the only problem with the .357. And plus, she's still empty. Weighs over five pounds when you load her with shells."

"Which, of course, I'd be wanting to *do* . . . "

He points his blunt trigger finger right at my lower lip: bingo.

The idea of having a gun has been vaguely appealing of late. Packing heat. Stopping power. You talking to *me?* I've heard that if a woman carries a gun, a violent male criminal will figure out a way to take it and use it on her. Shot with your own gun, and so on. But the way I figure it, you don't buy a gun unless you're willing to use it. A situation arises, you don't stand there negotiating, or trying to look unintimidated; you aim and pull the trigger. No warning shots, either. It's something I know I could do. In the next hundred miles or so I'll be in bear country again; for all I know, I might already be there. There are cougars around here as well. But I'd have to jettison clothes to make room for it, just at the point where I need to be adding some warm ones. Packing eight extra pounds on a bike is like hauling an oven on the side of a car. Most tents weigh less than half that, and at least with a tent I'd be able to center the weight on the rack. Whichever pannier I carried a gun in, it would throw the rear end way off-kilter. What I'd need is a rack for the front to balance the overall load; it would also make the gun easier to get to if Très Cheeseheads pull alongside me again. It sure would be satisfying to be able to respond the next time with something more stinging than irony.

"What do you think?" says the salesman.

"I think that's what I'm gonna do—do some thinking."

"So you like the little Colt."

"I do. But no. I still—"

"The Winchester?"

"No. I mean I still need to think just a little bit more about this."

I shiver a little in my T-shirt and shorts as I walk back to my motel. It's dropped about twenty degrees since I pulled into town around five. The sky in the east is matte black, but directly above me it's a crystalline, worlds-away sapphire.

The freckle-faced woman in the manager's office waves as I go by her window. I smile and wave back. When I checked in she told me how jealous she was of the trip I was on. "All that *road*," she said, shaking her head. "All of that time to just *think*."

I let myself into my room, put on my blue hooded sweat-shirt, make sure the door's locked again as I leave—and make sure I still have the key. I walk north toward the prairie, cutting through the parking lot of the McDonald's in which I ate dinner. A guy with belt-length red hair tied back with a purple bandanna sits by himself in a booth by the window reading *The Lady in Kicking Horse Reservoir*.

I remember brushing my teeth in Rugby that morning, and what happened just after. Ndele's white towel was draped from a hook behind the door. I touched it with my finger, then held it against my cheek: bleached, threadbare terrycloth still damp from his shower. I spread it out, turned it around. One spot near the middle was moister. I muzzled my nose in that place and inhaled. My whole face. I could smell us: skin, muscle, sweat, vaguely salty white shadows . . . Ndele.

I kick a small bottle, keep walking. My legs aren't terribly good at it; they're better at pedaling, lately. I assume that it's too cold for snakes. If a rattlesnake bit me, I'd probably die here tonight; but before I passed out I'd be in considerable agony. I might become paralyzed, be discovered alive in the morning, or three days later, lying in the dirt with drool running sideways across my blue cheek. Spend the rest of my life in the no-rehab ward of a hospital.

The night isn't perfectly clear, but I still can see stars, tens of thousands of them, fifteen times brighter than they ever appear in Chicago. I also see floaters in my vitreous humor, so what else is new. The bunched-up hood of the sweatshirt cushions the back of my head.

I finally spot the Big Dipper. From reading *National Geographic*, I know that a massive black hole swirls near the center of the Milky Way, at the dark empty backward-time heart of the galaxy. Our own little sun-star is somewhere underneath or behind me, shining through ozone and cirrus and smog onto Asia, while an infinitesimal fraction of its light bounces back off the three-quarter moon over here. The sun is off near the fringe of the cluster of stars I'm looking at, tiny and not very powerful, getting sucked toward the blackness as it burns itself out: its glomeruli and islets of Langerhans don't work anymore, so it's dying. It's developed retinopathy. It's experiencing end-stage renal complications as it continues to be irresistibly swept toward the center of its galaxy, only one of the limitless billions. It's having a slow-motion stroke. I can feel it, I think; it isn't just dizziness, either. Gravity's holding me upright. I feel a vague tilt toward the froth, feel myself becoming a note or a hole or a tree. I shift my weight from one pale, as-yet-unamputated foot to the other, and shiver. The sky spins around me. I sway but feel strong. I could fuck if I wanted to now—the guy in McDonald's, I bet. Have a child. Because maybe I'm already pregnant. I could live with Lee Marvin and raise it. I could run, write a book, finish my dissertation, start an entirely new one about Beckett and mortal dark humor and stars, about Beckett and diabetes and bicycles. I could really rethink this whole project.

I know that during the first 10^{-36} of a second the strong force got separated out from gravity and time, that 10^{-31} of a second later numerous three-quark protons and neutrons got generated as the universe cooled to a trillion degrees Kelvin. Other things happened, and according to the way we apprehend time, they happened rather quickly. Matter became the primary source of gravity, then decoupled itself from electromagnetic energy as the universe became transparent; my islets of Langerhans got zapped by my own motherfucking immune system. Radiant energy began to travel more freely, and many more galaxies formed, spinning off black holes and quasars and—the best stuff—dark matter, which now makes up more than 99 percent of the mass of the universe. I'm breathing the stuff in right now. Everything else—Route 2, Ndele, Alaska, the sabotaged business inside my body, the lights I can see in the sky—is just froth.

Dark matter. Yeah. To be part of a sun or a system that becomes a black hole. Bodiless. Out of the froth and into the dark, just like that. I hope so, at least.

What I am convinced of is that it doesn't make any difference what you believe, publicly or privately, officially or off-the-record, while you're kneeling in some varnished pew or strolling along the Evanston lakefront or trembling in the fetal position. Whatever long-term deal the universe had in store from the outset is what will befall you. There aren't going to be separate and distinct "personalized" afterlives for agnostics and Lutherans and Sunis and pantisocratics and gay Presbyterians, Catholics and diabetics and Hindus. Everyone will get the same deal, the same brand of afterlife, or everyone will become worm meat and rot gelid and consciousnessless forever. Be nothing. Have no sensations at all. The thought doesn't fill me with horror.

But I'd love to be part of the dark, since the froth part is not working out. But so how do you get there? By dying or living in a particular way? I don't think so—since how could *how* you approached it possibly make any difference? But what would it be like to be out there? It seems doubtful that you'd be able to experience things with anything resembling the physical senses, so what would that leave you? Memories, thoughts, more desires? No thank you.

I'm definitely up for a new way of knowing and feeling and wanting things, a new way of making things happen, or just letting things happen. Would all this be easier, or make any more sense, if I were "religious"?

Oh dark matter, dark matter. We all want to turn into darkness.

All of us? No. Though that's what I'm betting will happen. I hope. Forget all this stardusty, neverland bullshit.

In any event, I am ready.

I find myself back by Route 2, a few hundred yards west of town. I can see the yellow arches of McDonald's and the satellite dish outside my motel.

Two cars zoom by, making me suddenly realize that I could rent one myself. I could pick one up tomorrow morning right here in Americus and drive to Seattle in two or three days. Having a car might even make it easier to track down Mr. Rimes once I got there. I could check out that bookstore he told me about.

I could take the ferry to Juneau from Bellingham instead

of Prince Rupert. It takes only thirteen more hours to get up
to Juneau from Bellingham than it does from Prince Rupert,
and costs something like eighty extra dollars.

Avis and Budget and Dollar and Hertz all take Visa. The
Alaska Marine Highway takes Visa. So do hotels in Seattle and
Bellingham. So does Amtrak, for that matter. Plus all of the
airlines, of course.

> Omniscient, omnipotent plastic
> Oh gray, rectilinear credit card
> With rounded-off corners and dove holographic
> Sporting my overly confident signature

> Backed by the billions of Citicorp
> Of Sioux Falls, South Dakota
> 57117-6000
> Just save me and bill me, Amen.

A coyote starts yipping—laughing, I bet, at my pitiful qua-
trains. But I *can* do any number of things—declare bankruptcy
and trump my bad credit; fly to Las Vegas, play blackjack, win
back the money I've spent. I could also sit in my bedroom
back home and finish my dissertation. I could get a new job. I
could visit Mount Fuji in the company of three Shinto priest-
esses, or lie by myself in the cold on the side of the mountain
and wait for a storm to blow in. I could leap from the side of
the mountain. I could let myself go. I could refuse to speak
under any circumstances, even under doctor's orders, even if
my unloved betrothed took an ax and chopped off my finger. I
could refuse to test my blood, do my shot, to ever take care of
myself. I could take the train back to Chicago. I could ride my
bike west on Route 2.

This latest stretch of 2 winds parallel to the Milk River as it cuts through a mile-wide moraine, most of it strewn with gray-and-yellow boulders dotting the lumpy beige hills. Some of the boulders sit an inch from the side of the road, and I keep imagining rattlesnakes coiled in their shade, waiting for me to get spilled by the rut they've chosen their shade boulder for its proximity to—specifically, to a spot about twelve feet beyond, and slightly to the right of, the rut. That's snake logic for you.

I've been climbing slowly and steadily for the last two weeks, almost fifteen hundred feet since I crossed the Dakota border. I always thought of Montana as mountainous—why else call it Montana?—but I've now ridden more than halfway across it and have yet to see *one*. Not even too many hillocks or foothills or buttes. The change of elevation is so gradual that I've noticed it more in my legs; I find myself riding in thirteenth or fourteenth, a gear or two lower than I usually use on flat ground with no wind against me.

What you see along this stretch of 2 is a pretty much endless progression of wheat, much of it crosshatched in two shades of gold. Where wheat isn't growing, the prairie comes right up alongside the road: acres and acres of June grass and bluejoint, most of them strewn with round granite boulders. Some of the farmers have piled up the boulders at intervals in the middle of their fields or along barbed-wire fences, but in most of the fields they are randomly spaced, still lying out where the last glacier happened to drop them.

Later I ride past a cluster of little black *Giant*-style derricks rhythmically humping the landscape. No James Dean tending them, though, or waving sideways to me from his hip as I pedal on by. No Rock Hudson trying to screw him. No gushers, either, right now. I'd love to be watching as one just went off, but my sense is that it's not gonna happen this morning. Oh well.

If this were the last place I ever laid eyes on, it would not be the end of the world.

The shadow of my body and bike are etched in sharp focus against the bleached asphalt, angled now slightly in front of me. Until I can get it slanted behind me, I'll have the hottest, windiest half of the day still ahead.

I think about riding by moonlight. At Al's Bike Shop back in Chinook I had them repack the ball bearings and put on a new titanium chain, so I'm chugging right now with approximately point zero eight six more efficiency—but no light. They had lights, of course—the sleek little German solar-powered number, I noted, was almost two hundred dollars—but it didn't occur to me that I might have a use for one. There was also a neat pyramid of pee bottles on sale for $2.49—about 50 cents more than the one David had offered to buy for me at the REI store in Chicago. I wanted to prove I could rough it with the best of them—would Emma Pitt use a pee bottle?—so I neither scoffed at the idea nor encouraged him to buy one, and we left the store with a trunkload of other gear but without a $2.00 pee bottle. I have no idea—I have endless ideas—as to whether David himself would have used it that night, but . . . At Al's I also bought two pairs of gloves, a new chamois crotch liner, chamois fat, four plain white T-shirts, and a fresh supply of Power Bars. I'm no longer keeping meticulous track of my pale-yellow receipts.

The new gloves feel great on my hands: spongy and comfy and sleek. I pedal along in fifteenth and think about reincarnation. So far the leading choices today have been the hands of God and Adam on the Sistine Chapel, freshly cleaned, unretouched, much admired by multitudes of tourists craning their necks; that stroke of beige paint on the squared-off right nipple of Picasso's *Girl with a Mandolin*; a paper-bark maple; Emily Dickinson, closeted away in Amherst, no agues or pains, no diabetes, able to get all my work done, perhaps even some of it published; the president of Ireland, but with American-style constitutional powers; myself without diabetes, with my Ph.D., two books, and a tenure-track job at Cornell; Maria Callas; Sarah Vaughan; Maire Ni Bhranain; Kathleen Battle; the singer from Mazzy Starr whose name I always forget; some sort of incorporeal musical consciousness in a more or less local black hole where the direction of time was reversed but things still made sense and it wasn't too cold; a colder, more ferocious musical consciousness, a kind of Valkyrie, at the expanding edge of the universe, blazing out into the frothlessness at point nine four *c*; modal Miles Davis; hard-bop Miles Davis; Viktoria Mullova; Glenn Gould, never having to leave my studio in Toronto; Suzanne Deschevaux-Dumesnil Beckett; myself, exactly as I have been and am, exactly this second, right now, but without diabetes; myself with David, alive and intact; myself with Ndele, and he's really a basketball player, and his knee is okay, and his sister and I don't have diabetes; nothing forever, no past or future, having never been born or existed, no consciousness or life or desire; a dolphin; a tiger; an alpha female Arctic wolf, with two strong male pups; an alpha male Arctic wolf; a droplet of blood on the moon . . .

Skip that last one. The view—if droplets have views—would get old in a matter of centuries. There'd be nothing to do besides seep.

Yet that's pretty much what I feel like sometimes when I'm out here alone: a skin bag of off-kilter blood pedaling across lunar grasses.

I'm now near the end of a half-mile-long strip of Route 2 that is being repaved—about a week too late for my purposes. If the state of Montana could only have waited a week, I wouldn't have to inhale the petroleum fumes off the smoking new asphalt, or deal with the leering and shirtless flagmen, especially the one with the patches of hair around his nipples—the one who looks like he's tempted to stick the handle of his SLOW sign through my spokes and then jump me.

An Indian guy in a red tie-dyed T-shirt is hitchhiking just beyond the END CONSTRUCTION sign. We nod at each other, and he smiles like he knows me. I watch him recede in my mirror, waving when he waves, relieved to be breathing fresh air.

I arrive in a daze outside Felco, Montana, population 121. The sign has been pierced by two bullets, dented from behind by five or six others. I've seen a lot worse, but the town doesn't look all that promising.

I've been riding for almost six hours already, since seven-thirty this morning, through vast tracts of buffalo grass and blue grama, the occasional coyote and pronghorn. Two of the pronghorn were standing fifteen or twenty feet from the road, staring at me as I slowed way down, almost stopping, to watch them. I have no idea how I smelled to them—pretty nauseating, probably, since I eat things they'd think were disgusting. To me they smelled bitter, like almonds. Like they had too much cyanide in their systems; like they were killing themselves in slow motion on purpose with whatever it was they were grazing on. I'm probably wrong about this. Other than skunks, it's the first time I've smelled a wild animal.

The last time I stopped was in Shelby, eighteen against-the-wind miles ago. I want to make Cut Bank by five. Two of my water bottles are empty, and I could probably brew cappuccino with what's left in the third. My electrolytes and blood sugar are both way too low, and I've let my front wheel start to weave a few times: not good with piggybacked semis blasting past my elbow, sucking me in toward their maw.

From what I can see, Felco consists architecturally of a boarded-up gas station, a grocery without any lights on, two corrugated sheds, two frame houses both painted dark green, ten or twelve trailers on blocks. One tilted house is sinking down into its yard. No actual tumbleweed, though. And no barking mongrels so far. The next yard I ride past does have a swaybacked Appaloosa grazing alongside a trio of pink lawn flamingos; there's also a doorless sedan with goldenrod shooting up through the holes where the seats used to be. The rest of the chassis is mostly a lacework of rust.

It's Sunday, I think, and the Steer Bar's the only place open. Forty-five minutes ago I was slavering for an icy mango Snapple, strawberry Gatorade, iced tea with lemon and sugar; at this point I'll settle for tap water. I lean my bike against the tar-paper wall, adjust the bungee securing my helmet and sleeping bag, squat down and bounce on my toes. When I stand up I notice, exactly at eye level, a succinct pastel memo: 4Q.

I look around, stretch, get my bearings, shifting my weight from one tingly foot to the other; my thigh muscles want to keep pedaling. If I tried to walk fast I'd tip over, so I stand here and stretch for a while. Something's up. I detach my three water bottles, dig out my wallet, swallow a buzz of dry nerves, and go in.

At the bar is a man in a cowboy hat, two men in feed caps. No women. No one in the room besides me who is not at the bar in a hat. I don't see a bartender, either. One standard-issue, rope-wound longhorn rack hangs above the bar; keno and poker machines off to the right, all unplugged; above them a mounted cutthroat trout and two glass-eyed pronghorn, one with an antler snapped off. A printed cardboard sign taped to the paneling encourages me to play KENO! KENO! Another sign offers directions: LIQUOR UP FRONT, POKER IN THE REAR.

Thirsty and helmetless, I advance through the gloom toward the register. I'm scared, but I also resent being scared. All three patrons have turned on their stools and are frankly checking me out. Feed Cap 1 looks kind of ornery. I hold in my chest, square up my shoulders, half smile. I want to look sexless but cordial.

Suddenly, eight or ten feet to my left and a little behind me, in slanting gray light, there's a car. My muscles tense involuntarily, preparing to leap from its path; there's also a five-second rush of adrenalin before I understand that it's no longer moving. It's a lime-green Del Sol convertible with a black plastic bra framing its headlights. The top's off, of course. But no driver. No passenger. Its blue-and-red Wyoming plate proclaims WHOA. The economy-car-sized hole in the wall just behind it is shrouded with taut strips of bubble wrap. Two small circular tables are overturned on the floor amid tar-paper shingles and splintered beige paneling. A third pronghorn head mounted on a shard of paneling has survived the collision with both of its antlers intact.

I stand here and stare at the car. No shattered glass, no sprays of blood on the windshield or dash. The bumper is dented, concave, but other than that the car seems undamaged. Very clean, too. Even shiny. It looks like a raffle prize at a badly lit JDF fund-raiser. An unopened bottle of maraschino cherries lies on its side an inch from the fat left-front tire.

This town needs new signs, I decide. Better signs. BEGIN CONSTRUCTION. STEER BAR. CAUTION CHILDREN. I try to breathe evenly, clutching my bottles and wallet, refusing to let myself have a reaction. The room smells like beer and new car.

Feed Cap 2 pulls from one of his overalls pockets a rolled-up strip of the plastic that the wall's been repaired with. He squints, fiercely concentrating, shifting his gnarled thumb and index finger.

Pop.

Pop.

Cowboy Hat finally drawls, "That's an accident, but nobody was hurt." He laughs for a moment but stops when I smile.

I glance toward the car, assuming that's what he's referred to. I lower the timbre of my voice and try to sound knowledgeable when I ask him, "Still run?"

"S'pose so," he says. "She sure *looks* pretty good, assumin' a person happened to go *in* for that sort of thing. But we don't have the *keys.*"

"Don't know then, now do we," says Feed Cap 2, tilting his eyebrows and popping another one smartly. The report's like a log going off in a fireplace. It looks like he's trimming his nails.

"But she looks pretty good in that *bra*," says Cowboy Hat. "Wunt you say?"

Yes I would. But I don't.

"Pretty *darn* good, I would say," amplifies Cowboy Hat.

"Where's the driver?" I ask them. "I mean, you couldn't just walk away from—"

"Don't know."

"We don't know. Just found her *parked* here when we opened the place after this mornin's *services*."

Pop.

Doesn't one of these gentlemen know how to hot-wire an ignition? Couldn't they put it in neutral and push it back out? Have they not called the cops? Why didn't the air bag, or air bags, deploy? Why do men insist on assigning to automobiles a feminine gender? Another question I don't ask is: Shouldn't the plastic go up *after* the car's been removed? There are two or three others.

"Figured it was yours," Feed Cap 1 tells me. The first time he's opened his mouth.

I tell him I'm riding a bicycle, presenting my bottles as evidence.

"Be, that as it, may," he pronounces ex cathedra. Blitzed.

Hugging the bottles against my damp shirt, I try hard to fathom his point. *Pop.* My legs and back are cooling down fast, getting stiff.

Feed Cap 2 asks me, "But so that ain't why you come back then?"

"I haven't 'come back.' I just got here." Though it's time to be going, I think.

Feed Cap 1 belches. "Scoozma." He covers his mouth with a fist, belches more daintily. "Whoa."

Pop.

"How far you ridin' it to?" Cowboy Hat asks me. "You don't mind my askin'."

I nod, shake my head, tell my story. I add things, subtract things. The three men supply me with water.

Back on my bike in the dazzle outside, I squint at a blasted gray moon hanging low in the sky above the shed across the road. It's four-sevenths full, on the wane. Stratus clouds, looking like curdled gray haze, drift left to right, headed east. A few thousand feet higher up some jumbo cumulonimbus jobs scud along out of the north much much more quickly. I hope that it doesn't mean rain.

Last night on CNN there was a piece about a trio of hand-somely funded gerontologists—all three themselves quite handsome and affluent-looking—in San Francisco who are try-ing to extend the life span of humans to a hundred and eighty years. I'd like to make fifty or sixty. If I was born a decade or two in the future, doctors would use gene-splicing therapy to cure me in utero. If I'd been born a few decades earlier, before insulin therapy, I would've been dead by the time I was five.

A lot of my heroes died young. (If they hadn't, maybe they wouldn't be my heroes.) Kafka was forty, I think. Chopin and Mozart were both thirty-eight, Keats twenty-six, Rimbaud even younger. Sylvia Plath was thirty, Anne Sexton forty-five. Anne Frank was only sixteen. Mozart wrote *Figaro*, the string quintets, the "Trio Divertimento," the "Requiem" . . . and Mozart is dead, so how bad can being dead be? Frida Kahlo and George Eliot and Miles Davis and Marguerite Duras and Dante Alighieri and Samuel Beckett and Sarah Vaughan and Hannah Arendt and Suzanne Langer and Abraham Lincoln and Maria Callas and Billie Holiday are dead. So—really now—how bad can being dead be?

When Nabokov characterized the life span of humans as a "brief crack of light between two infinities of darkness" he got it about right, I would say. Not that I *know*, but I find his take very convincing. Ditto for Emily Dickinson's "Born—Bridalled—Shrouded/In a Day." Her solution is also convincing: "Caress a Trigger absently/and wander out of life." I would love to. And Beckett's work is pretty much one long take on how short life is: "giving birth astride the grave" is just one of his more pungent images. It also seems funny to me.

The aspects of the Trilogy that used to interest me most were its writtenness, its formal elegance and austerity, the aplomb with which it deconstructed itself, or encouraged itself to be deconstructed. Then for years I was obsessed by the notion that *Molloy*, *Malone Dies*, and *The Unnamable* didn't really comprise a discrete, separate trilogy properly so-called, but in fact were part of a continuum including *Murphy*, *Watt*, *Mercier and Camier*, and *How It Is*.

Five years ago I shocked myself by winning the department's Hopewell Selby Award for my master's thesis, in which I "succinctly and convincingly demonstrated" that in terms of narrative dynamics, prose rhythms, and the "accelerating inertia" and physical deterioration of the eponymous narrators, the difference between parts I and II of *Molloy*, so long as the order of the parts was reversed, was exactly analogous to what occurs vis-à-vis Molloy and Malone, and Malone and Mahood. The Trilogy was thus more usefully understood as Four Novels: *Moran*, *Molloy*, *Malone Dies*, and *Mahood (or The Unnamable)*. Not exactly beach-blanket reading, of course, yet apparently of sufficient academic interest to get me admitted into the Ph.D. program, where I've languished ever since.

I now read the novels as a supreme comedy sequence, an on-paper monologue of preternatural funniness, and at the same time as a deadly serious self-help book. Beckett refuses to assume that everybody is young and beautiful and healthy. He assumes just the opposite: that the loss of one's health is a given. He continually waxes hilarious on the desire to have never been born, on the idea that sexual intercourse is physically and metaphysically disgusting, or at least problematical. I also love the way he transcends—neuters—gender. "There's so little difference between women and men, between mine at least." Which is even more true, of course, the older people get. It also helps make it okay for a chick to write a dissertation on a dead white male writer.

Naive, unschooled readers have always employed these criteria: can they "see themselves" in the characters, "identify" with their problems, share their little fantasies, etc. I used to express my contempt for such middle-class narcissism, such corporate narrative sentimentality, and the consumerist value structures they invidiously engendered. Maybe I'm changing my mind because I want to inhabit a fictional universe in which I am normal.

There is also this factor: Samuel Beckett is only the handsomest man of the twentieth century. Iron-gray hair raked straight back on the top but still standing up, buzzed on the sides and in back. Cliffhanger cheekbones, bird-of-prey beak, brilliant and calm and ferocious blue eyes. Not that it matters, of course, how he looked. No, of course not. My feelings about Sam's appearance contradict my most cherished notions about how things like haircuts and how tight your skin fits should never count. They usually still manage to, somehow.

Five miles west of Cut Bank I start to get light-headed, woozy. Too dizzy to ride anymore. Should I head back to town or keep going? The next town ahead is McCrook, at least twenty miles up the road. As I suck down a carton of AJ, I turn and look back. No trace or shimmer of Cut Bank. No evidence of humans, in fact, on any horizon. Maybe everyone else on the planet is dead. Maybe I'm the most alive person around anymore. Wouldn't that be something?

My original plan was to touch base with Michelle every day if I started to feel sick. That soon became every other day, then every other day but today.

I called Michelle twice the first week. We talked about the sights I'd seen, how far I'd ridden, the food I was able to get my hands on, and she helped me adjust my dosage. Knowing me, I think I also promised her that I'd get a blood and urine workup before I left Montana—either that or as soon as I get back to Chicago in September, or else . . .

The wind has died down now, a little.

I pedal.

*   *   *

There are worse things to have, I'm aware. I wouldn't trade diabetes for a spinal cord injury, for becoming a quadriplegic; not only could I not buy a gun or get Nembutal, I'd need other people just to eat, turn a page, take a pee. I wouldn't rather be mentally retarded. I've also seen from up close the way pancreatic cancer can waste you: keep you in serious pain for ten months. So options like these would not be close calls.

What about being a young, healthy girl in Rwanda or Burkina Faso? The provisos, of course, are that I couldn't go marry some rich guy or get myself educated; I'd have to stay poor my whole life, live in a pastel shack alongside a sewer, lice in my hair, clitorectomized, eating rodent meat and donated cereal and drinking rancid water, brushing flies from my eyes, never leaving my village—unless I were chased into a refugee camp by some unfriendly tribe with machetes. No way. But I'd definitely prefer being healthy in places like Belfast or Kashmir or Sarajevo to having diabetes in good old safe turn-of-the-millennium America. It depends on what you find honorable and what you find humiliating. Personally, I'd rather have my life threatened by a bomb or a mortar or a gun in the name of some cause than incinerate myself in slow motion over nothing—because some enzymes got their signals crossed three or four decades ago.

To keep from feeling *too* sorry for myself, I try to remember what other people go through. My friend Marcy Bookchin got lymphoma when we were sophomores in high school. The first fifteen pounds she lost made everyone jealous, especially when she managed to still keep her breasts; when she continued losing weight, we assumed it was bulimia, which in those days had its own quasi-sexy cachet. Plus Marcy kept doing her homework, getting A's on her projects and tests; she was smart, thin, and beautiful, and her skin was translucent. She went into the hospital the first week of December and died Christmas Eve.

Petty thieves get gang-raped and have their throats slashed in prison. Children get abducted and buried alive; they get drowned by their mothers while strapped in their car seats. They get born joined at the head, or blind, or without arms or legs. Linea Domsworthy, the older sister of a girl I knew in grammar school, was born with a spinal abnormality that caused her to have no buttocks. This would be difficult under any circumstances, and I have no idea how it affects her overall health or her life expectancy, but it's got to be especially difficult living here on Planet Reebok in the Era of Athletic Buttocks.

One of the girls in my freshman dorm at Northwestern had four nipples: two in the regular places, one lower down on her rib cage, another one up near her collarbone. I can't remember her name—Sharon or Shanna, I think—but I do remember some of the more vicious if obvious nicknames ascribed to her, and which she must have overheard at some point. I'm sure she had numerous wardrobe dilemmas, especially during the summer, not to mention the various First Times she had to steel herself for, desperately rehearsing her "casual" introduction of the subject, the harrowing moment of unveiling.

The people I'd like to have banished to the thirty-fourth circle of Hell are the ones who're convinced they've got health problems the minute they come down with strep throat, liver spots, crooked teeth, root-canal-caliber cavities, gingivitis, ulcers, acne, insomnia, cellulitis; the folks who groan and curse and shake their heads as they recount, mucus-voiced, the history of their colds. Then there are the mini morality plays on the TV commercials: a man buys the wrong recreational vehicle—the Ford, not the Chevy; to make matters infinitely worse, Michael Jordan gets out of his Chevy, notices the poor sucker's Ford, shakes his head, and whistles his disdain. In another Chevrolet commercial, the wife comically refuses to forgive her husband for buying the inferior sedan when they could've had the Chevy for about the same price; the punch line of that one is, "At least they still have their health."

In McCrook's Motel 6 I eat a small dinner, give myself three fewer units of Lente, and wind down by reading in bed. It's almost ten-thirty, but there's still some gray light through the curtains.

GOING TO THE SUN

I'm rereading the section about Jacques Moran and his son, Jacques Moran: *Where are we going, papa? he said. How often had I told him not to ask me questions. And where were we going, in point of fact. Do as you're told, I said. I have an appointment with Mr Py tomorrow, he said. You'll see him another day, I said. But I have an ache, he said. There exist other dentists, I said, Mr Py is not the unique dentist of the northern hemisphere. . . .*

I'd like to have a son. Some little guy to cook for, watch movies with, who could teach me how to play catch, do geometry . . . Having a son would not be half bad.

Daughters can be difficult, in my experience. Daughters are tougher. You worry about them more, since they tend to have less than optimal control in a lot of situations: the boys they go out with are stronger than they are; the boys are usually driving the car; the boys can't get pregnant. Daughters can get monumentally vicious and weird on you during high school. You also can die before they do.

Someone has left an old *Spy* under the telephone book. The cover has a photo collage of Hillary Rodham Clinton in S/M drag: dog collar, riding crop, shiny black-vinyl brassiere. Inside there's an undoctored photo of Madonna in a similar getup leering down at the photographer. *That's* where I've seen Ndele's nostrils before . . .

Okay. I can either call the vice president of Motel 6 and complain about the scandalously shoddy housekeeping, how his innocent female guests are being corrupted by the concupiscent smut his minions leave lying around, how he could be liable for failing to protect me from exposure to women in dog collars, insist that at the very minimum he refund my $32.66—or I can snuggle down under the covers and have a few yuks with this *Spy*.

Two-fifteen, and I'm still belligerently, comprehensively awake, unable to read one more syllable of Beckett or *Spy* or the Fun-Pak for northwest Montana.

Instead I am learning perforce to do self-massage. I press my palms and fingertips in circles over my temples, or rhythmically back and forth around the orbits of my eyes, pressing hard against the bone with my thumbs. I probe every contour of my sockets, the stiffness and give of my cartilage. When I start to obsess about eyes, it guarantees that I won't sleep. The next day they burn all day long from my not having slept and get worse, and I worry about them some more.

Self-massage seems to work best when the room is dark, with fresh air coming through a window. I'm also pressing a damp cloth across my forehead and eyes. If I were about to have a stroke, would fresh air or damp cloth or darkness make any difference? Maybe I could try some aroma therapy. Would smelling some lemon verbena or clematic vitalba head off a stroke? I could call up Michelle and ask her, but I already know what she'd tell me: Check into the nearest hospital and ask for Dr. So-and-So—right now. I lie in the dark and massage my own skull, trying to locate the roots of the nerves that are throbbing.

The headaches I've been getting for the last several days are different from any I can remember. Not that the pain is much greater—it feels like it's *deeper*, closer to the center of my brain. The blood running through me is tainted, imperfectly filtered, way out of balance. Each time it throbs I can feel clots of plaque getting thicker, obstructing more blood. My pulse pounds away at them, trying to find a way through.

I'm going to die soon. It hits me like a bowling ball in my solar plexus. But harder.

All of a sudden I scream—not a word, just a long, cursing sob. I don't care who hears it. It's roaring right out of my chest. I can't help it.

I want to be cured of this thing as of Monday. I want not to ever have had it.

I've been having death dreams lately, almost every night. Some of them, like the one back in Elder, wake me up gagging on acidy bile. There are two or three basic scenarios, and most of them end the same way. I run into David somewhere—in a Stop-N-Save out here on Route 2, in a room down the hall from my office. At the outset it's not always clear that it's him;

sometimes it's Lee; sometimes it's an anonymous man I'm attracted to for purely physical reasons—his chin, his abdominal muscles, his legs—and I criticize myself in the dream for being so callow. I want love, I keep telling myself. But the sexual dimension of the dream usually holds sway for a while. The man and I will touch each other's faces, start kissing. Almost immediately, I get pulsed and wet in my sleep, in the dream as well as between my legs, but I *know*. That's the thing. I'm aware in my sick, fuguing brain of how it's going to turn out, even though the erotic momentum of the dream won't let me stop or wake up; even the part of my mind that's not dreaming desperately wants to prolong it. It's David. He's finally real, and I'm with him again. My bones ache, I'm so overjoyed. I pull up his T-shirt, run my hand lightly across his chest, making X's and O's on his sternum, tracing the shape of his pectoral muscles, his abdomen. His body is perfect, intact. He is back! I've been waiting so long, though I've known every day that this would happen. I feel entirely vindicated, in control of all parts of my life. Even though both of us know he has an erection angling up toward his belt, I'm refusing to touch it just yet, and he likes that. I'm teasing him, knowing he's dead, making him breathe the live air more and more jaggedly. Sometimes he's holding my nipples, making me get up on tiptoe while he's biting the side of my neck. I bite him back, scratch him, draw blood. I'm literally tearing him up, and he loves it. But his fingers and lips are so cold—they feel like Formica—and I know, even in the dream, that he's dead. I don't have diabetes anymore, but David is dead. I'm violently sick to my stomach. The problem in the dream becomes how to demonstrate to David that I love him, I'm better, I'm perfect again just like he is, not torn apart anymore, that I desperately want him, when I'm about to start vomiting. I turn my head sideways, gagging back bile, but he yanks me around by my hair, makes me face him. "Penny, I'm dead. We both know that. Don't make me beg you." I try not to listen, to escape his fierce grip, prove that what he's saying's not true. Doesn't work. All I can do is savor the sound of his voice, though I cannot accept what he's saying. "Just when things are starting to work out, it's time for some German to book.

Wonder why. Look at Coltrane. My turn now, your turn later, all that." By this point he usually has faded away. I'm lying on a hospital bed with tubes in my arms; the catheter needle is five inches long, so I stab myself deeper each time I move; if I so much as shiver or flinch it will rip through a vessel, a bone; and, of course, I cannot keep from flinching. Then David will be with me again, though it's never entirely clear whether we'll be able to *have* one another; I don't even know what that means. I also can't tell where we are. Sometimes it's a room in a house or apartment we've borrowed, but I don't recognize any of the pictures or furniture. I often can see his green eyes. I know that he loves me. Sometimes he tells me he loves me; yet he doesn't look sad, or in love. I gather he never has loved me. He wanted someone to camp with, to fuck with, to help him forget about Emma. He liked me, but not half as much as he needed me. He needed me to help himself die.

When I wake up I'm clammy and shivering and the back of my throat is on fire. I usually have this dream, or one like it, around five in the morning. I wake up and remember one or two parts of it, and it's not a relief when I realize that I was dreaming. The sound of Saint's voice always fades, but other things—his chest, the catheter, the house where we're staying— will take on a life of their own. I never can get back to sleep.

I wonder whether on some nights I have it but just don't wake up, or have it and fail to remember. I think I prefer to wake up.

Sometimes I make up obvious, stupid little prayers in response.

> Now I lay me down to sleep with no one to lay me
> again.
> Captopril's healing my Velcro glomeruli
> In the name of the father, I hope.
> Not my eyes! Not my eyes!
> Gene sequencers, please please please hurry.
> Work weekends, work overtime, hurry!
> Deliver us from evil, Lord hear my prayer, or what-
> ever.
> Vidito videto a man,
> Cogito ergo amen.

I pedal through Think, Montana, a two-block-long town complete with actual tumbleweed, a hot-pink door banging in the wind, a big turquoise "4Q" graffito on the wall of an abandoned Cenex station. The entire town, in fact, looks abandoned.

As I ride toward the last place in town, a beautiful young woman opens the door and steps out onto the tiny front porch. Her red hair blows loose around her shoulders and neck, and she has on a pale gingham dress. When I slow down in front of the beige clapboard house, she drags on a cigarette, then languidly waves with that hand. Does she know me? The glare of the sun off her face and the dress makes her look vaguely inhuman. I cough, then wave back. But what would she do if I stopped? What would I say? Perhaps I could fill up my bottles, though I've moved well beyond her by now, and to pull a fast U and go back would just seem too weird. Plus I think I see mountains ahead: brownish-gray forms a smidgen above the horizon, with tiny white patches catching the sun at odd angles. Snow? Whatever it is, I keep going.

The woman is still on her porch. I can feel it. Her arms are so thin as they hang from the sleeves of the dress; her collarbone is frail but pronounced. I think I can actually smell her: ash from a menthol cigarette, freshly mown lawns, garlic shrimp. There are no lawns or shrimp around here.

Don't look back, I tell myself firmly. But it's clear that I'm losing it. I have to concentrate harder on steering past pot-holes and cracks. Stay focused, as jocks on TV always say. As Ndele would probably put it.

The young woman waves with both hands as I ride out of sight. There's a wan, crooked smile on her face. She blows me a kiss, then rotates her pelvis and hitches her cunt toward me lewdly.

I upshift a gear and keep going.

Room six, Motel 6, Bobmars, Montana. Two kids making out in the seat of a pickup not five feet from my window. My drapes are drawn and it's dark out, so they think I can't see. Or don't care. Maybe they're proud of their little performance. The boy has tattoos on his shoulder, revealed by a tight dago "T." The girl is in similar garb, but with garish white hair. No tattoos.

I must be getting sicker than I thought if I'm populating these towns with mirages. I'd better start testing for ketones. I'm not exactly sure what hallucinations might be a symptom of.

Maybe I just miss Chicago. Besides my apartment, my books, and my Jane, I miss being able to choose from more than two movies on cable. When I go into bookstores I want there to be more than eighty-five titles, even if I'm just in there browsing. Especially if I'm just in there browsing. And I miss the live music. There are two dozen clubs I can walk to from my apartment. When I finish grading papers, I can go up Clark or over to Halsted and see jazz, blues, rock and roll, folk stuff, poetry readings, and drink fifty-cent margaritas on ladies night.

Sometimes I miss having people around—a hundred thou-sand folks within hailing distance at any given moment. I also miss taxicabs, restaurants, the superb, jagged, Etch-a-Sketch loopline. I like being within a ten-minute cab ride of my doc-tors' offices, even if I don't miss actually taking those cab rides.

I certainly don't miss the weather, especially at this time of year: moldy, polleny, nasty, humid, and long. Three months of deplorable hair days. Plus the air reeks and buzzes, continually attempting to figure out ways to keep you from breathing it.

With all the foul moisture it's holding, there's not much room left over for actual oxygen. A lot of nights it doesn't get below eighty-five, and I lie there and sweat through my sheets, then an inch or two into my mattress. At least during the winter, even when the windchill gets down to sixty-nine below, there are things you can do to protect yourself. You can even turn it into a look: men's boots, long underwear, wool headbands, sweatshirts under your sweaters with hoods poking up through the neck holes. At bedtime you make some hot chocolate, open the window three fourths of an inch, leave on your wool socks and sweatshirt, and snuggle up under the comforter.

I certainly don't miss riding my bike in the traffic, squeezed between buses and cabs on my left and block after block of drivers'-side doors, any one of which might be rashly swung open in front of me. I don't miss going blinder from staring at a CRT screen seven hours a day, re-rearranging my notes. I don't miss the hair boys and airheads on the local news reporting each night about two rapes in Gary, two drive-by shootings in Pilsen, two strangled homeless women in East Rogers Park, two children asphyxiated in a fire at California and Madison, and a lottery winner in Uptown, followed by weather and sports.

According to my friends on the Weather Channel, it's ninety-five humid degrees today in Chicago, and at this time of year it doesn't cool off much at night. It's sixty-two here. If I stepped out the door of my room now, there'd be a breeze blowing down from Canada, and I could look up at three million *stelle*. Of course, I'd also see stars if I banged my head against an unfamiliar towel rack, as I did in the place back in Parshall.

I've reached a decision about my stalled dissertation, I think. A year ago today I had around twenty-five pages of adequate prose. I had four hundred pages of notes, short on coherent paragraphs or even grammatical sentences, long on quotes from the novels and secondary sources. In my mind it existed as white dots on a royal-blue screen eighteen inches from my eyes, the actual words somewhere behind the blue screen, in (on?) a hard drive, deep in my WordPerfect system of glossaries, merged codes, and menus. I had the ability to block and copy parts of what I'd written, try them out in different places, compose variations; without this capacity, I wouldn't've had twenty pages.

In the meantime, translucent floaters and spirals meander like dust motes across my field of vision. Where is this happening, exactly? In my brain? In the back of my eye? It *looks* like they're two or three inches in front of me, moving sideways away from me. After five or six hours of riding or writing, or trying to write, you can't really blink them away.

I imagine myself back in Chicago, sitting at my desk with a white plastic rotating fan blowing muggy air across my forehead and chest, not getting work done. Eighty-three degrees, ten forty-five in the evening. My hair is a stringy, wet tangle. The end of my project is getting harder and harder to picture. By midnight I'm down to panties and a T-shirt—*You down for that look?* says Ndele—reading or trying to sleep. At five after three or three after five I go down the hall to the kitchen and find myself hunkered, totally spaced, in the half-open door of the fridge, scanning five wrinkled grapes and what's left of Jane's two-week-old tuna casserole, hoping for Oreos, pudding, banana bread—which would, of course, be in the bread box I've already searched three, four times, ignoring the caramel-corn rice cakes—though whatever I find would require an extra few units of insulin, but so why not some Equal with corn flakes, now that the finches are dicking and cheeping . . . ? Somehow this isn't the image I'd had in mind during my first years of grad school of the quirkily brilliant Beckett scholar at work, steadfastly preparing her first magnum opus.

Then it occurs to me, a bolt from the blue: I should not write my dissertation on the fourfoldedness of the Trilogy. The very idea of that project suddenly seems so preposterous that I cringe, actually physically cringe, from amazement and humiliation. What in God's name was I thinking of?! I should be writing a book about what Beckett has to show about the comic and cosmic inevitability of the deterioration of the body—about accepting, even wishing for, mortality, as a return to our natural state of nonbeing. . . .

Twelve minutes later, after a hundred-yard jog to Dag's Foremost Liquors, I'm pouring Cuervo Gold over ice to celebrate my new writing project. I already have a buzz on from how elated I am, how endlessly relieved, to be dropping my sorry-ass project. *Ugh!* Already fluttering with moist contemplation, I sip. It bites for a second, but that doesn't keep me from sipping again. And again. My whole head expands with ideas and tequila. Because I'm *exactly* the person to write this damn book! It is, moreover, a book that needs to be written. I can tell that it's going to win some awards, maybe get me in line for an NEH or a Guggenheim. I'm even convinced it will *sell*.

Toasting myself with two more gold sips, I re-reaffirm my decision: What mortal person who likes a good laugh would not buy and read it? In the meantime, if it turns out to be acceptable to Lee and the rest of my committee as an appropriate subject for a dissertation, so much the better. If it doesn't, tough titties. Because this is the book I'll be writing.

The Cuervo reminds me of the time twelve or thirteen years ago when I inadvertently tracked down the place of my conception: room 701 of the Americana Hotel in Cozumel. I was helping my sixty-two-year-old father move his books from one apartment to another. His rent had gone up, the new place was roomier—something. The bookmark in one of his *Paris Review*s turned out to be two MasterCard receipts stapled together—a souvenir of that wonderful evening five months before he and my mother got married, nine months before I was born. Two hundred and sixty-eight days after they'd mastered the moment.

One receipt was for "2 CHI FAJ 6 BAR" from Ernesto's Fajita Factory; the other was the hotel receipt. I shudder to think of this now; I also can't stop myself. I always assume they were drinking margaritas—what else does one order at Ernesto's Fajita Factory? They could have been drinking Dos Equis, of course. They could have been drinking Corona. But I usually picture the six margaritas, although sometimes it's four margaritas and two straight-up Cuervo Golds. But neither of them were ever big drinkers, at least not that I can remember.

And then, all too soon, it's back to room 701 and off with their clothes. My father mounts my mother. I never have seen his erection, and I don't really picture it. (I belong to what's apparently a very small club: women who can't remember being molested by their fathers.) There's *something* there between them, but the X-rated stuff stays in shadow. Nothing kinky goes down. Straightforward missionary position, my mother's knees raised, one slightly more than the other, while they rather mechanically do it. My father's white buttocks move faster, then slow down and shudder. It's awful.

For the actual ejaculation part I often picture the scene in the movie that Travis Bickle takes Betsy to in *Taxi Driver*: a Technicolor screen full of microscopic close-ups of a few dozen spermatozoa wriggling energetically around a lone ovum, all this activity incomprehensibly narrated by some Swedish sexologist. Cut to: My father gets off of my mother, though a trapeze of come still connects them. This sequence even has its own voice-over joke. *Fuck my mother. My father did—once. Fuck my father. Everyone else did.* They presciently wind up in separate beds, fall asleep. Sometimes my mother will lie awake smoking, a motif I may have picked up from another movie. Sometimes the smoke she's inhaled is what causes the cell change in me. Sometimes it was there all along in the ovum. Or the wrong spermatozoan arrives and bores its way in before anything can stop it. Too late! The microscopic image is enlarged by ten thousand, so I'm able to watch as the actual protein or enzyme gets aligned the wrong way. And I'm fucked.

PART 5

Parked outside a Quik Stop in Hanna are a pair of *muy* serious cross-country bikes: aero bars, four jumbo water bottles each, front and rear panniers spattered with mud, pumps and tent poles and sleeping bags bungeed to front and rear racks. I'm powerfully tempted not to go in, but because I left Bobmars this morning without packing a snack, I have to buy something to eat.

The bikes must belong to the couple that's back by the cooler: tan, hearty, slender, decked out in Patagonia $H_2NoPlus$ wind gear. In love. I'm not riding fast enough to have passed such uberfolk as these, so they must be headed east. Wherever they're headed, I'm not in the mood for a disquisition on touring aesthetics, or comparing notes on chromoly versus graphite aero bars, or the advantages of Mr. Tuffy tire liners. I'm not in the mood to hear war stories.

I buy two bananas and a carton of OJ, hold the brown bag in my teeth, and wheel my bike back toward the picnic table I spotted as I rode into the station. It's about twenty feet off the highway, shaded by four leafy oaks.

A blue Honda stops just ahead of me and a muscular guy with a Beckettian beak and a raven-black ponytail gets out of the passenger door. Except for the overly chic two-tone tennis outfit he's sporting, he looks like an authentic Indian. He's holding a raven-haired toddler in two up-scooped hands, extra careful. A pristine plastic diaper swings from his teeth like a gigantic bleached shrimp as he jogs, child in hand, toward my table.

A woman—his wife, I assume—gets out on the driver's side. She's laughing and calling, "Code brown! Code brown!"

"Absolutely code brown," says the husband.

I stop a few feet from the picnic table but try to communicate that it's exactly where I was planning to sit down and eat: what else would I be doing with this bag in my mouth?

They ignore me. The husband lays the child faceup on the table and proceeds to change its diaper. He's good at it too: tender and quick and efficient, tearing open the stays on the used one, holding back the child's legs as he wipes its rear end with an unsoiled corner.

As I watch and edge closer, the husband looks up and grins. He knows he's taken my table, but *it's just for the moment, you see.* I smile and say nothing. The woman pretends I'm not there.

I can make out the three small mauve bulbs of their son's balls and penis, and smell the acidic beige shit he was smeared with a moment ago. I assume that we all can.

The little boy gurgles and yells with delight as they change him.

On my way into Browning, I ride toward a squadron of Indian boys playing basketball on a short gravel driveway. Their basket is screwed to a cinder-block wall: no backboard, no net. They're going at it pretty ferociously, skidding and banging into the wall and each other, kicking up clouds of gray dust. As I click slowly past them, the tallest one stops, stands up straight, holds the ball; then all of them swing around and gawk, making no bones about checking me out. None of them looks to be older than twelve, but that doesn't keep them from frankly appraising me. Are twelve-year-old Indian boys interested in women in *that* way? In a woman my age? Maybe they find me vexing in some other way—white woman invading their territory. The moment seems less than propitious for comprehensive sociobiological interviews, but if they said something to me, I'd respond. But they don't. They stare and confer sotto voce, and the tallest one nods. He throws the ball violently down—*thwack!*—then catches it in front of his chest. I keep riding.

Route 2 gets dusty and wide as it shambles through Browning. Dogs lope and sniff through the alleys. The street-lights are fixed to the top of thirty-foot poles, but just about everything else is one story. BIG BLACKJACK. The Montana Restaurant and Casino, Teepee Village Shopping Center, Ben Franklin, The Jug. POKER! KENO! I'm looking for a place to have lunch. Town Motel? I don't think so. Johnny's Supper Club? Blackfeet Trading Post? Teeple's? I do see a few newer pickups and cars, but most of the vehicles look at least twenty years old. A rust-colored mutt is licking his balls as he lolls beside one of the ancienter models. I pedal.

A guy with long straight black hair limps diagonally across the parking lot of Tim's Body Works. He has on red sweat-pants with a graffitoed and smudged plaster cast at the end of one leg. He looks like the hitchhiker I saw back near Chinook. When I nod, he nods back, but I don't think he rec-ognizes me. He heads toward a group of young guys hanging out under the triangular, tilted-up canopy of an old Cenex sta-tion. There's a fluorescent tube on inside, but it doesn't look open: no gas pumps, for one thing, just bare ten-inch-high concrete islands. A hand-painted sign on the wall says BROWNING VIDEO CLUB, NEW MEMBER WELCOME. The guy alongside it is holding a cellular phone to his cheek; one cow-boy-booted heel is propped against the peeling blue wall; the other leg's perfectly straight. His colleagues, including my friend with the cast, are sipping from bottles in brown paper bags. One of them's staring me down—and now so is the guy on the phone.

Beep. Leave a message. 4Q.

I picked up some cranapple juice and a sliced turkey sandwich at the IGA deli, but I need to sit down and think while I eat. All I can find is my four-dozenth bird-beshat picnic table, this one a few hundred yards north of the IGA, just outside the Red Crow Kitchen. My table is ten yards away from an orange-and-yellow trailer propped uncertainly on stacks of red bricks; a radio's playing inside, and a small girl has peeked once or twice from the window. I hope and assume I'm not trespassing.

At least there's a view around here. The Rockies fill up half the sky in the west, under low misty clouds drifting south. There's diesel and pine in the air, and another sharp smell I can't identify. Mountain? After twelve hundred miles of strictly horizontal horizon, it's like I've arrived on a whole other planet. A dickcissel chitters close by, *dick dick, dick dick*, and there are three kinds of wildflower between the Red Crow and my table. If I were toting a vase, I'd be tempted to pick a bouquet.

I spread my big map on the table, weigh down the top with my juice jar. I've arrived at my first major fork in the road. Route 2 keeps going west, circling under Glacier National Park, then heads northwest through Kalispell, Lolo, and the Kootenai National Forest into Idaho. (Idaho! I'm definitely in the mood to get out of Montana.) Route 89 goes west another fifteen miles to Kiowa, then turns and runs almost straight north past the park into Canada; another branch, called Going-to-the-Sun Road, cuts west through the park from St. Mary. Looking up from the map, facing west, I can see the huge road signs hanging out over the highway: 2 WEST, EAST GLACIER; 89 NORTH, ST. MARY. Piggybacked trailers whiz underneath with their lights on.

Decisions, decisions. I can reach the Alcan Highway in Canada, the one that will get me to Prince Rupert, by taking either 2 or 89. When I highlight both routes with red marker, the one heading north on 89 then cutting northwest at Calgary seems slightly shorter. It would also get me out of Montana and into Canada by this evening, or at the latest by tomorrow ... Gravel crunches behind me. I recognize the footsteps but look to make sure.

It's Ndele.

"Girl, where you been?"

I stare at him, letting his presence sink in. He seems slightly taller and thicker. The design on the side of his head has grown out. He looks like the guy in the CNN photo: Ndele Rimes. He has on a new pair of oval sunglasses. I'm pissed but I can't keep from grinning.

"I been camped out here waiting on you almost three goddamn days."

I nod and stop grinning. Almost. I swallow the food I've been chewing, put down my sandwich. He's just so damn pretty.

Two Indian boys are standing beside him, scratching their toes in the gravel. The taller kid's holding a basketball; it's the one who was checking me out as I rode into town. The shorter kid, who now has his back to me, has little red lights in the heels of his sneakers. *Blink blink*.

Ndele peels twenties from a thick roll of bills: three for you, three for you. The taller kid pockets his money while staring at me.

"I thought you said she had blond hair," he says to Ndele, making zero effort to keep me from hearing, then tosses the ball to his friend.

Nobody says anything. The shorter kid bounces the basketball, catches it. He does it again, then brings it up close to his face and examines its globelike convexity, apparently looking for some small undiscovered country wherein the exchange rate will allow him to live like a prince on his sixty dollars for the foreseeable future.

"Actually," I say, "it *is* sort of blond when I've washed it."

"Yeah," Ndele tells the kid. "That's right. You blind? What's your problem?"

The shorter kid bounces the ball, crushing a country or two. The taller kid glares at the gravel.

"Yeah," I say, fluffing my hair.

Both boys examine me skeptically—hair, face, and torso—in a descending sequence of brief, furtive glances. Then shrug.

I put my hand in back of my head, strike a pose. "Are you blind?"

"*No*," says the taller one, furious. The other kid toes the gray dirt.

"These are my lookouts," Ndele informs me, helpfully changing the subject.

I nod but say nothing. I also don't get up from the table or invite him to sit. My plan is to speak to him the second I figure out what I might say.

He puts a big hand onto each lookout's shoulder, gives them both little shakes, trying to get them to look at him. Uh-uh. No way. "But I described the *bike* pretty accurately, didn't I?"

Shrug, shrug, exhale, toe the dirt.

"This is Thomas—Doubting Thomas—and the Trickster. Penny Culligan." The taller one is eagle-eyed, skeptical Thomas. I owe him for spotting me. The Trickster has scars on his arms, neat grids of X's and checkmarks. I don't owe him as much, but he's darling. His skin is the color of twelve-year-old pennies. He's almost as dark as Ndele.

I smile. "Pleased to meet you, confederate spies that you are."

Both of them mumble and shuffle their feet.

"Blackfoot spies?"

Thomas glares up at me: wrong!

"Say hello," says Ndele, shaking their shoulders again.

They perfunctorily do as they're told.

"So, Mr. Trickster, what did he tell you I looked like?"

Ndele rolls his eyes. Shy-sullen shrugs from the Trickster.

"Did he say I was tall, thin, and gorgeous?"

Thomas nods, shakes his head. Trickster shrugs.

"He happen to tell you he didn't say good-bye when he left me at the jail?"

Thomas's narrow black eyes become much less narrow: the jail?! He looks up at Ndele, who remains noncommittal. Then he looks at his money and counts it again: one, two, three. Trickster counts too, dropping a bill in the process. As he bends down to grab it, he blurts out, "Blond hair, nice boobs, black bike with—"

"And cuts on her knees and her hands," says Ndele. "You guys take off now. We square?"

They nod and say yeah, but just stand there.

"We're square," says Thomas.

"Hey, you did great," says Ndele. "You both did fantastic."

They shrug and begin—first Thomas, then Trickster—to slowly stalk off. Ndele watches them go.

"Although why emphasize my stigmata?" I ask him.

He looks at me briefly, then spins on one foot and takes two lightning steps across the gravel; his hand flashes out and he steals the ball from Thomas. Grunts, high-pitched curses, a flurry of action. Ndele plays keepaway from both of them, dribbling and shifting direction and pivoting while both of them chase him and lunge for the ball. He dribbles it between his legs, behind his back, always an inch out of reach of their fingers. And it's clear that they've been playing together, and that Thomas and Trickster can't get enough of it—Ndele either, for that matter. And it's clear he's a physical genius, feinting and dribbling like an explosive, well-disciplined maniac. He finally allows Trickster to steal the ball back. The boys whoop and curse, defiantly claiming victory as Trickster runs off with the ball. Blink blink, blink blink . . .

"I thought you told me you were a basketball player."

He snorts, makes a face. He's not even breathing hard. "Guess I'm still too slow to recognize where the double-team's coming from."

"I guess. Or to know how to say, 'I'll be seeing you.'"

"Defense creates offense," he says, changing the subject again, this time using an Arkansas drawl. "We get steals, easy run-outs, donks . . . That's *your* guy."

We stare at each other. I have no idea what he's talking about. Is this his bad version of Clinton?

"May I join you?" he says.

I open my hand toward the opposite bench of the table. He looks back to see where Thomas and the Trickster are, then sits down directly across from me.

"Where's your car?"

He squints—is this a hard question? Because I've got a few

harder ones—then slides to his left, apparently to keep the sun from shining into his eyes when he looks at me. He finally points to a red Taurus parked about twenty yards away. A white mountain bike is attached to a two-bike trunk rack. "Speakin' of yo' man Mr. Pip."

"Of whom?"

"Mr. Pip 33."

"Whatever you say, Mr. Rimes. That's your car?"

"Rented it last Tuesday, until—"

"What I meant was, where's the Mercedes?"

He winces. "Still in pieces, I think. May as well be. Minot cops and my insurance company both wanna just glue it back together, but there's no way I ain't gettin' a new one. Only *had* the damn car for five days."

I stare at him as he talks, waiting for a voluntary explanation of why he left Minot without saying good-bye. Looking past his shoulder, I notice the Trickster and Thomas spying on us from beside an old station wagon.

"Where's your gun?"

He groans, shakes his head. When I repeat the question, he gestures toward the Taurus. "Wanna go for a bike ride? There's some really wild trails around here. Some people ran into a moose just this morning."

"Ah—no. Not really in the mood for a bike ride."

He looks at my poor, battered Trek. "We're only twelve miles from Glacier Park. That's where I'm staying, you know, up in St. Mary, so—"

"What was Thomas supposed to tell me when I finally showed up?"

"Supposed to come get me, fast as he can, let me know. *If* you showed up." I can tell he's a little put out that I'm grilling him. "I was starting to think—"

"I showed up," I tell him, using both hands to indicate my physical presence kitty-corner from him across the gray picnic table. "What was he supposed to tell *me?*"

"Ask you to wait. Say I was here, you know, waiting for you."

I put my hands back on the table.

"Okay?" says Ndele.

I cock my middle fingernail against my thumb, then snap it forward, flicking a nub of dry bird shit from the warped middle plank of the table; it zings past Ndele's left ear.

"That I wanted to see you," he says, ignoring my little bombardment. "That I wanted to talk to you."

I lift up the map, then the napkin my sandwich is on. There are no other suitable nubs.

"You know," he mumbles.

"No, I don't know."

"That I wanted to talk to you."

I look past his head toward the mountains. Smoky white clouds drift across them. I shiver and hug myself. "Why didn't you wait for me, to tell me what happened in Minot?"

He exhales enormously, but as a prelude to nothing. We both watch a busload of tourists enter the parking lot of the Museum of the Plains Indian. Rotund white oldsters file down the steps of the bus, squinting and milling about in their strange pastel outfits. When Ndele finally answers he speaks rather hesitantly, pausing for long, awkward beats:

"People from the team, lawyers, came, bailed me out. Cops, they wanted to charge me with attempted murder, extradite me back to fuckin' Indiana or someplace. Didn't know what they were talking about. Some fuckin' cop mis-recorded the serial number, so they thought I stole the Mercedes, shot some guy in the face for the thing. My own goddamn car. I told them I wasn't no shooter."

"So you did have a gun?"

"Shit, man. You kidding?" He's shaking his head: What bus did *I* just get off? "Thought I needed one to protect myself crossing this great land of ours—and I *did*. What's your stigmata?"

What? . . . Oh. "Wounds that you get when you're cruci-fied, or pierced with a spear in your breast. In your heart. I thought we were talking about guns."

"Thought I was too. Thought that's what a stigmata *was*. Some kinda pistol or something. The brand."

"Okay. So which brand did you have? They told me what it was back in Minot, but in all the commotion I seem to've forgotten. A Glock?"

"Penny, I know it was dumb. I *know* it was dumb. But there's no way I ever ... " He shakes his head. Holds it. He looks at me. "No way. And the guys from the Sonics believe me. May even've got them to drop the charges by now. Calvin Gates put up my bail in person, had his own little jet at the airport, hustled me outta there before the cameras show up ... I went up to find you, but they'd already let you out. I didn't know where to go to look for you."

"No ideas at all as to where I might be?"

"They told me they let you go too."

"This is before or after they forced you to go to the airport without talking to me?"

"Before. Soon as I got outta that room."

I shiver again, in the sun, though my flesh feels ungoose-bumpy—dead. "Go on," I tell him.

He looks at me, then down at the planks of the table, at my upside-down map. He's sorry; I feel it. I keep staring back at him, hard.

"I figured ... " He pauses, massaging a cheekbone with a ringless six-inch-long ring finger.

"Go on."

He went on. I had to encourage him, but a lot of what he said came out without too much nudging. In the meantime we relocated ourselves to Diamond Lil's Cafe. I watched out the window as people returned from their jobs in convoys of pick-ups. The pink-and-cobalt sunset over the mountains seemed to make no impression on anyone.

Our waitress now brings me hot water with two white anonymous tea bags, then sneezes. I thank her. She has on a salmon-colored smock over a black corduroy work shirt with the sleeves scissored off at the shoulders. Above her left breast, in lieu of a nameplate, is a button that says MAKE ME LATE FOR BREAKFAST. She is not Diamond Lil, I decide.

As Ndele gradually relaxes with his Lipton's iced tea, he needs fewer and fewer follow-up questions to proceed with his alibi, which is essentially twofold: his team's lawyers had hustled him out of Minot before he had a chance to confer with me; and his girlfriend, Yolanda, was pregnant.

". . . plus my mother's telling me the same thing as the guys from the front office: Got to Marry the Girl. Got to Do the Right Thing." He's either genuinely crestfallen to have to be telling me this, or he's truly a masterful thespian. I cannot rule out either reading. And then out of the blue he perks up considerably, starts talking like a marble-mouthed old woman: "Ain't none of us be sayin' nothin' less'n you marry dat girl fore I whip yo narra butt good'n proppa. Oth'wise ain't gone be worryin' 'bout none a yo problems, you hear?"

"Yes, I do. And Yolanda's still back in Virginia?" I want to change the tone, not the subject.

He nods.

"You love her?" It's schmaltzy and pushy to ask this, but right now it seems all that matters.

He blinks, sips some tea, but he isn't avoiding my eyes. I appreciate that. I appreciate it even more when he shakes his head twice: he does not.

I can't help grinning. It gets worse when I try to frown. I have to remind myself that he hasn't proclaimed he loves *me*. I ask him, "Is that why you called me 'Landa' that night?"

"Like I said, you got a vivid imagination."

"Be that as it may."

"Whatever *that* means. You do, man. I mean, I don't hardly know her. We just got together *one time*. It was after the Bullets game, and we were, you know . . . "

"Sounds just like us."

"We didn't meet after no game."

"Like I say—sounds just like us."

"With you it was different, believe me. Nobody's playin' no games here."

I believe I believe I believe him. But should I? I probably shouldn't.

"Besides, she's a *cat* person," he adds, sort of half to himself. He shudders at the very idea.

"We talking about Yolanda or Debbie?"

"Or who?"

He's forgotten our Debbie already? "How was it different?" I ask him.

"Who's Debbie?"

I push my chest forward and drawl my best Debbie: "Ain't these the pussenest little puttytats you ever laid eyes on?"

He shakes his head, gets it: *that* Debbie. I'm suddenly mad at myself—guilty—since not only had he not flirted with her, he'd heroically resisted her open-door policy. I try to apologize with the tone of my voice: "How was it different with us?" (Maybe he's using *his* tone of voice to tell me he loves me. I resolve to listen more closely.)

But Ndele says nothing. He tilts his head and raises his eyebrows: Isn't it obvious?

No, in a word. It is not.

"Hey, man. I stayed. I *wanted* to stay. I came back." Annoyed that I'm dragging this out of him. "You always think I'm splittin' on you, don't you?"

"Aren't you?"

"No."

"No? Not in Minot? How exactly do you mean?"

"You *always* think that. You noticed that? Shit, 'how you mean.' Mean, like the time I went out for the munchies and beer." He pauses and grins at me, chalking up points for himself. "'Course I only was *gone* twenty minutes." More points. He sips his iced tea, letting these cold, hard facts register. "Fact is, I did show up that time *and this time*."

"Not to mention the first time."

I can tell that he's more than a little surprised by my amicus brief. And delighted. "That's right."

"Where did you find your two lookouts?"

"Two? Try about twelve? Got me ones down in East

Glacier, St. Mary . . . "

I have to admit that I'm flattered and decide to use actual words.

"You should be, girl. Damn!"

"I am. And I'm real glad you found me. I am." When I put my hand over his wrist, I remember the force surging through him. "It's just that—"

The waitress arrives with another hot water, asks for the third or fourth time if we're ready for menus. Ndele informs her that we're just having tea.

"Yolanda won't have an abortion?" I say when she leaves us alone.

"Shee-it." Shakes his head, looks away. His wrist feels inert, almost cold. "Too late for that now."

"Before, though. Why didn't she then? Didn't she care what you wanted?"

"She tells me she's having the kid whether I want it or not. Next thing I know she's got this big lawyer from down in D.C."

"And it didn't make any difference that you told her you wanted to wait—"

He snorts: That's a good one.

"That's one way to propose, I suppose. 'Surprise! You're a dad! Will you marry me? Because if not . . .'"

He shrugs, shakes his head: I'm naive.

"But what's wrong with, 'Hey, girl, excuse me, but I happen to be a part of this decision-making process.'"

"Penny, I tried that. Believe me."

I nod. I believe him.

"Just remember, with you, *for* you, whatever, I'm back. On my own, or whatever."

"For me you came back."

"Hey. Here I am."

"I guess that you did. Yes, you did. Here you are."

"Ain't that the main difference?"

"Whether or not a person is 'here'? I'll have to think about that."

Ndele rests his chin on his fists. He's apparently willing to let me.

"I can honestly say I don't know." It's weak but the best I can do.

"Penny, I'm serious. I mean, what are we talking about here?" The light in the room has become horizontal. "Just fuckin' tell me, okay?"

"I don't know. Can we go someplace now, get some dinner?"

He immediately rotates his narra butt off the stool, exhaling subtle impatience—like he's been taking some classes from Lee.

"You think *I'm* not serious?" I ask him.

"I hope that you're serious. I am."

Is he old enough yet to be serious? How could he possibly love me after less than a day in my company? There's an aspect or two of my life he might want to know about.

We head for the register. "Well, I think that that's good," I say finally.

"Well, shit. Glad you think so."

"Because I think I have to tell you a serious story."

Before I got to the heart of the story of Saint, we drove to the cabin Ndele had rented in St. Mary. Two of his windows looked out over the eastern end of the Going-to-the-Sun Road, which according to my map runs fifty-two miles through the park. St. Mary Lake, stands of fir trees, purple mountains' majesty, the Road winding through it: I wished I was more in the mood to relish the postcardly vistas.

We ate dinner in a lodge down the road, and I told Ndele all about Saint. I told him about how we first met at school, how we "borrowed" his mother's car and drove to St. Louis to see McCoy Tyner and Frank Lacy and Jackie McLean. I told him about the camping trip, what he looked like in the hospital, what he asked me to do to him there. What I did to him.

Ndele was sympathetic, but he didn't seem all that amazed. Maybe he was pretending for my sake not to be horrified, but I don't really think that was it. He was eating lime sherbet while he listened to me. He'd nod, lick his fingers, ask questions: What songs did Ray Charles sing? Was David's penis torn off *entirely*? How many units of insulin? He gave me to infer that men in the prime of their lives get torn limb from limb all the time, that people killing people they loved just wasn't all that remarkable. Maybe he's right, assuming that's what he was thinking. Maybe I read him all wrong. It certainly wouldn't have been the first time.

We each have our own single bed in the cabin, and that makes me feel much more comfortable. The headboards are fashioned from boughs of white pine, with see-through shellac painted over the papery bark. My bed is under one window. I have my back against the headboard, hugging my knees to my chest. Ndele is sprawled on his side, head propped up on his hand, facing me in the dim light. He's taken off both of his complicated green-and-black sneakers, but only one of his socks. His toes look like decent-sized fingers as he arches and wiggles them.

"That's why you were riding to Alaska," he says.

"That's why I am. Among other weird reasons. But mainly."

"The guy's pretty ballsy, I'd say, deciding to handle things that way." The foot with the sock on it juts half a yard past the edge of the mattress. "Took him some big-time, serious guts to ask you to do him like that. Though I think if I ended up that way myself I'd probably wanna cash it in ASAP. There's fuckin' grizzly bears in the park we're in now. Right out there."

"I know."

We stay here a while without talking. I assume that the subject's been changed, and I'm glad. I've had to pee badly for the last twenty minutes, and it seems like this might be the moment.

"Didn't no one suspect you," says Ndele, wiggling the toes in his sock, "with the insulin and all?" He sounds like he's just getting comfortable.

"I think maybe his uncle suspected. Who knows. He was so amazingly bad off to begin with."

"Why you think he suspected?"

"Just the look he gave me at the funeral. But I do know his mother didn't suspect me. If she did, she would've had me prosecuted till the cows *and* the bulls wandered home."

"I thought they could trace shit like that."

"I still don't know whether anyone did an autopsy. Nobody ever pressed charges. And you're the first person I've told—the first man." This prompts no reaction. "I'm still sort of shocked that I did it sometimes."

"You think you shouldn't've done it?"

"Not exactly. Just that it's weird, the things you'd never suspect you could talk yourself into. Or deal with. Not that I'm so convinced I have."

"Like what Francie and you gotta deal with every day."

"Well, like I say . . . " Has one of us changed the subject again?

"But you guys never even *did* anything," he says, "you never did *any*thing, that caused you to get diabetes."

Oh. Is that so? But isn't this usually the case? In any event, I gotta *go*.

"You know what I mean?" says Ndele.

"Yeah, I do. And sometimes it pisses me off. But it isn't like David 'did anything.'"

"I guess so," he says. He blinks while he thinks about it. Then stares. "Pisses Francie off big-time."

"You think you can deal with it, you think that you can't—you're right either way."

"Unless your body tells you otherwise."

"Un*til* it's told you otherwise. Like with your knee. Till it's *told* you otherwise."

He's nodding and flexing his knee as I get up and go in the bathroom. I try to pee silently, holding back, aiming for porcelain, then realize how senseless this is, with the things that he knows about me.

*   *   *

I stare out the window at the last blush of sunset above the dark mountains: jagged blue-black singularities in a crooked but staggering row. Ndele is watching it too. We're both all talked out.

I love being back inside his microclimate—his rippling stillness of sweat, lime deodorant, and something else. Baking soda? No. Something warmer, like blanket or pepper or basil.

In a minute he turns me around, pulls me against him, just holds me. When he kisses the side of my mouth, I pull back away from him.

"What?"

"I don't know." I don't see the point anymore—though maybe we don't need a point.

"What don't you know?"

I trace the Nike logo on his shirt with my finger. "You know, just—swooooosh."

"I's a company man through and through."

I trace a bit harder now, using my nail. "Swoosh goes the goddess of victory."

"The goddess?"

"The goddamn goddess of victory," I tell him. "That's right." His nipple is directly under the baby-blue logo. Cocking my middle finger, I flick it dead center. "Imagine."

He's trying to kiss me again, but I turn my face to the side. His chin touches down near my temple.

"Did you know about this? It's what every good nurse does." I seize his right nipple, the one with no logo—defenseless. "To their patients' penises when they happen to get erections? Just *boink*." I let go his nipple, then flick it again. "When they start to get rambunctious? Makes 'em lie right back down like good little boys."

"Is that what you want it to do?"

I look at the black-on-black mountains. Below, wending east on the Road, car headlights glimmer like fireflies.

"If I knew what I wanted you to do, for us to do, I think I'd be one happy camper."

"And you're not."

I run all ten nails down his ribs. Shake my head.

"'Cause you don't."

"I don't think I've ever felt . . ."

"Say it," he tells me.

"Nothing. Just sad."

"Even with me, us, together?"

I put my hands under his shirt.

"Has it ever occurred to you—and I want you to tell me the truth about this—" I seize both his nipples.

"Pen—I promise I'll tell you the truth."

I roll them between my thumb and index finger, and I don't loosen up when he gasps; I twist them and pull on them harder. "That I'm, like, jinxed?"

When he presses against me, his temperature radiates through the stiff, folded denim. His heart thumps against my bare wrist. "Maybe that's why I'm so hot for your sweet nurse's ass."

"So you agree that I'm jinxed?"

When I twist in the other direction, he gasps, shuts his eyes, but does not move my hands away.

Harder.

"Jinxed or a jinx?" he says finally. "There's a difference."

"Either way. Either one. Do you?"

I let go. He untenses and shivers, groaning two wondrous chords of basso relief and frustration. His heart's beating hard.

"*Do* you?"

He looks at me doubtfully: Where am I going with this? Do I jinx all the men in my life?

We don't know.

"You think that you're jinxed," says Ndele, "you think that you're not. Either way, you're probably right."

"That's correct. Or touché. Either way . . . "

He kisses my hipbone and lingers there, nuzzling and tonguing me. No. Then my navel. My lowermost rib.

"You have to take care of Yolanda," I tell him. "Make things work out—either way. We can talk when I'm back from Alaska."

It's midnight. We're too raw to fuck anymore. To make love to each other. To fuck with each other. I don't know what to call it, or think.

"Shit," says Ndele. His naked legs stir in the distance. "Do the right thing, huh? Still?"

"What choice do you have?"

He's sliding the edge of his teeth along my hipbone again. "When will you be back?" he asks with my flesh in his mouth.

"Labor Day. August."

He nuzzles the bones between my spread breasts. "And you promise you'll call me?"

Promise? I'm writhing. But I'm also observing myself—standing a few feet away with my arms crossed in front of me, feeling his teeth on my nipple, watching myself pull away from him; horny as a giant black hornet, but cool, analytical, even a little bit distant. I'm marinated in our sweet, tangy juices and telling myself that I'm *distant*? This is all much too good to be true.

In the meantime Ndele is sliding an arm through my legs and winching my back with his other one, raising me up while I mindlessly, helplessly—wait! He's cradling me while we kiss. I struggle and kiss him. He holds me. I feel like I'm floating—I'm dying. We kiss. He lays me back down on the bed. Suppose, just suppose, I stopped fighting him—

Promise to call him? Stop fighting? What can that possibly mean when Ndele is kneeling in front of me, kissing and licking my raw, inflamed labia, biting me, whispering, lifting me up by . . .

I cling to his neck for dear life.

Nine forty-five Wednesday morning. The Taurus is loaded and ready to go. Ndele has to be back to his summer-league team and the rehab facility in Seattle by Friday. I've got the key to the cabin.

Ndele starts the engine. He's wearing a Nike cap backward. I have on one of his extra-long, XXL, extra-loud shirts (the hem's hanging down past my knees) and his Sonics cap, frontward. Ex ex ex ex, I keep thinking. Ex-what?

I hand back his sunglasses, which I wore during breakfast. I always feel great in his shades.

"Thanks."

"You're welcome."

"Just be careful up there with those crazy Canadians."

"Don't worry."

He tries a Canadian accent: "Don't let yourself get picked up by, hey, any a dem dere gun-toting Afro-can Ameri-can carjackers, you know, hey?"

I raise my right hand, "swear" I won't.

As we begin to kiss good-bye, the bill of my cap hits his forehead. The cap starts to fall, but I reach behind my back—and I catch it.

Ndele leaves his lips melodramatically hanging mid-kiss as I check out my fancy new cap, rolling the bill back and forth. I fit it back onto my head.

All of a sudden he's serious again. He has been for most of the morning. "And, so, I'll call you?"

"So long as you don't call me Landa again."

"Never did, girl." His hand flashes out, smacks my hip. "And you know it."

"Good luck in camp with your knee," I say, holding his hand. "Try to recognize where the double-team's coming from, boy. And watch out for those half-court ambushes."

He laughs *at* me, not with me. "So who are you now, Bobby Knight?"

"Who's he?"

"Oh, just some deranged, hyperventilating Hoosier."

"Oh." I let go of his hand.

"Good luck with your gamma hemoglobin and your proteins."

"Yeah. Merci. I think I might need it."

Ndele puts the Taurus in gear and backs up. "And take care of that business with Saint."

I swear.

He swings around in the driveway, then turns left onto Route 89, heading south. A couple of hours ago, just before breakfast, we made love on the floor of the cabin again. I try not to think about that.

The mountains and trees are so wild around here, it's strange to see telephone lines. The tops of the pine trees sway half a foot in the breeze. I can smell them. To the west there is snow near the tops of the mountains, white hieroglyphics glaring back down through the green. I'll be up there myself in five hours.

From halfway up the hill behind the cabin what sounds like a very small poodle starts yipping, and some young children giggle. "No, Daisy. No!" So there must be more cabins up there. I wonder if they have heard *us*.

The sun's banging down on my forehead. I squint, shade my eyes; the sunglasses aren't enough. Three girls cruise into St. Mary on bikes as I watch the red Taurus get smaller. Before it disappears, I go back in the cabin to pack.

Having paid the $3.50 for an entry permit to the park, I have 32 cents left in cash: a quarter, a nickel, two pennies. The receipt is good for five days' admission. No discounts for bicyclists or single-day rates were available.

The Going-to-the-Sun Road is two lanes of cherry new blacktop; there isn't much of a shoulder, but both lanes are wide enough for a bike and a car with a reasonably considerate driver. I can see the Road rising steadily at least ten miles ahead of me, clinging to the southern face of three jagged mountains. I'll be in the sun all day long.

I decided during breakfast to take the Road west the fifty-two miles through the park, then take 93 north out of Whitefish. The Road is mostly uphill for the first eighteen miles, till it crosses the Continental Divide at Logan Pass, then downhill the rest of the way—the first time this trip that going east to west will be to my advantage. The views are supposed to be something, but mainly I took it because it splits the difference between 89 north into Canada and Route 2's loop south of the park. I was getting quite sick of old 2.

Now that I'm out on the Road, I'm glad that I took it. No more Quik-Stops or Speedways or girlfriends or boyfriends or shots. The pedaling isn't overly strenuous, especially when I'm down on my easiest sprocket, though I'm trying to stay in the middle one so that I'll actually cover some ground. You apparently use different muscles going uphill than you use against the wind, since the tops of my thighs are feeling a new kind of strain. It's also the first time I've ridden my bike with a tenderized vagina. Every few minutes I slide back or forward a half inch or so, to a slightly wider or narrower place on the saddle, so my bones can abut it at different locations. It makes me feel less raw and bruised.

Maybe what I should write is an article about maintaining one's diabetes regimen, and or the integrity and complexion of one's crotch, while riding a bicycle from Chicago to Alaska. According to Flann O'Brien (whose name and idea I'd bring up in the article), after a while your bike literally becomes part of you because "mollycules" from the saddle get transferred into your crotch, and vice versa. I believe this has already happened, with Ndele as well as my saddle. I picture the fervid

Ndelecules bonding themselves to my enzymes as I shift into seventh and pedal along through the afterburn.

As I'm rounding the first major bend in the Road, I have to navigate alongside a seven-car backup, a veritable not-Going-to-the-Sun traffic jam. The impediment turns out to be a troupe of two dozen senior citizens on mountain bikes. Whatever the cycling equivalent of a stroll is, that's what these people are out for. I admire and envy them, every last one, as I pass them. The people in cars can *back off*.

An ambulance roars by, lights flashing, no siren, heading down into St. Mary, or wherever the closest hospital east of the park is. It reminds me that, unlike Route 2, the Going-to-the-Sun Road (so far at least) has no little clusters of white crosses to mark fatal crash sites. I assume that some must have occurred.

Do I really want to go up to Juneau? I don't think I've made it even halfway yet. I must be delirious. Why else would I want to go back to that hospital? But maybe that's what my life has come down to: I go to the hospital. As the Anglo-Irish would say, *David was in hospital when he passed away. Sam was in le hôpital. Molloy had been taken by ambulance from a ditch somewhere in the wilds of Wicklow to his mother's old room, Malone was alone in his boardinghouse room, The Unnamable died on the way to the hospital.* I don't want to go to the hospital.

On my right there's a forest of cedar and aspen, with dozens of ripped-apart trees; they look struck by lightning. Higher up there are gnarled, stunted hemlock and pine trees with most of their branches snapped off. Then the tree line abruptly cuts in and there's nothing but granite and sandstone mottled with patches of snow.

On my left, to the south, is St. Mary Lake. It's immense— almost two miles wide and fifteen miles long, at least according to the info-placemat under my oatmeal this morning. In real life it fills up the floor of the immense U-shaped valley I'm pedaling along the rim of. The entire panorama is almost absurdly picturesque. The mountains are veined with bright quartz cutting horizontally through the crenelated rock near the top, then fringed with dense blue-green spruce as they slope toward the lake, where they loom upside down on the surface. One tiny island—a dozen blue spruces, some bushes, flat boulders—near the middle of the lake is also reflected, forming a diamond-shaped evergreen Rorschach inside the upside-down mountains.

Every half mile or so scenic overlooks have been built to let people park and take snapshots. So far every one has been crowded with nature people: binoculars, telescopes, monopods, handicams, and plenty of khaki and Gore-Tex. Signs leading up to the overlooks have pictures of cameras on them so people will know what to do.

I pedal along in the third-lowest gear of my middle sprocket, taking in about as much scenic splendor as I can digest. The dirt on the side of the pavement (where the shoulder should be) has recently turned from olive to rust red, though I'm not looking down all that often. Squadrons of swallows soar and dart just ahead of me, turning on dimes in midair, zeroing in on mosquitoes and cheeping their one-note fughettas.

I pedal. There've been four short downhill stretches this morning, but it's entirely flat or uphill now. The incline's about five degrees, and I have to work harder and harder, standing up on the pedals when I feel energetic, downshifting when I get pooped. St. Mary Lake is already fifteen hundred feet below me, but I can't see the end of it yet. The sun is above my left shoulder.

A miniature old-fashioned tour bus rumbles by, much too close. With its white canvas top rolled back above the sightseers—there must be eighteen or twenty of them, sardined into five rows of seats—it looks like a stretch Model-T, only red. I can hear the driver's amplified voice informing his charges about "the severely glaciated arete" and "Bird Woman Falls." Oh does she? So why don't you *drive* that precisely? An identical bus follows thirty yards behind him, and this driver gives me more room.

*   *   *

On my right, up ahead, by itself, about a third of the way up the slope of a huge quill-shaped mountain, there's a red-orange flame. It looks like a maple in autumn, but it's too far away for me to make out the shape of the leaves. The fire is even more startling against all the earthenware colors. The Burning Bush at this time of August? I guess.

A Harley growls up alongside, then past me, not going terribly fast, with a corpulent couple propped on its stepped leather saddle. The wife, or the woman, is driving. The man's hairless ankle peeps out between the end of his black leather pants and his kelly-green sock. I can tell they're enjoying the scenery, conversing on microphones inside their helmets. In love. They may have made love just this morning.

Besides the ambulances and buses and motorcycles, plenty of cars also pass me, going in either direction. I guess I was expecting a little more solitude as I rode through the mountains, though it's easy to see why this Road is so popular.

Then the sign—at least one of the signs—I've been waiting for since I first entered southern Wisconsin: CONTINENTAL DIVIDE 7 MILES. As old JFK might have put it, I pedal with retrebled vigah.

A half hour later St. Mary Lake has thinned to a glistening river far, far below me. I'm sweating. South of the river is a vast rolling tundra dotted with bear grass and wildflowers, surrounded by more jagged mountains.

A guy with curly black hair has set up a box camera on a rise to the left of the Road. The drape hanging from his tripod billows and falls in the breeze. The closer I get, the more the guy looks like Bob Dylan—or Bob Dylan's sad-eyed, less cynical son. With his corduroy pants and actorish, film-person shirt, he seems out of place around here; he looks like he belongs in TriBeCa. I can't tell from his expression whether he's waiting for the light to change or for something dramatic to happen. Perhaps I should have an affair with him.

A few hundred yards beyond the melancholy photographer, I have to slow down for a switchback; the Road barely clings to a sheer wall of granite. It's a little like making a U-turn on the roof of a very tall building. You swing out too far to the left, going one mile an hour too fast, down you go.

The switchback proceeds through a round, narrow tunnel: *in the darkness you don't know, you never know* . . . Water drips onto the pavement from cracks in the rock overhead. The click of my gears echoes back off the walls as my tires track through the dark pools. The air is much cooler in here.

The posted elevation of Logan Pass is 6,646 feet, but at least 3,000 feet of mountain still rise directly above it, with numerous patches of loosely strewn boulders all ready to bounce down and plow through the roof of some car, or squish some poor, tired, innocent cyclist. The wall right beside me is relatively smooth granite and limestone, much of it splotched with green-and-purple algae. The mountains across the valley have what look to be steel-gray mohawks with highlights of blinding white snow. The sun shines more brightly up here.

The Divide. I have made it. Every stream, puddle, and river behind me runs east; everything in front of me trickles out toward the Pacific. I can feel the thin air do its thing as I try to maintain my momentum. But all things considered, I'm pretty damn proud of myself. I've just climbed a not unsteep eighteen-mile-long hill in less than three hours, though the much bigger deal is that the hardest part of my insane little road trip is behind me. Everything's downhill or flat from here to St. Rupert, at least theoretically.

So.

After eating my lunch I cruise through the parking lot of the Logan Pass Visitors' Center, checking out license plates, tour buses, fancy titanium mountain bikes bungeed to doors of ranch house–scale campers. One plate, from Oregon, proclaims GRTMRCA. A plate from Indiana says DAVE.

I even spot the two little girls who serenaded me at the gas station back in Minnesota. And since they also recognize me, I figure I can't have deteriorated *too* badly in the last month or so. They wiggle their fingers while flashing me upside-down peace signs. I flash them one back, right-side up; wiggle wiggle. I can tell they're at least as amazed as I am that we've run into each other again. As I slowly click past the back of their station wagon, deciding whether to stop and have a chat, I hear their hoarse mother: "It's still not a nice thing to say, whether she heard you or not." There are boys in the car, older brothers. Maybe she was talking to them.

As I exit the lot heading west, there's a black-and-white sign you could neither miss nor misunderstand: NO BICYCLES NEXT TWELVE MILES, 11 A.M. TO 4 P.M. Who made this rule? And what do they want you to do in the meantime? It's not even five after two. If I waited till four to start down, I wouldn't make it to the first motel until . . .

Sorry.

The Road runs downhill for less than an eighth of a mile before banking into another coiled switchback. Although this one isn't holding on by its fingernails to the side of a cliff, it's indecently crowded with cars—cars parked sidehill and crosswise, alongside no-parking signs, trunks sticking up from a ditch. Three grandma types are using long twigs to carve their initials in a patch of snow, but the principal activities along here involve photographing, sketching, speaking to, cooing over, and videotaping a pair of baby mountain goats who are lapping a puddle streaked with a rainbow of antifreeze. The nanny is some yards away, with her snout through the grill of a burgundy Jeep. She's apparently licking the radiator.

Once I'm beyond the switchback, the grade becomes steeper: eight, even ten degrees in some stretches. Since I don't have to pedal, it's mostly a matter of staying in a high enough gear in case I do have to pedal, and steering precisely enough to avoid bashing into the craggy granite wall whizzing by a foot from my elbow. It's white-knuckle time on the brakes; if I let one hand relax even fractionally, my bike rockets forward too fast—a temptation I can't always resist. I feel like I've earned a reckless and effortless spin down a hill. Whenever the left lane is clear, I ride over there; it's easier to avoid skinning my elbow, or braining myself, on the granite, and I can see more directly over the side of this mountain. Shadows of clouds drift across the evergreen floor of the valley; as soon as they pass, the sun glints on the river again. The guard wall next to my left ankle is built from rectangular flagstones cemented together in an up-and-down pattern, like the top of a rook, about eighteen inches high in the higher sections, twelve in the lower. A car would have to hit it at just the wrong angle and be going quite fast—forty or fifty, I'd guess—to go over the side. A bike would go over more easily, especially if it happened to hit one of the twelve-inch-high sections.

As I think about that, the Sonics cap gets blown off my head and starts sailing and twirling toward the river. It takes me at least sixty yards to finally stop, then a sweaty three minutes to walk my bike back to what I think was the spot. A hawk glides along almost motionless a half mile below me as I lean and peek over the guard wall: a river, trees, rock, all of it far, far below. But no cap. The drop gives me vertigo, but I don't close my eyes or back up. I've never seen things from this angle before, and the sweep of this place is so gorgeous it's downright erotic. Going thirty-two feet per second per second, how many seconds would it take to hit bottom? Say, seven?

I start down again in the left lane, still scanning the air for my cap. When a small truck appears up ahead, I have to move over. Long, spindly waterfalls—I can't see the top of them— splash down every few hundred yards, soaking this half of the pavement.

A small Asian man is walking a pair of coffee-colored Dobermans alongside a thirty-foot-high snowbank. At first I thought the dogs were gamboling about without leashes, but now that I'm closer I see that they have collars attached by thin nylon cords to a pair of black reels—not that this tiny gentleman, or anyone, could reel them back in if either, let alone both, of them decided they wanted to *go*. So I'm nervous, and I know dogs can sense that. When the female squats to pee, the male wheels and sniffs her—ignoring me, at least for the moment. They really are beautiful animals: sinewy, muscular, and apparently able to mind their own business, for now. The huge bank of snow just above them glitters and drips, though half of it's covered with mud and debris. I picture the Asian man unleashing the Dobermans. I can also picture a swift, thorough avalanche, and I give the whole scene a wide clearance.

As a minivan passes me, the jut-jawed driver hooks his thumb back up the hill, like he's hitchhiking—*me?*—in reverse. "Can't you read the fuckin' signs?"

I ignore him, keep riding. His schoolmarmish mother or wife, sitting primly behind him, shakes her finger at me: naughty, naughty. I smile back at her beatifically, keep right on cruising downhill.

I'm only pretending not to be rattled, of course. People like that make me nervous, and I know they can sense it. To reassure myself, I finger the logo on Ndele's big shirt—my big shirt now, I suppose—and *swoosh* goes the goddess of victory. The speed and the air whip my face, make my eyes water a little. I use both my hands on the brakes, trying to get more control. It's suddenly impossible for me to imagine him not marrying Yolanda, and I'm not sure either one of us would deal with all that very well, even though it's essentially what I've told him to do. But where is the logic in any of this? Because while to be vindictive is bad, to be vindi*cated* is good. Is it not? What about, then, to be impregnated? I think I'd rather be impregnative than pregnant, the fucker instead of the fucked, at least at this particular point in my fucked-up and personal history.

If I were a man I could simply knock up a woman or two, or twenty-two hundred and seventy-seven, even make a few extra deposits at the local sperm savings and loan, the local sperm no-load mutual fund or money market account with free checking and no-annual-fee platinum Visa, to make extra sure I got plenty of my wonderful genes into the next generation. As it is . . . Or, instead of turning right when I get off this mountain, I could keep going straight to Seattle. I could be there in four or five days if I hustled; could call him and tell him I'm coming. I could get on a plane in the morning in Kalispell. Yes! That's what I'm going to do.

If Saint were alive, this would kill him. Not that he'd have anything against Mr. Rimes personally, or have anything against all this philosophically. If Ndele's knee holds up, he'd probably turn out to be one of Saint's heroes. Even so, I suspect that he'd think this was all going down a bit soon. On the other hand, as much as I love him, as crazy as I am about both these guys, it really ain't none of their business. It's mine, and I'm going. I can always remind Saint *or* Ndele of what old J. Marshall Hendrix once said: Don't Be Late.

This morning I watched the sports with Ndele. No mention of him this time around, which was good. No news about basketball, period. A nineteen-year-old black kid has the lead in some big-time golf tournament, and that got Ndele's attention. Plus, the White Sox have the best record in baseball, so I'm certain my dad will be happy. The Tour de France has only one leg to go. The Tour de Montana as well, and the rest of the leg is downhill.

A ranger has stopped just ahead of me and is signaling for me to pull over.

I do.

"Ma'am, I'm afraid there's no bike riding along here at this time. You know that."

The first excuse that occurs to me is that there's an emergency of some sort in Apgar or Lake McDonald Lodge— someplace at the other end of the Road I have to get to before five o'clock. There are telephones back at the visitors' center, of course, plus there's a phone on his passenger seat. He also might offer to drive me. Diabetes—is that an excuse?

"I know," I tell him, "I know. My husband's waiting for me just up ahead, in our camper. Down by that bend? But I just *had* to see what it felt like to ride on this road?"

He isn't amused, but he may be convinced. "So you know you'll have to put that bike back onto the rack?"

I hold up my hand, swearing. "I promise. We're parked

right down there." Pointing. "I apologize. I'll get off right away. I just had to ride a few hundred yards on this thing."

"Ma'am, just make sure you ride straight to your camper."

"I will."

I'm still at large five minutes later. Fluffy white cottonball clouds have drifted in front of the sun, which is beaming down through them in what looks like a parody of Bountiful Sunshine. Though the fluffy clouds are hardly moving, there must be more wind just above them, since some blue-gray-and-white cumulonimbus clouds are scudding along much more quickly. When I glance again over the guard wall, a long swatch of fog is hugging the river below me. So even the weather can't make up its mind what to do.

Items: Saint is still dead. Samuel Beckett is still dead. Billie Holiday and Emily Dickinson are still dead as well. Ndele and Lee are alive. In the meantime, before I am dead, I want to be a notorious writer and a thoroughgoing babe. I may be becoming a mother.

I'll probably never feel better than I'm feeling right now. Bottom line: My body is still a going concern. The planet I'm on not only looks good, it works. While its gravity zips me along, its sun warms my forehead, my torso, the tops of my sweaty brown wrists; if I turned over one of my wrists, it would heat up the khaki-pink inside. In the meantime this breeze keeps me cool. My hand muscles burn, supplying some low-grade endorphins. I can also see where I'm going. And I do all these things voluntarily—no nurses' assistance required. My lunch fuels me pretty efficiently; I have bottles of water for when I get thirsty. As my lungs breathe and process this crystalline air, they feel vaguely tingly and sweet. Even my blood still gets cleansed more or less efficiently, at least well enough to let me make it the rest of the way down this hill.

The problem, as always, is time. Time always does the opposite of what you want it to do, so there's no way to trick it. If I'm looking forward to something—a hot shower, baba ghanoush, a buffalo cheeseburger, seeing Ndele again—it will drag like a

fatherfucker. But if I want to forestall something even nebu-
lously disagreeable, it rushes up at me with a sickening, kaleido-
scopic vengeance, and that's how it always will be. So amen.

A black guy glides by on a huge golden Honda; it isn't
Ndele. (I've also been checking on oversized white guys, plus
any silhouette without a lot of hair on the skull. I never know
where he'll pop up.) The Honda is decked out with fancy mirrors, antennae, a sound system blasting mean-sounding
gangsta rap, and XXL hard-body saddlebags. Viewed from
behind, it's as wide as a Civic sedan.

I begin to move faster again, concentrating hard as I steer
through acute, hairy turns. But I also feel giddy abandon, the
rush of all this effortless velocity, as well as my new outlaw status.

I roll even faster through a straight stretch with very steep
downgrade, veering out toward the center of the clear eastbound lane. I doubt my rear brakes could stop me right now,
and if I squeezed the fronts any harder I'd somersault over the
handlebars. If I go over the guard wall, my Trek has the
wrong avionics to negotiate that particular flight plan.

An oncoming car honks its horn long and hard, and I
swerve to my right and flash past it. Without the cap, my hair
is blown almost straight back; I know this because my
shadow's right there on the asphalt, but I can also feel every
one of the thousands of miniature tugs on my scalp. The
wind's whir and bellow registers deep in my ears: pretty fast.
My tires buzz over the asphalt, staying ahead of my shadow by
a neck and a handlebar bag.

I'm determined to make something happen. When a car
coming up from behind me forces me to move over, my right
elbow grazes the wall, but just barely; I don't even think I'm
bleeding. My face does get slapped by a stray splash of water-
fall. Yow! Most of the water keeps falling below me through a
grate between the road and the mountain. There's a river
down there, is there not? And so, since this is where some of
its water must come from, then . . . My brain isn't used to
deciphering such vertical, craggy topography.

My speedometer reads twenty-three, twenty-four as I

zoom toward a stretch of wet granite. This must be the Weeping Wall I read about back in St. Mary: thirty or forty feet high, a buckling cubist arrangement of dripping slate rectangles scrimmed with dozens of separate white mini falls cascading onto the Road. As I rocket downhill through the spray, each little tweak of the handlebars has seismic ramifications. Hold steady! My way-too-big shirt flaps behind me. In the meantime I'm mesmerized by the blur of purple-and-yellow lichens against the glittering black granite, by the sweep of the valley below me. I get slapped in the face by a small, icy falls. Another one splashes my chest, bounces up off the road, sprays my legs. It feels pretty great, but I'm scared. My tires and rims are too wet.

I swerve, almost flip, as I go through an S-curve, but I regain my balance, zoom on. As the Road straightens out and gets drier but steeper, my front wheel rises up off the asphalt. It's just what I need: more degrees. The bike's almost literally flying.

The end of *The Unnamable* comes streaming spasmodically back to me, *perhaps it's done already*, as the black wall of rock keeps hurtling toward my right eye. Any adjustment I'm tempted to make in my steering will have to be terribly subtle.

And now here comes a tunnel, a long one: *where I am, I don't know, I'll never know, in the silence you don't know . . .* In the dark is where I am, holding on. I do not love life anymore. I do not love life *for the time being*. But I've never felt stronger or sexier or happier. So? Or so what. I've become the Patience Liver, filtered of poisons and impurities by a patient's flawed liver—by two headlights coming straight at me as I'm flying alone in the dark. But there's light—literal, actual light—at the end of the tunnel. My eyes work. I head for it.

Ah.

Do I have enough gumption to see this thing through with Ndele? To the very, very end? We will see.

I'm heading, at thirty-six miles an hour, toward my second millennium, and I really don't know if I'll make it. *You must go on, that's all I know*, that my bike's moving faster, picking up speed every foot, every second. The tires are making a loud, high-pitched whir I haven't heard before. I'm really not ready for this. When I change lanes again and glance over the side, the fog is rising off the floor of the valley—meaning what? I'm going so fast I can't think straight.

I can. I can't live with diabetes, since it's slowly but efficiently slaughtering me. I can't live without it, since they haven't found a cure yet. They say that you can't take it with you. I say, I hope not. Because up there, or down there, or out there, wherever, it's apparently anything goes. So I'm going.

I did kill my David with an angry and generous fix. All my love. If I didn't have diabetes I couldn't have done it. I'm about to lose my health altogether, though I never really had it to begin with. But still. It would've been nice to have had it.

Thirty-eight. Thirty-eight. Thirty-nine. A hundred yards ahead there's a sharp right-hand turn. Adrenaline buzzes up through my carotid arteries and into my temples. My tonsils. The finest-grained gravel and tiniest bumps in the road, in the Road, why don't we do it in the Road, rattle straight up to my brain. It's broken I'm going to fix it.

I steer. I hold on. The wall on my right is a blur of horizontal smudges and streaks. All I have to do is *touch* the rear brake and my whirring front wheel bounces an inch off the asphalt. Oh boy. I lean back and squeeze slightly harder. Five inches. I flash past the ranger who told me to get off the Road.

I loosen my grip on both brakes and hunker down over the handlebars, aiming myself at the turn. I'm already pretty far into it, bouncing baby wheelies at thirty-nine, forty, centrifugal forces whipping me out toward the guard wall. I'm fishtailing, skidding, but which way's the right way to lean?

I'm fighting it, braking now, whoa, pulling back hard on the handlebars, trying to get some control. But isn't this what I've always been doing? Leading up to exactly this point? Or down to that point? I don't know.

It's broken I'm going to fix it. This air! All this air! I'm terribly happy, but frightened.

You must go on, I can't go on, I'll go on. Or whatever.

I'm going.